GIDEON FALLS STATIONS OF THE CROSS

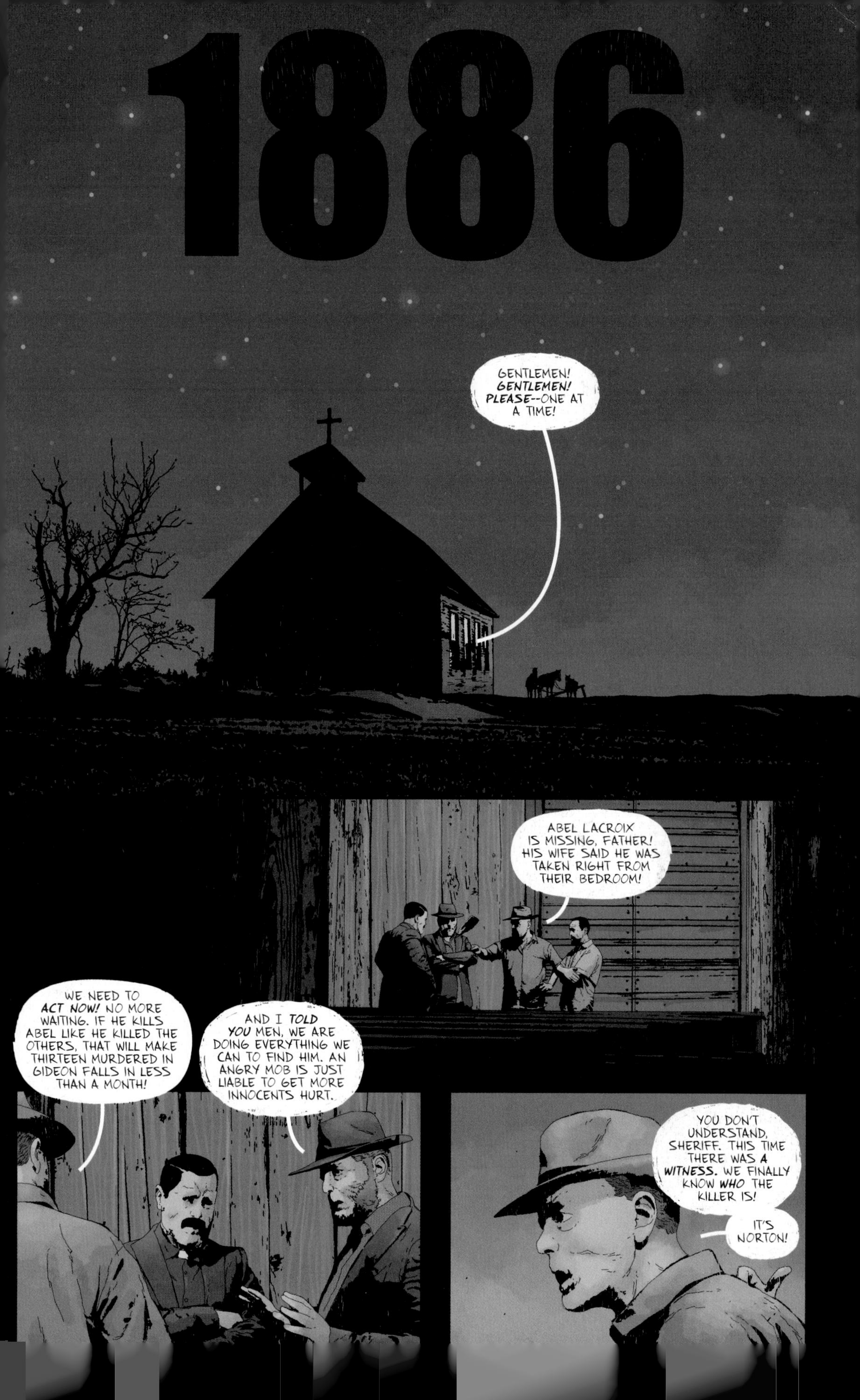
1886
GENTLEMEN! GENTLEMEN! PLEASE--ONE AT A TIME!
ABEL LACROIX IS MISSING, FATHER! HIS WIFE SAID HE WAS TAKEN RIGHT FROM THEIR BEDROOM!
WE NEED TO ACT NOW! NO MORE WAITING. IF HE KILLS ABEL LIKE HE KILLED THE OTHERS, THAT WILL MAKE THIRTEEN MURDERED IN GIDEON FALLS IN LESS THAN A MONTH!
AND I TOLD YOU MEN, WE ARE DOING EVERYTHING WE CAN TO FIND HIM. AN ANGRY MOB IS JUST LIABLE TO GET MORE INNOCENTS HURT.
YOU DON'T UNDERSTAND, SHERIFF. THIS TIME THERE WAS A WITNESS. WE FINALLY KNOW WHO THE KILLER IS!
IT'S NORTON!

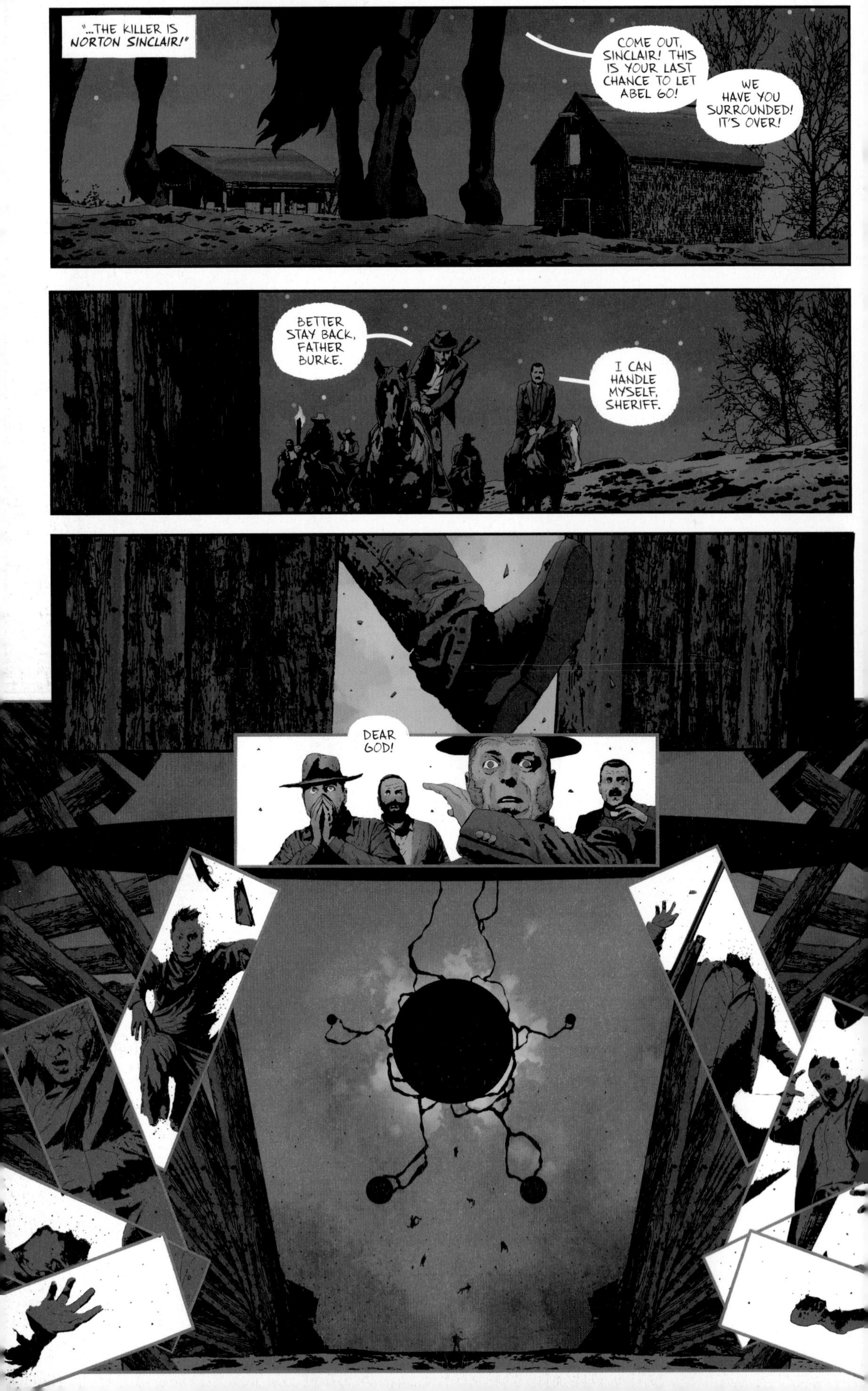
"...THE KILLER IS NORTON SINCLAIR!"
COME OUT, SINCLAIR! THIS IS YOUR LAST CHANCE TO LET ABEL GO!
WE HAVE YOU SURROUNDED! IT'S OVER!
BETTER STAY BACK, FATHER BURKE.
I CAN HANDLE MYSELF, SHERIFF.
DEAR GOD!

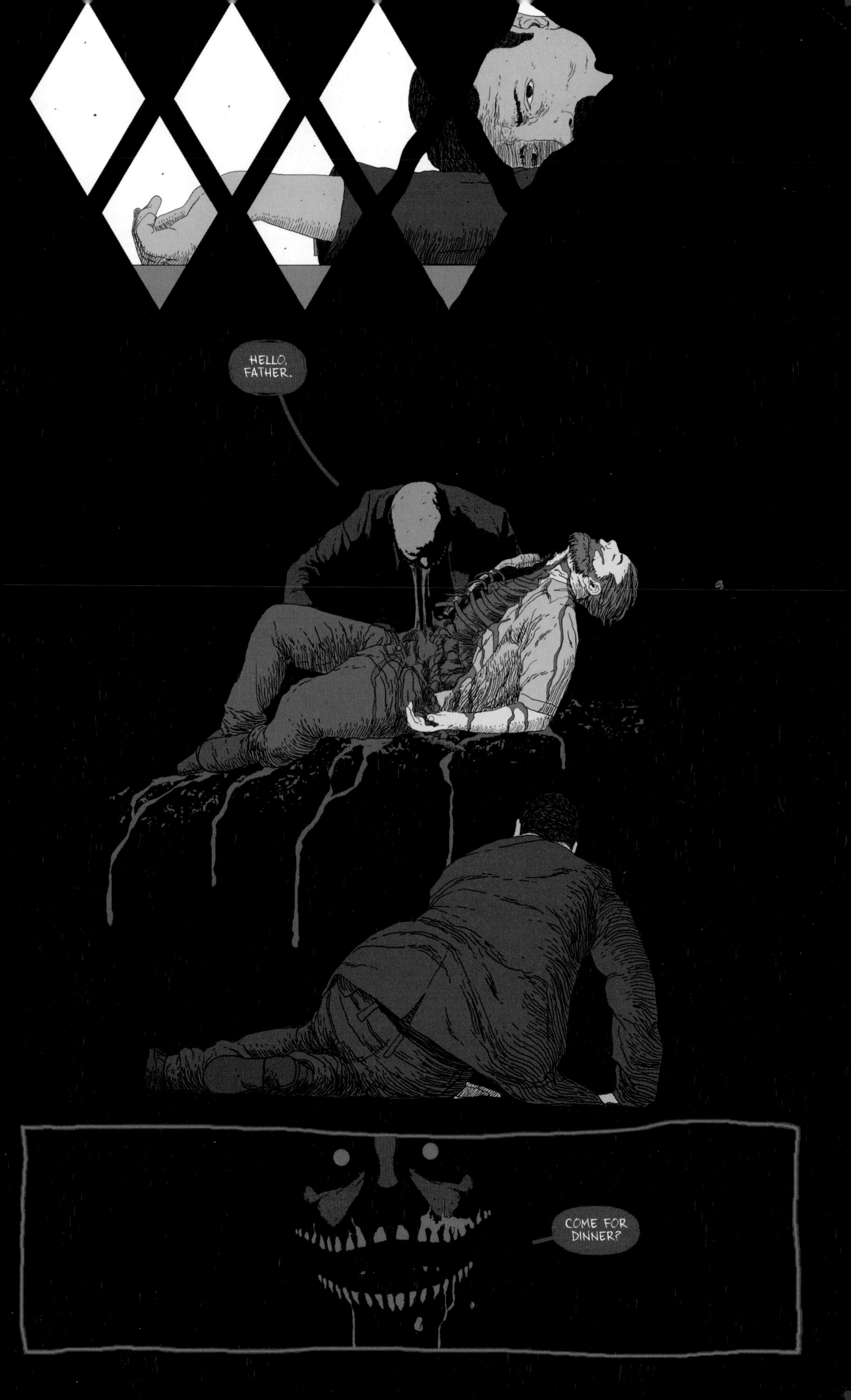
HELLO, FATHER.
COME FOR DINNER?

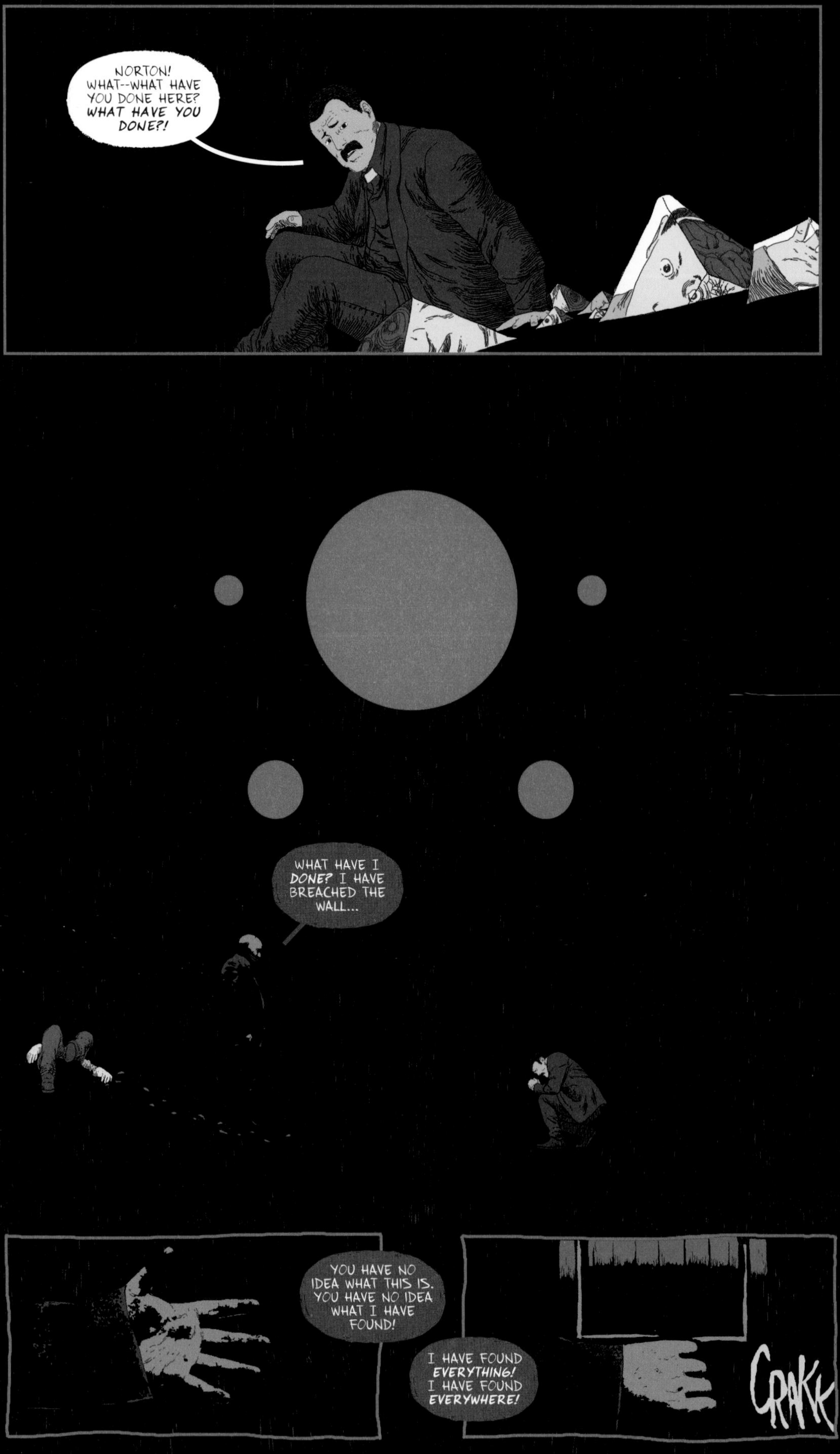
NORTON! WHAT--WHAT HAVE YOU DONE HERE? WHAT HAVE YOU DONE?!
WHAT HAVE I DONE? I HAVE BREACHED THE WALL...
YOU HAVE NO IDEA WHAT THIS IS. YOU HAVE NO IDEA WHAT I HAVE FOUND!
I HAVE FOUND EVERYTHING! I HAVE FOUND EVERYWHERE!
CRAKK

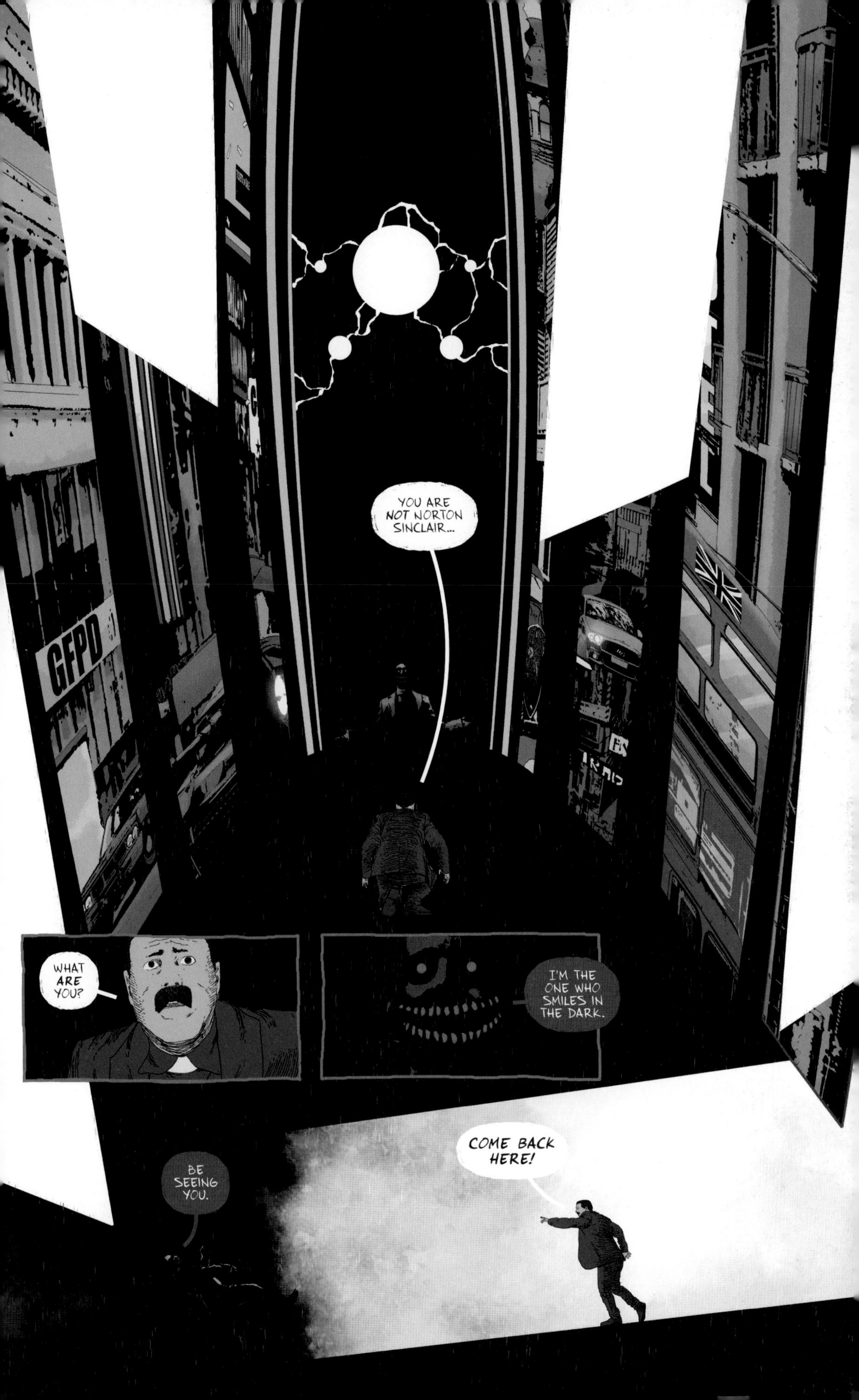
GFPD
YOU ARE NOT NORTON SINCLAIR...
WHAT ARE YOU?
I'M THE ONE WHO SMILES IN THE DARK.
BE SEEING YOU.
COME BACK HERE!

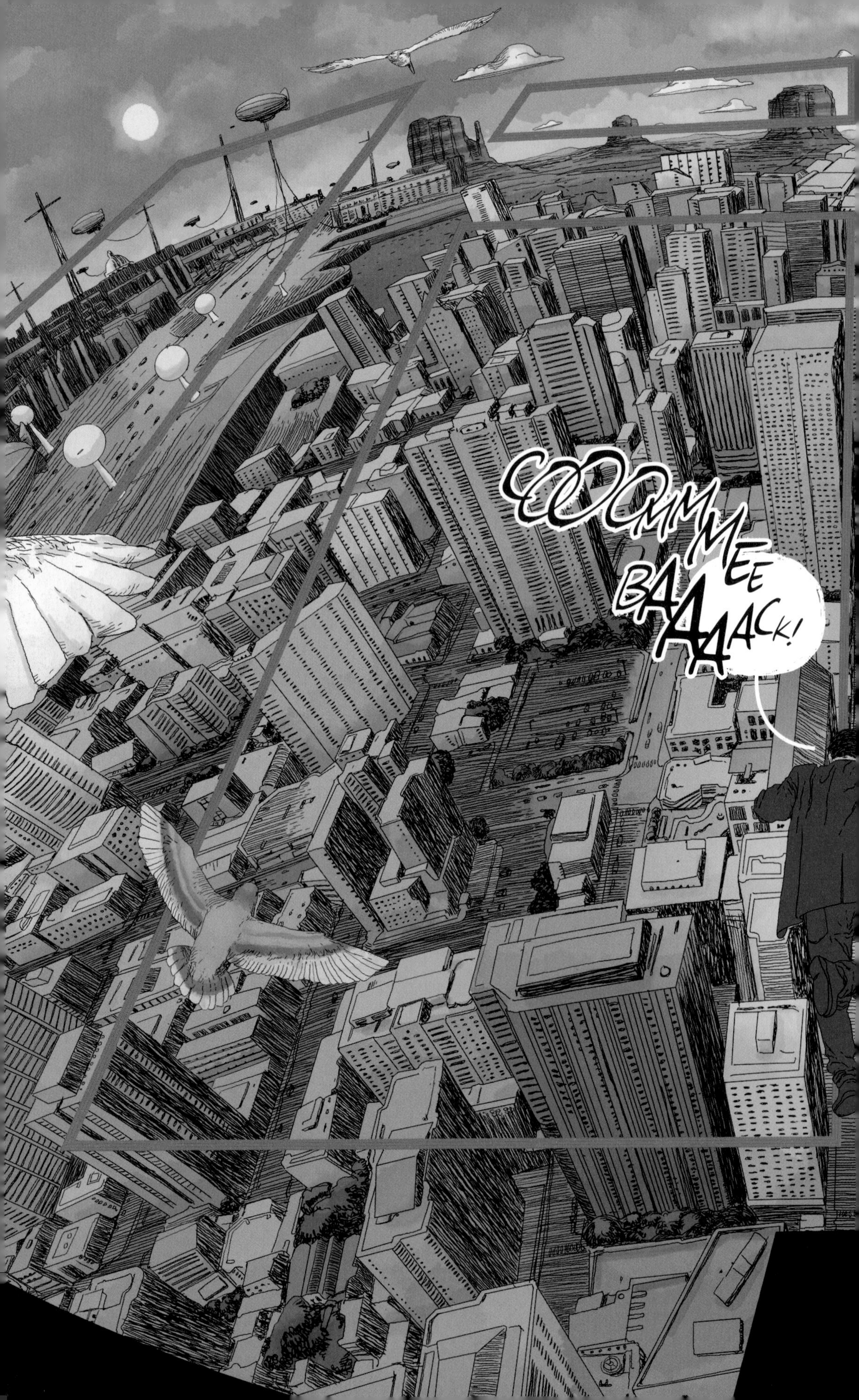
COOMMMEE BAAAACK!

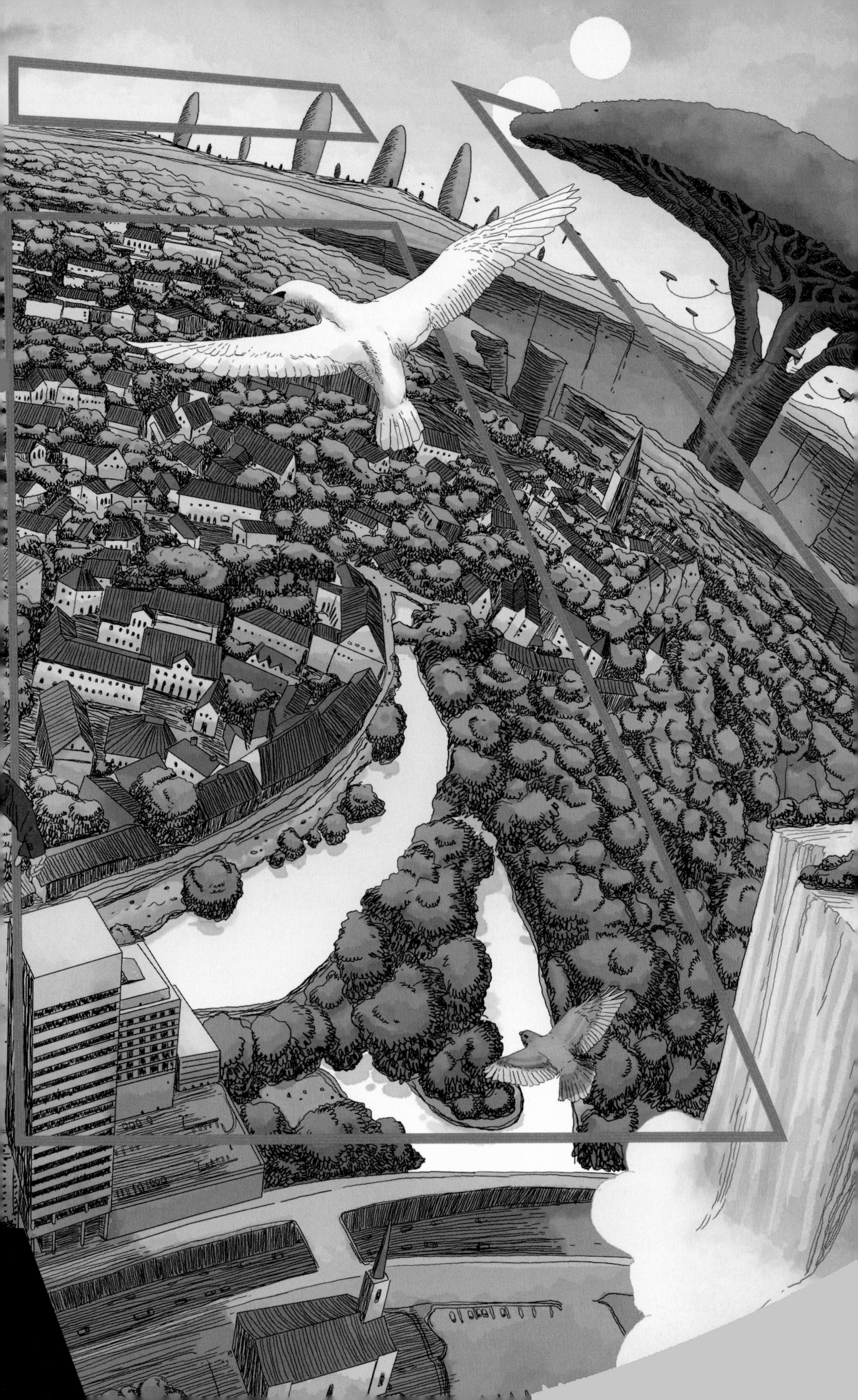

Jeff Lemire
Andrea Sorrentino

with colors by:
Dave Stewart

lettering and design by:
Steve Wands

and edited by:
Will Dennis

GIDEON FALLS

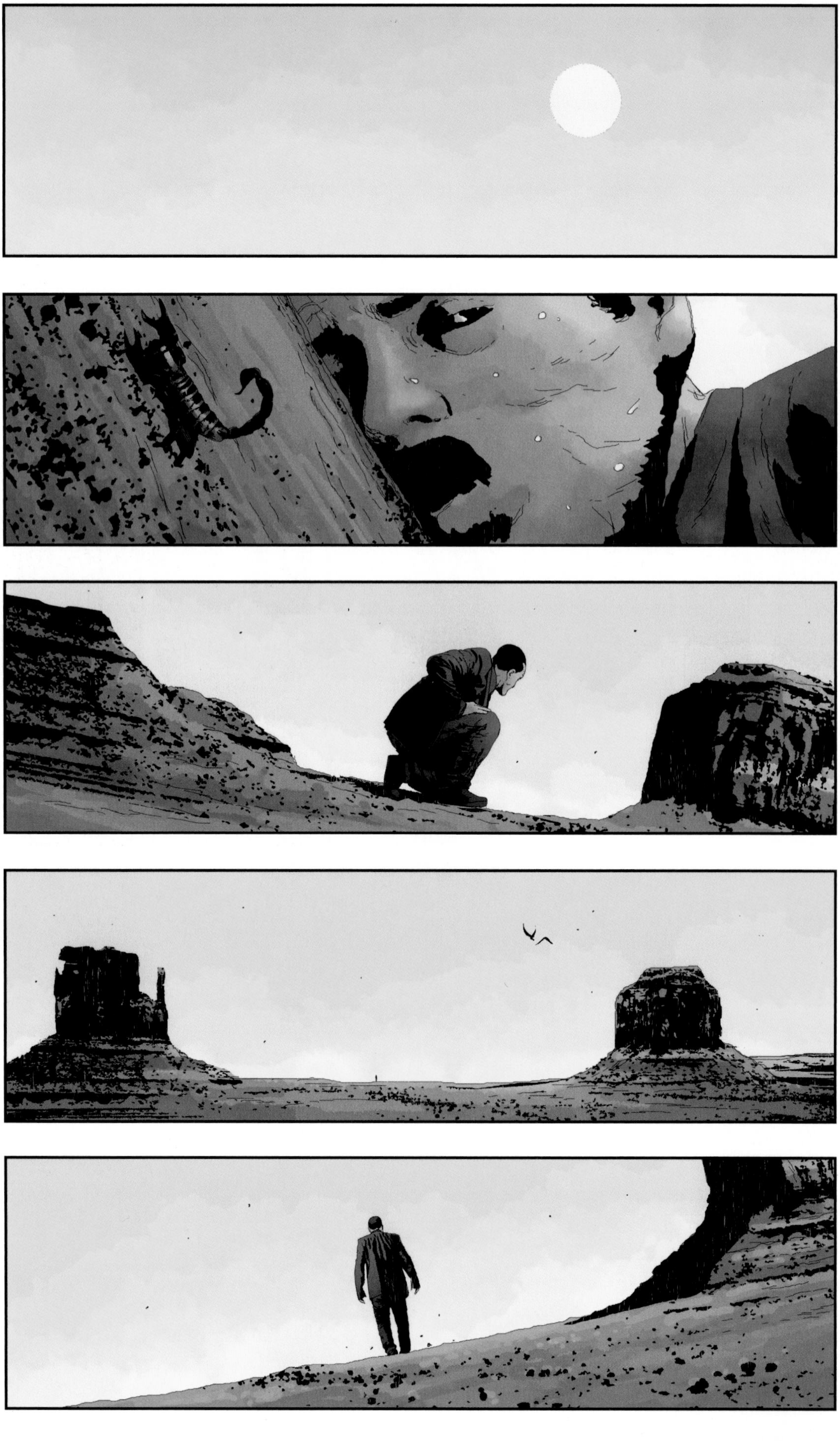

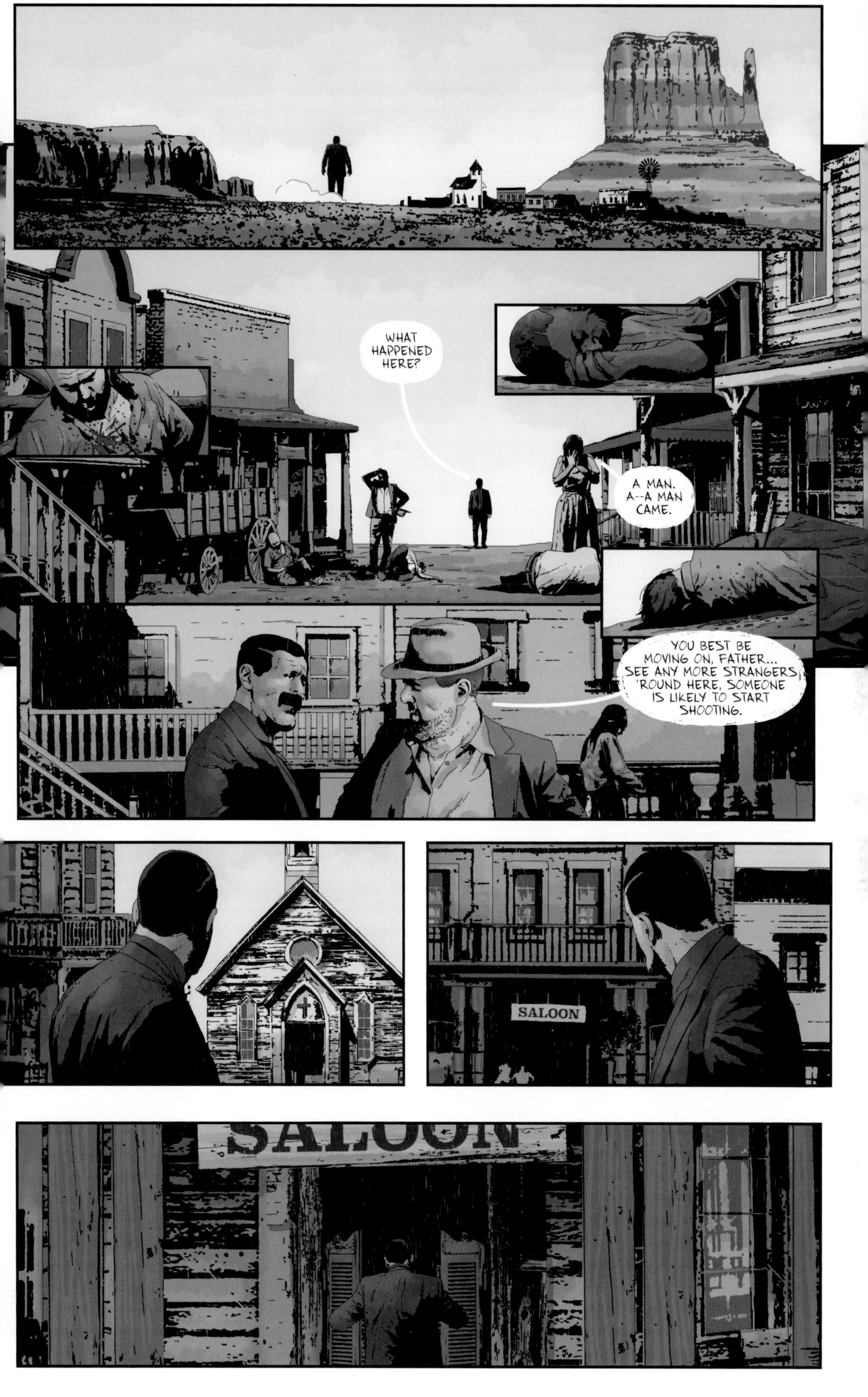
WHAT HAPPENED HERE?
A MAN. A--A MAN CAME.
YOU BEST BE MOVING ON, FATHER... SEE ANY MORE STRANGERS 'ROUND HERE, SOMEONE IS LIKELY TO START SHOOTING.
SALOON
SALOON

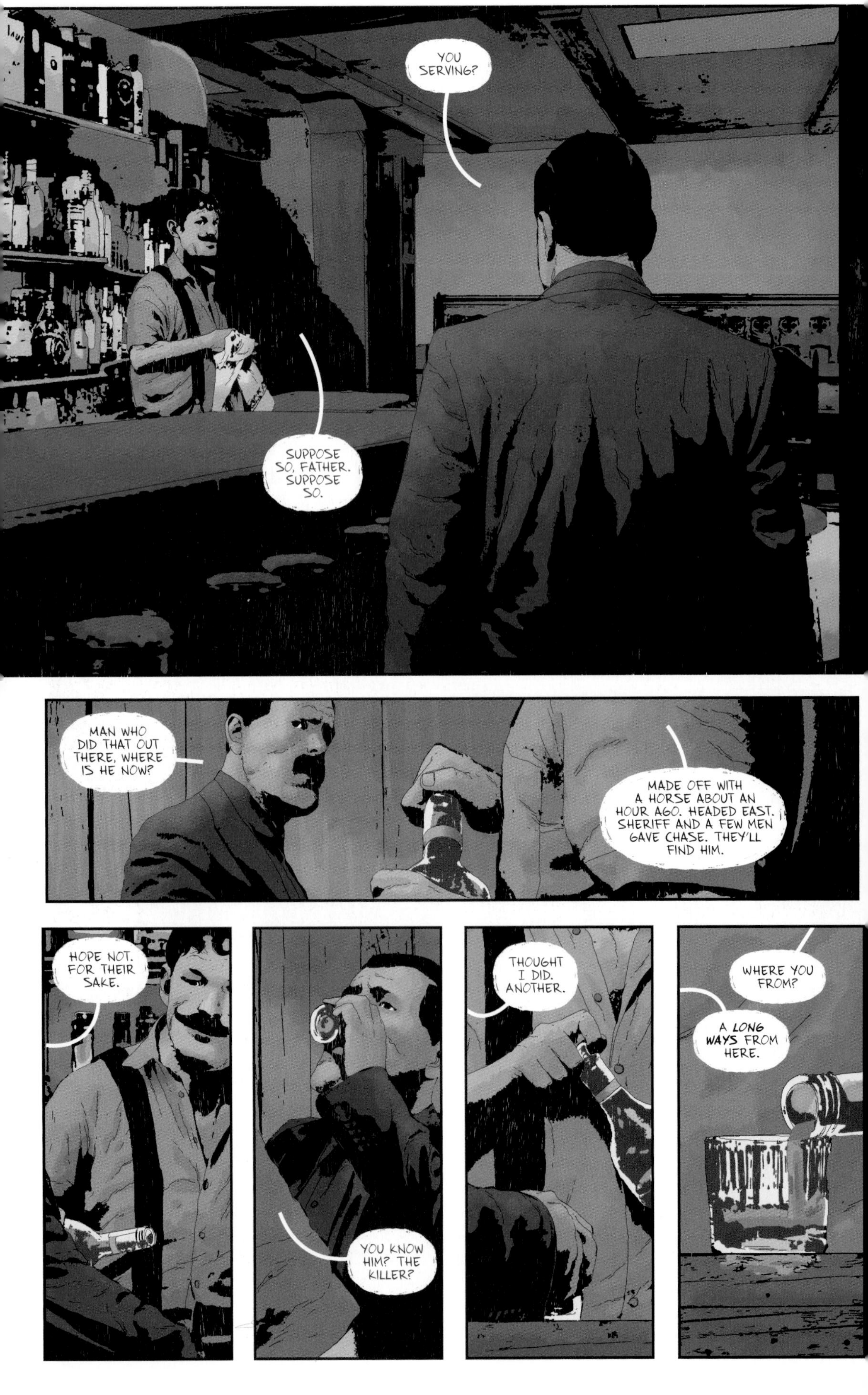
YOU SERVING?
SUPPOSE SO, FATHER. SUPPOSE SO.
MAN WHO DID THAT OUT THERE, WHERE IS HE NOW?
MADE OFF WITH A HORSE ABOUT AN HOUR AGO. HEADED EAST. SHERIFF AND A FEW MEN GAVE CHASE. THEY'LL FIND HIM.
HOPE NOT. FOR THEIR SAKE.
YOU KNOW HIM? THE KILLER?
THOUGHT I DID. ANOTHER.
WHERE YOU FROM?
A **LONG WAYS** FROM HERE.

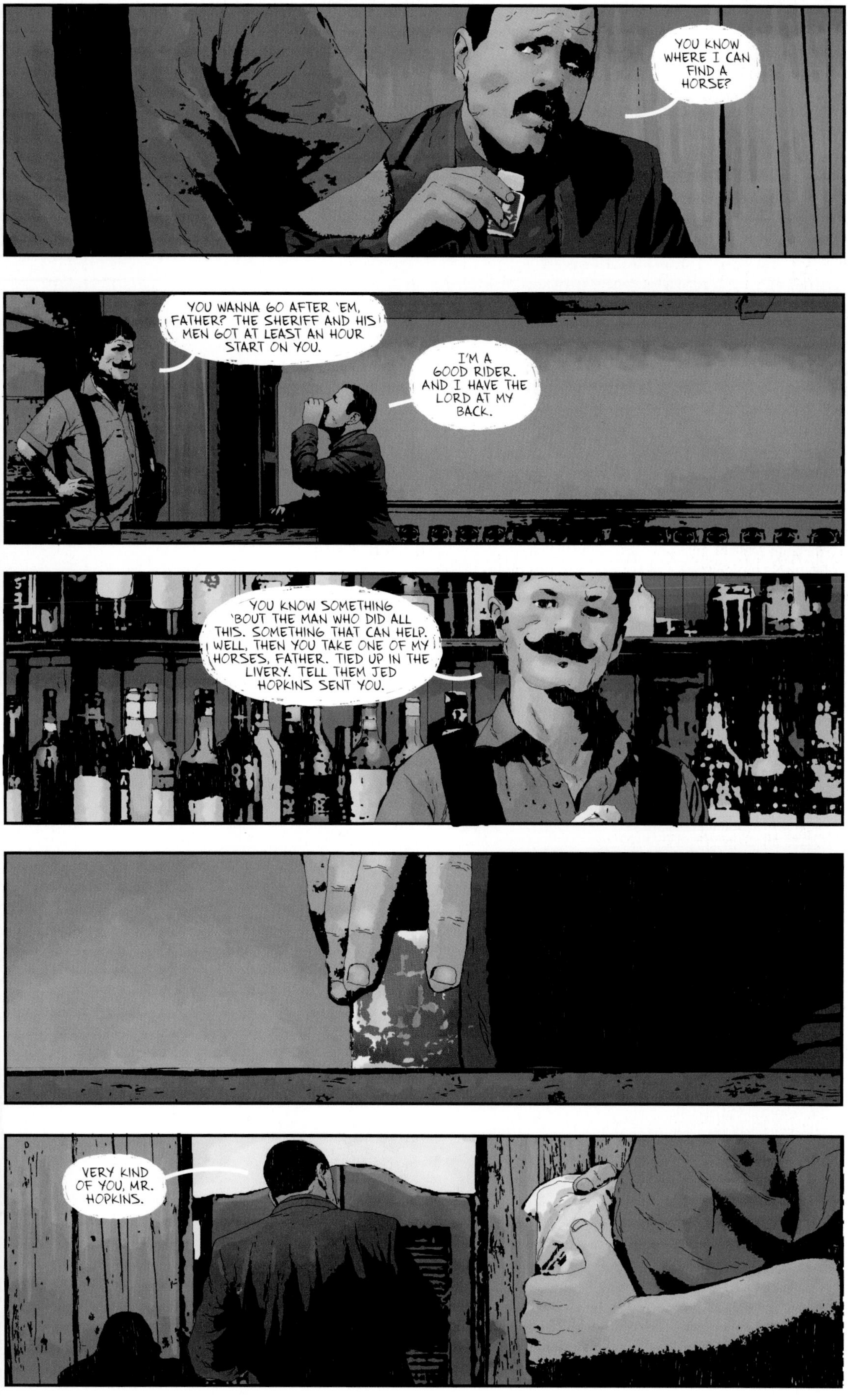
YOU KNOW WHERE I CAN FIND A HORSE?
YOU WANNA GO AFTER 'EM, FATHER? THE SHERIFF AND HIS MEN GOT AT LEAST AN HOUR START ON YOU.
I'M A GOOD RIDER. AND I HAVE THE LORD AT MY BACK.
YOU KNOW SOMETHING 'BOUT THE MAN WHO DID ALL THIS. SOMETHING THAT CAN HELP. WELL, THEN YOU TAKE ONE OF MY HORSES, FATHER. TIED UP IN THE LIVERY. TELL THEM JED HOPKINS SENT YOU.
VERY KIND OF YOU, MR. HOPKINS.

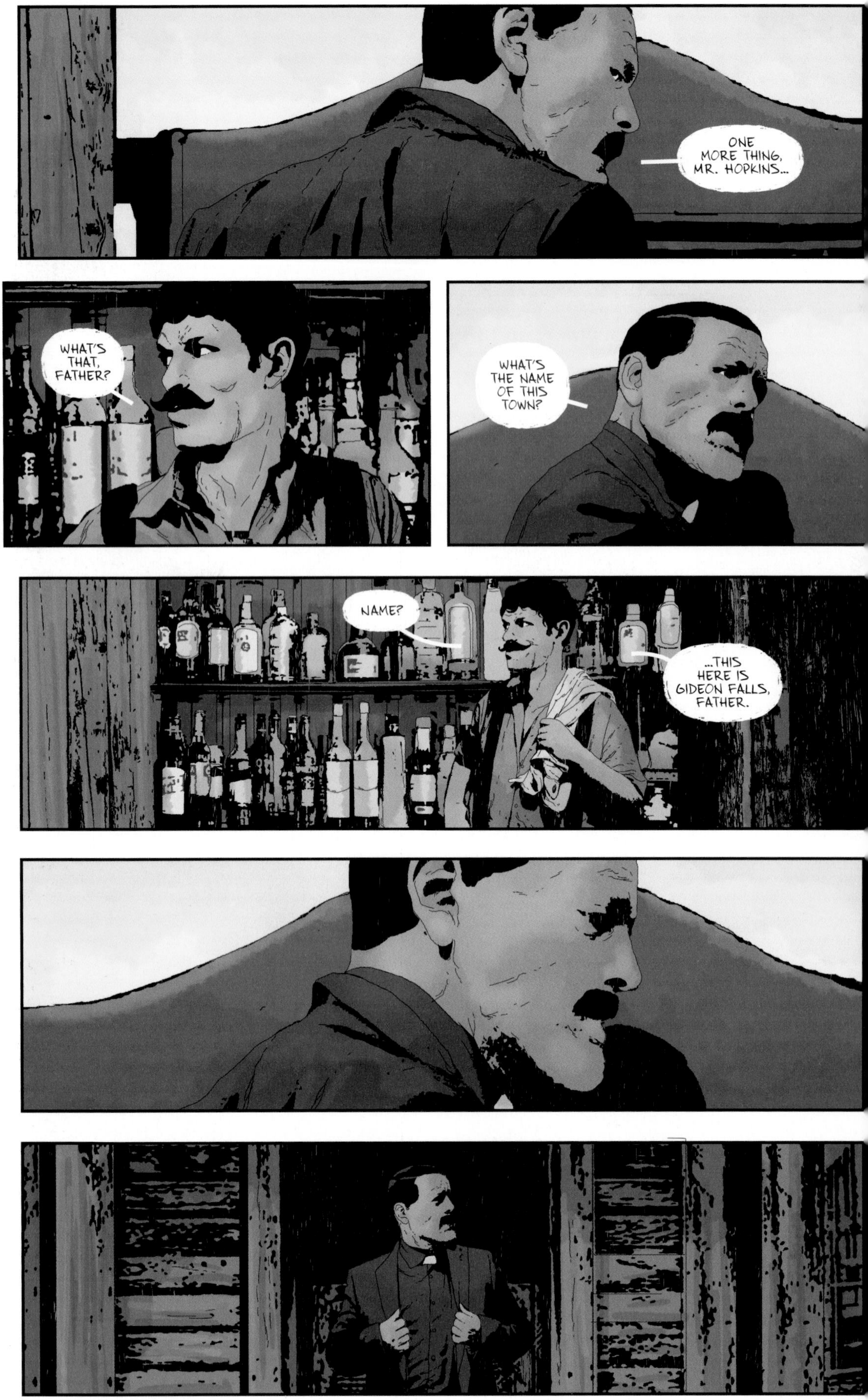
ONE MORE THING, MR. HOPKINS...
WHAT'S THAT, FATHER?
WHAT'S THE NAME OF THIS TOWN?
NAME?
...THIS HERE IS GIDEON FALLS, FATHER.

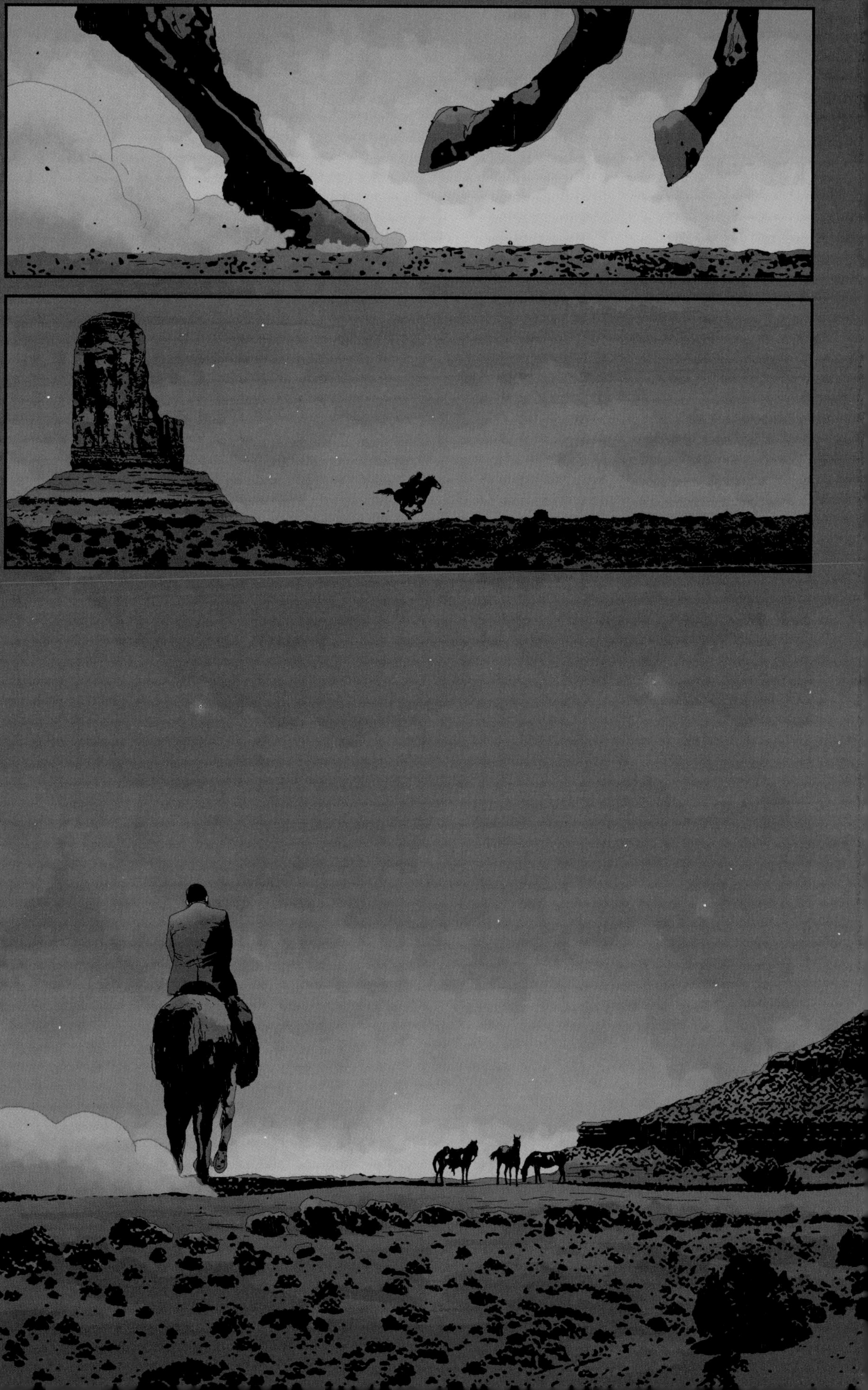

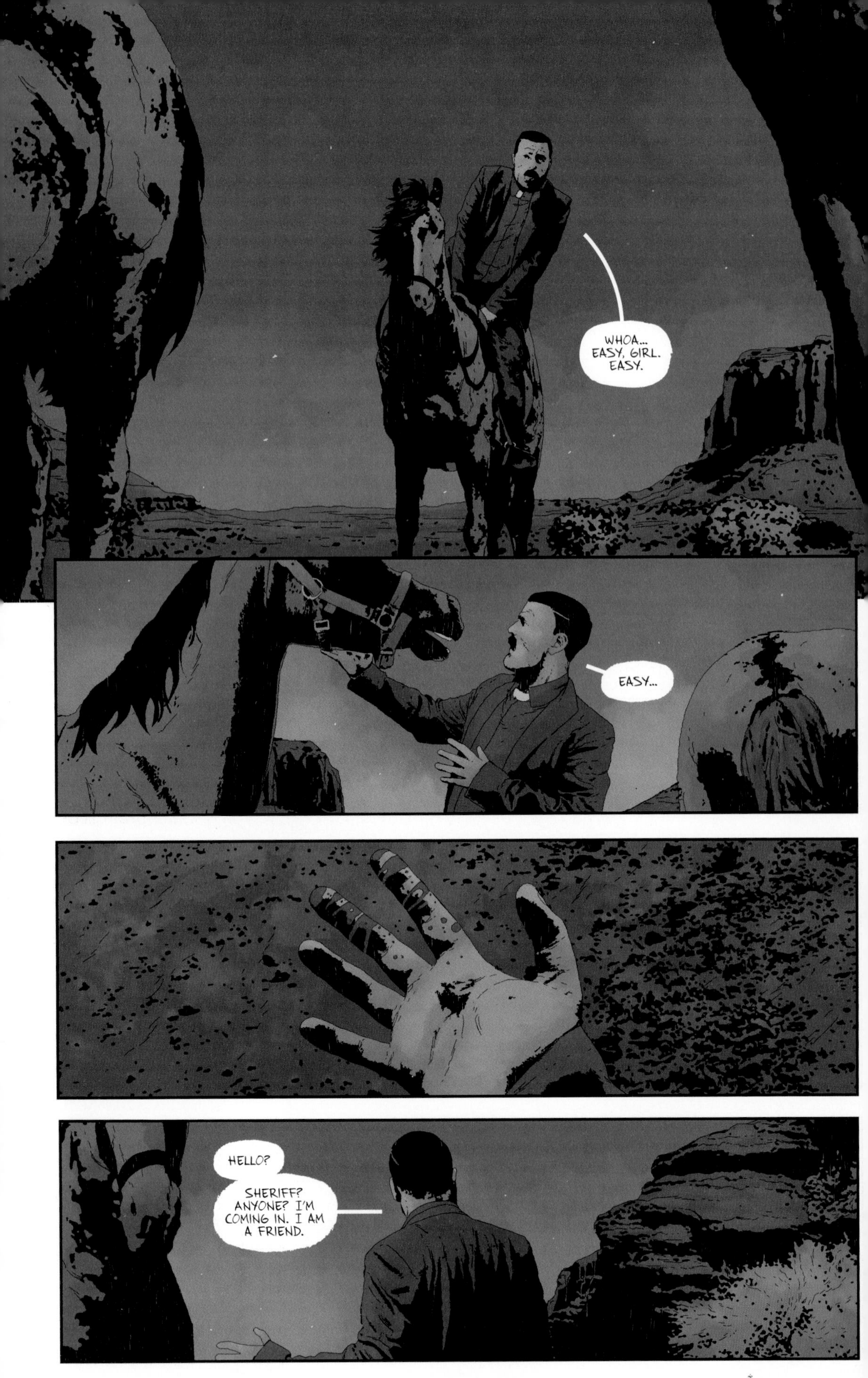
WHOA... EASY, GIRL. EASY.
EASY...
HELLO?
SHERIFF? ANYONE? I'M COMING IN. I AM A FRIEND.

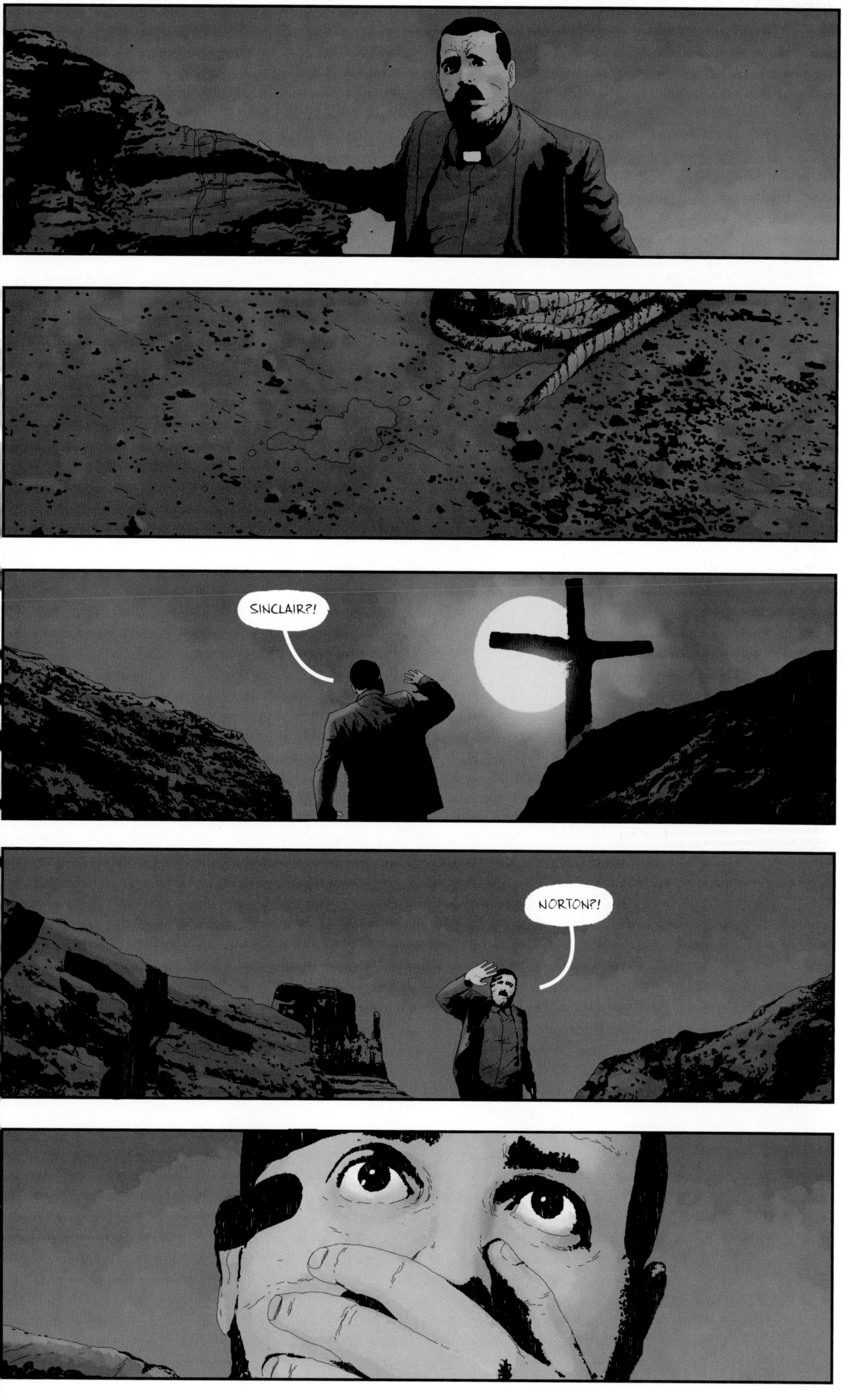
SINCLAIR?!
NORTON?!

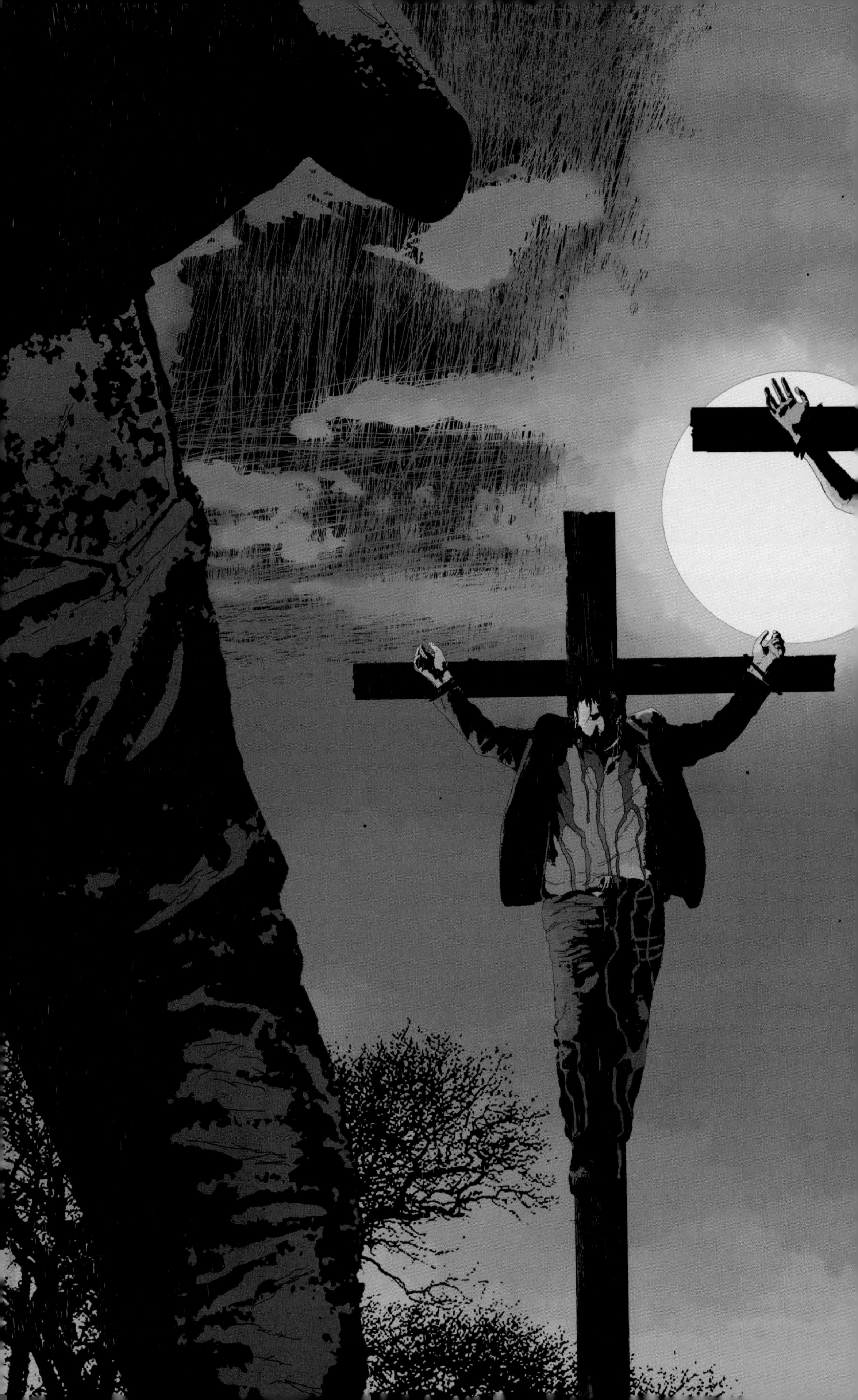

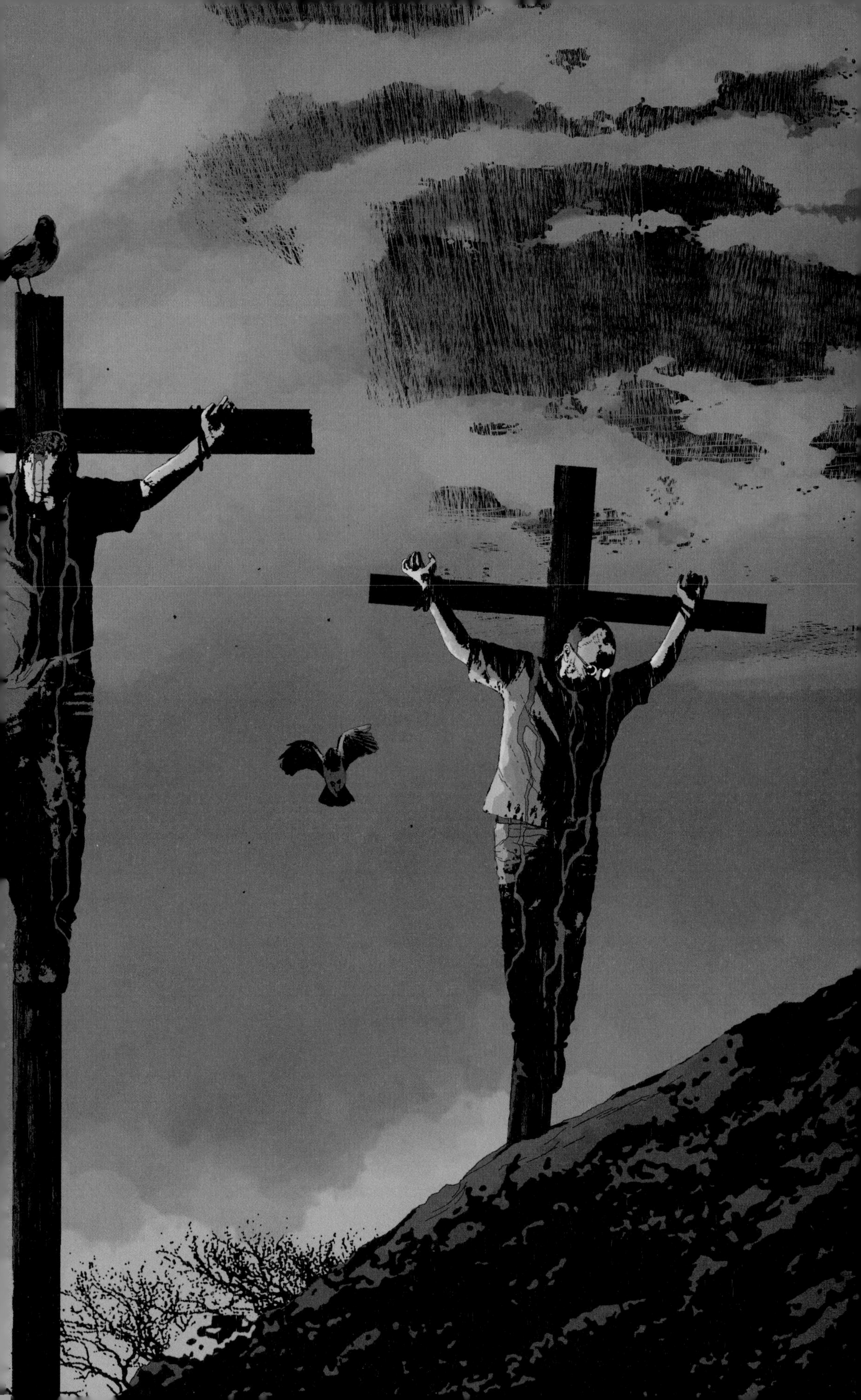

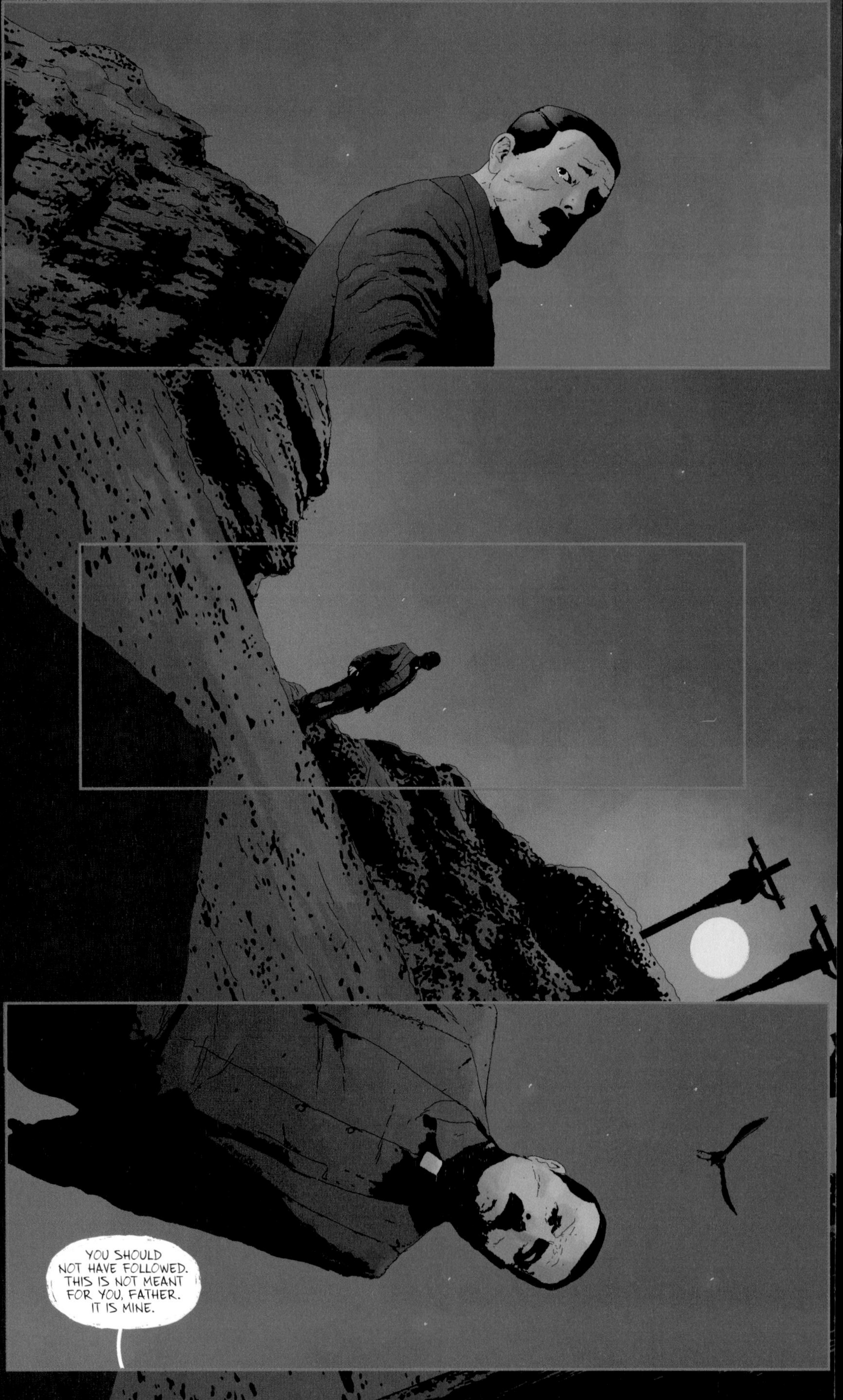
YOU SHOULD NOT HAVE FOLLOWED. THIS IS NOT MEANT FOR YOU, FATHER. IT IS MINE.

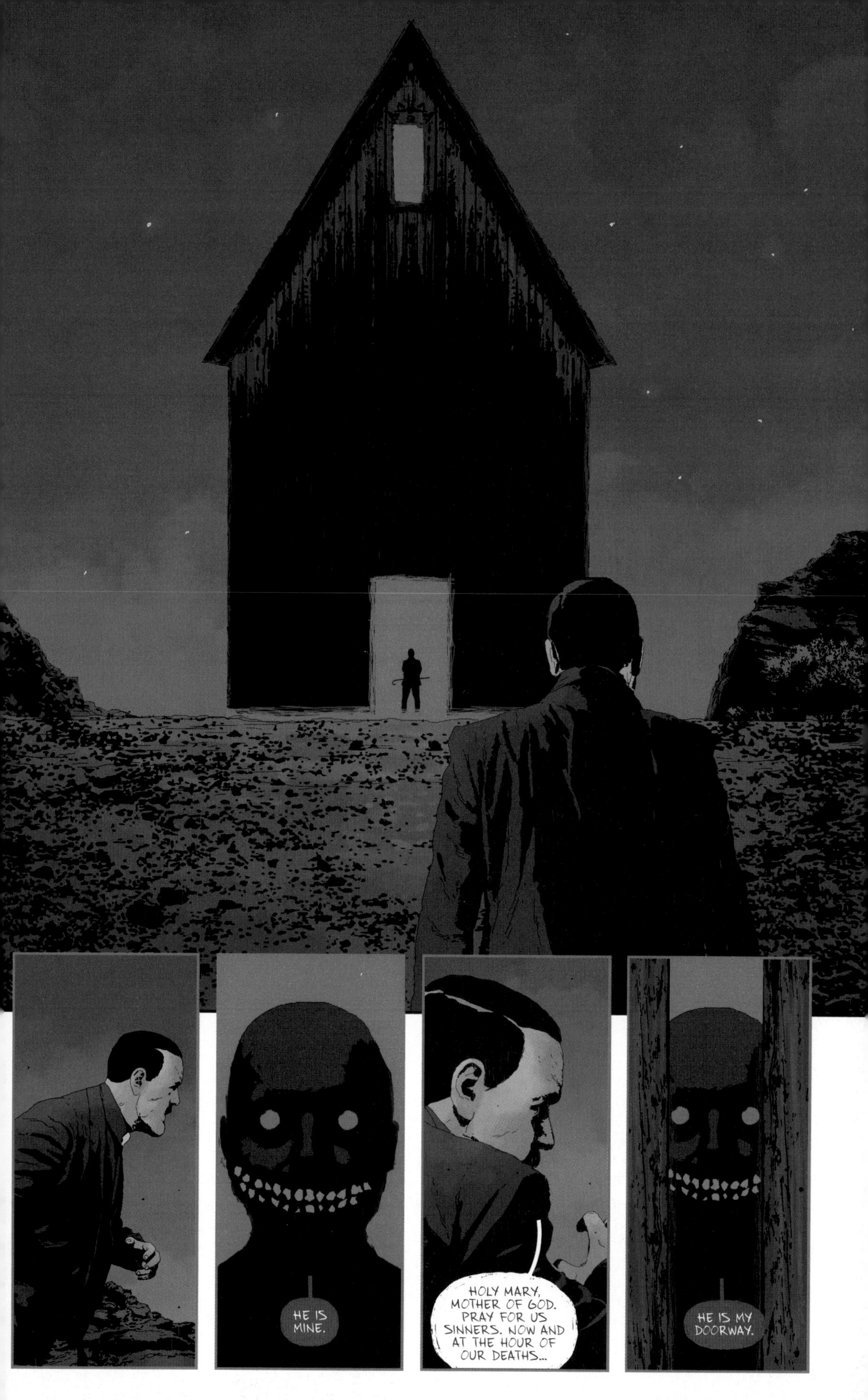
HE IS
MINE.
HOLY MARY,
MOTHER OF GOD.
PRAY FOR US
SINNERS. NOW AND
AT THE HOUR OF
OUR DEATHS...
HE IS MY
DOORWAY.

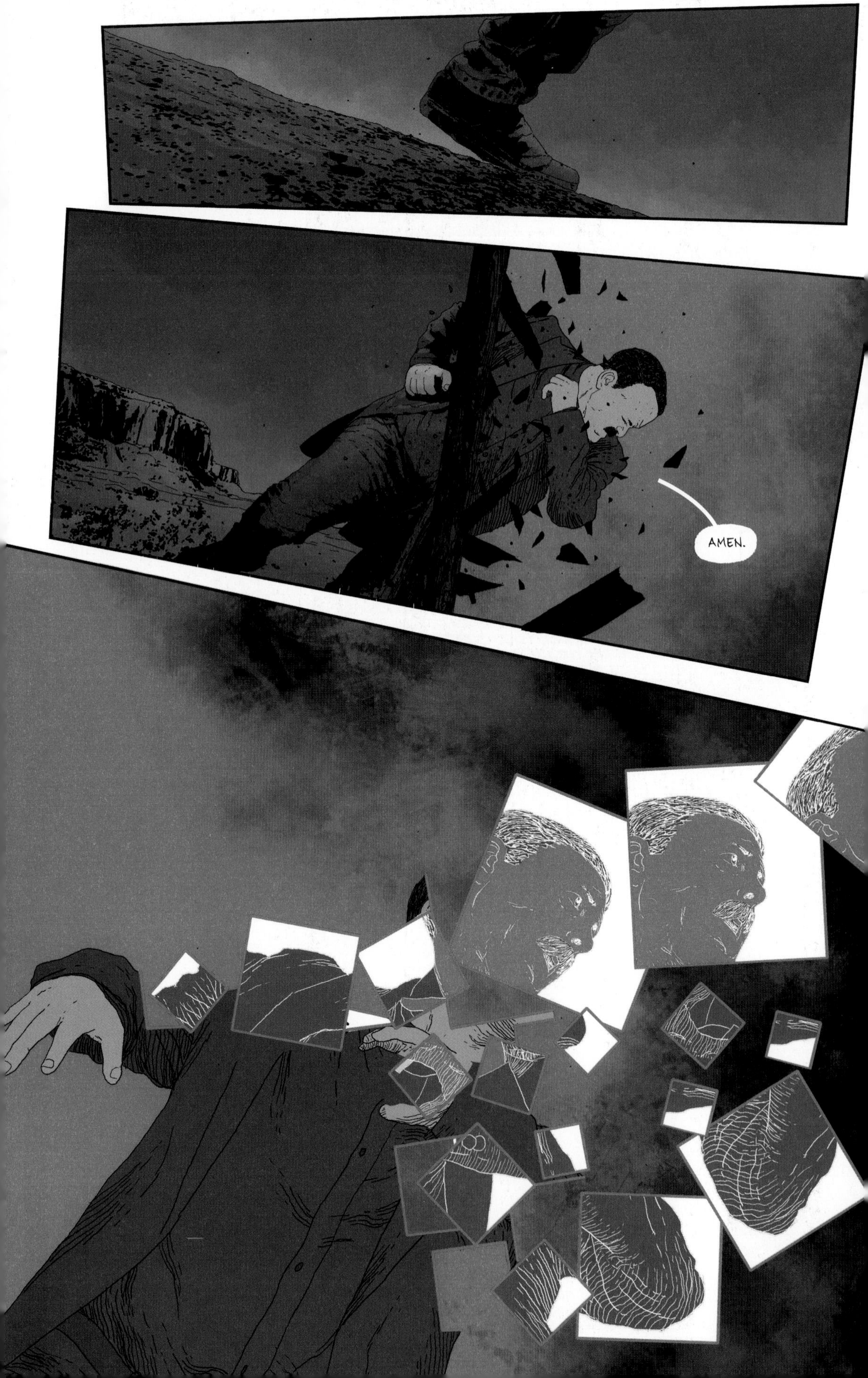
AMEN.

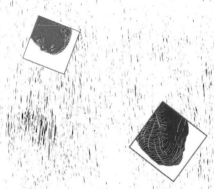

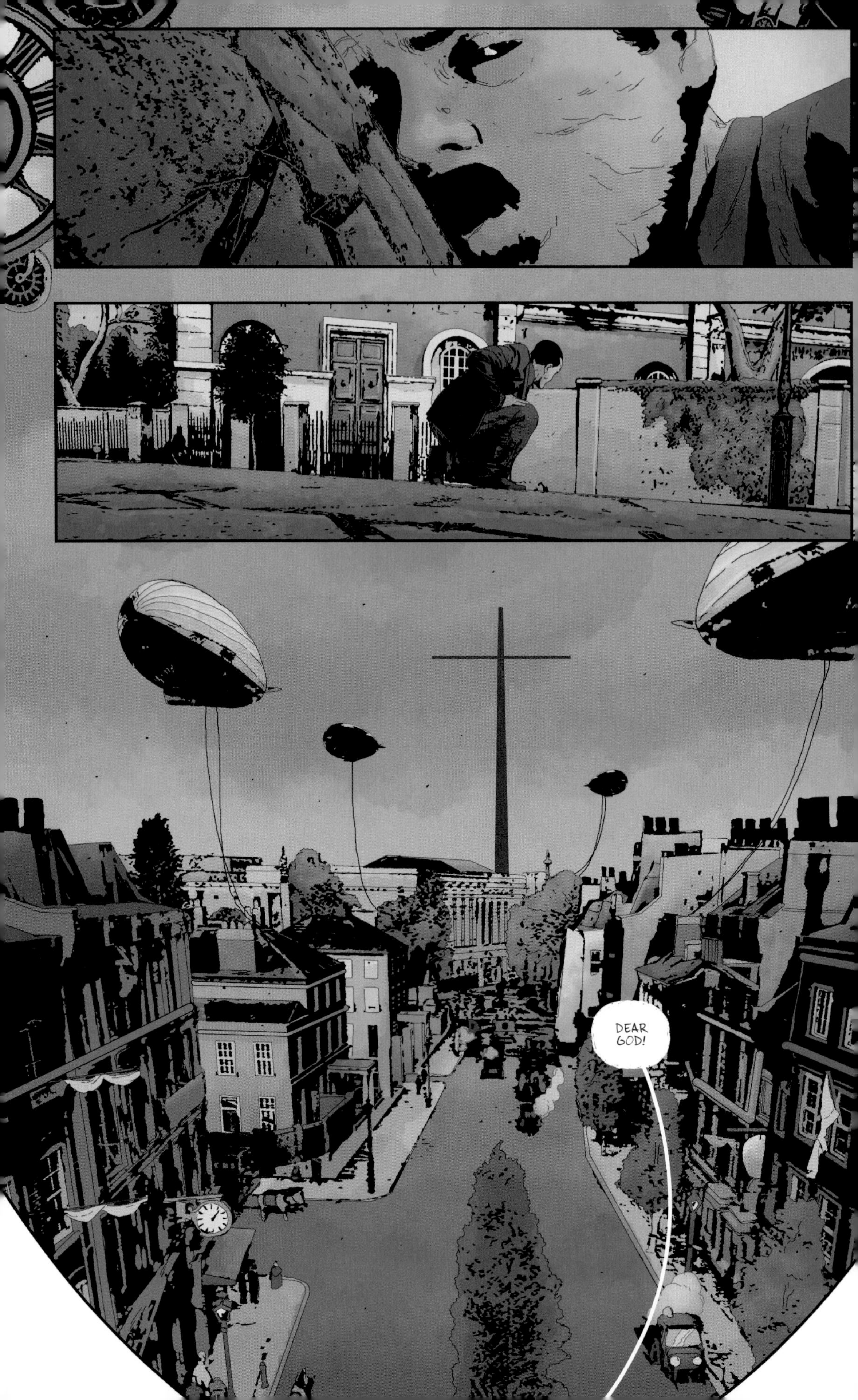
DEAR GOD!

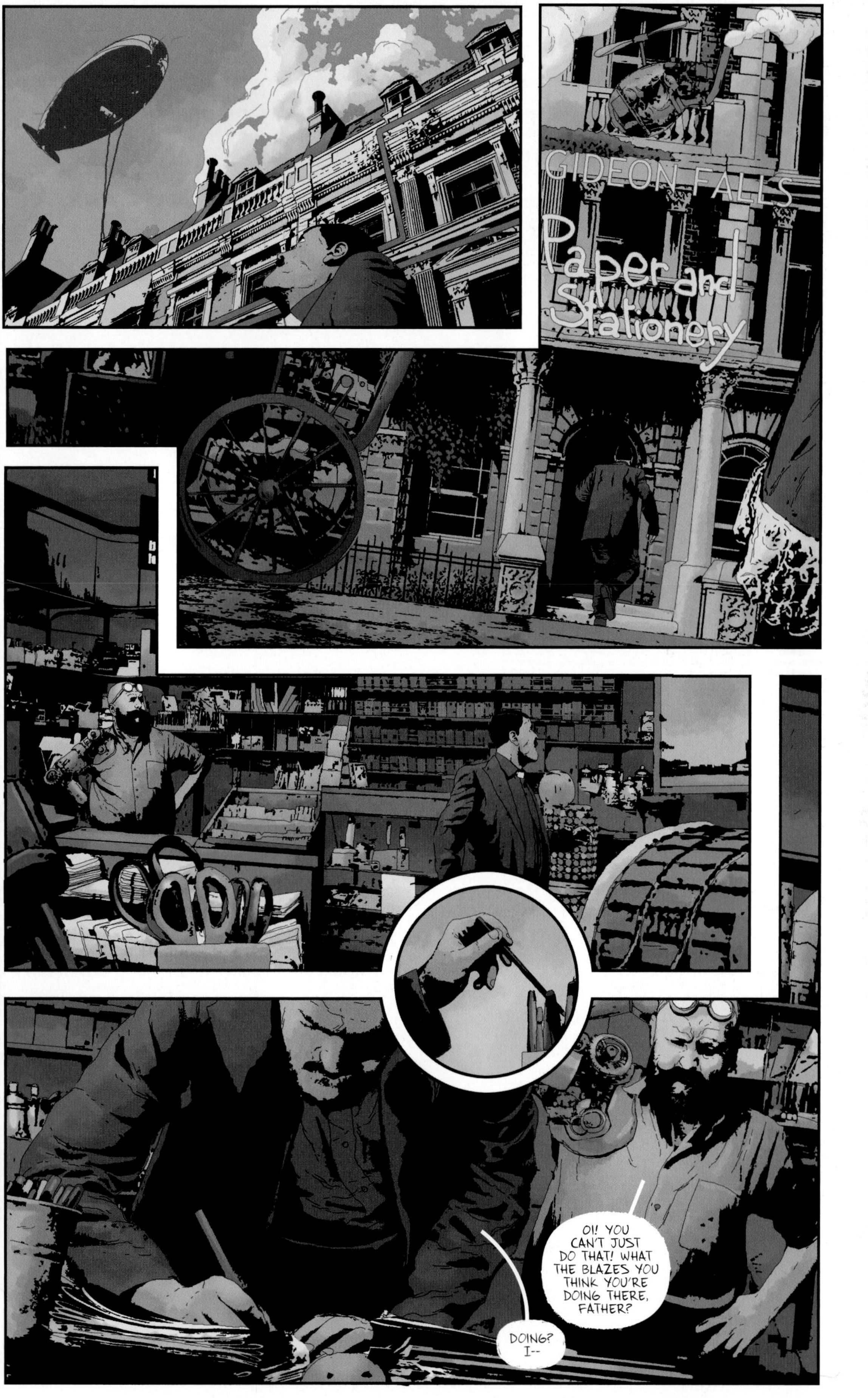
GIDEON FALLS
Paper and Stationery
OI! YOU CAN'T JUST DO THAT! WHAT THE BLAZES YOU THINK YOU'RE DOING THERE, FATHER?
DOING? I--

GIDEON FALLS
the city
of the future
GIDEON III
-STEAM-
SINCLAIR'S BARN
GIDEON II
-FRONTIER-
HOME
--I'M MAKING A MAP.
GOD HELP ME, I THINK I AM GOING TO NEED IT.

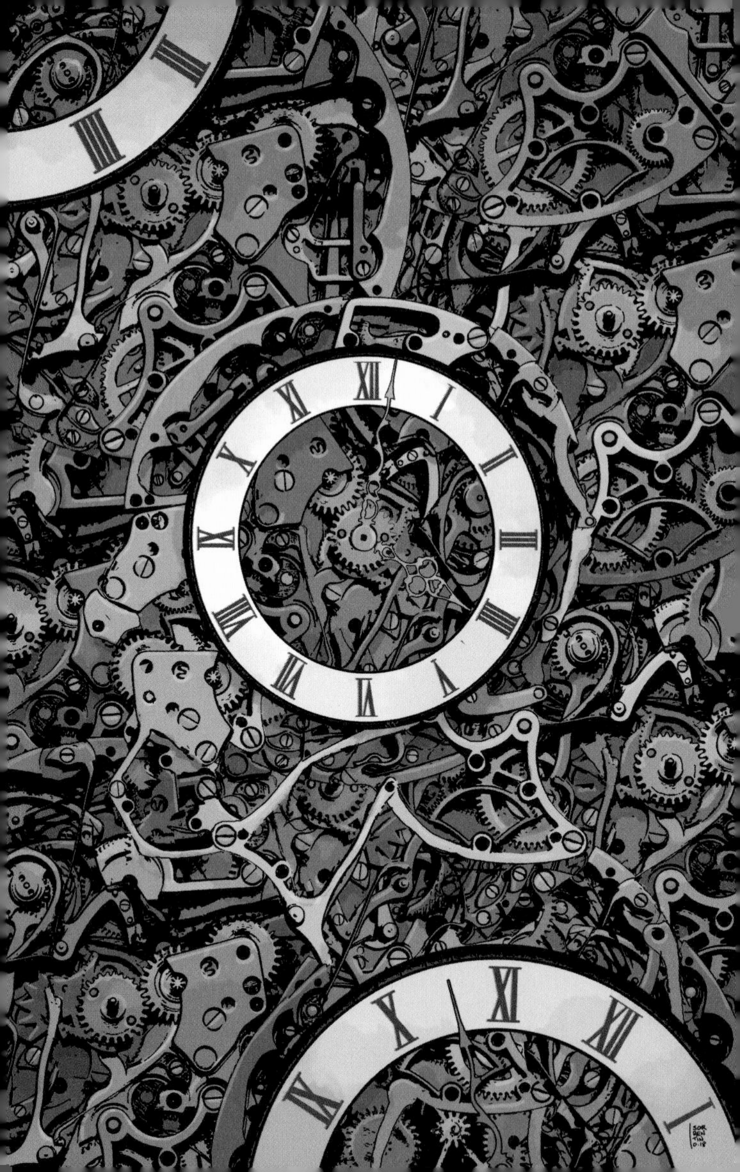

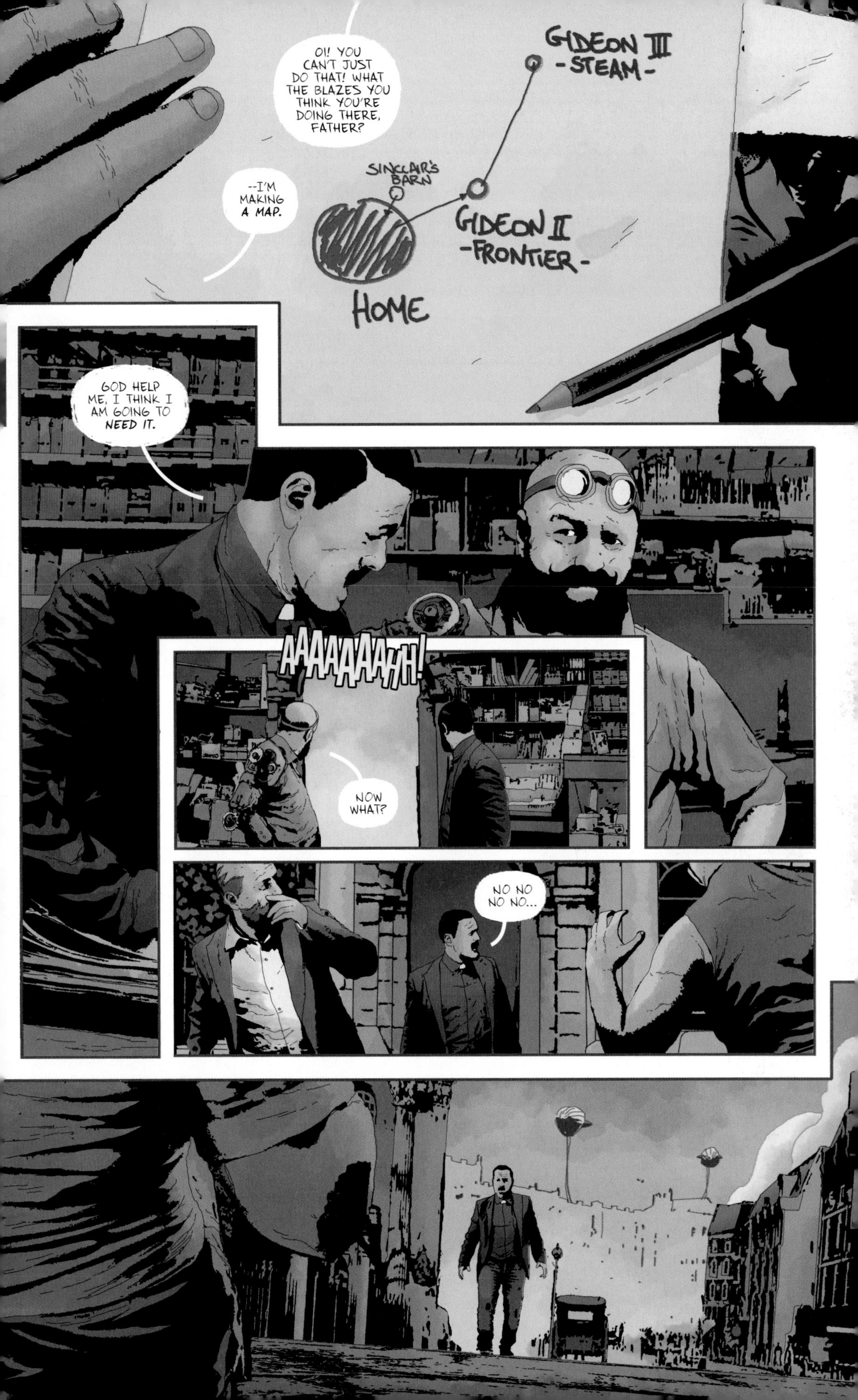
OI! YOU CAN'T JUST DO THAT! WHAT THE BLAZES YOU THINK YOU'RE DOING THERE, FATHER?
GIDEON III -STEAM-
SINCLAIR'S BARN
--I'M MAKING A MAP.
GIDEON II -FRONTIER-
HOME
GOD HELP ME, I THINK I AM GOING TO NEED IT.
AAAAAAAHH!
NOW WHAT?
NO NO NO NO...

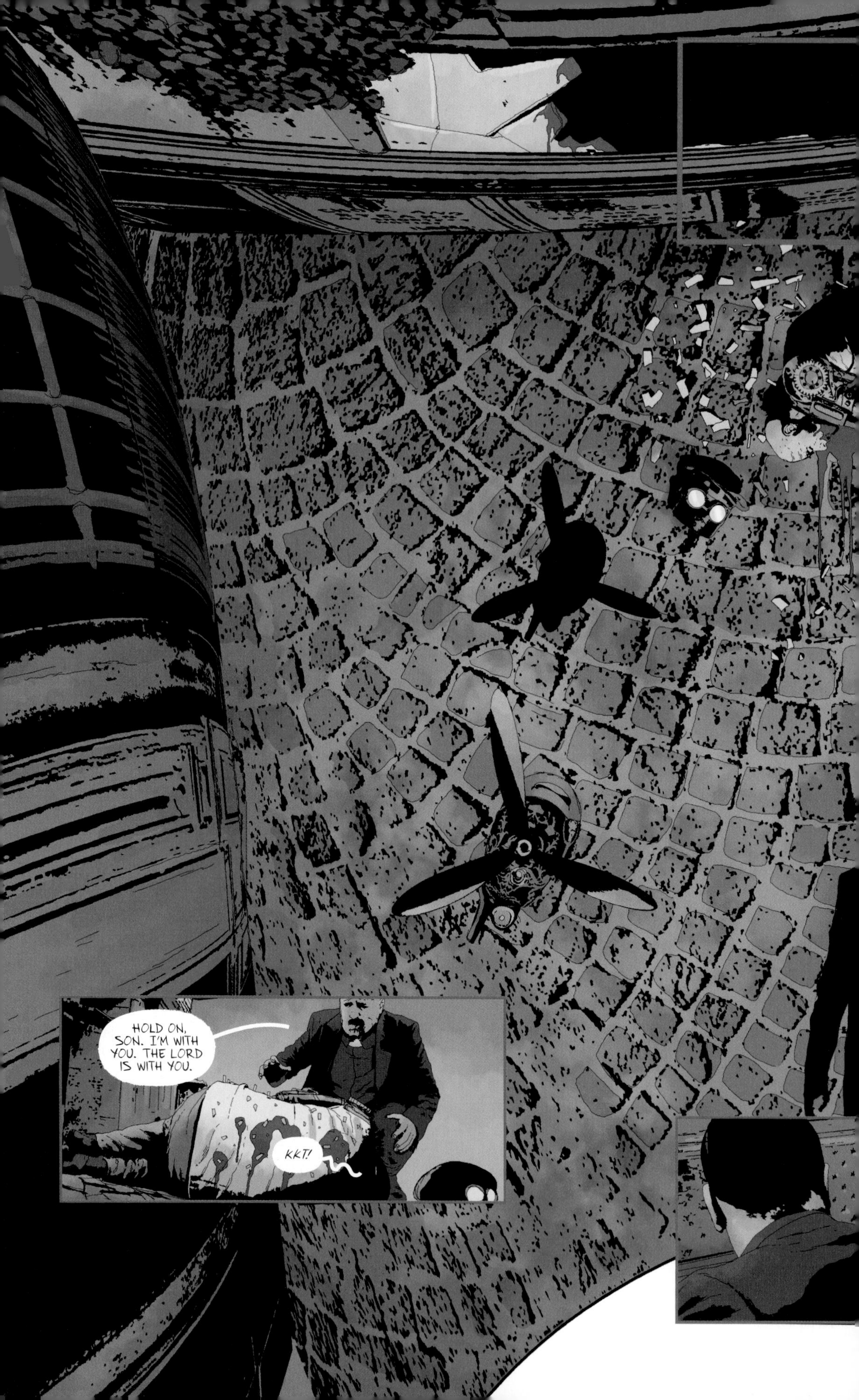
HOLD ON, SON. I'M WITH YOU. THE LORD IS WITH YOU.
KKT!

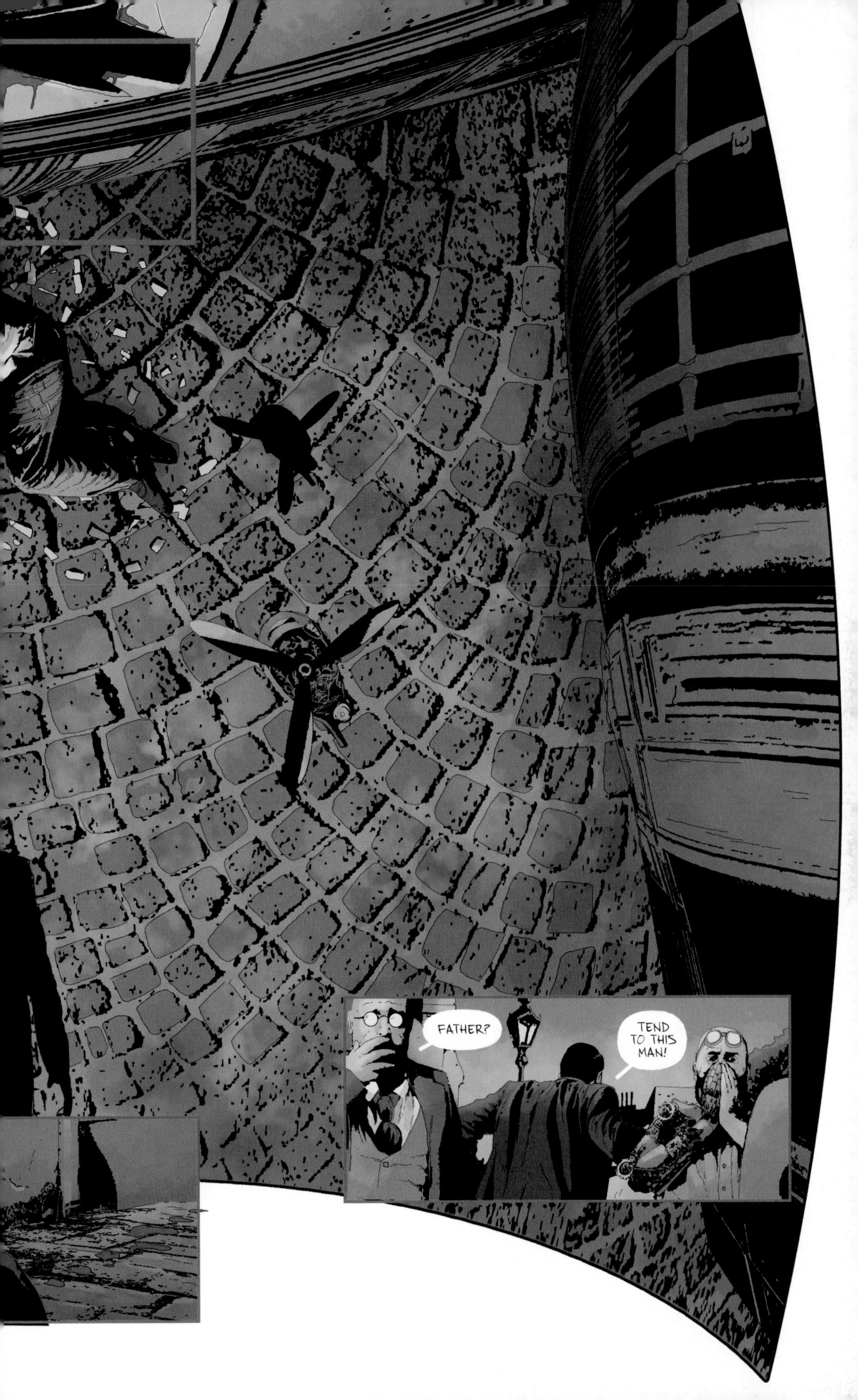
FATHER?
TEND TO THIS MAN!

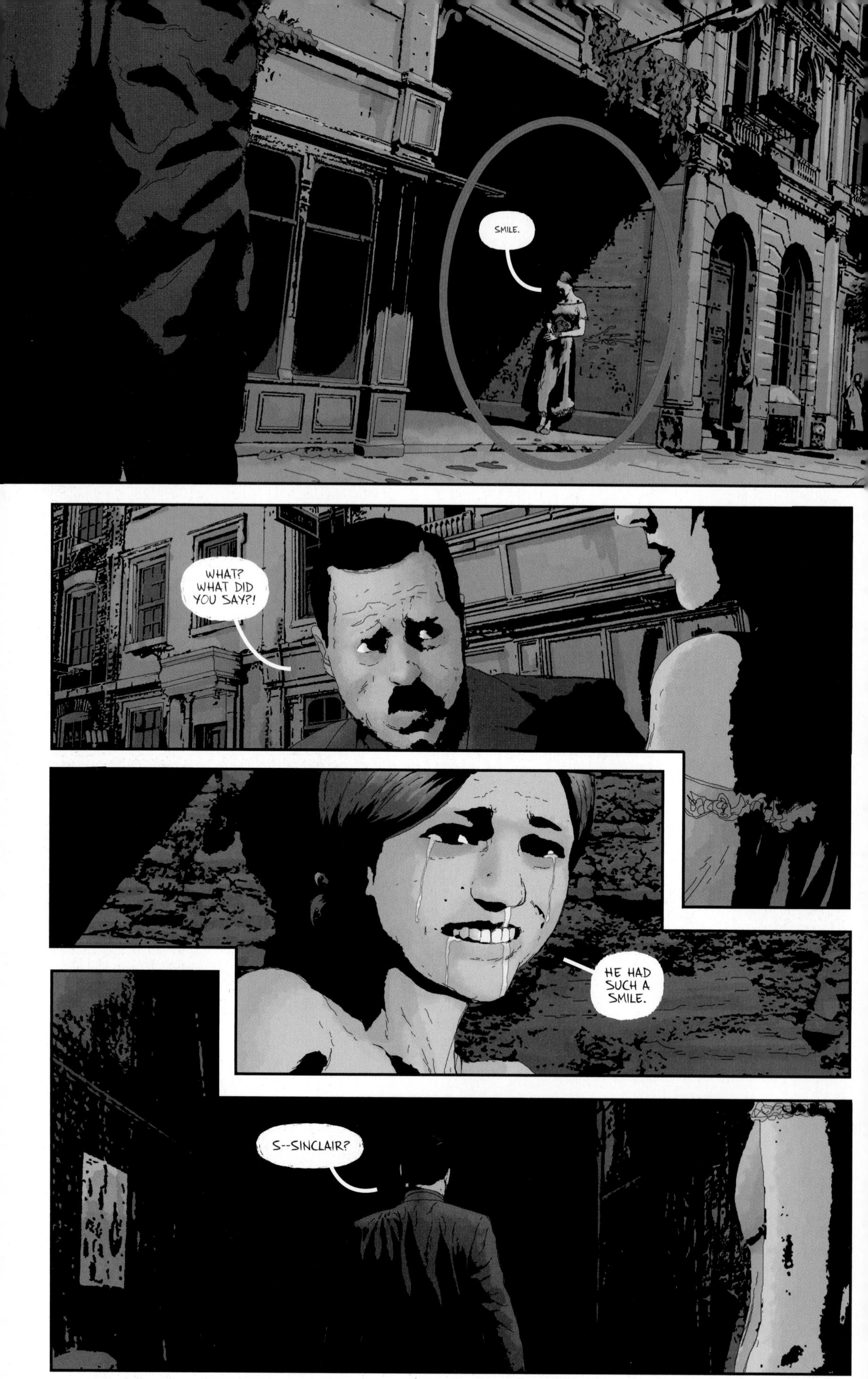
SMILE.
WHAT? WHAT DID YOU SAY?!
HE HAD SUCH A SMILE.
S--SINCLAIR?

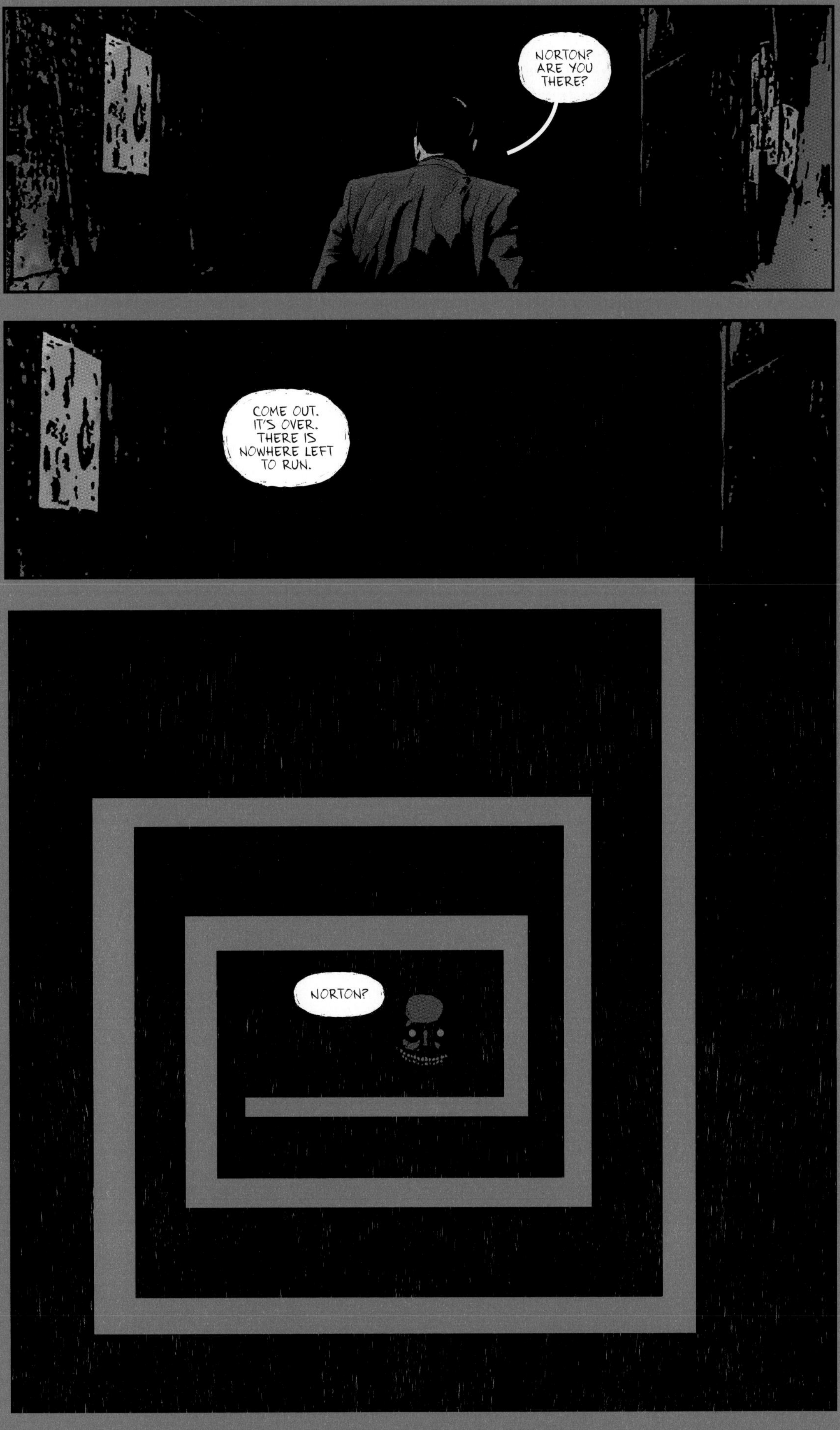
NORTON? ARE YOU THERE?
COME OUT. IT'S OVER. THERE IS NOWHERE LEFT TO RUN.
NORTON?

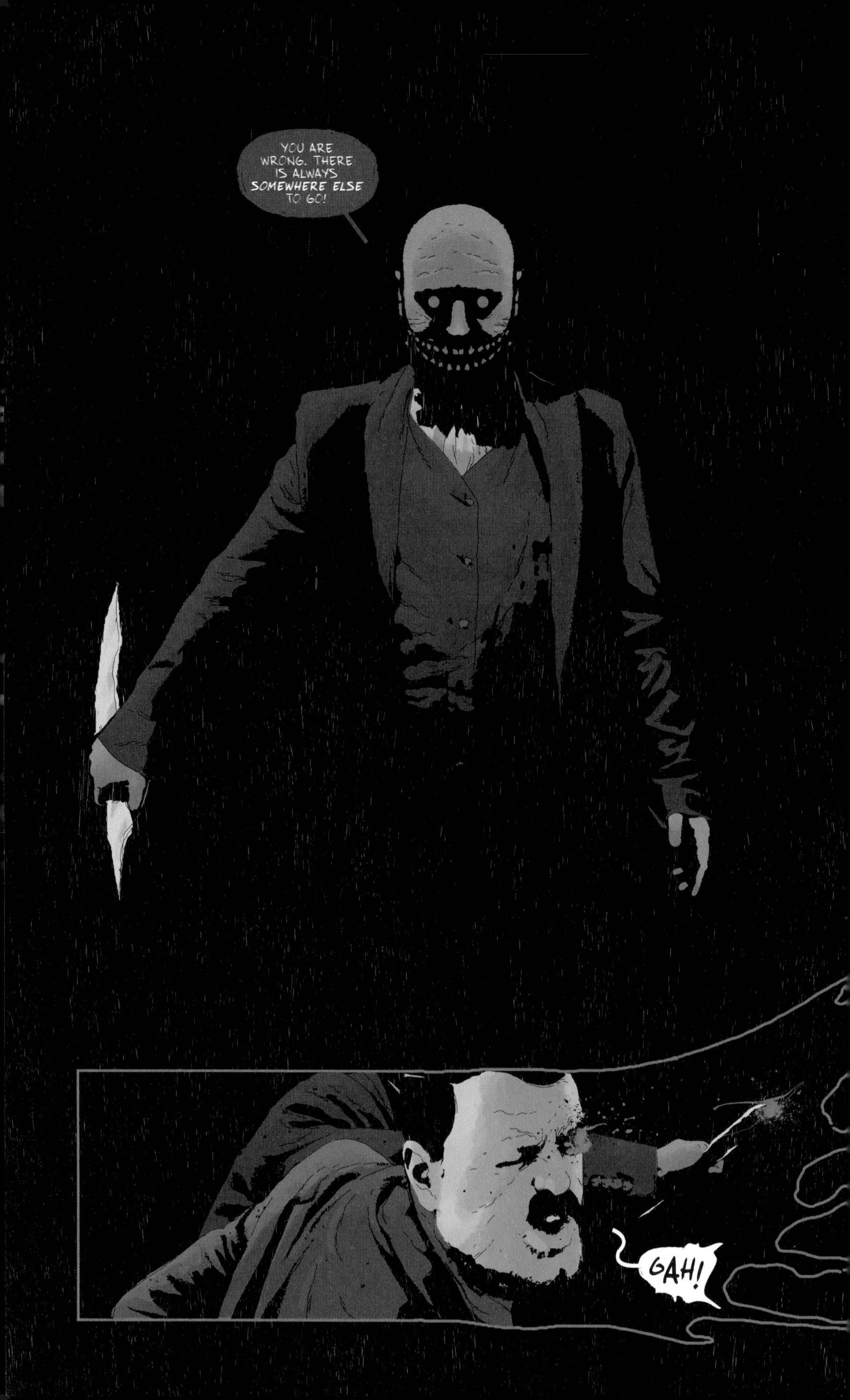
YOU ARE WRONG. THERE IS ALWAYS SOMEWHERE ELSE TO GO!
GAH!

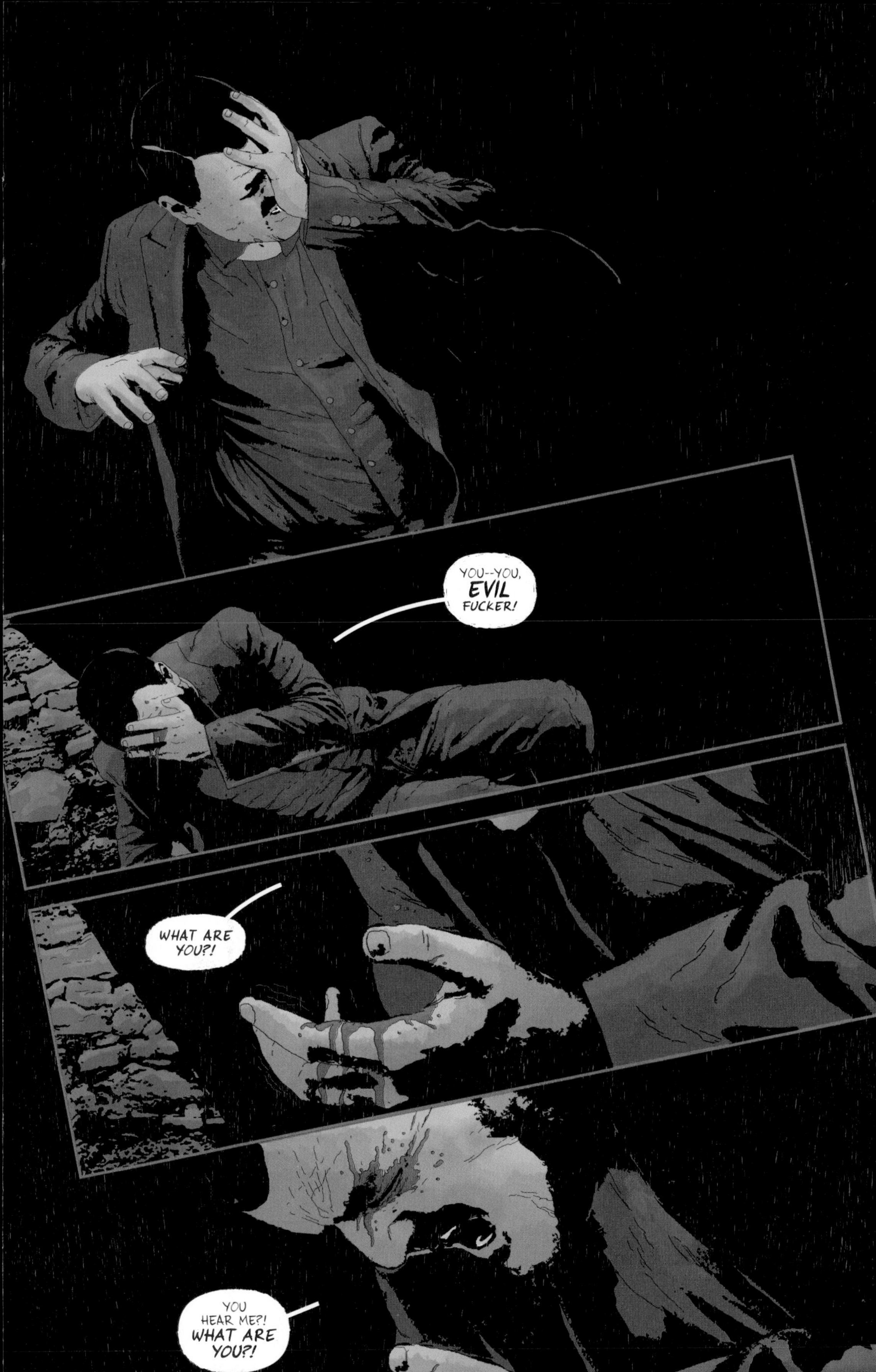
YOU--YOU, EVIL FUCKER!
WHAT ARE YOU?!
YOU HEAR ME?! WHAT ARE YOU?!

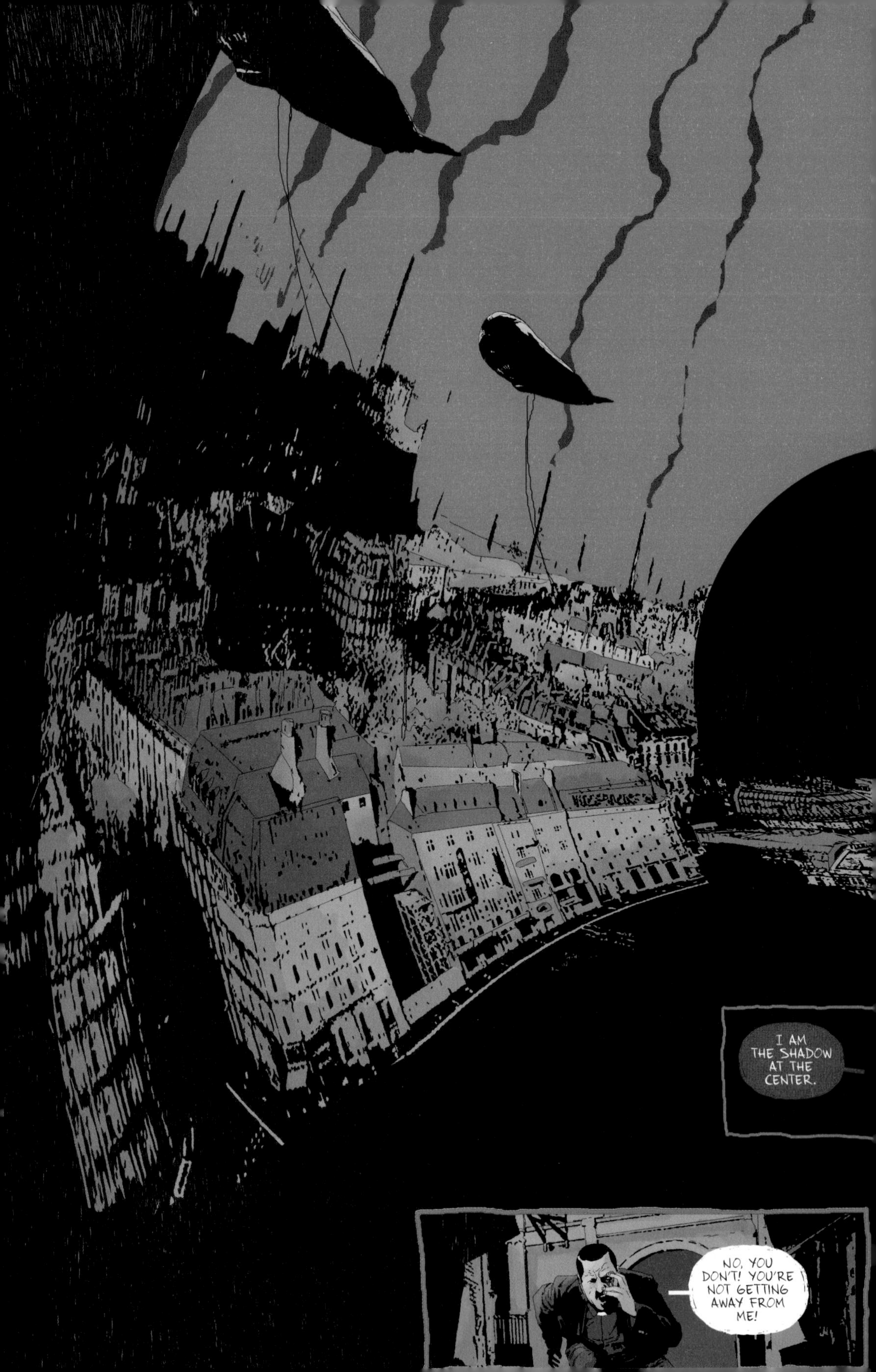
I AM THE SHADOW AT THE CENTER.
NO, YOU DON'T! YOU'RE NOT GETTING AWAY FROM ME!

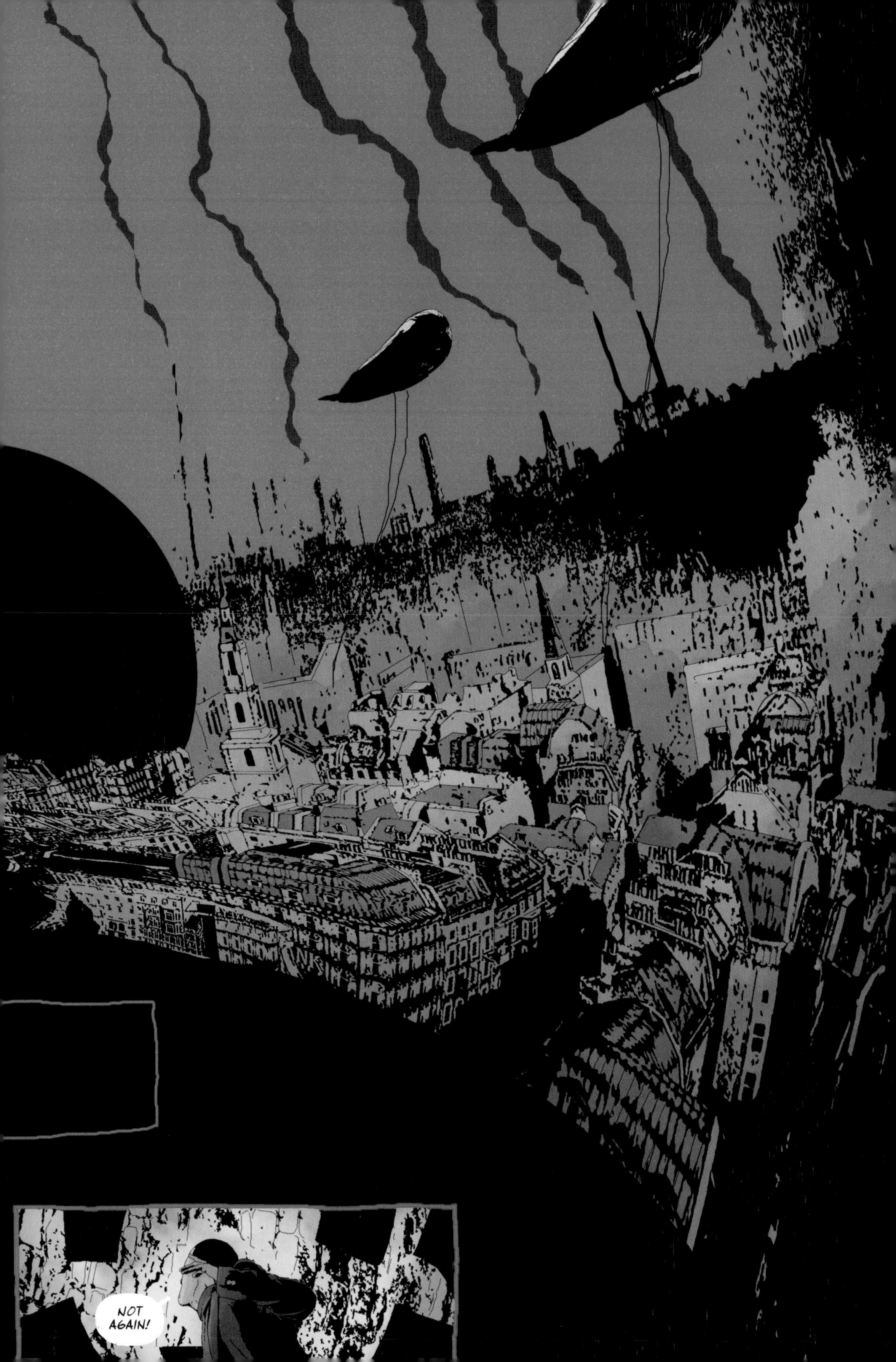
NOT AGAIN!

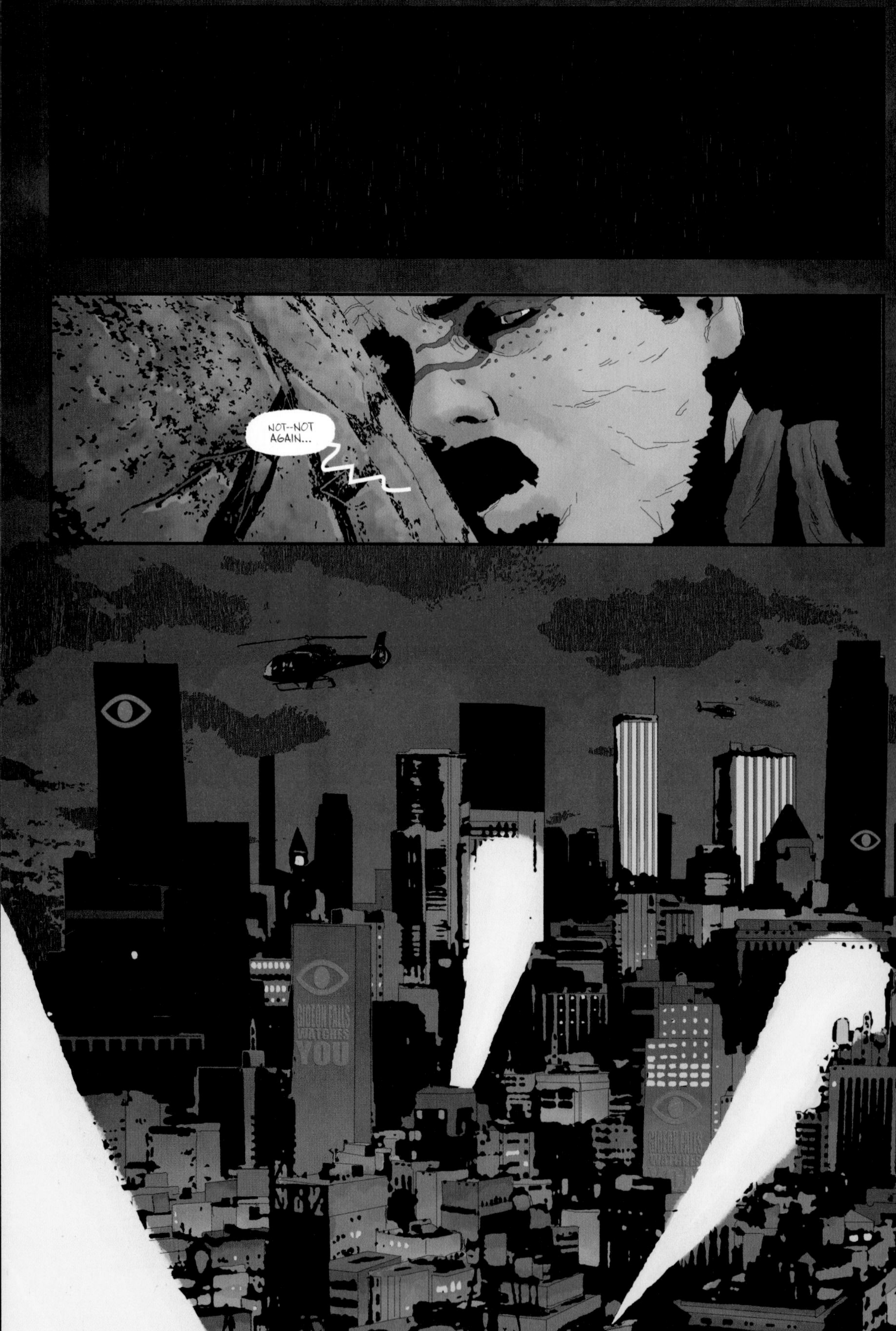
NOT--NOT AGAIN...
GIDEON FALLS WATCHES YOU

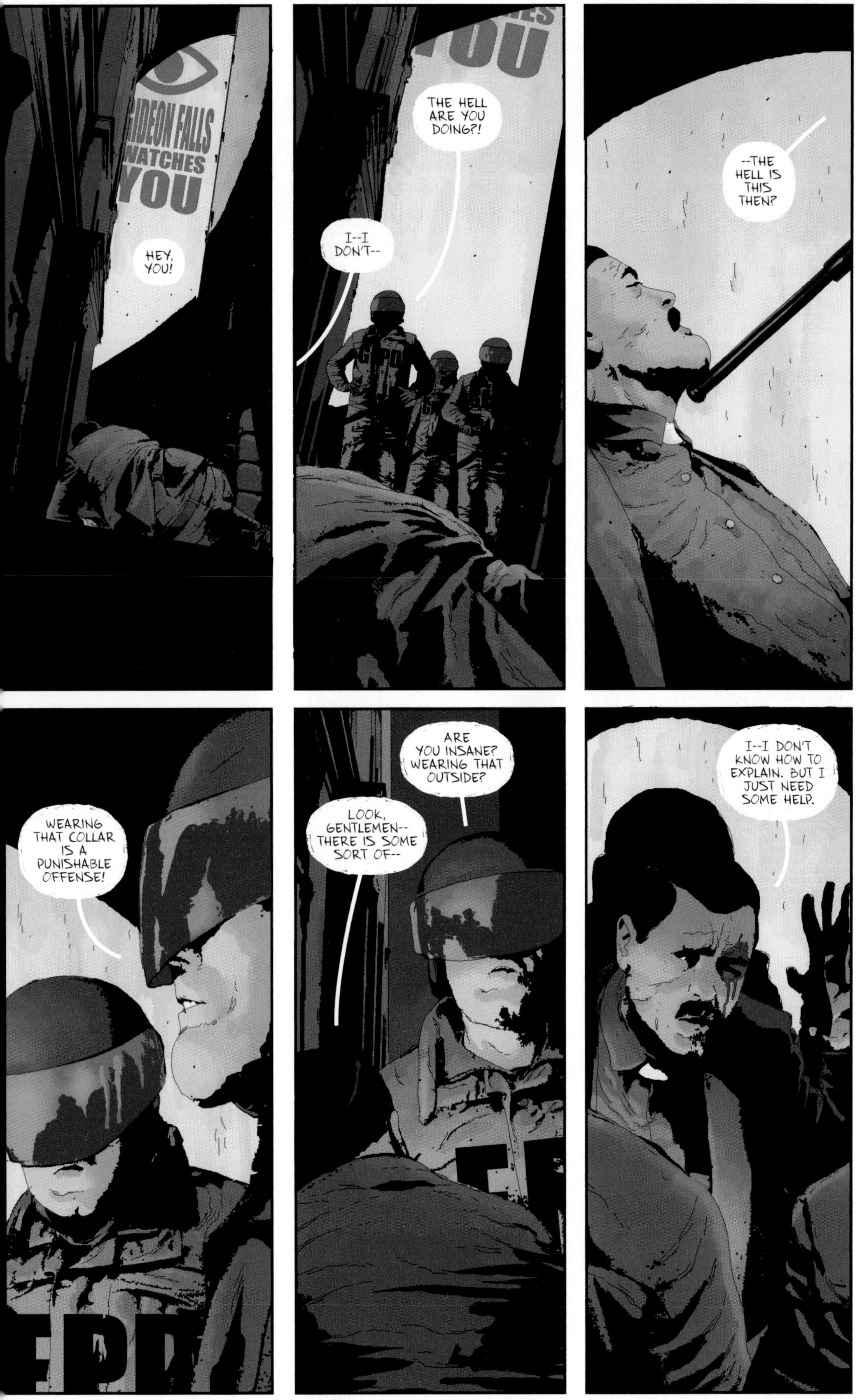
GIDEON FALLS WATCHES YOU
HEY, YOU!
THE HELL ARE YOU DOING?!
I--I DON'T--
--THE HELL IS THIS THEN?
WEARING THAT COLLAR IS A PUNISHABLE OFFENSE!
ARE YOU INSANE? WEARING THAT OUTSIDE?
LOOK, GENTLEMEN--THERE IS SOME SORT OF--
I--I DON'T KNOW HOW TO EXPLAIN. BUT I JUST NEED SOME HELP.

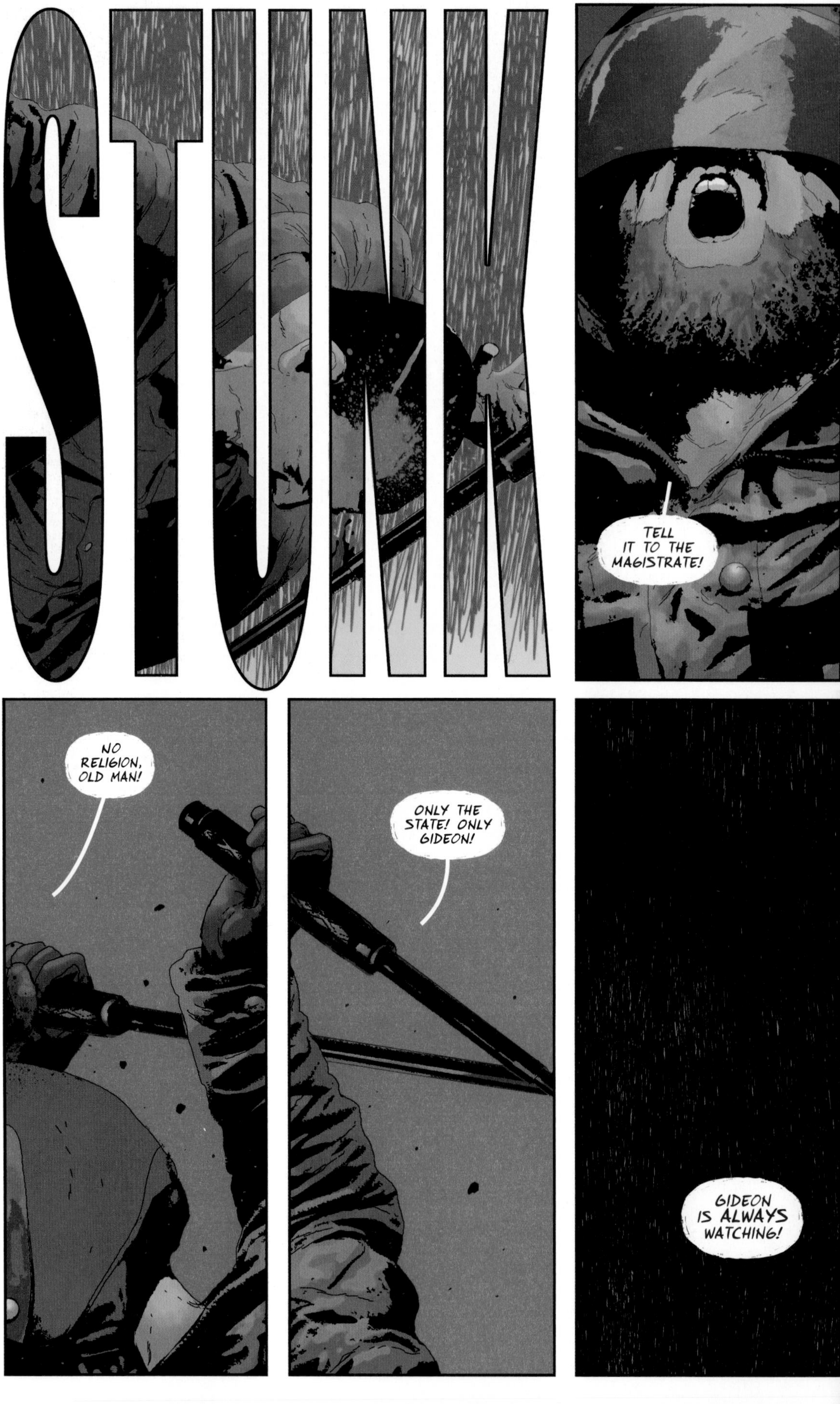
STUNK
TELL IT TO THE MAGISTRATE!
NO RELIGION, OLD MAN!
ONLY THE STATE! ONLY GIDEON!
GIDEON IS ALWAYS WATCHING!

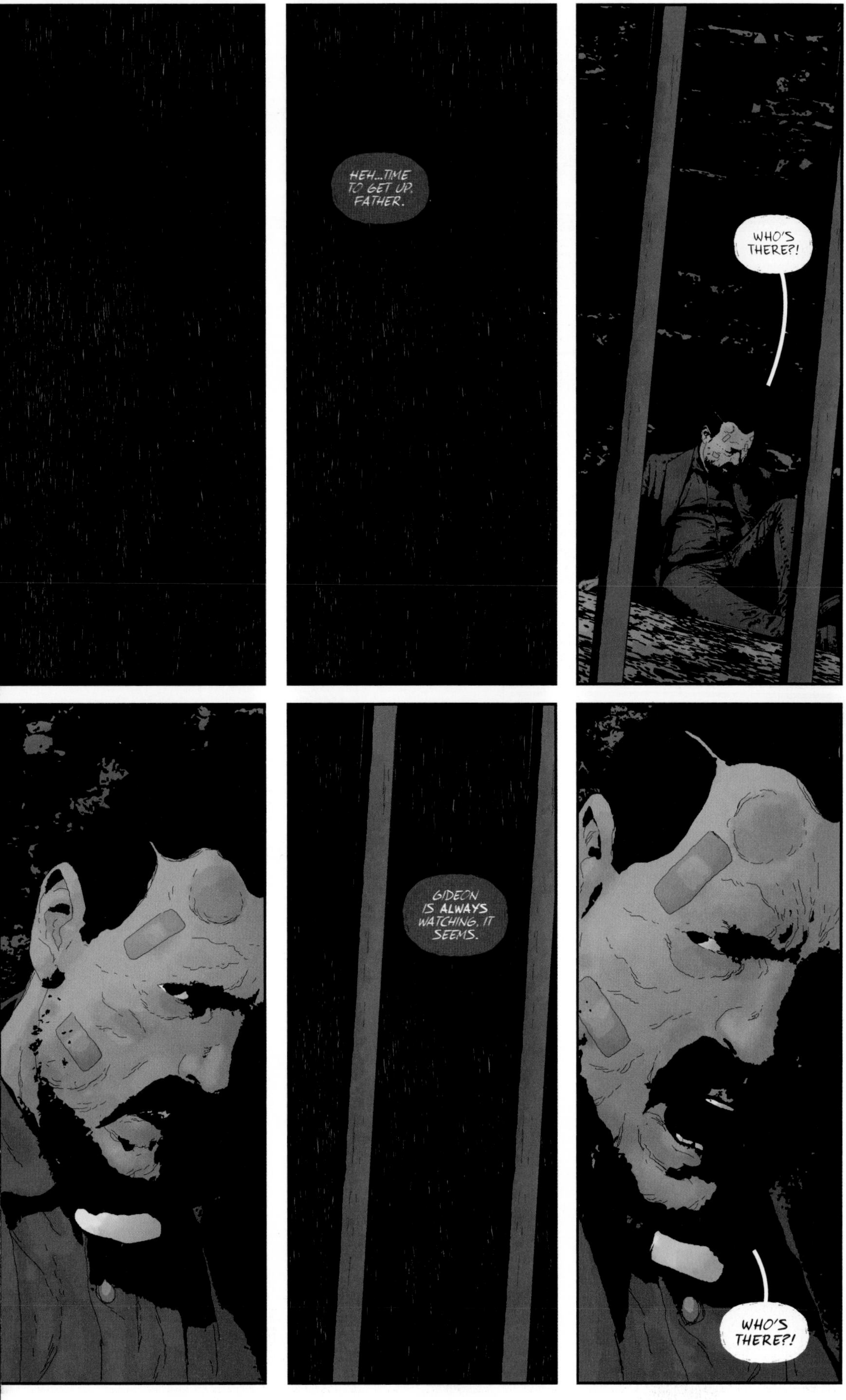
HEH...TIME TO GET UP, FATHER.
WHO'S THERE?!
GIDEON IS **ALWAYS** WATCHING, IT SEEMS.
WHO'S THERE?!

YOU ALREADY KNOW WHO.

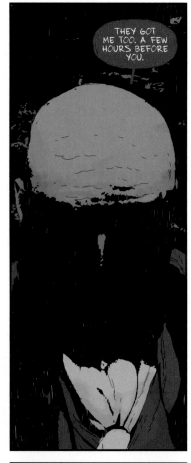

THEY GOT ME TOO. A FEW HOURS BEFORE YOU.

SINCLAIR...THIS--THIS ISN'T YOU. YOU ARE A GOD-FEARING MAN. I KNOW YOU. YOU NEED TO FIGHT THAT THING THAT IS INSIDE OF YOU.

WHY DIDN'T YOU DIE?

WHAT?

YOU SURVIVED THE PENTOCULUS.

HE SAID ONLY I COULD DO THAT. HE SAID I WAS SPECIAL.

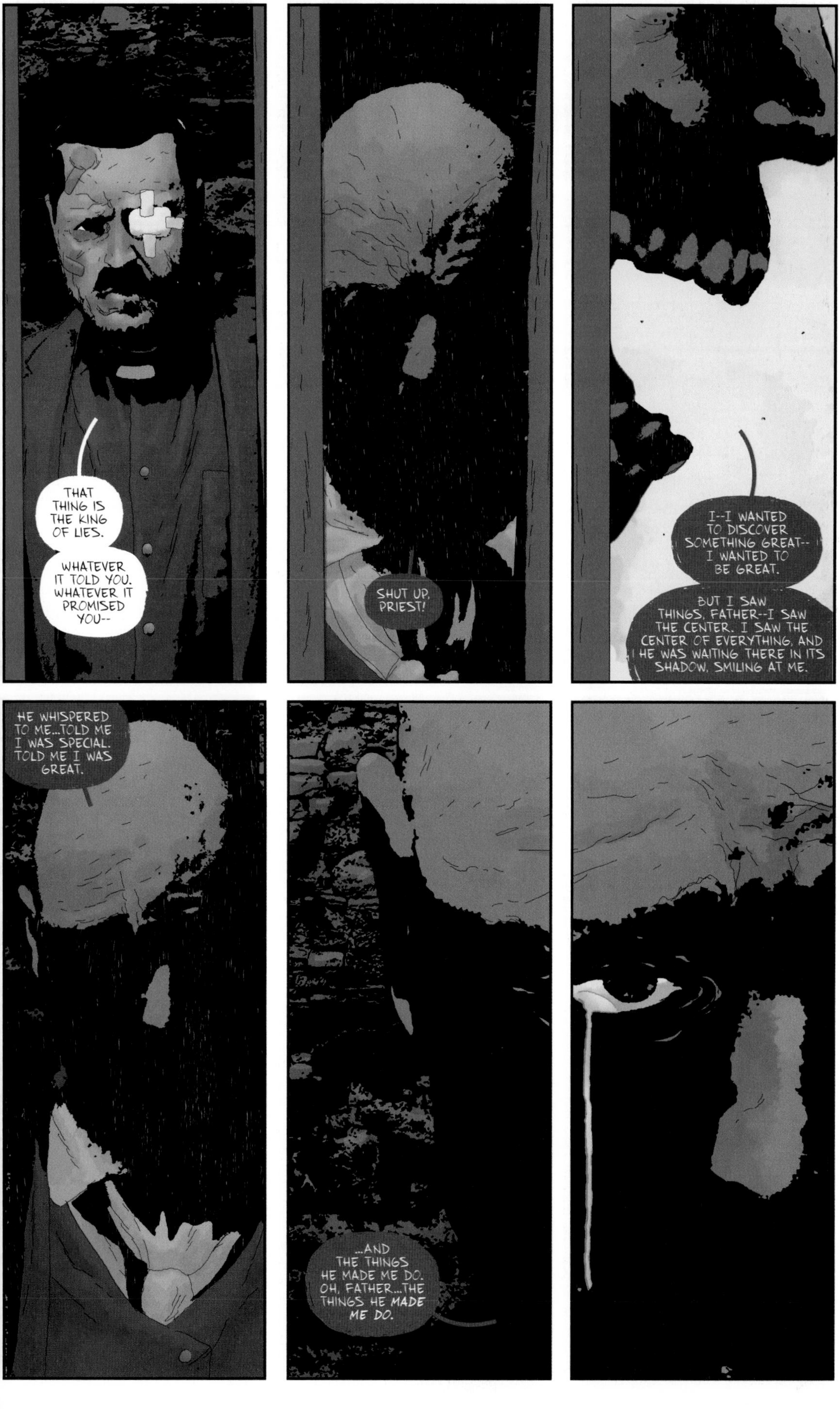
THAT THING IS THE KING OF LIES.
WHATEVER IT TOLD YOU. WHATEVER IT PROMISED YOU--
SHUT UP, PRIEST!
I--I WANTED TO DISCOVER SOMETHING GREAT-- I WANTED TO BE GREAT.
BUT I SAW THINGS, FATHER--I SAW THE CENTER. I SAW THE CENTER OF EVERYTHING, AND HE WAS WAITING THERE IN ITS SHADOW, SMILING AT ME.
HE WHISPERED TO ME...TOLD ME I WAS SPECIAL. TOLD ME I WAS GREAT.
...AND THE THINGS HE MADE ME DO. OH, FATHER...THE THINGS HE MADE ME DO.

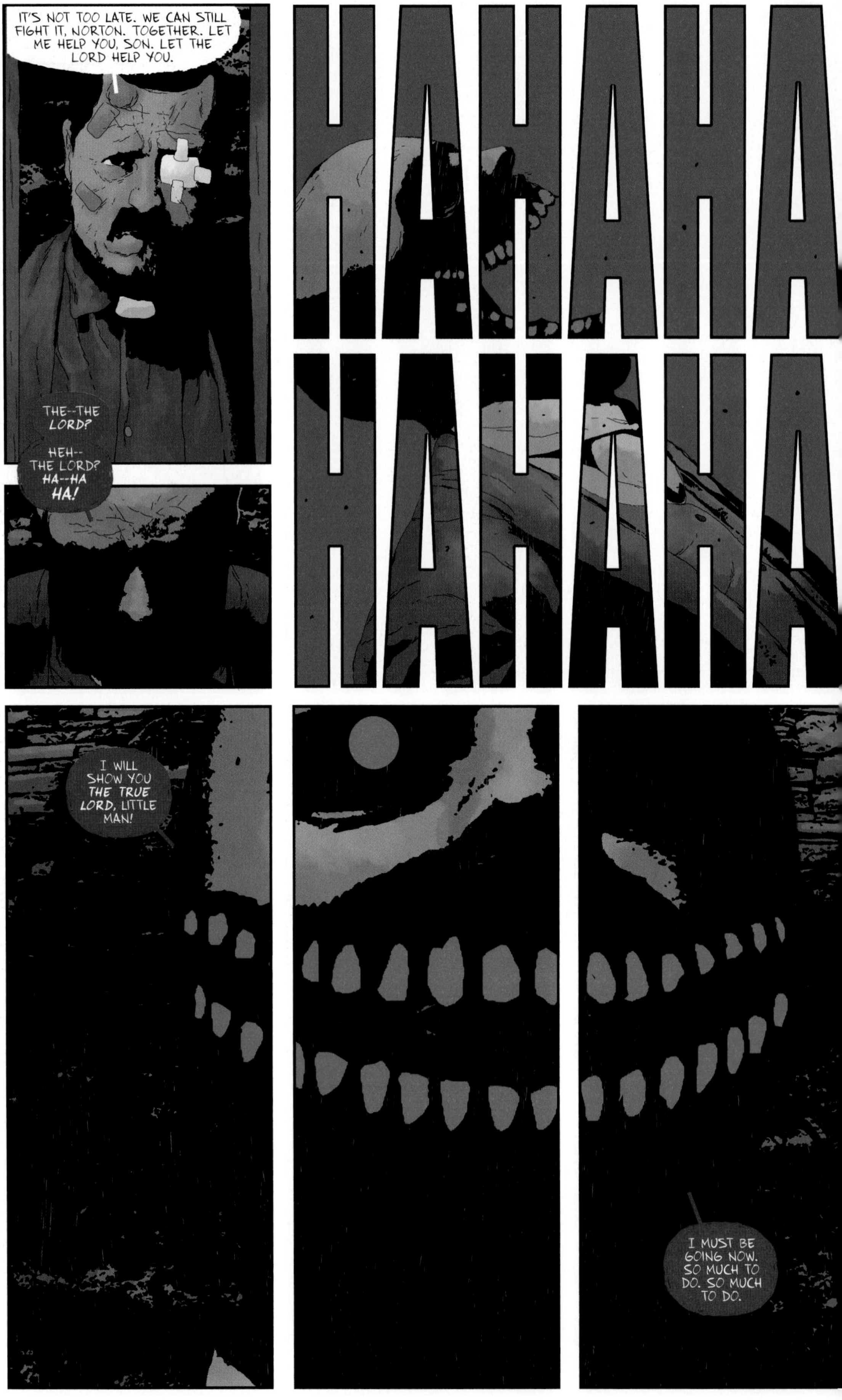
IT'S NOT TOO LATE. WE CAN STILL FIGHT IT, NORTON. TOGETHER. LET ME HELP YOU, SON. LET THE LORD HELP YOU.
THE--THE LORD?
HEH-- THE LORD? HA--HA HA!
HAHAHAHA
HAHAHAHA
I WILL SHOW YOU THE TRUE LORD, LITTLE MAN!
I MUST BE GOING NOW. SO MUCH TO DO. SO MUCH TO DO.

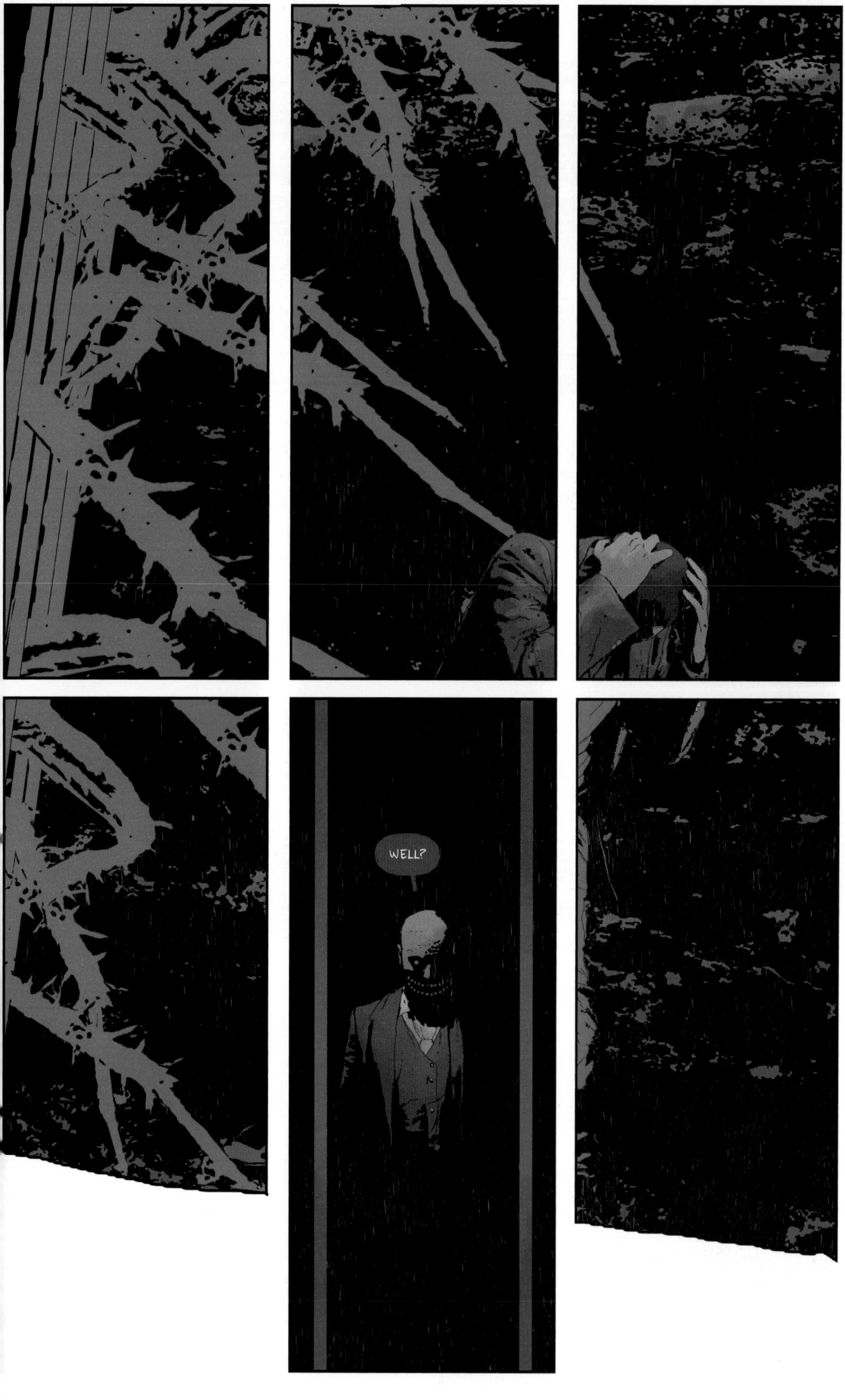
WELL?

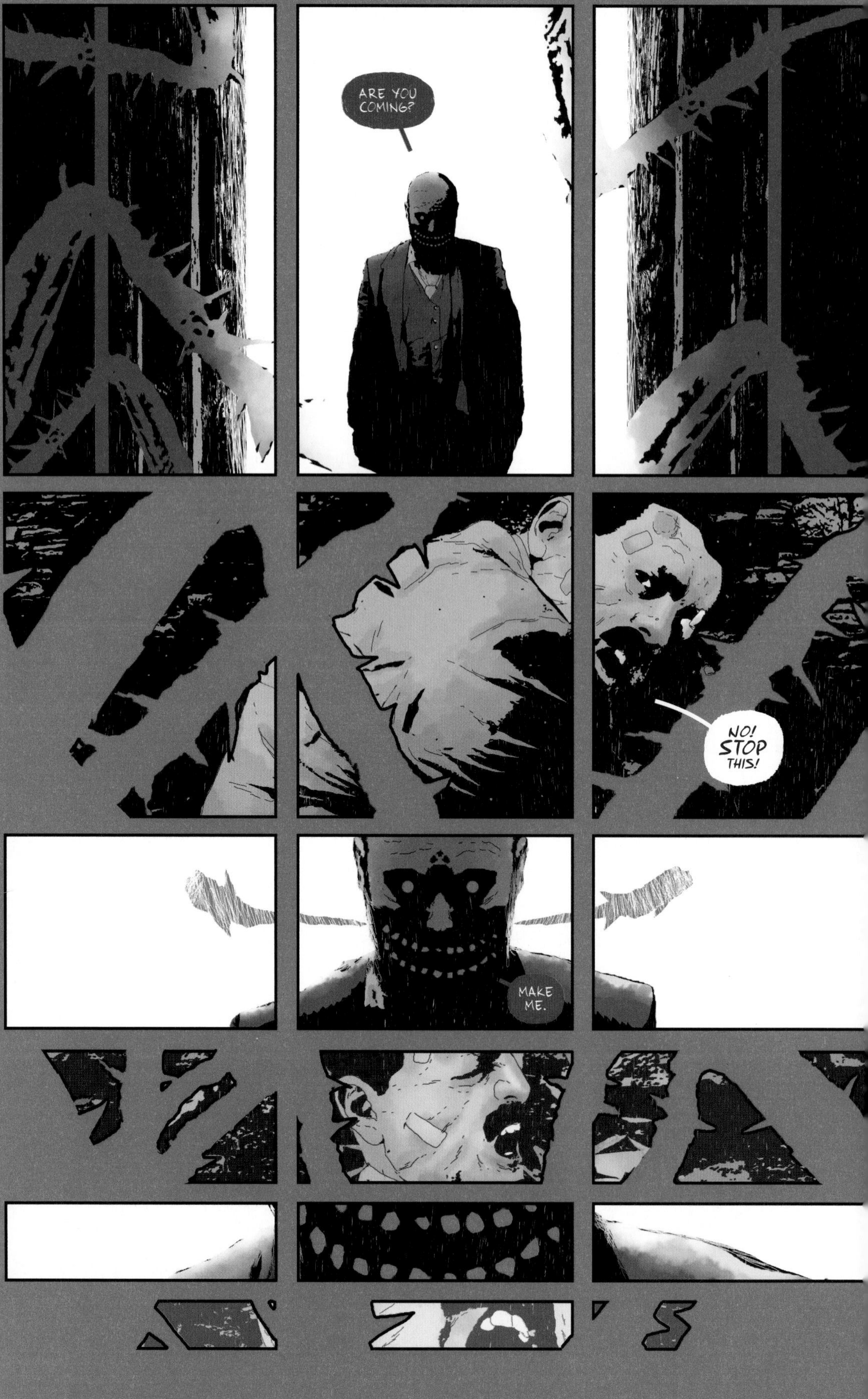
ARE YOU COMING?
NO! STOP THIS!
MAKE ME.

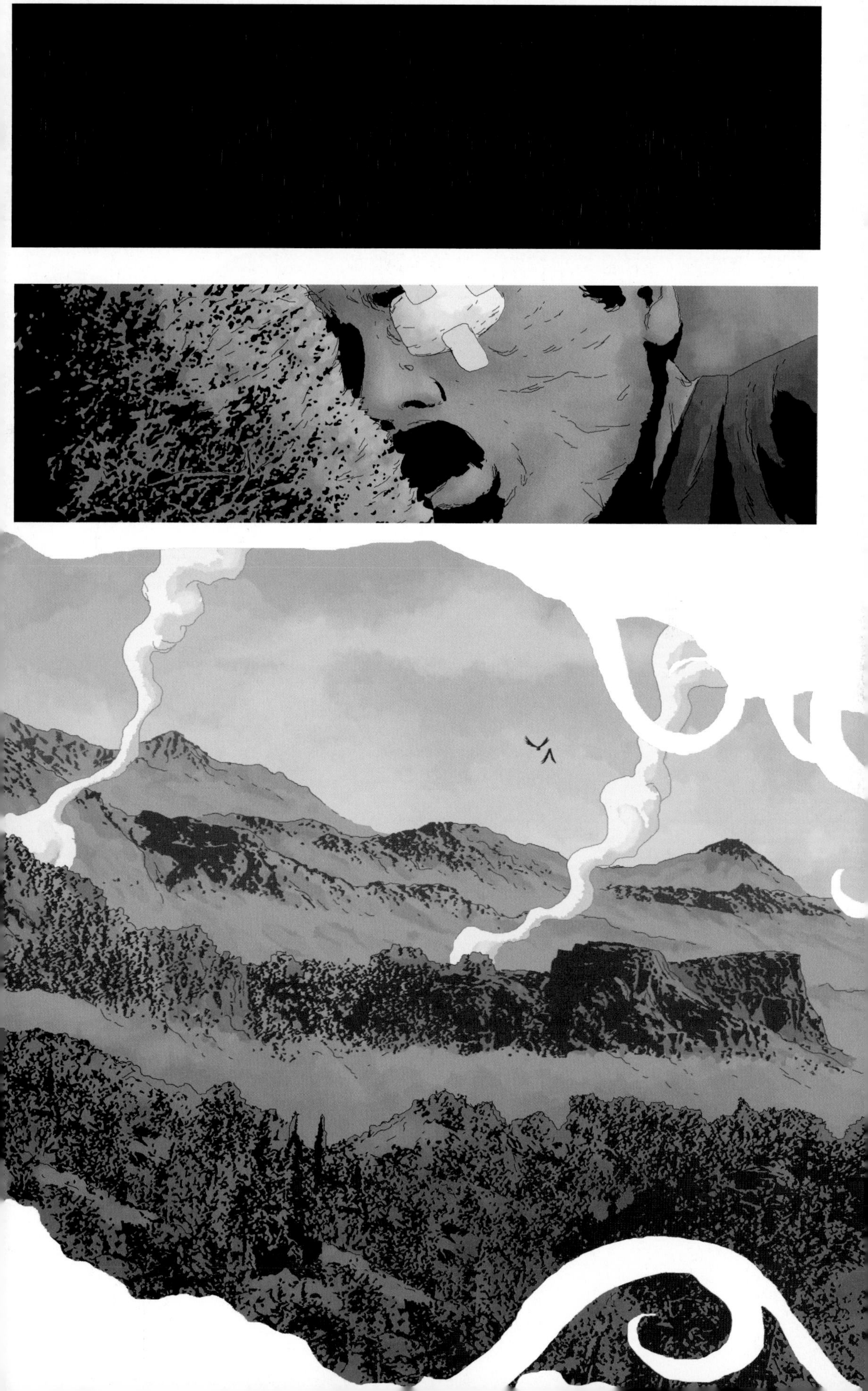

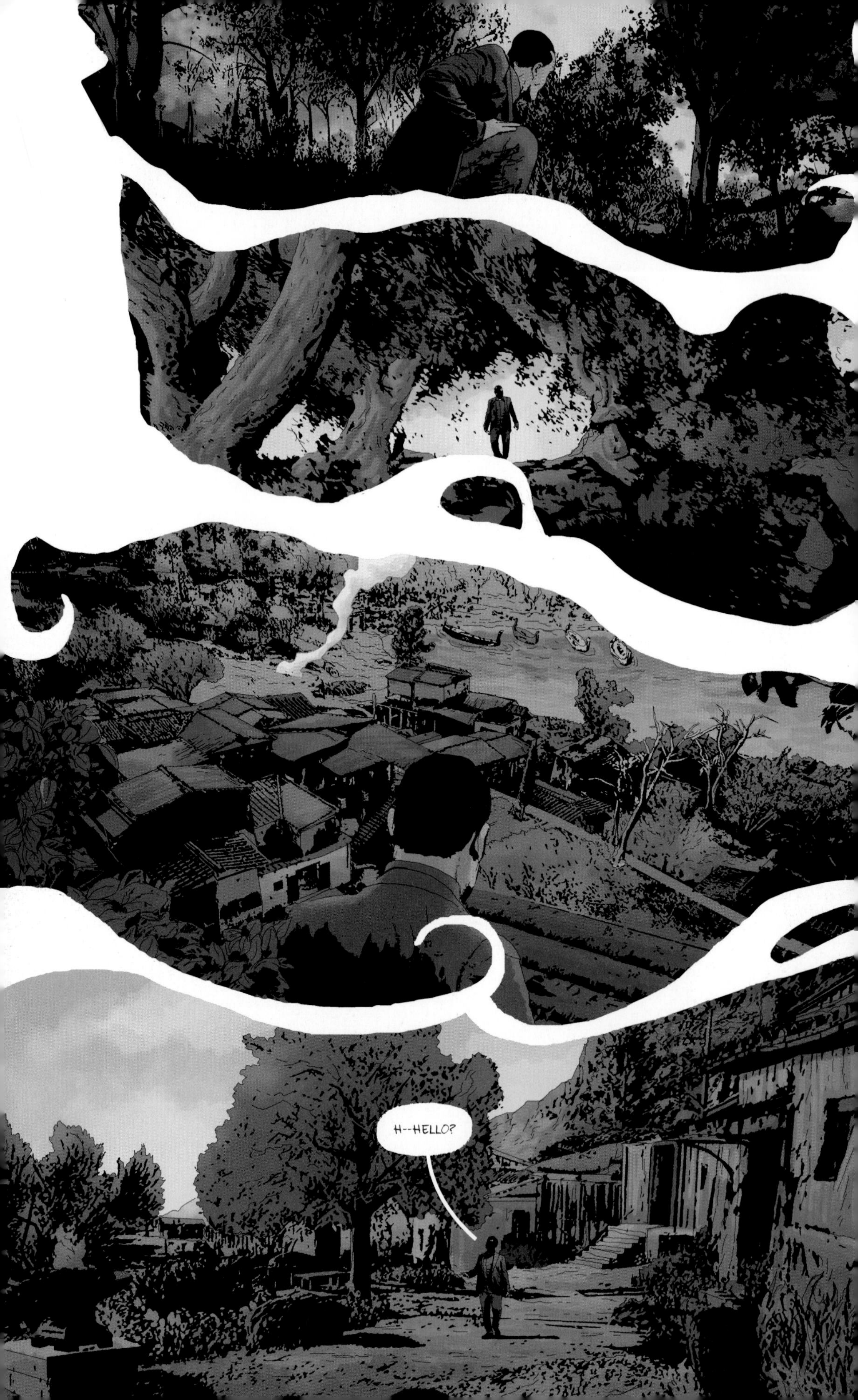
H--HELLO?

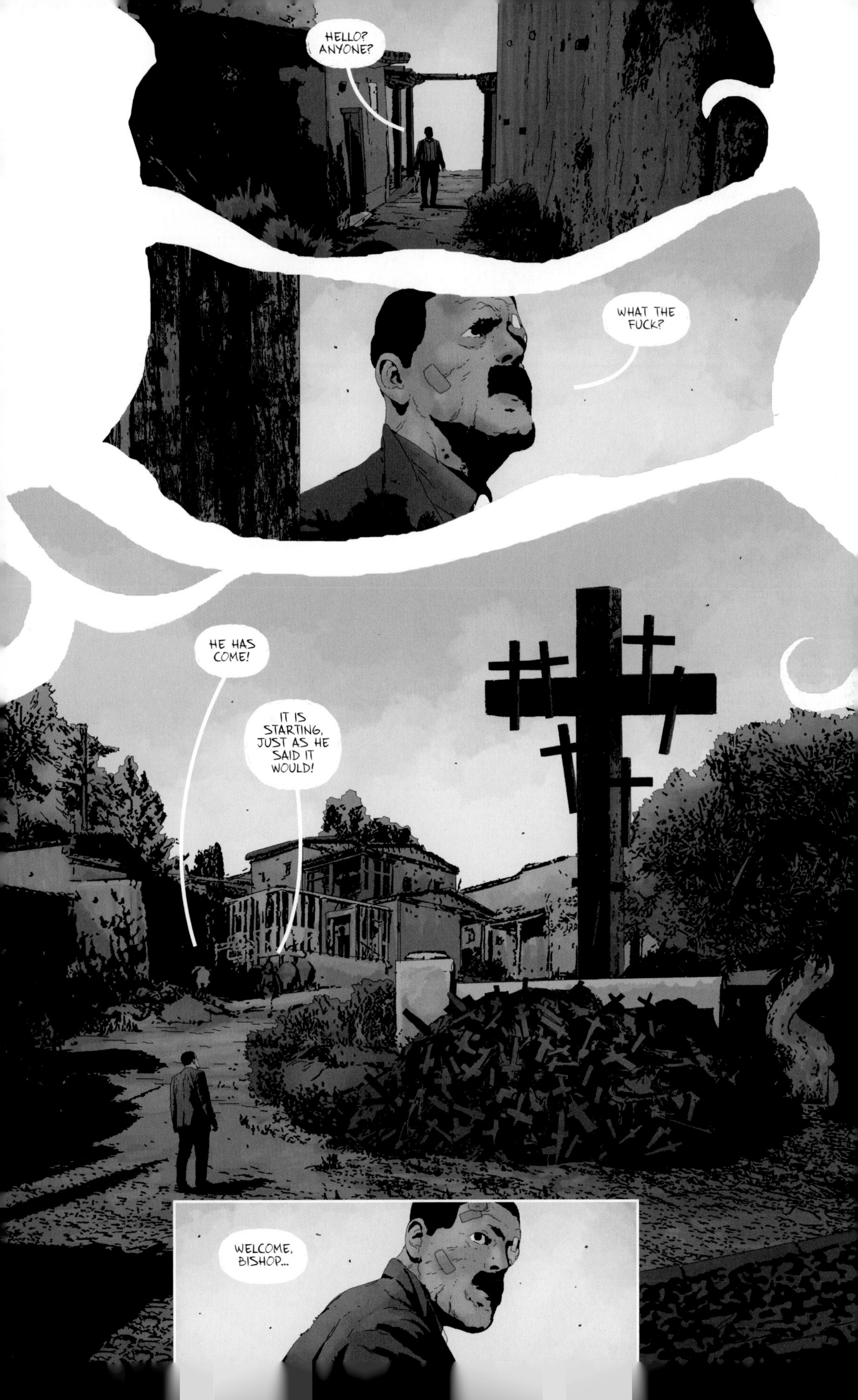
HELLO? ANYONE?
WHAT THE FUCK?
HE HAS COME!
IT IS STARTING, JUST AS HE SAID IT WOULD!
WELCOME, BISHOP...

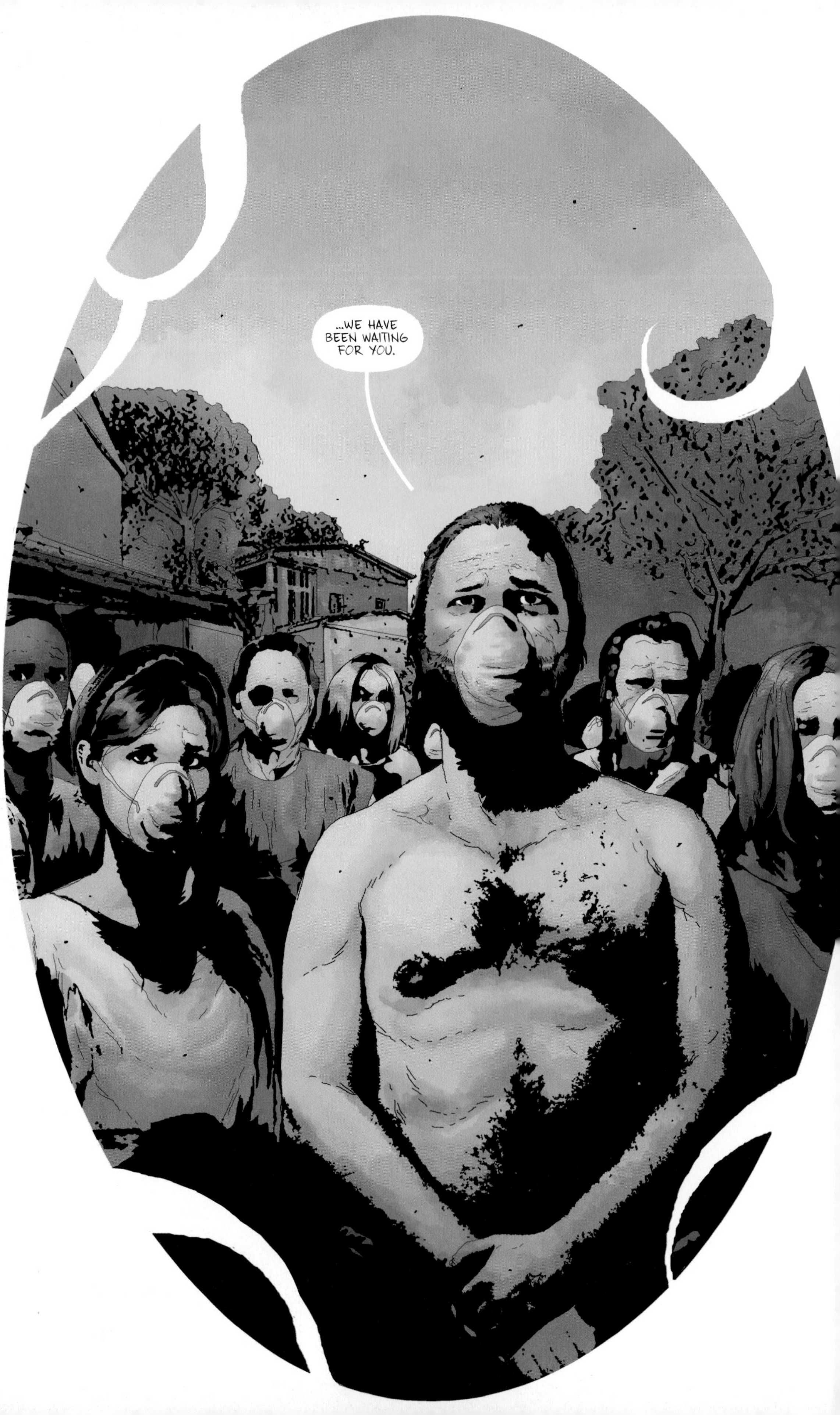
...WE HAVE BEEN WAITING FOR YOU.

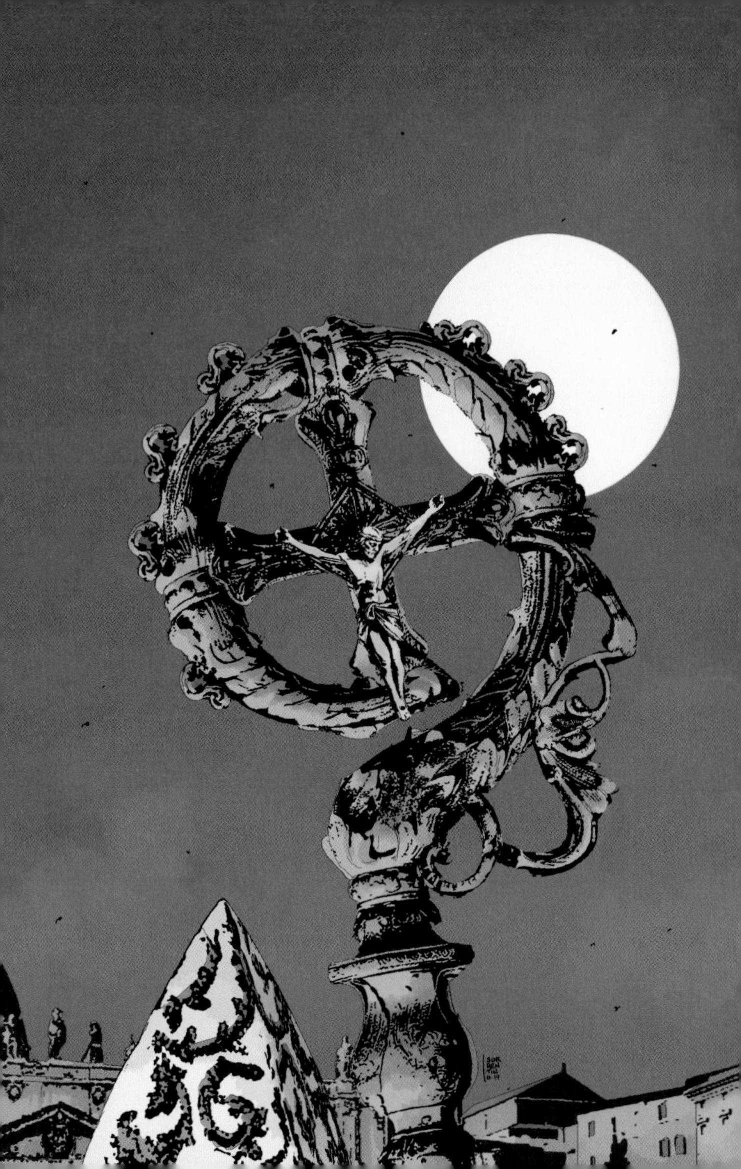

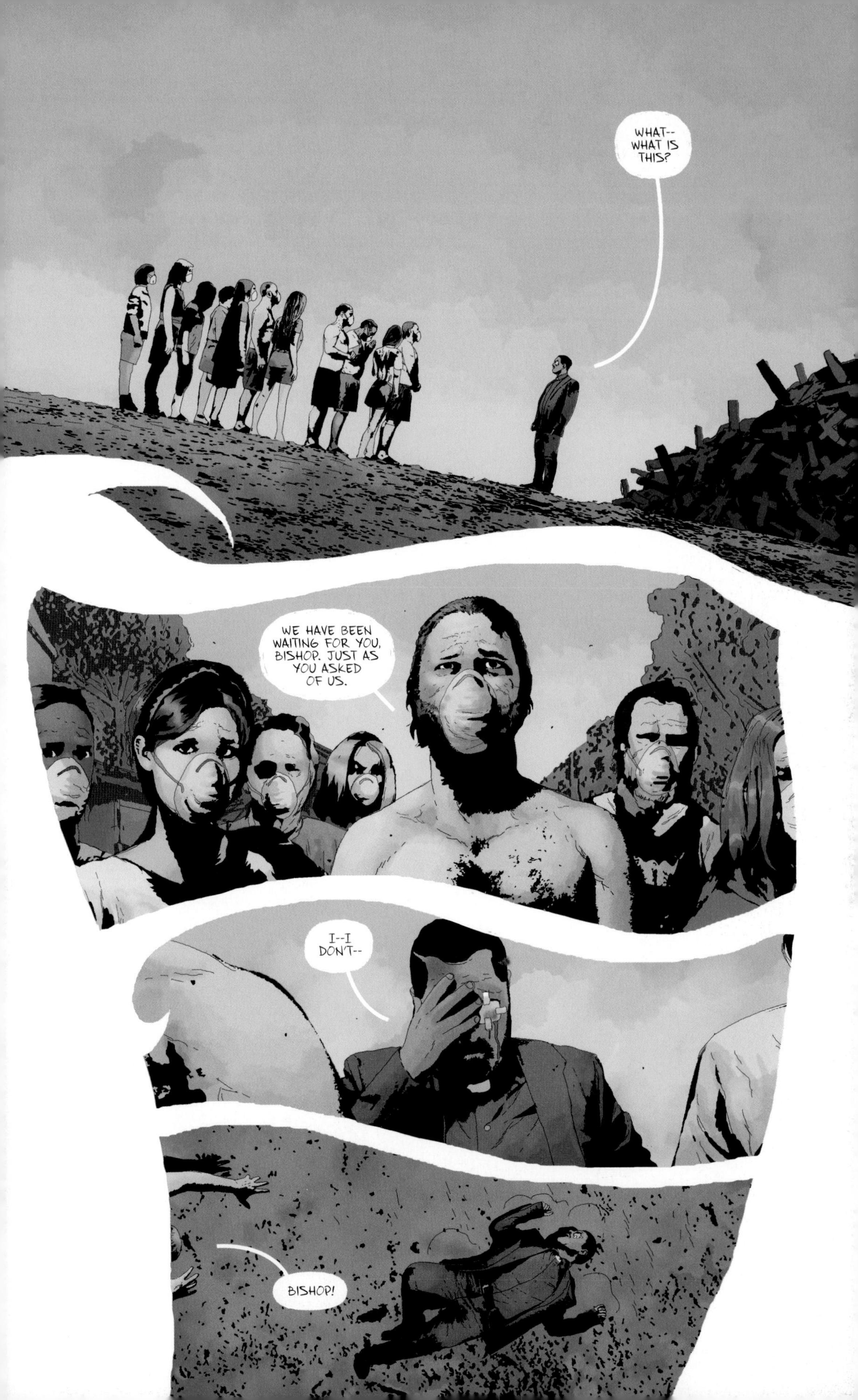
WHAT--
WHAT IS THIS?
WE HAVE BEEN WAITING FOR YOU, BISHOP. JUST AS YOU ASKED OF US.
I--I DON'T--
BISHOP!

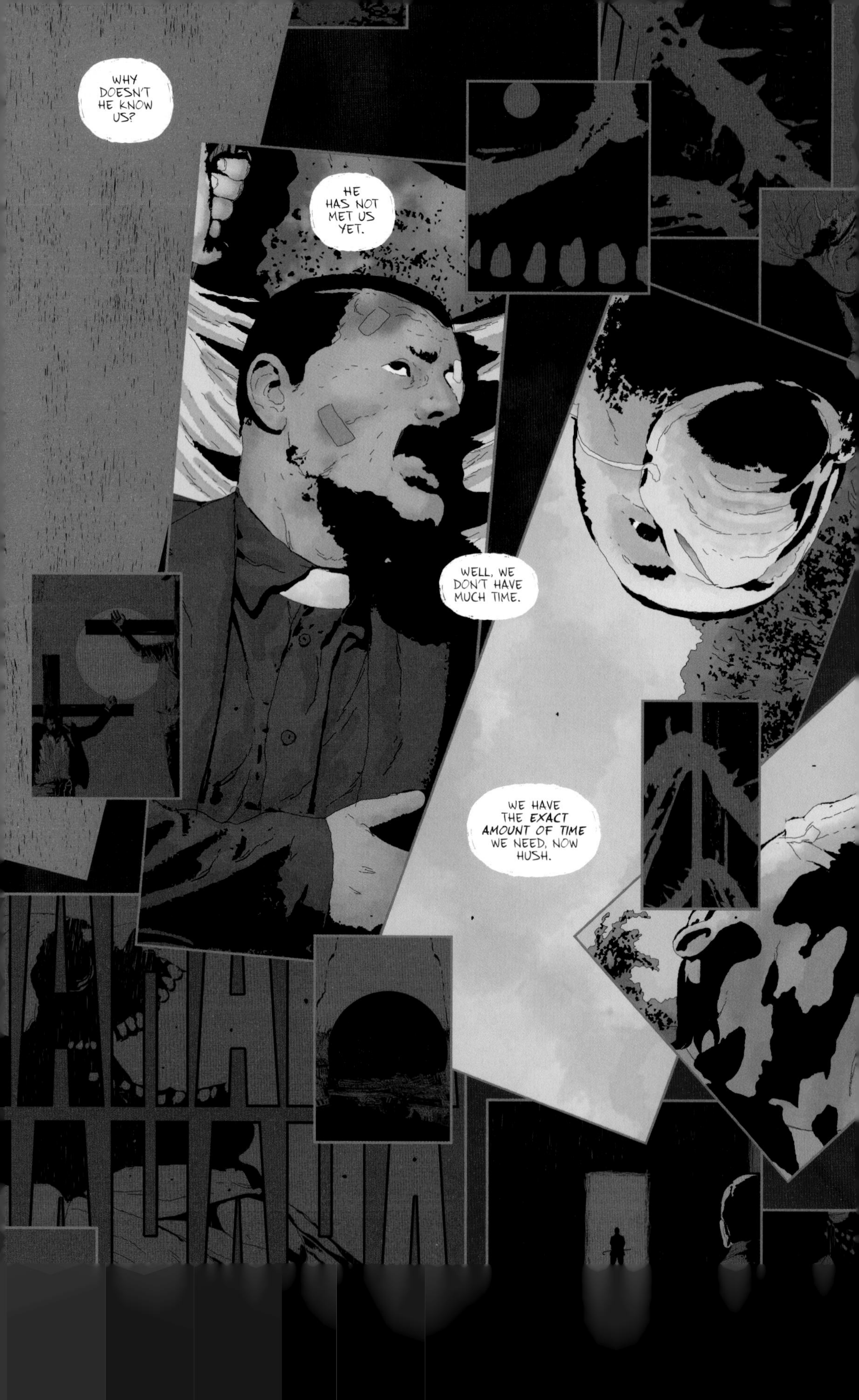
WHY DOESN'T HE KNOW US?
HE HAS NOT MET US YET.
WELL, WE DON'T HAVE MUCH TIME.
WE HAVE THE EXACT AMOUNT OF TIME WE NEED, NOW HUSH.

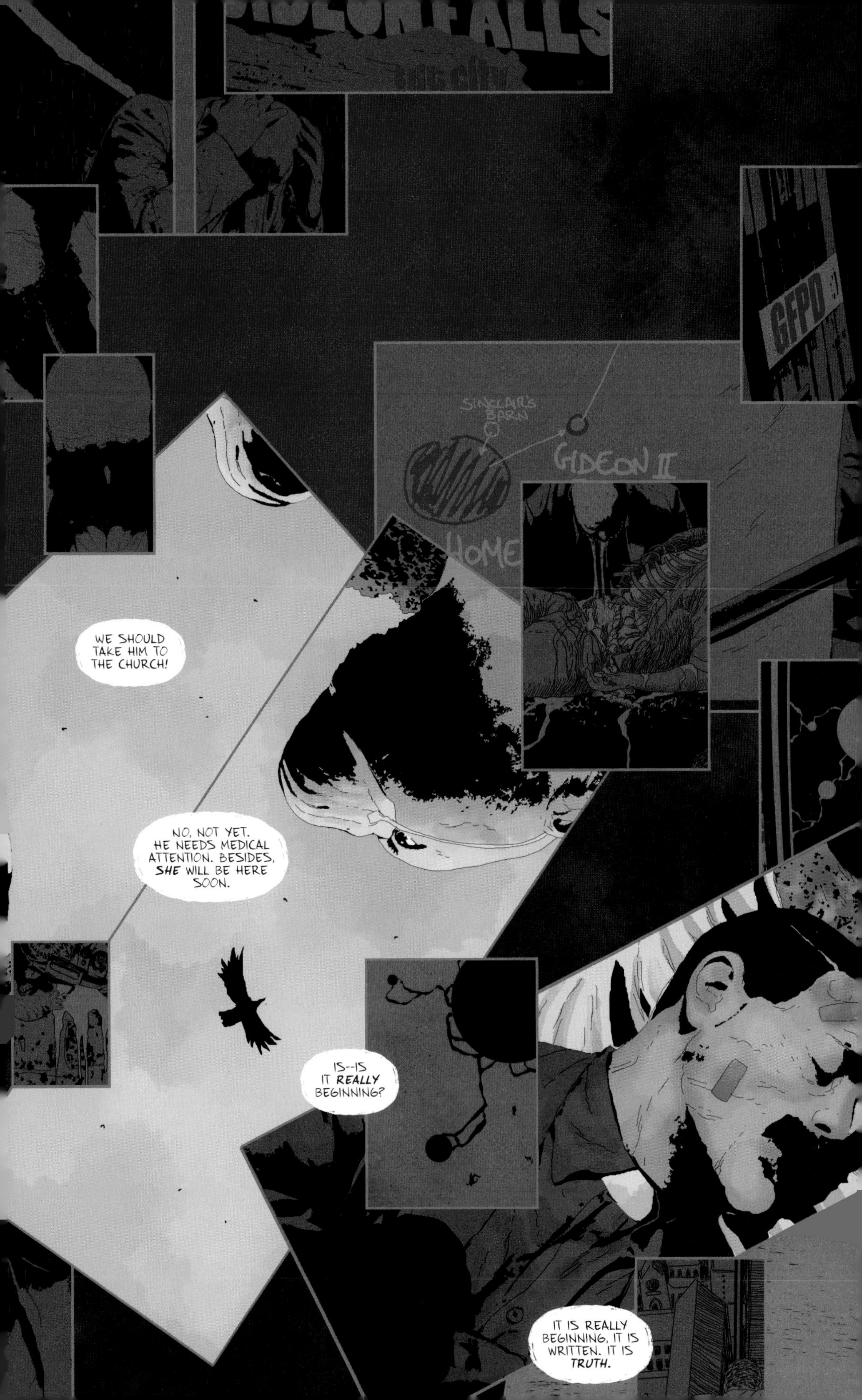
GIDEON FALLS
GFPD
SINCLAIR'S BARN
GIDEON II
HOME
WE SHOULD TAKE HIM TO THE CHURCH!
NO, NOT YET. HE NEEDS MEDICAL ATTENTION. BESIDES, SHE WILL BE HERE SOON.
IS--IS IT REALLY BEGINNING?
IT IS REALLY BEGINNING, IT IS WRITTEN. IT IS TRUTH.

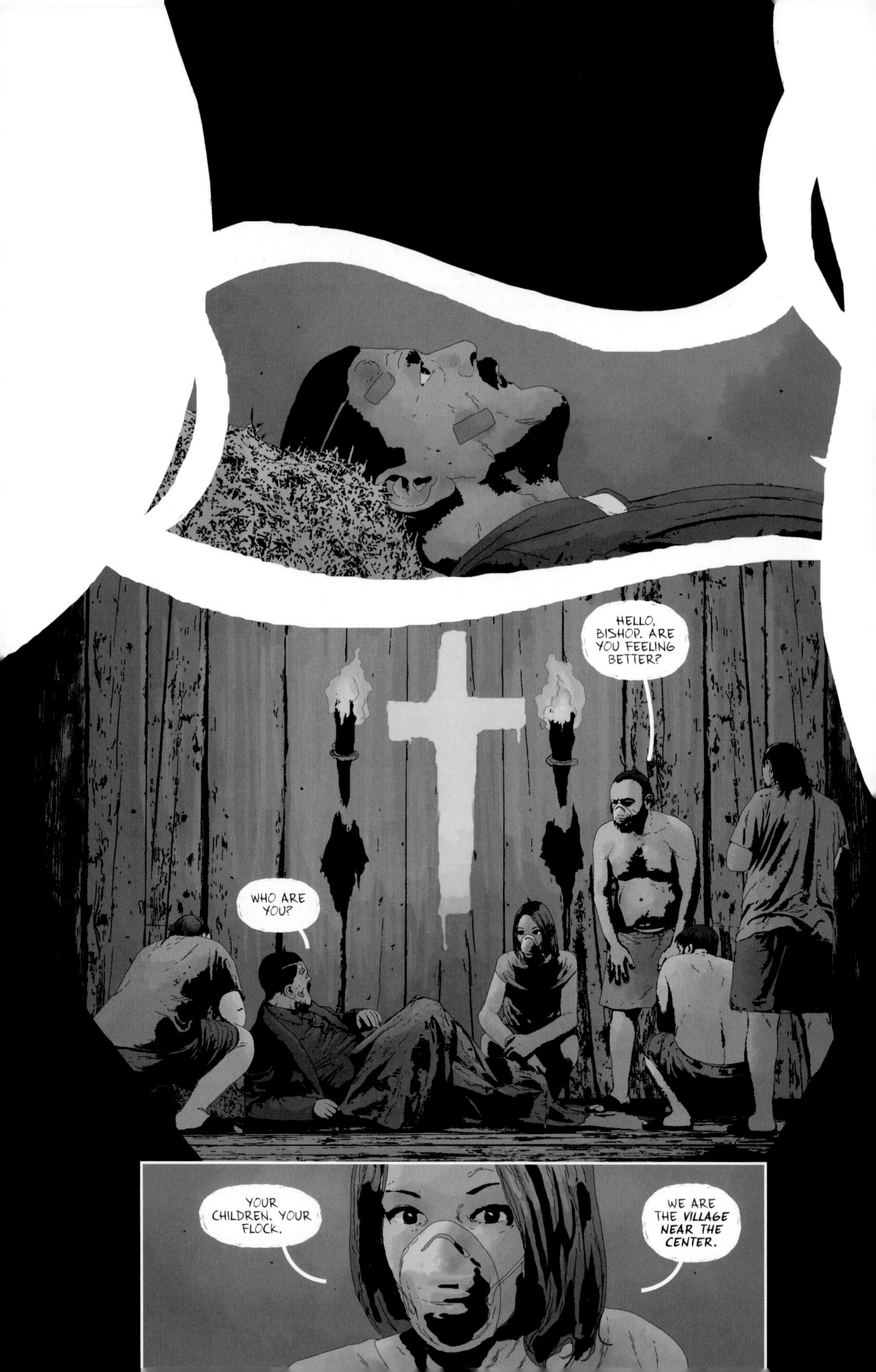
HELLO, BISHOP. ARE YOU FEELING BETTER?
WHO ARE YOU?
YOUR CHILDREN. YOUR FLOCK.
WE ARE THE *VILLAGE NEAR THE CENTER.*

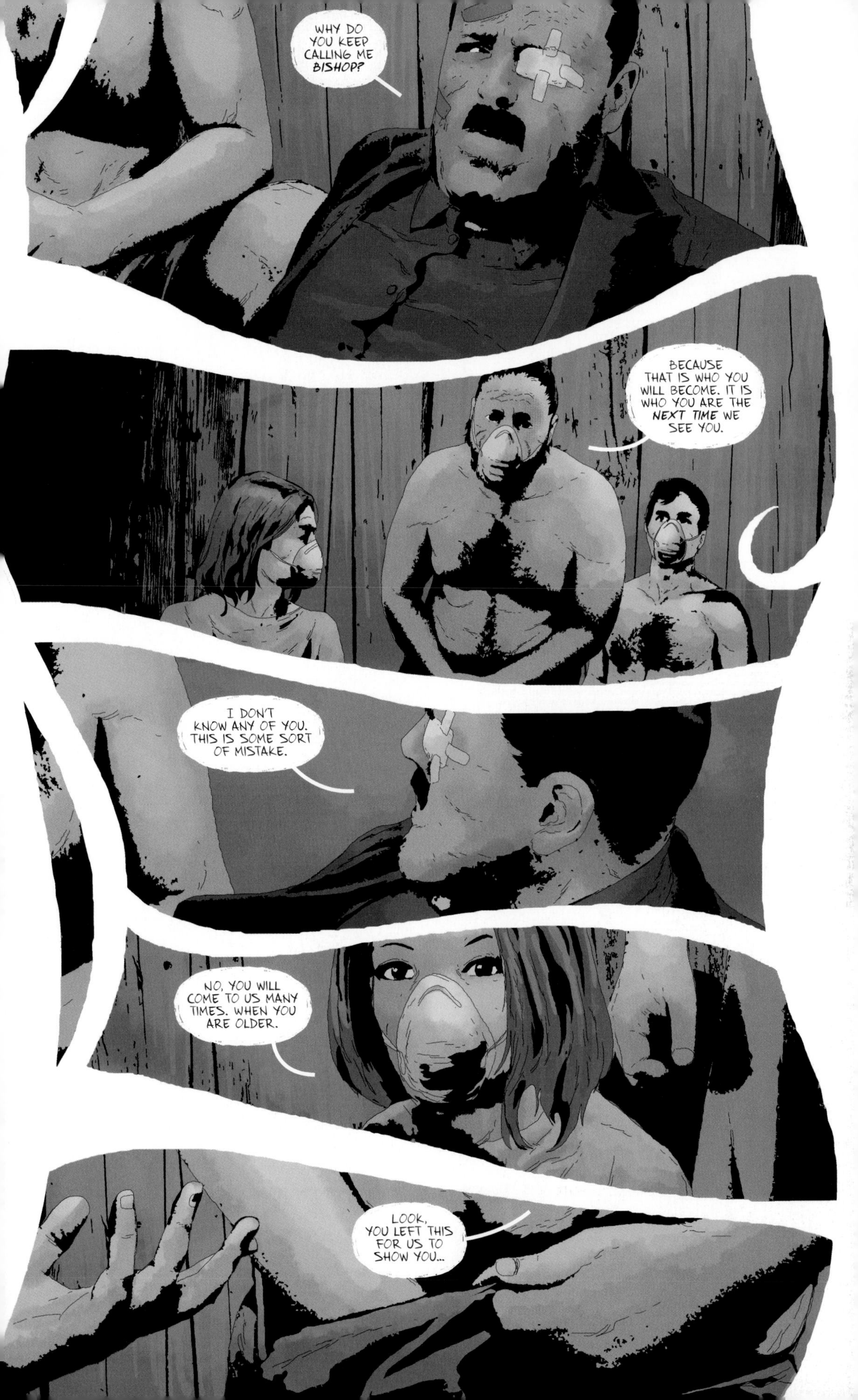
WHY DO YOU KEEP CALLING ME BISHOP?
BECAUSE THAT IS WHO YOU WILL BECOME. IT IS WHO YOU ARE THE NEXT TIME WE SEE YOU.
I DON'T KNOW ANY OF YOU. THIS IS SOME SORT OF MISTAKE.
NO, YOU WILL COME TO US MANY TIMES. WHEN YOU ARE OLDER.
LOOK, YOU LEFT THIS FOR US TO SHOW YOU...

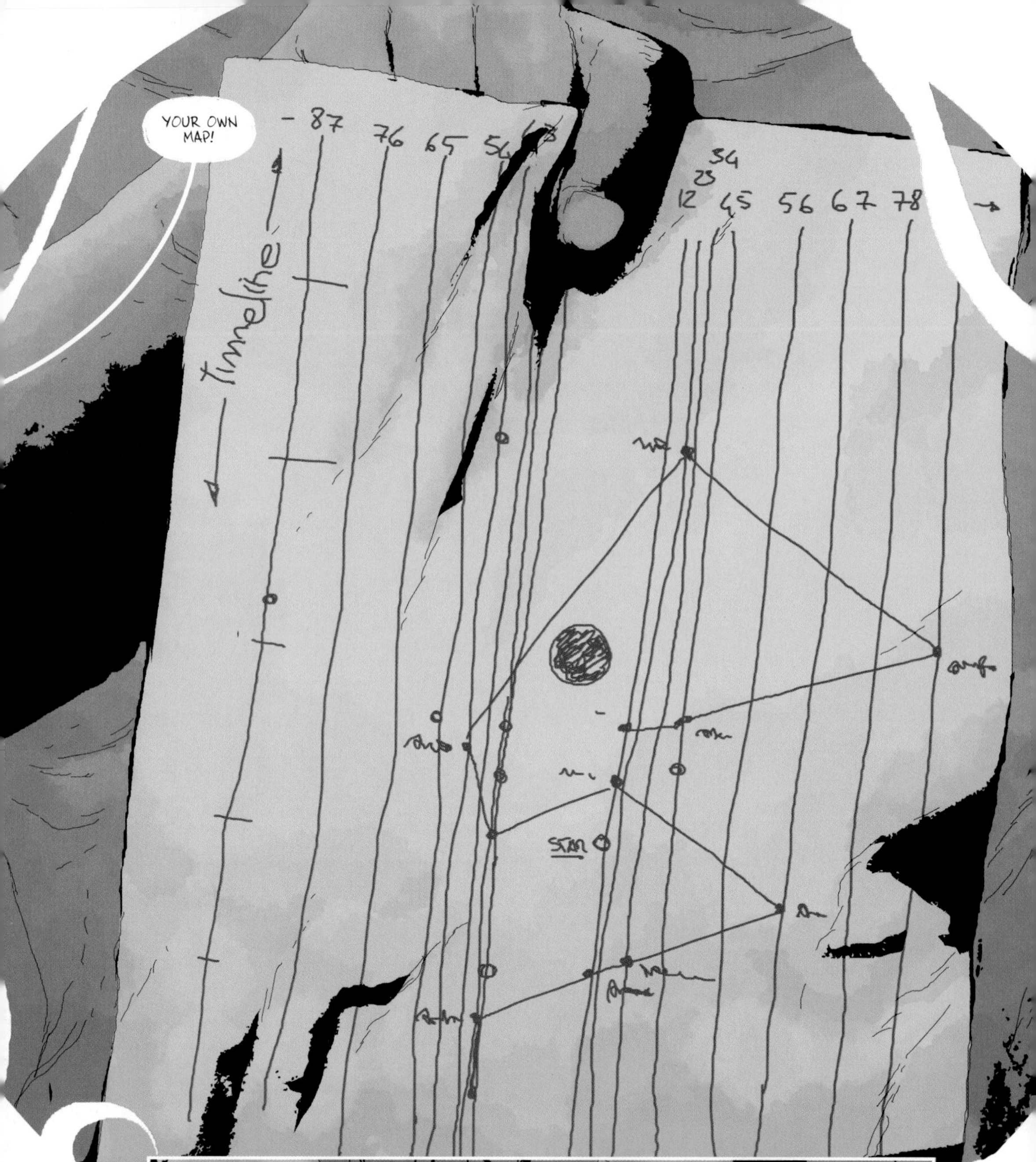
YOUR OWN MAP!
- 87 76 65
34
23
12 45 56 67 78
Timeline
STAN

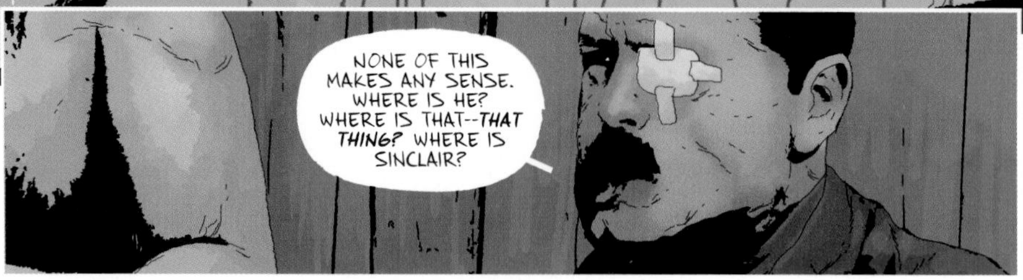
NONE OF THIS MAKES ANY SENSE. WHERE IS HE? WHERE IS THAT--*THAT THING?* WHERE IS SINCLAIR?

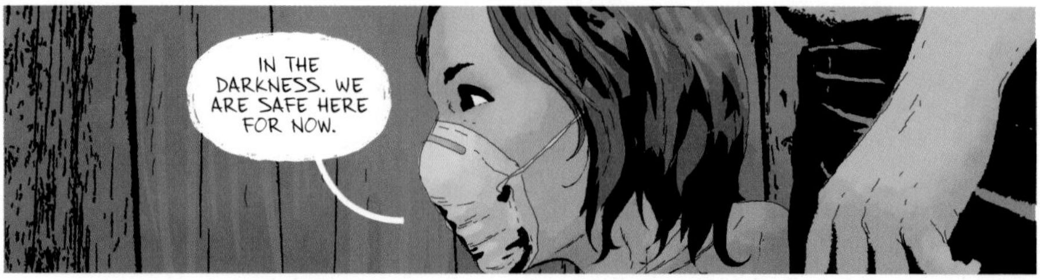
IN THE DARKNESS. WE ARE SAFE HERE FOR NOW.

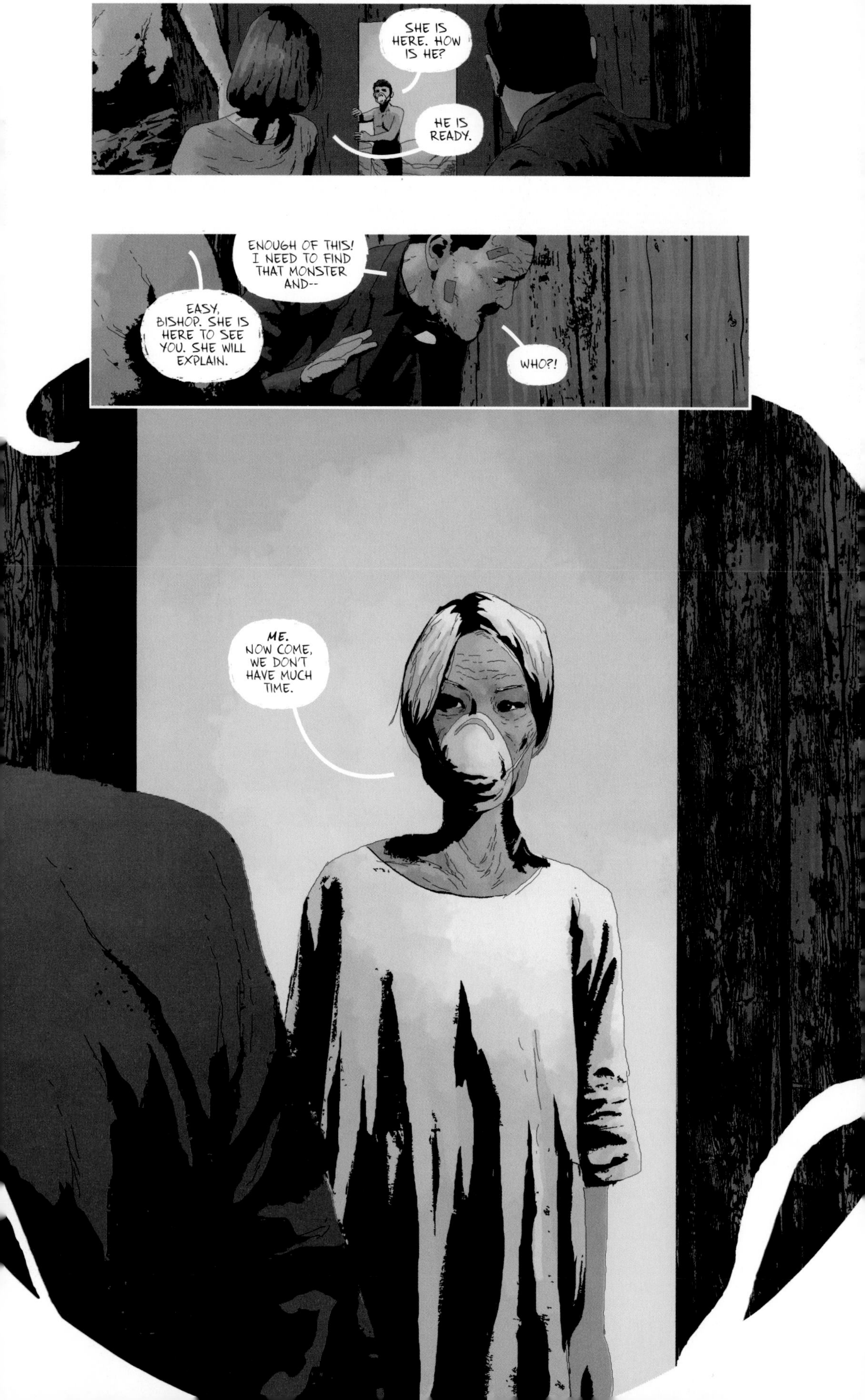
SHE IS HERE. HOW IS HE?
HE IS READY.
ENOUGH OF THIS! I NEED TO FIND THAT MONSTER AND--
EASY, BISHOP. SHE IS HERE TO SEE YOU. SHE WILL EXPLAIN.
WHO?!
ME. NOW COME, WE DON'T HAVE MUCH TIME.

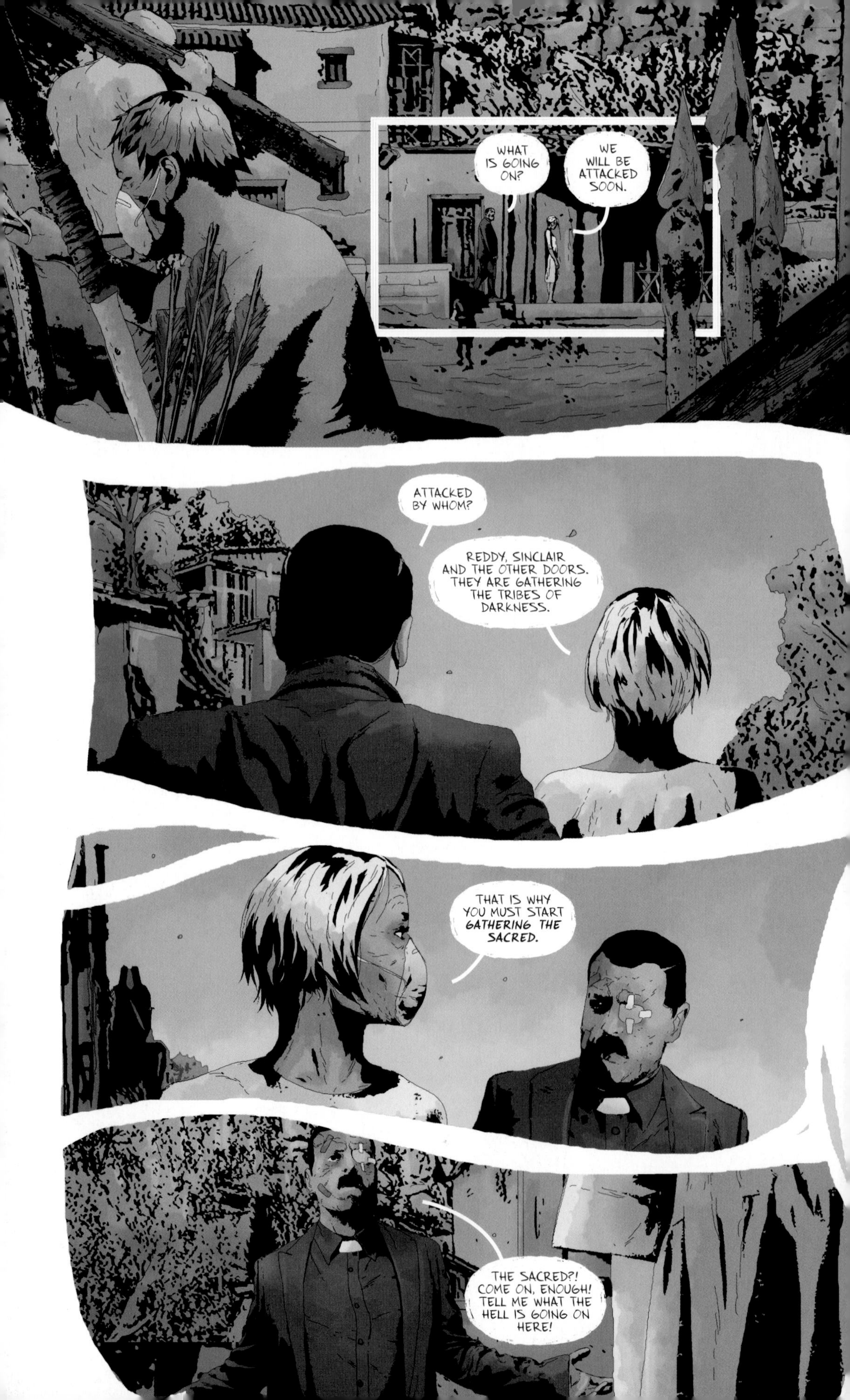
WHAT IS GOING ON?
WE WILL BE ATTACKED SOON.
ATTACKED BY WHOM?
REDDY, SINCLAIR AND THE OTHER DOORS. THEY ARE GATHERING THE TRIBES OF DARKNESS.
THAT IS WHY YOU MUST START GATHERING THE SACRED.
THE SACRED?! COME ON, ENOUGH! TELL ME WHAT THE HELL IS GOING ON HERE!

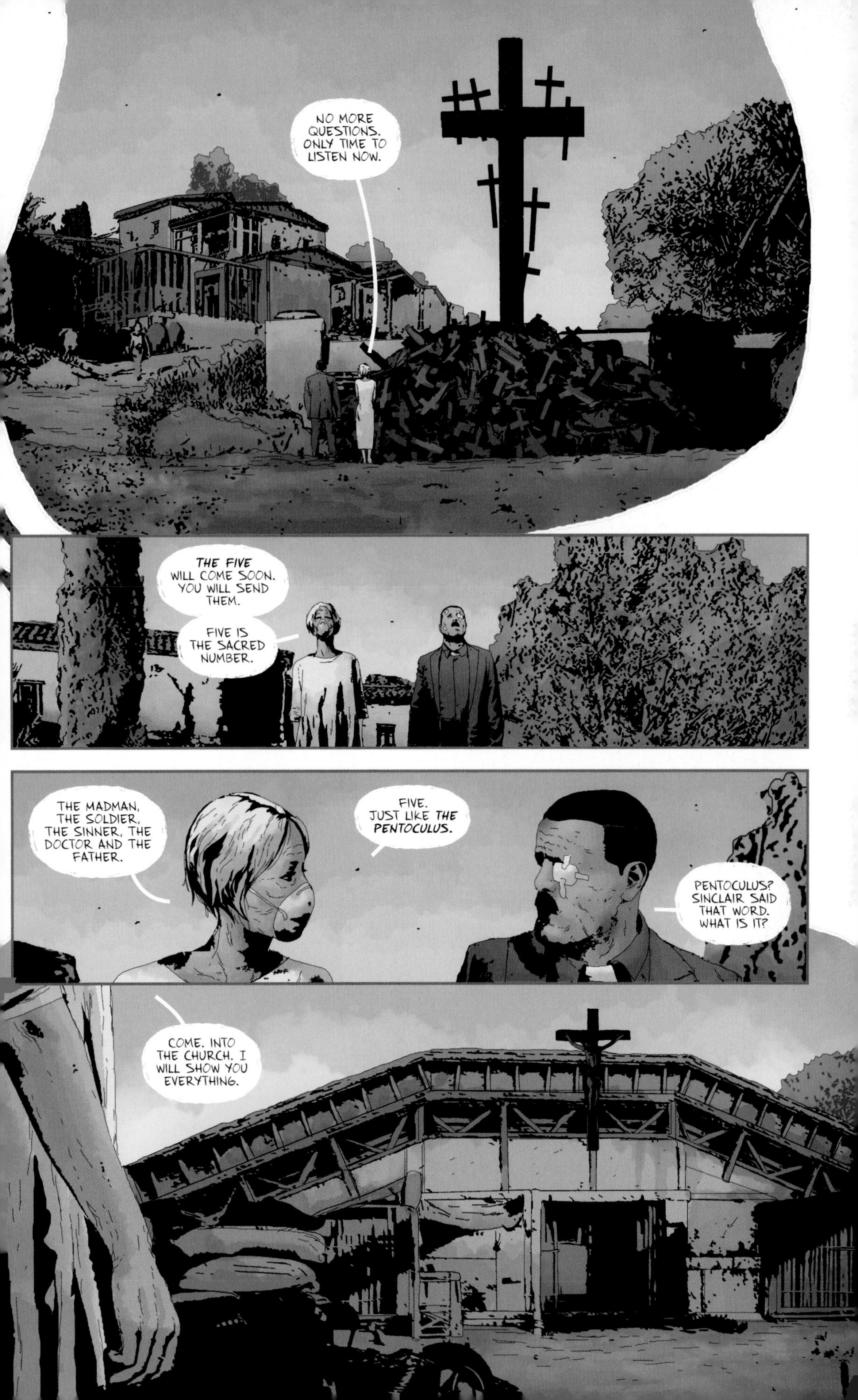
NO MORE QUESTIONS. ONLY TIME TO LISTEN NOW.
THE FIVE WILL COME SOON. YOU WILL SEND THEM.
FIVE IS THE SACRED NUMBER.
THE MADMAN, THE SOLDIER, THE SINNER, THE DOCTOR AND THE FATHER.
FIVE. JUST LIKE THE PENTOCULUS.
PENTOCULUS? SINCLAIR SAID THAT WORD. WHAT IS IT?
COME. INTO THE CHURCH. I WILL SHOW YOU EVERYTHING.

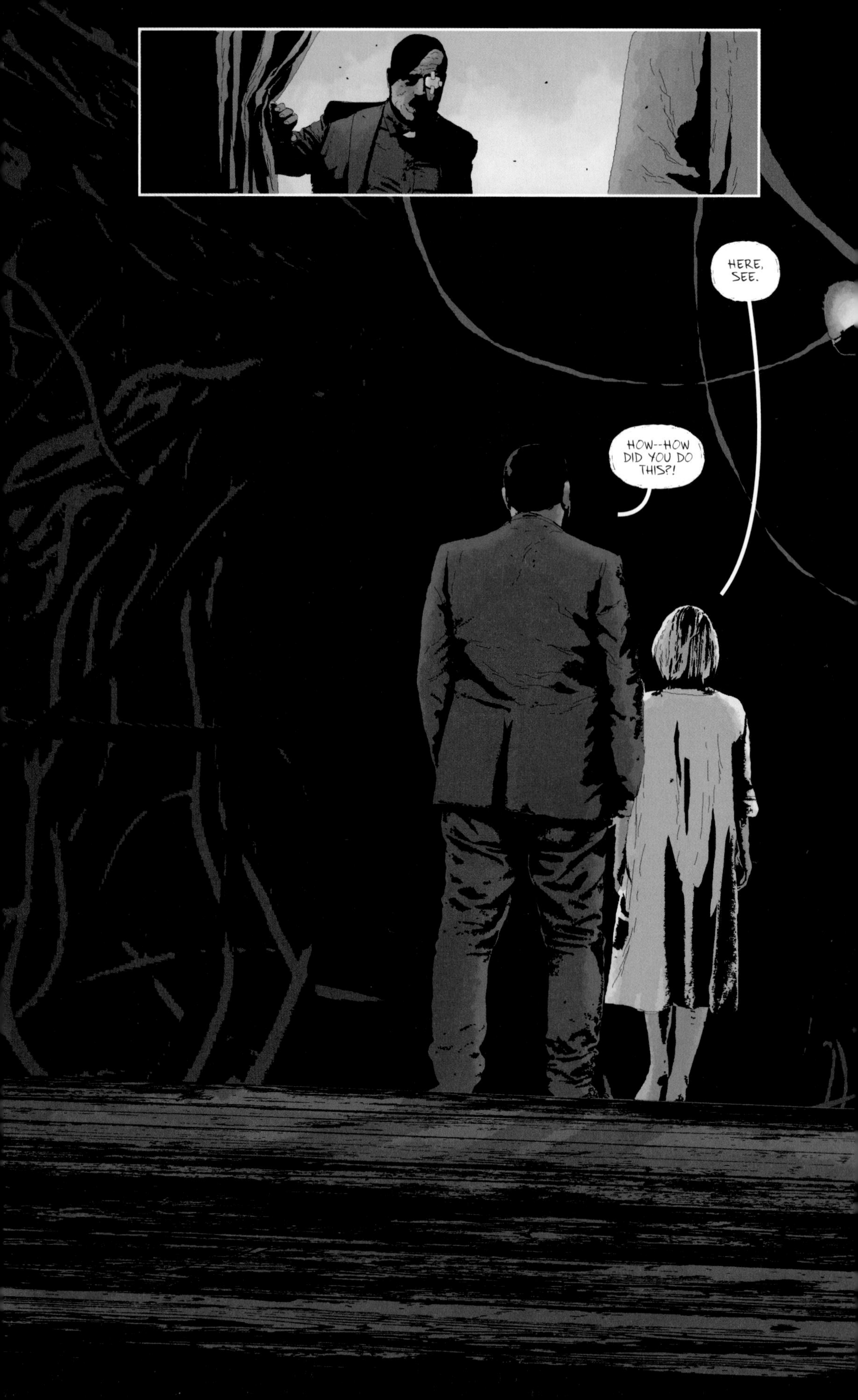
HERE, SEE.
HOW--HOW DID YOU DO THIS?!

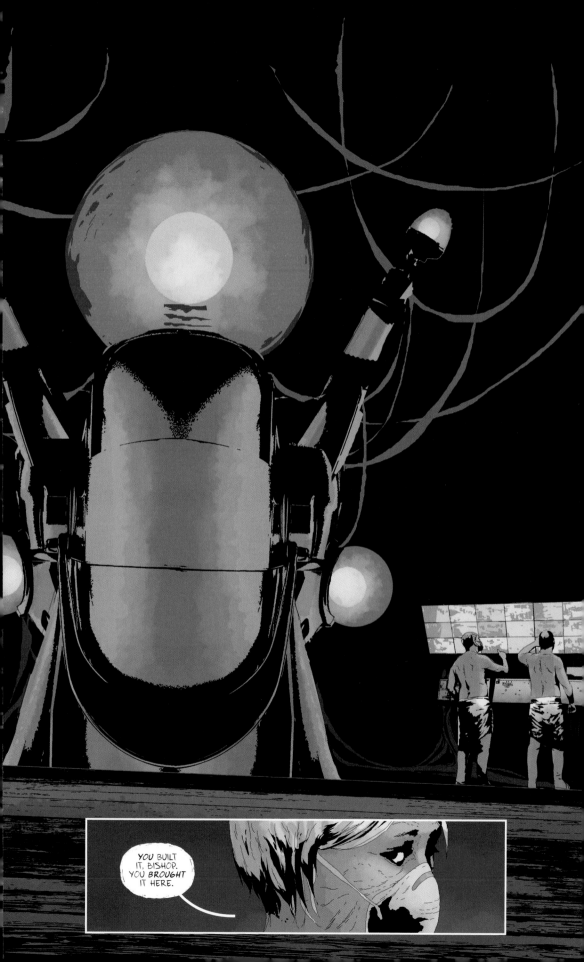

YOU BUILT IT, BISHOP. YOU *BROUGHT* IT HERE.

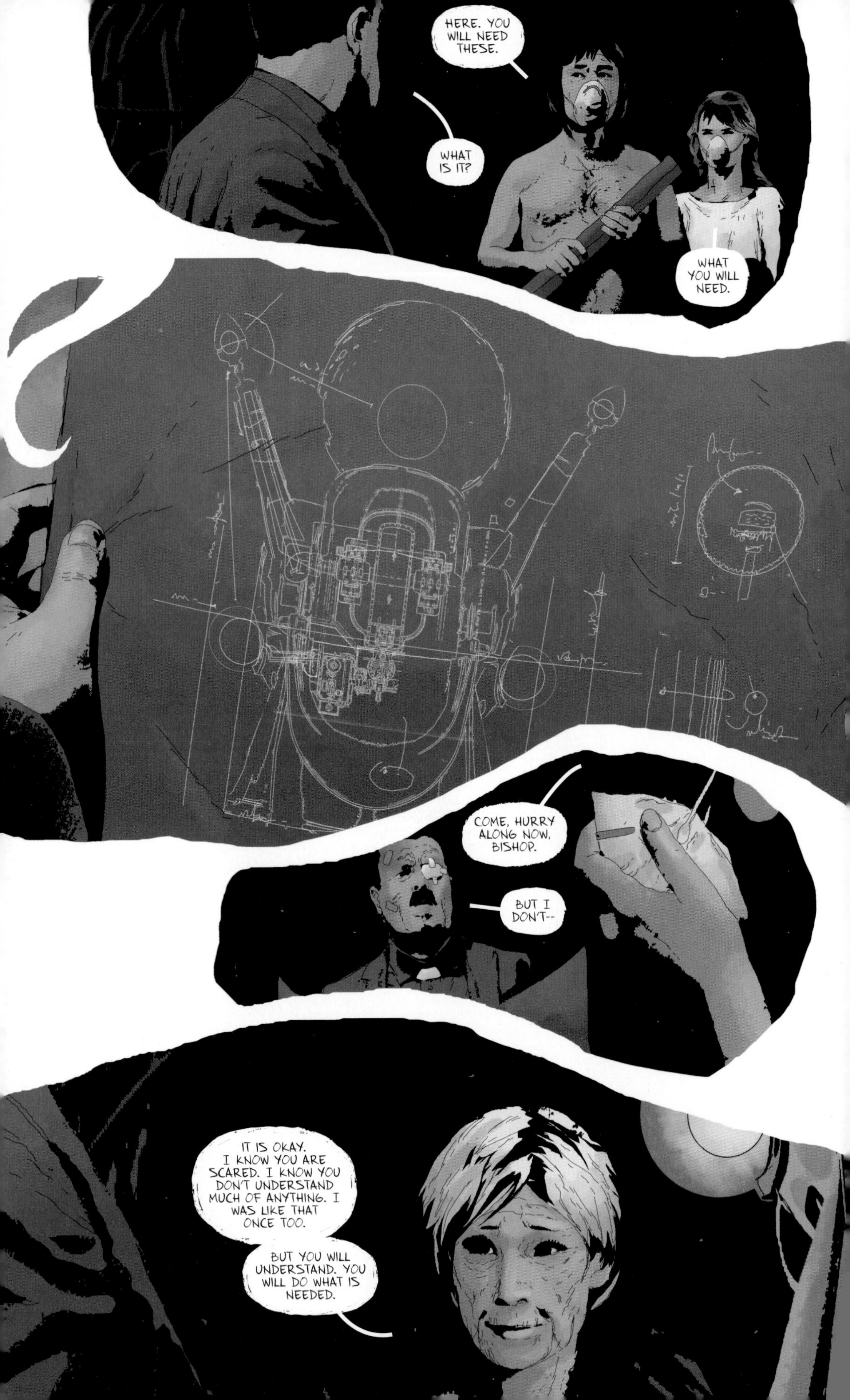
HERE. YOU WILL NEED THESE.
WHAT IS IT?
WHAT YOU WILL NEED.
COME, HURRY ALONG NOW, BISHOP.
BUT I DON'T--
IT IS OKAY. I KNOW YOU ARE SCARED. I KNOW YOU DON'T UNDERSTAND MUCH OF ANYTHING. I WAS LIKE THAT ONCE TOO.
BUT YOU WILL UNDERSTAND. YOU WILL DO WHAT IS NEEDED.

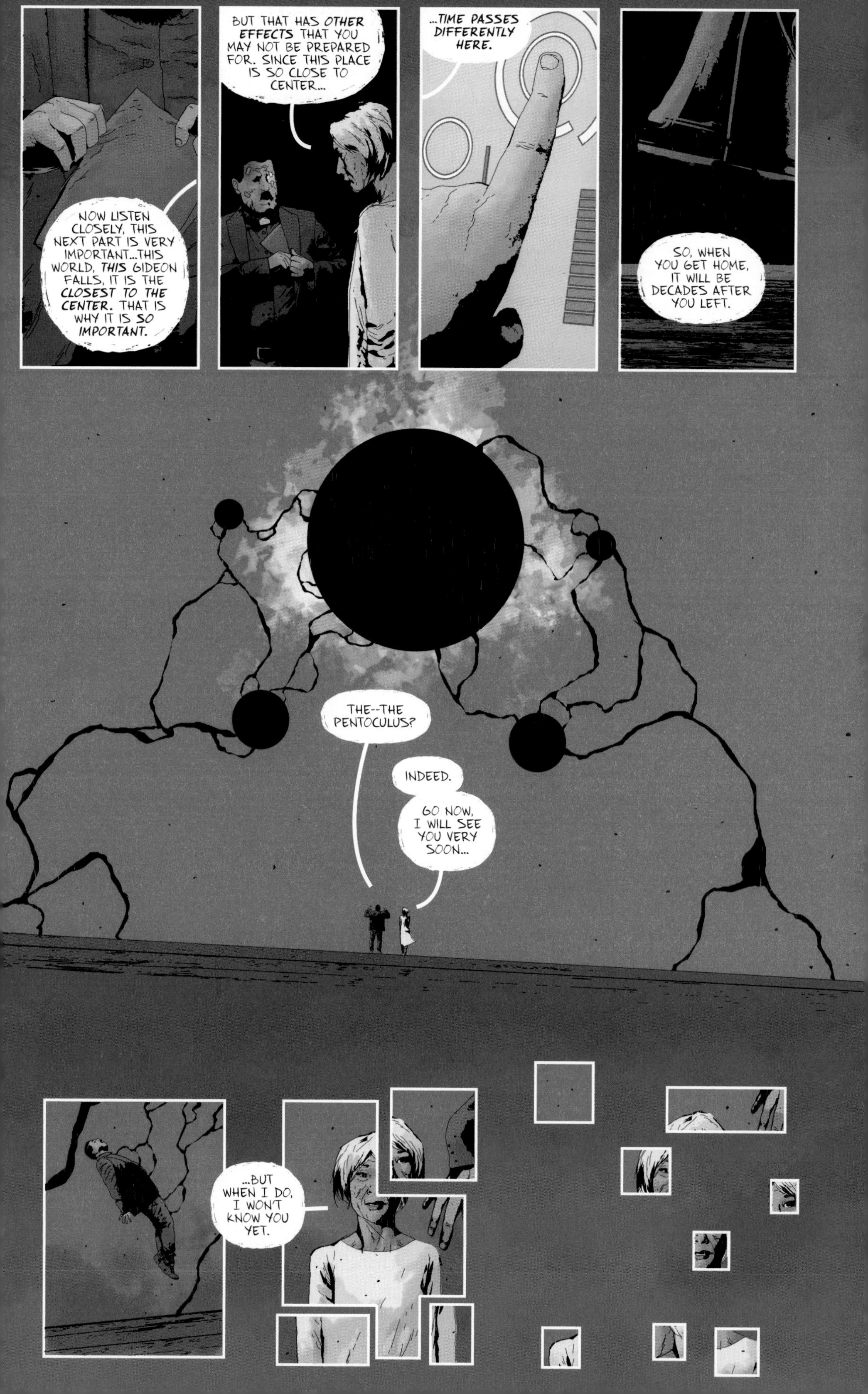
NOW LISTEN CLOSELY, THIS NEXT PART IS VERY IMPORTANT...THIS WORLD, **THIS** GIDEON FALLS, IT IS THE **CLOSEST TO THE CENTER**. THAT IS WHY IT IS **SO IMPORTANT**.
BUT THAT HAS *OTHER* **EFFECTS** THAT YOU MAY NOT BE PREPARED FOR. SINCE THIS PLACE IS SO CLOSE TO CENTER...
...**TIME PASSES DIFFERENTLY HERE.**
SO, WHEN YOU GET HOME, IT WILL BE DECADES AFTER YOU LEFT.
THE--THE PENTOCULUS?
INDEED.
GO NOW, I WILL SEE YOU VERY SOON...
...BUT WHEN I DO, I WON'T KNOW YOU YET.

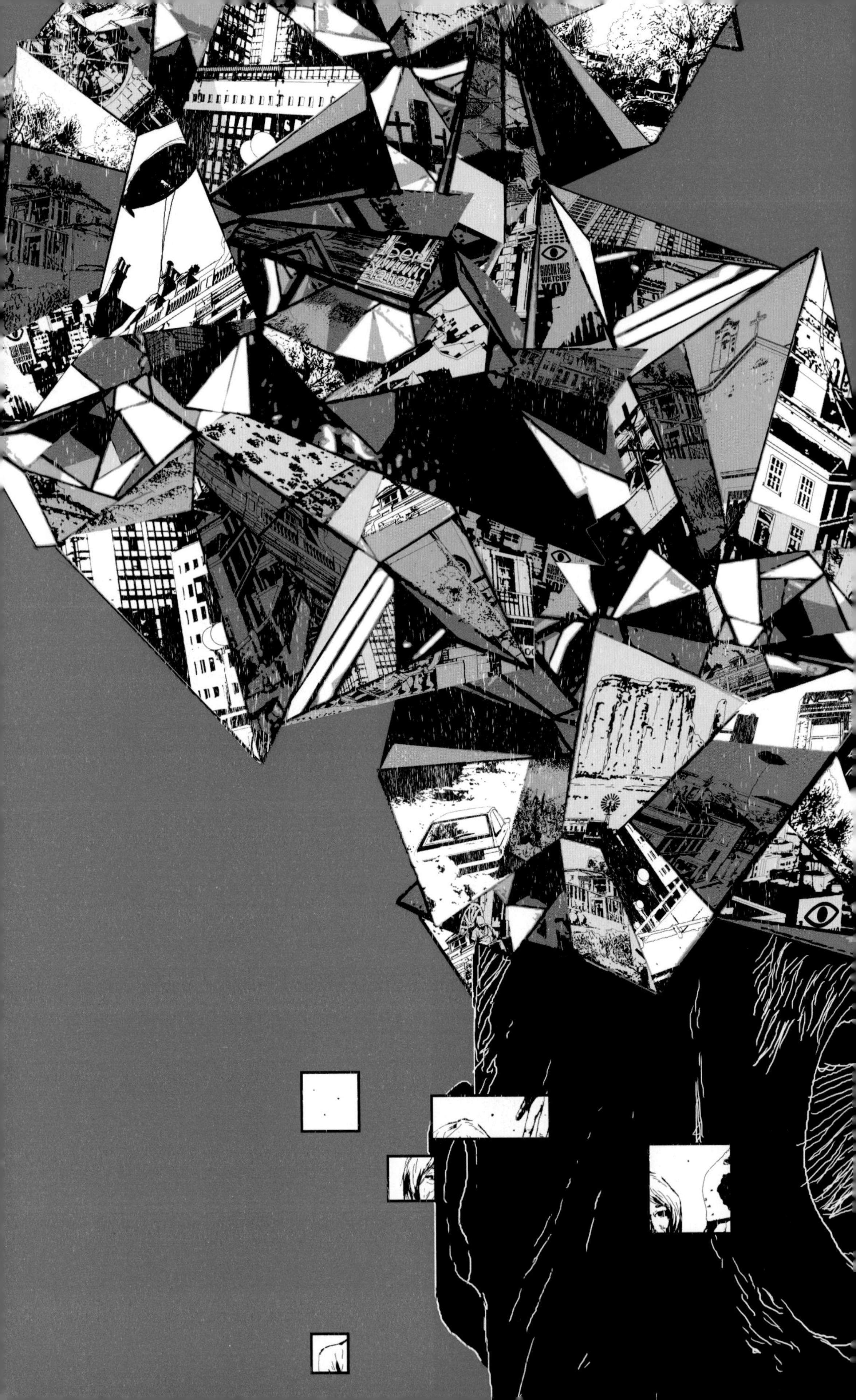
GIDEON FALLS
WATCHES
YOU

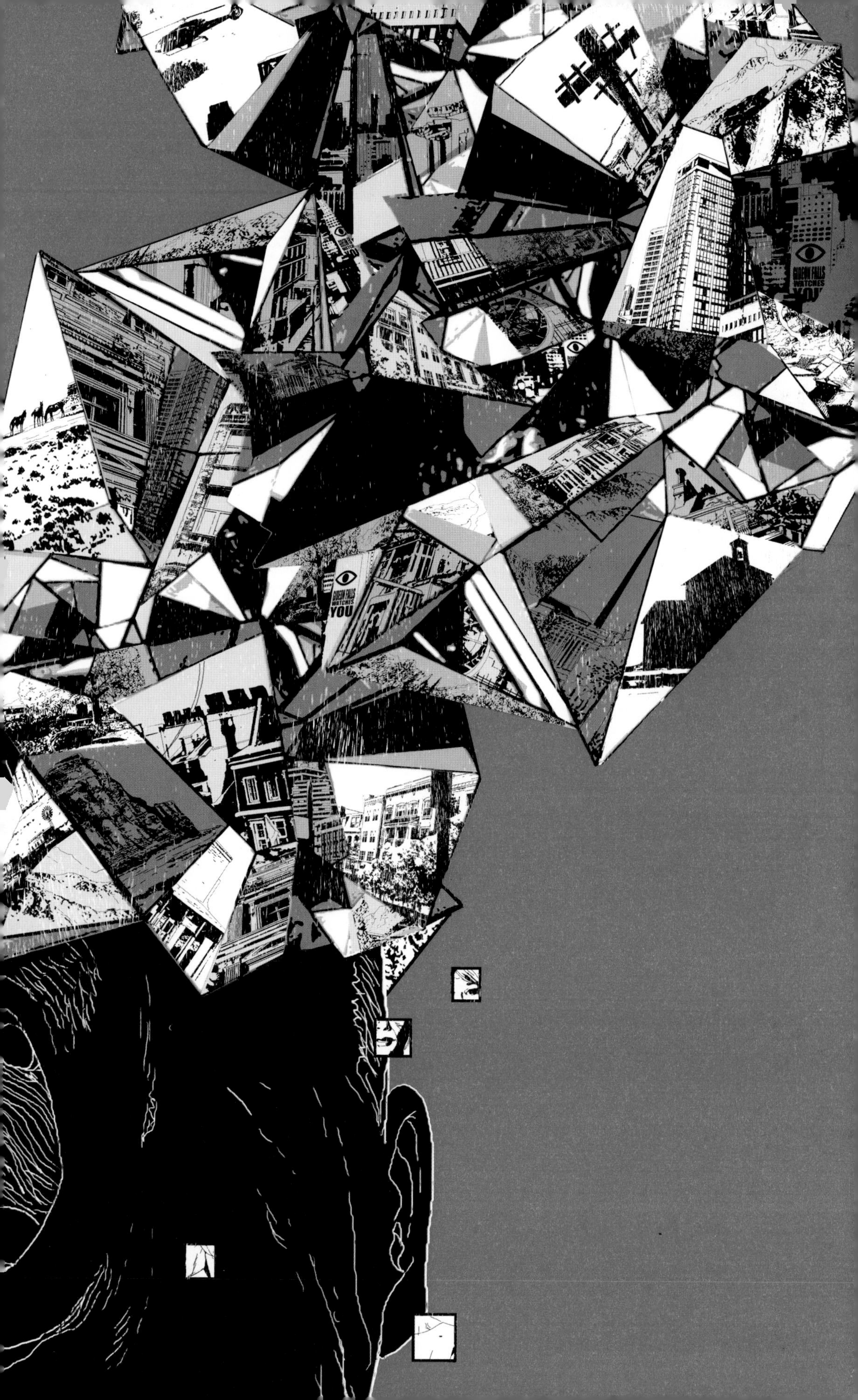
GIDEON FALLS WATCHES YOU

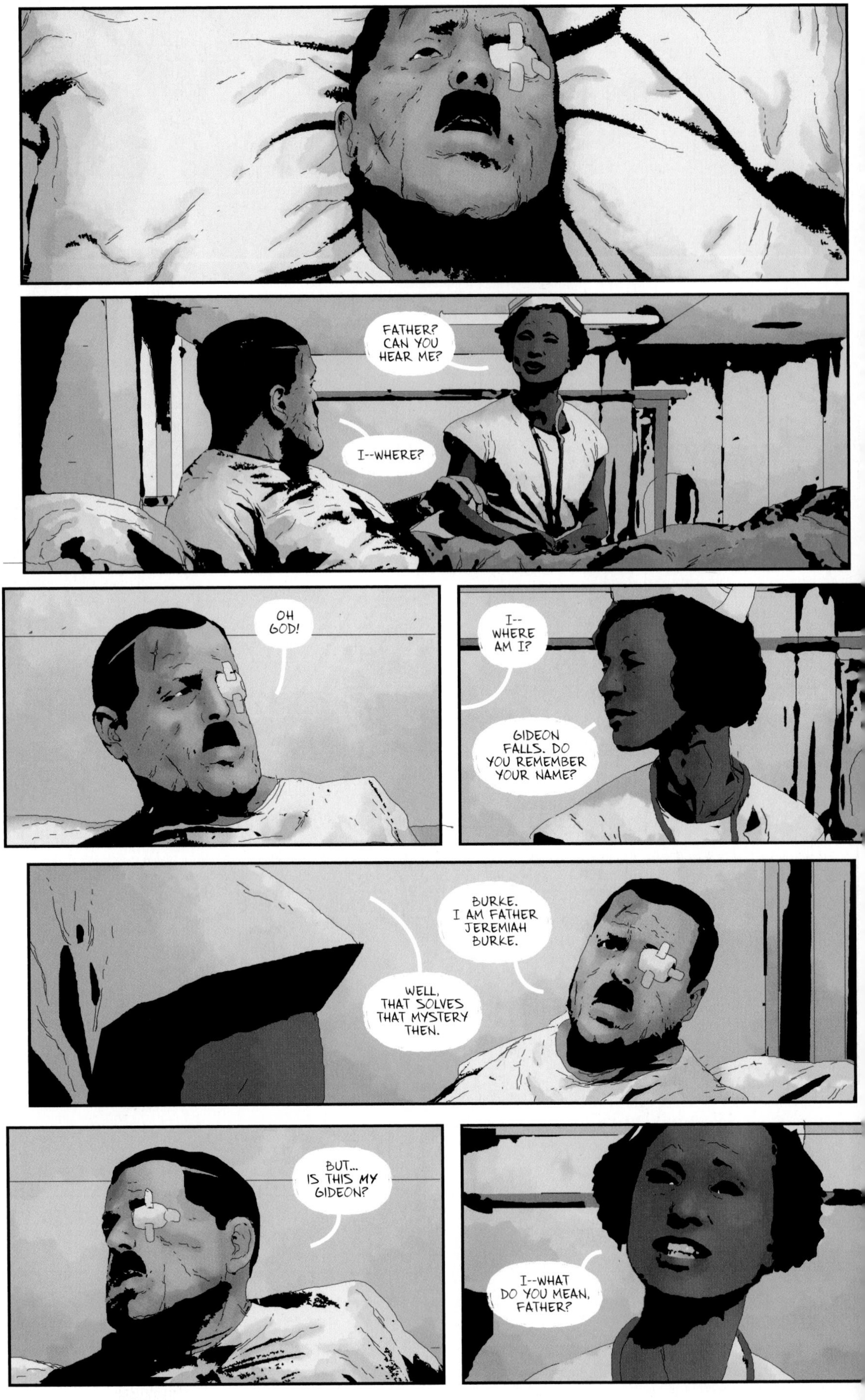
FATHER? CAN YOU HEAR ME?
I--WHERE?
OH GOD!
I-- WHERE AM I?
GIDEON FALLS. DO YOU REMEMBER YOUR NAME?
BURKE. I AM FATHER JEREMIAH BURKE.
WELL, THAT SOLVES THAT MYSTERY THEN.
BUT... IS THIS MY GIDEON?
I--WHAT DO YOU MEAN, FATHER?

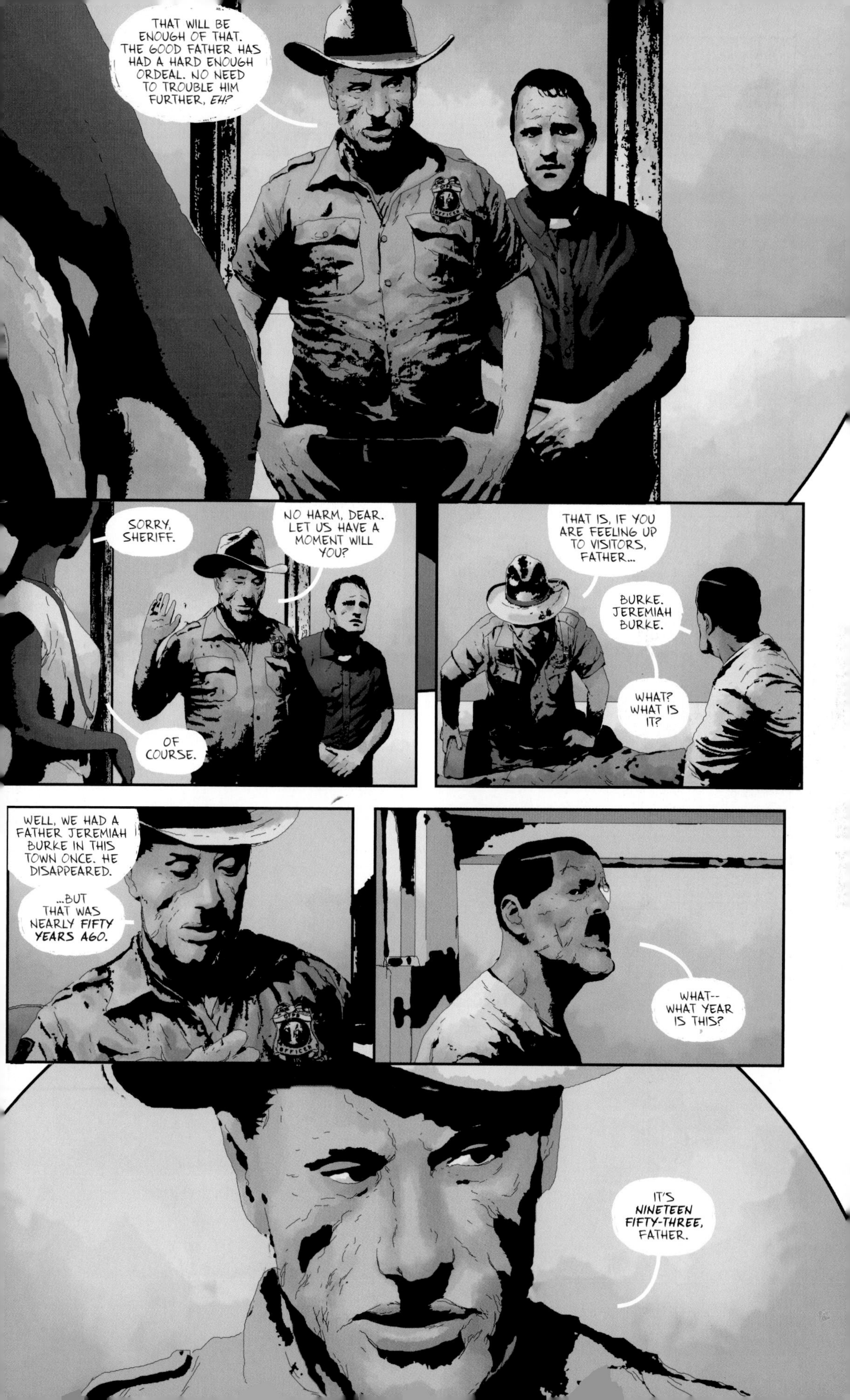
THAT WILL BE ENOUGH OF THAT. THE GOOD FATHER HAS HAD A HARD ENOUGH ORDEAL. NO NEED TO TROUBLE HIM FURTHER, EH?
SORRY, SHERIFF.
NO HARM, DEAR. LET US HAVE A MOMENT WILL YOU?
OF COURSE.
THAT IS, IF YOU ARE FEELING UP TO VISITORS, FATHER...
BURKE. JEREMIAH BURKE.
WHAT? WHAT IS IT?
WELL, WE HAD A FATHER JEREMIAH BURKE IN THIS TOWN ONCE. HE DISAPPEARED.
...BUT THAT WAS NEARLY FIFTY YEARS AGO.
WHAT-- WHAT YEAR IS THIS?
IT'S NINETEEN FIFTY-THREE, FATHER.

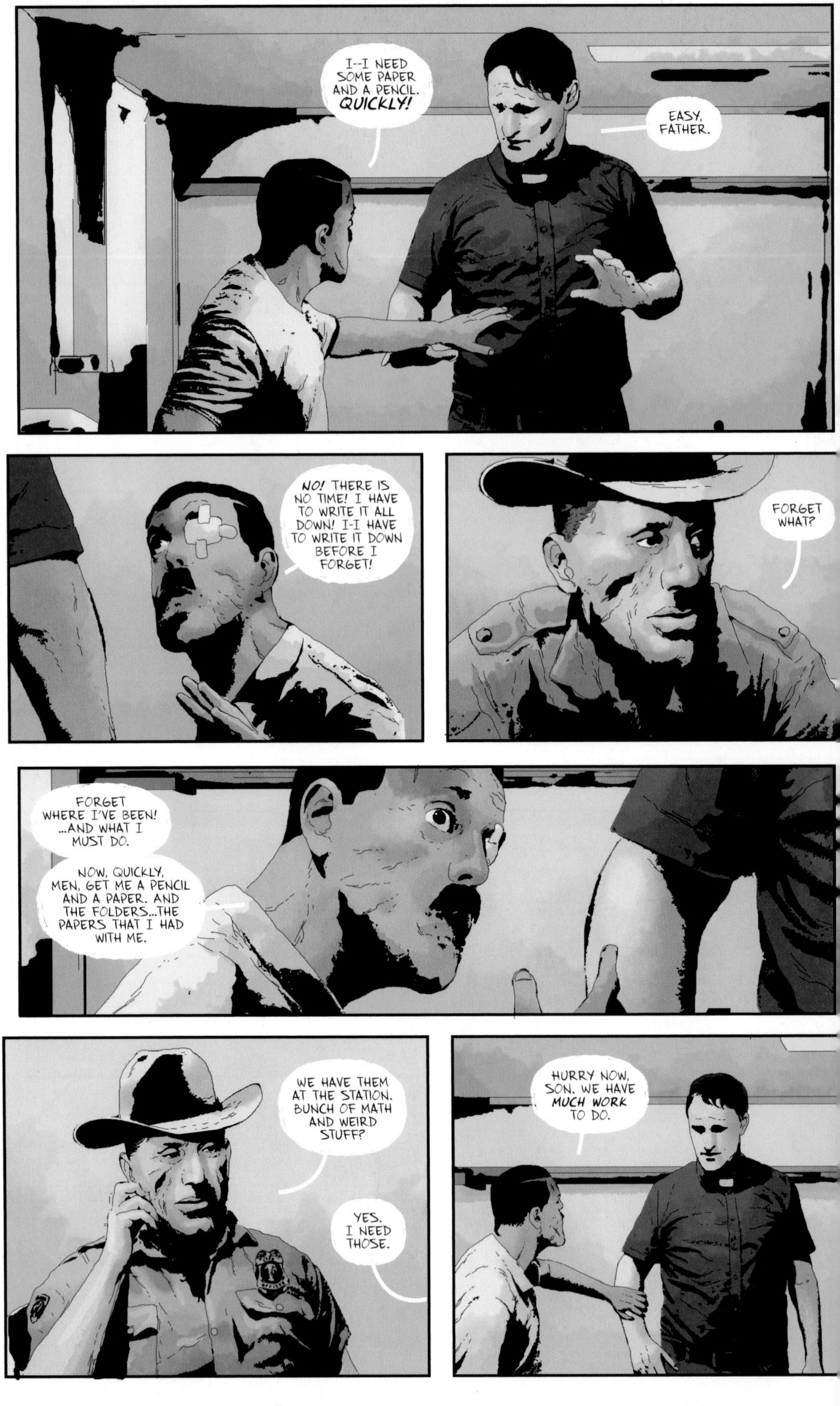
I--I NEED SOME PAPER AND A PENCIL. QUICKLY!
EASY, FATHER.
NO! THERE IS NO TIME! I HAVE TO WRITE IT ALL DOWN! I-I HAVE TO WRITE IT DOWN BEFORE I FORGET!
FORGET WHAT?
FORGET WHERE I'VE BEEN! ...AND WHAT I MUST DO.
NOW, QUICKLY, MEN, GET ME A PENCIL AND A PAPER. AND THE FOLDERS...THE PAPERS THAT I HAD WITH ME.
WE HAVE THEM AT THE STATION. BUNCH OF MATH AND WEIRD STUFF?
YES. I NEED THOSE.
HURRY NOW, SON. WE HAVE MUCH WORK TO DO.

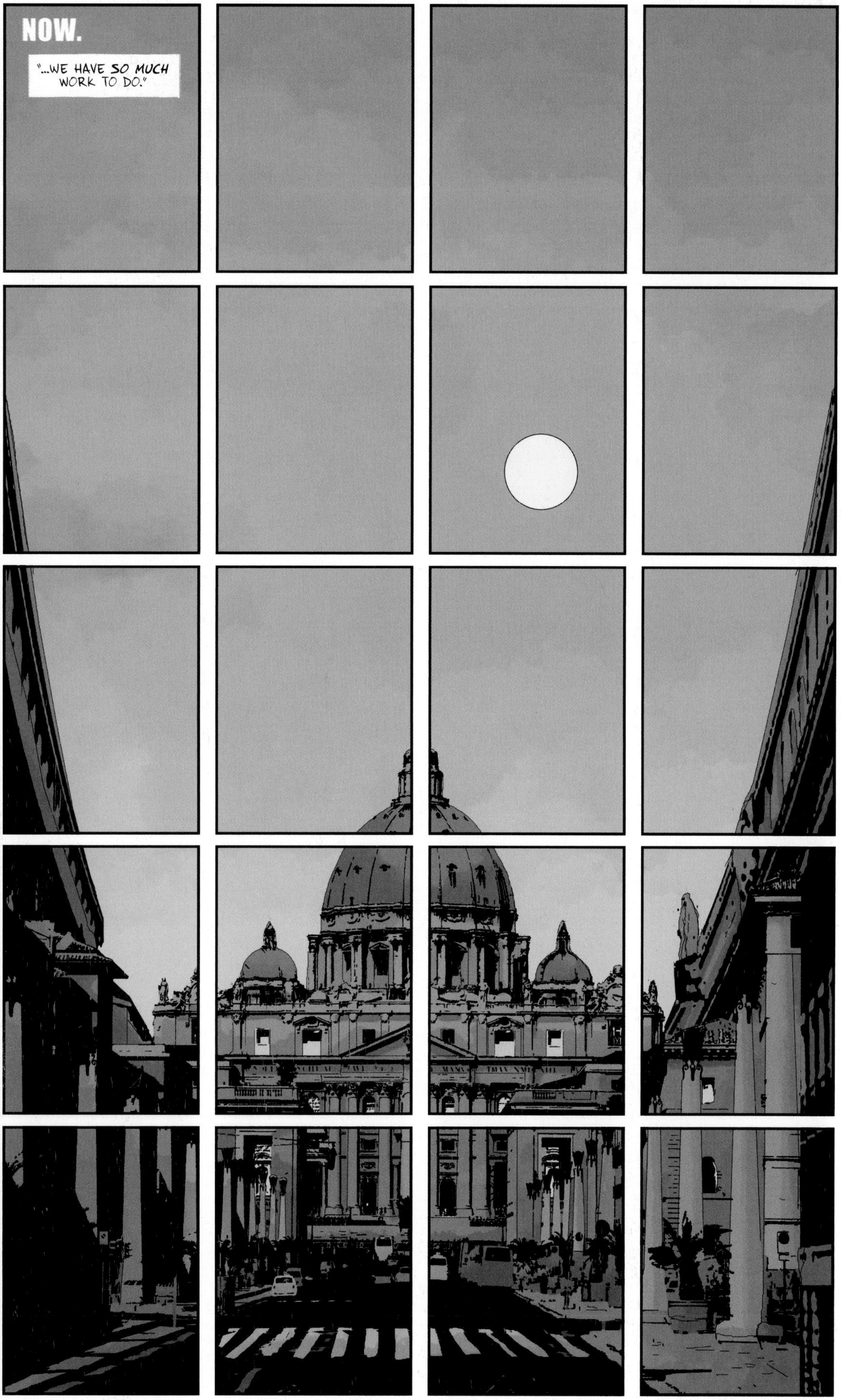
NOW.
"...WE HAVE SO MUCH WORK TO DO."

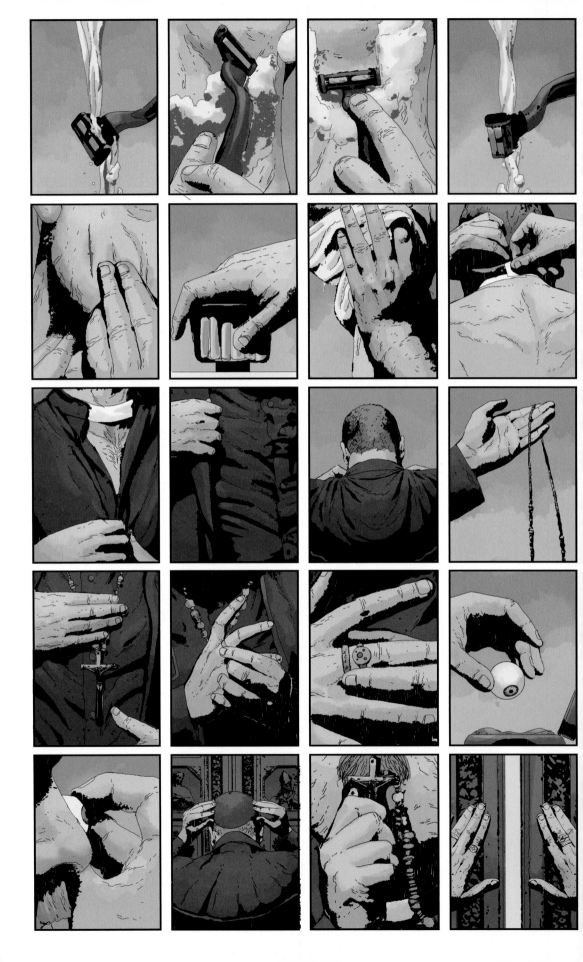

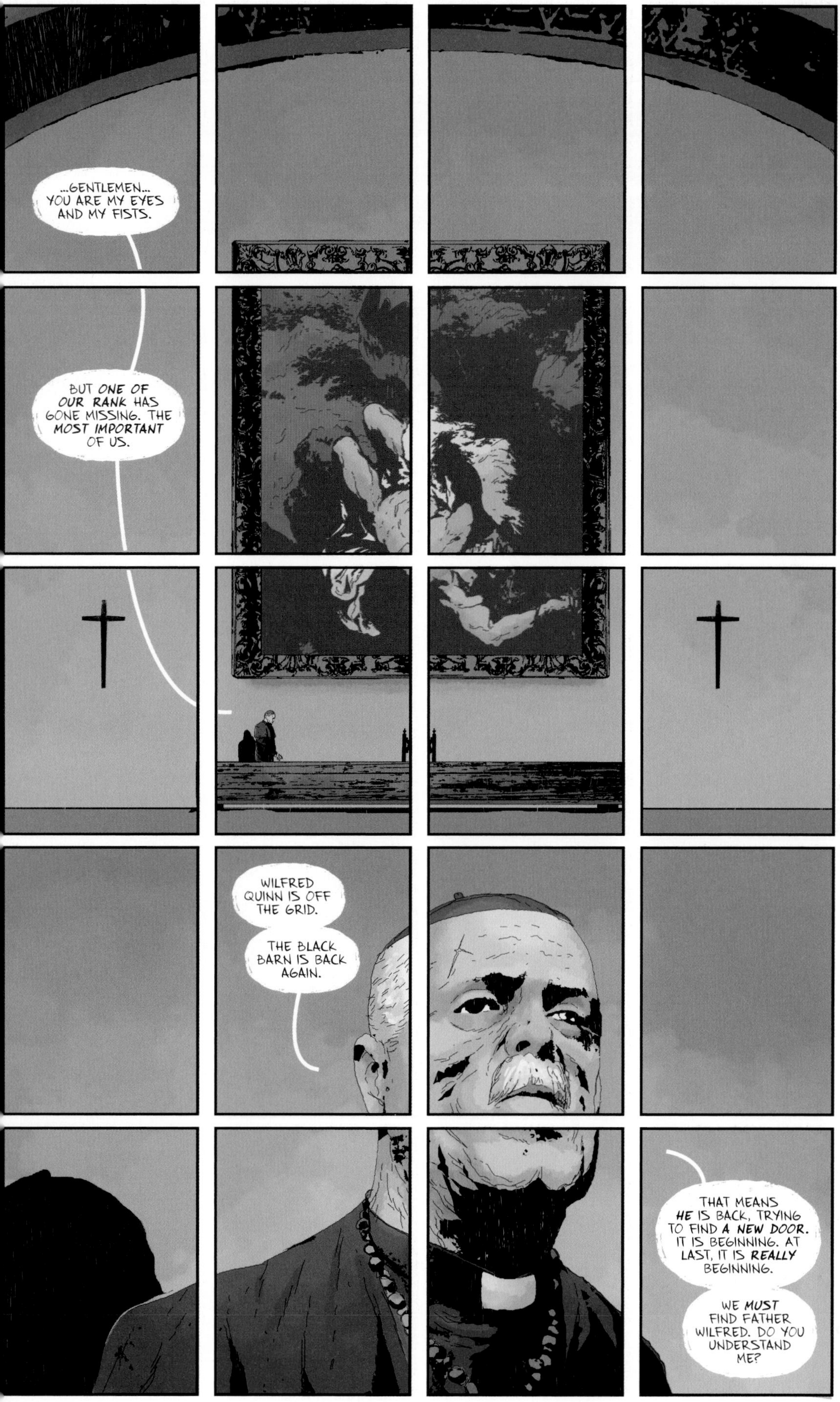

...GENTLEMEN... YOU ARE MY EYES AND MY FISTS.
BUT ONE OF OUR RANK HAS GONE MISSING. THE MOST IMPORTANT OF US.
WILFRED QUINN IS OFF THE GRID.
THE BLACK BARN IS BACK AGAIN.
THAT MEANS HE IS BACK, TRYING TO FIND A NEW DOOR. IT IS BEGINNING. AT LAST, IT IS REALLY BEGINNING.
WE MUST FIND FATHER WILFRED. DO YOU UNDERSTAND ME?

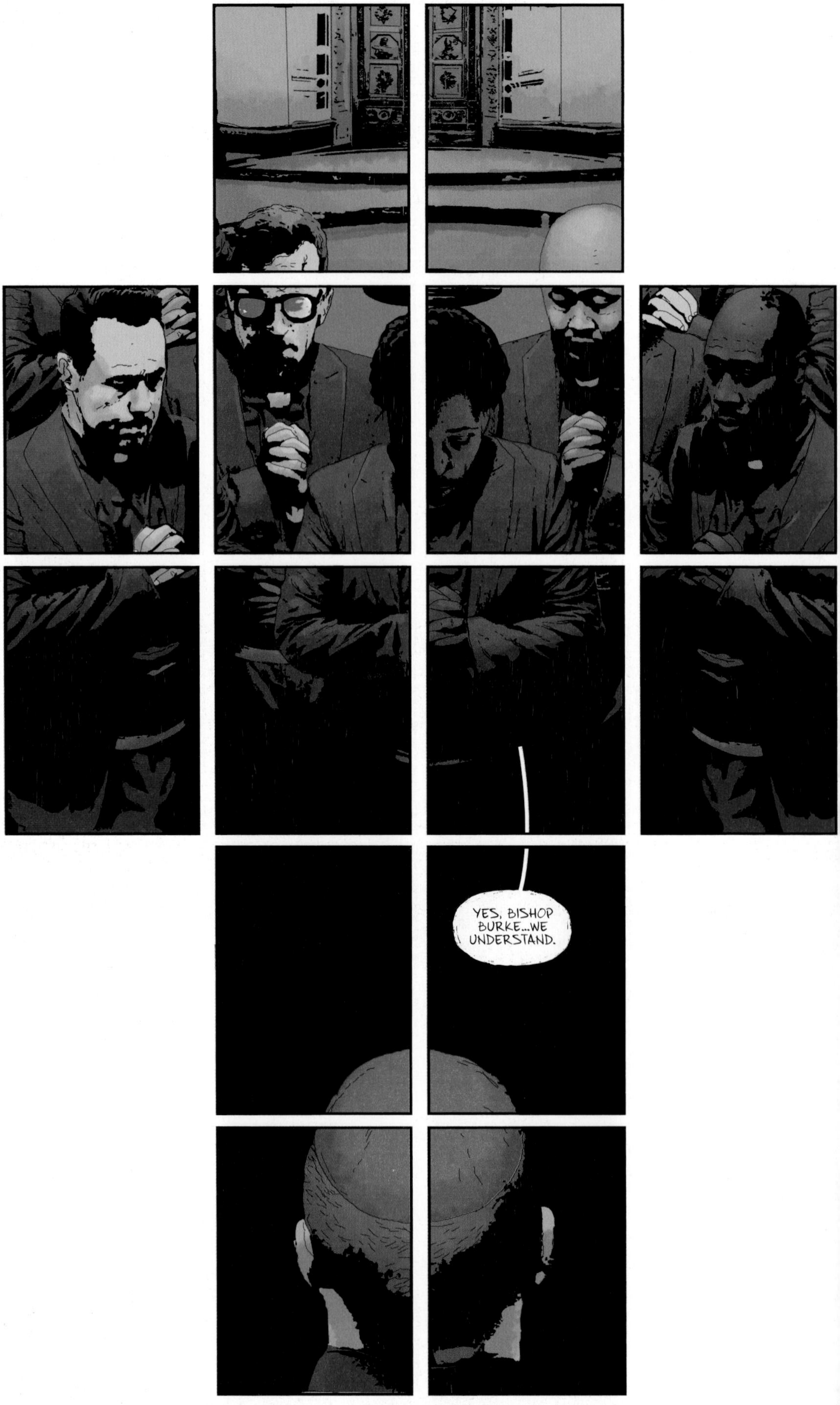
YES, BISHOP BURKE...WE UNDERSTAND.

GIDEON FALLS

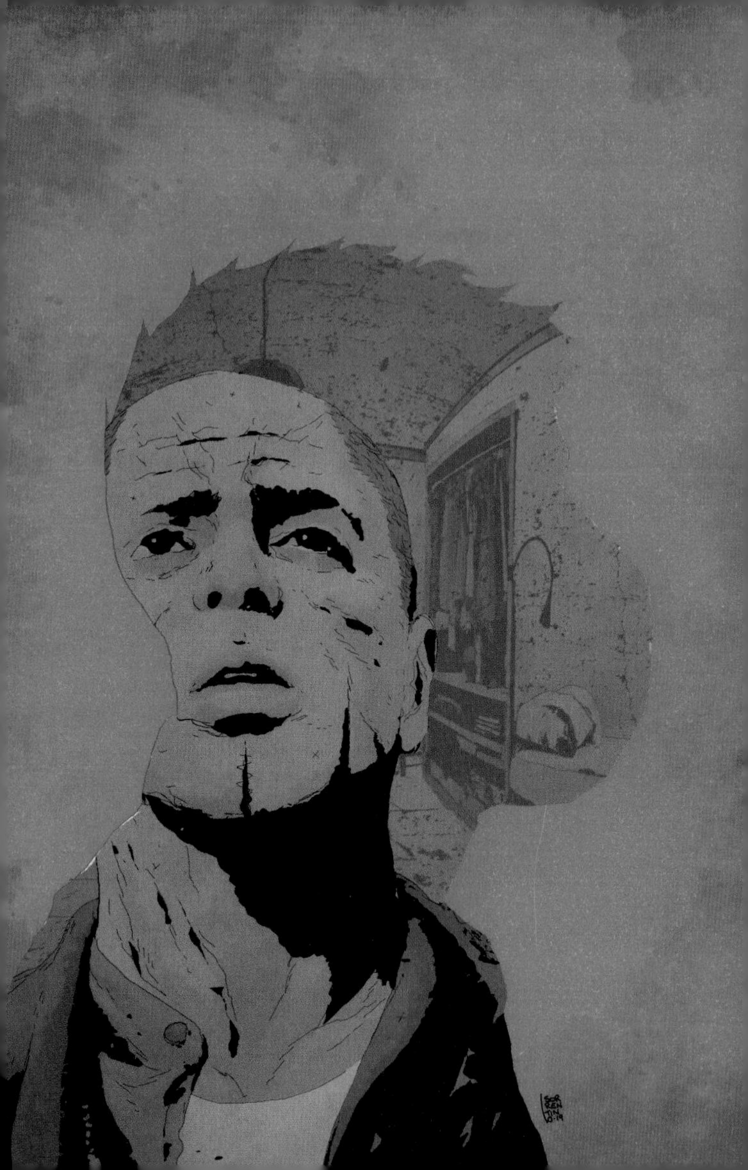

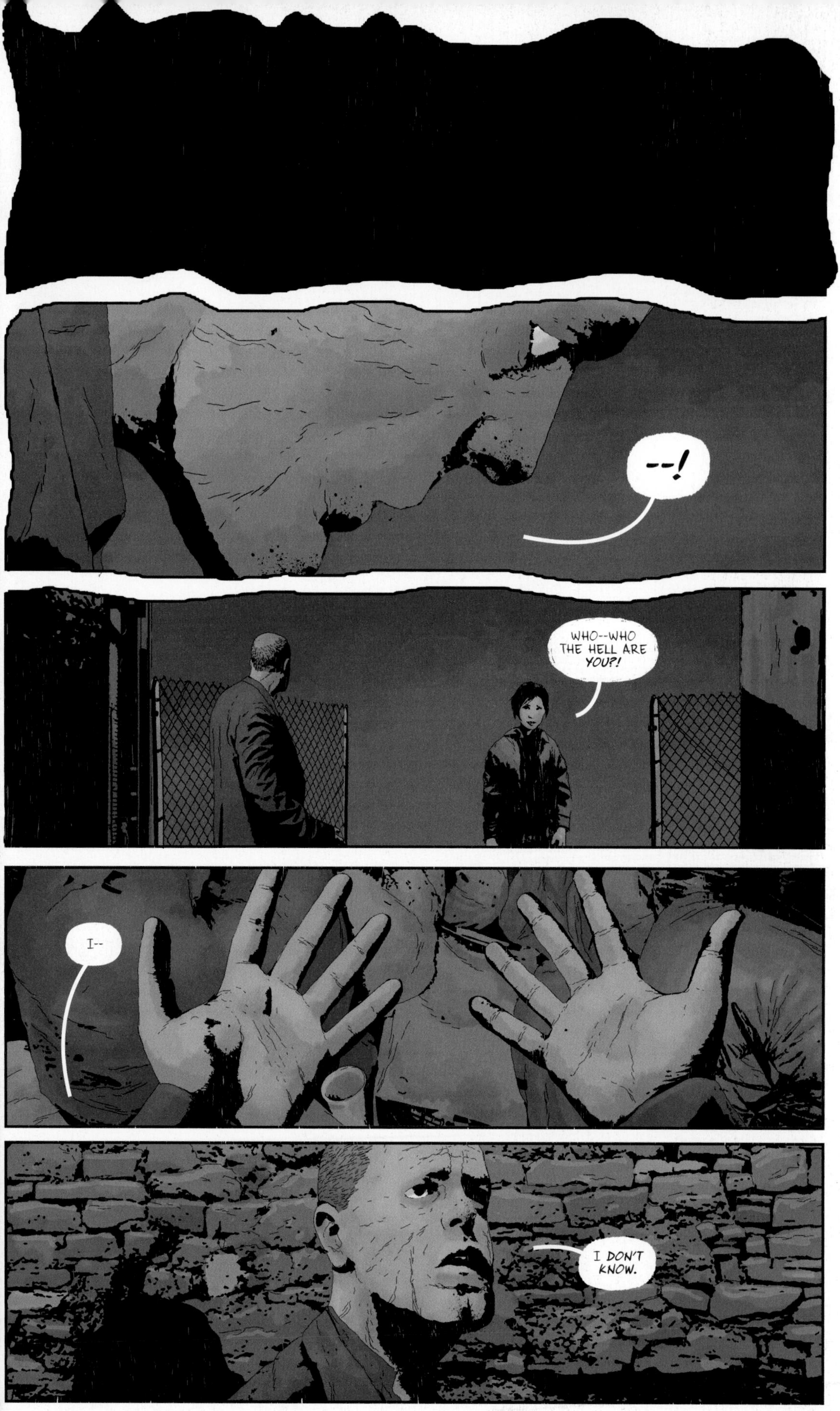
--!
WHO--WHO THE HELL ARE YOU?!
I--
I DON'T KNOW.

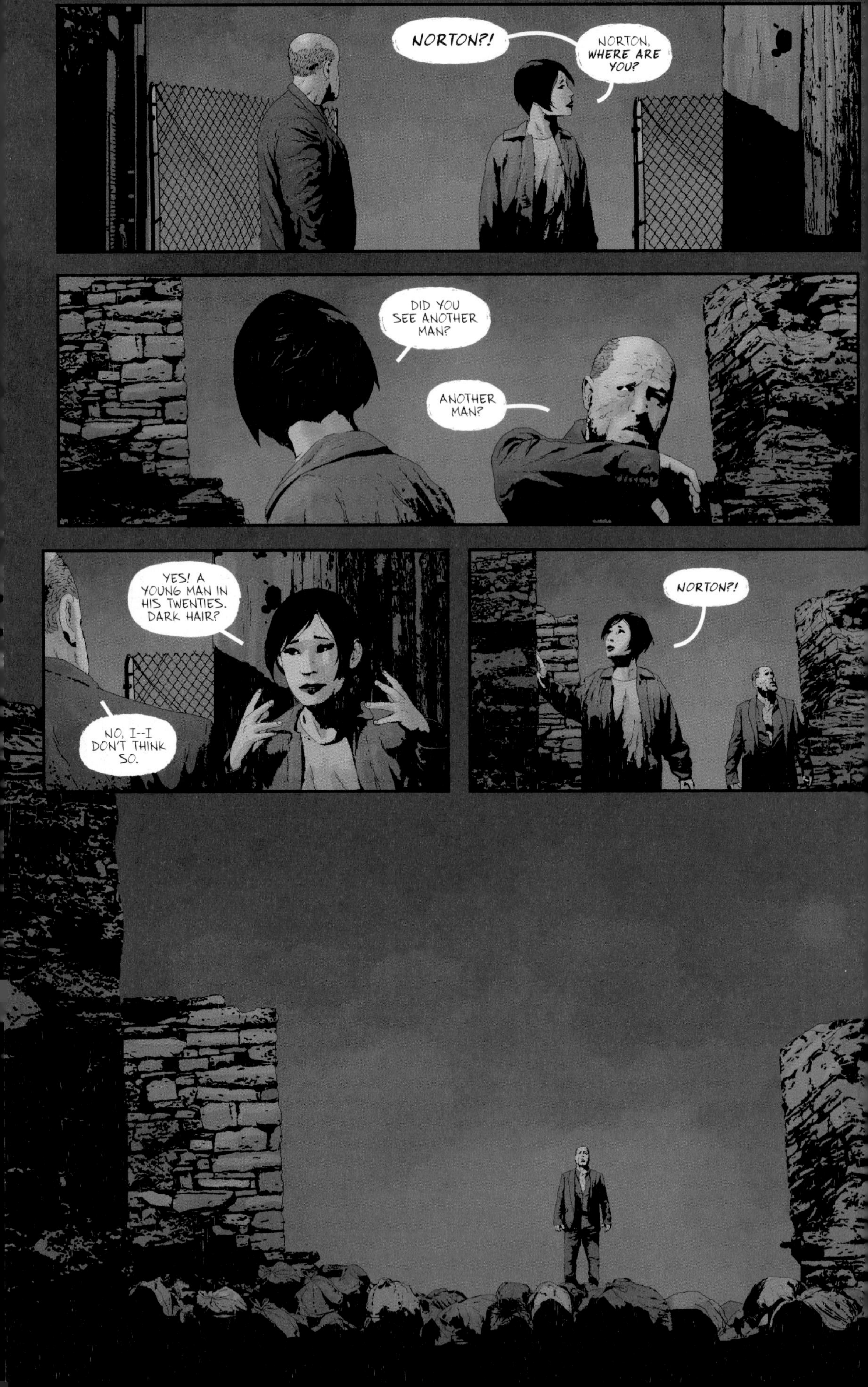
NORTON?!
NORTON, WHERE ARE YOU?
DID YOU SEE ANOTHER MAN?
ANOTHER MAN?
YES! A YOUNG MAN IN HIS TWENTIES. DARK HAIR?
NO, I--I DON'T THINK SO.
NORTON?!

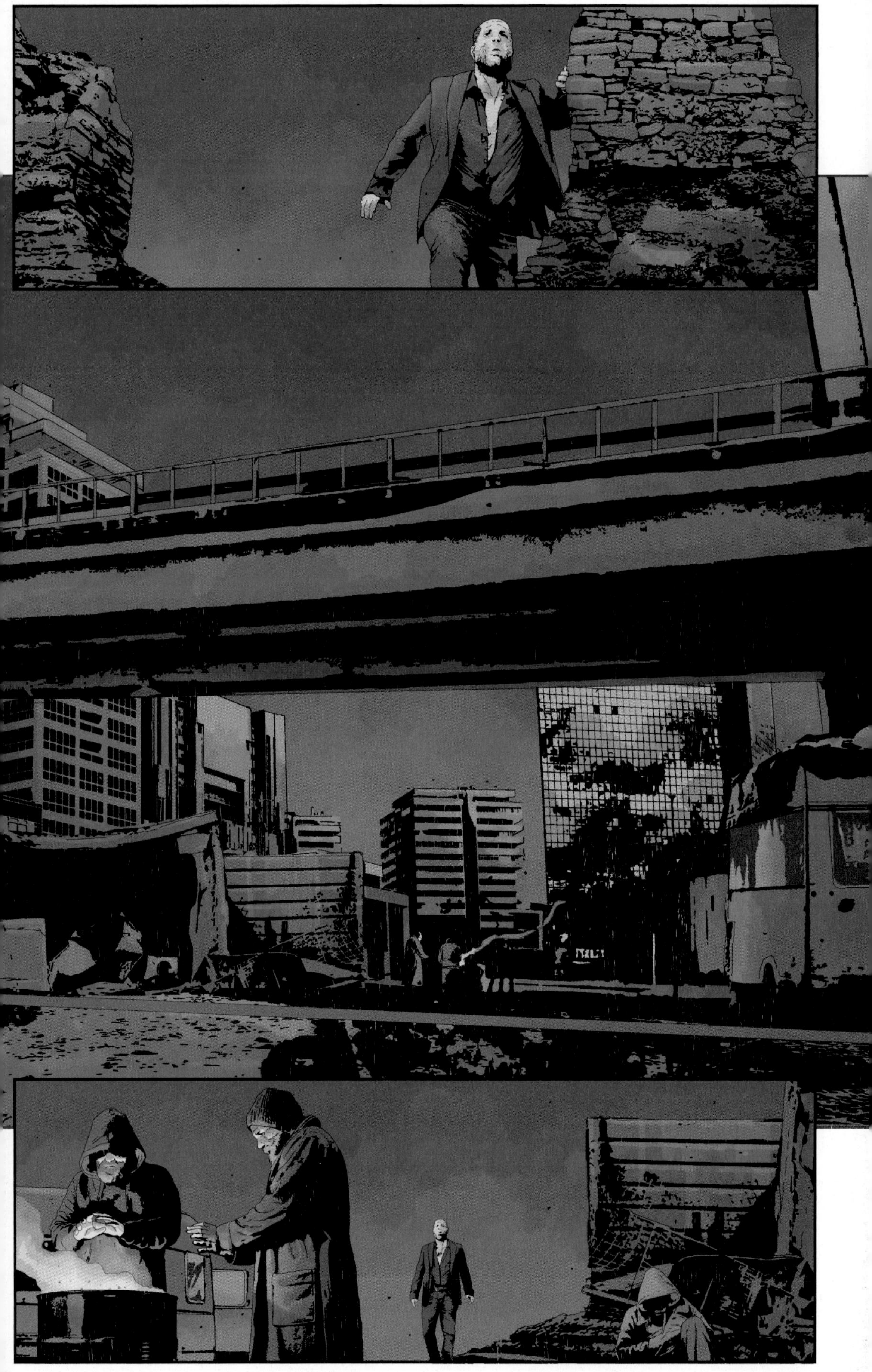

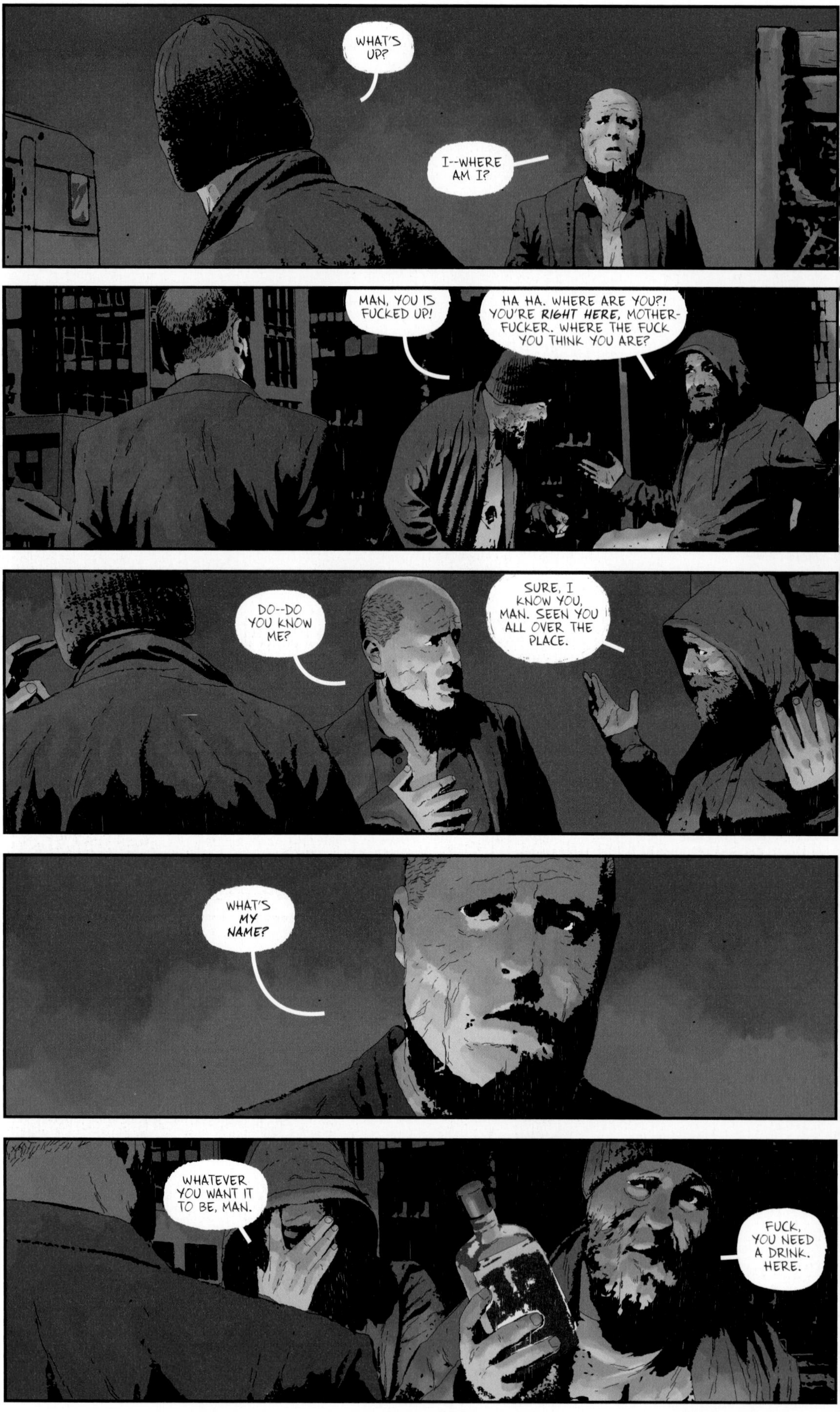
WHAT'S UP?
I--WHERE AM I?
MAN, YOU IS FUCKED UP!
HA HA. WHERE ARE YOU?! YOU'RE RIGHT HERE, MOTHER-FUCKER. WHERE THE FUCK YOU THINK YOU ARE?
DO--DO YOU KNOW ME?
SURE, I KNOW YOU, MAN. SEEN YOU ALL OVER THE PLACE.
WHAT'S MY NAME?
WHATEVER YOU WANT IT TO BE, MAN.
FUCK, YOU NEED A DRINK. HERE.

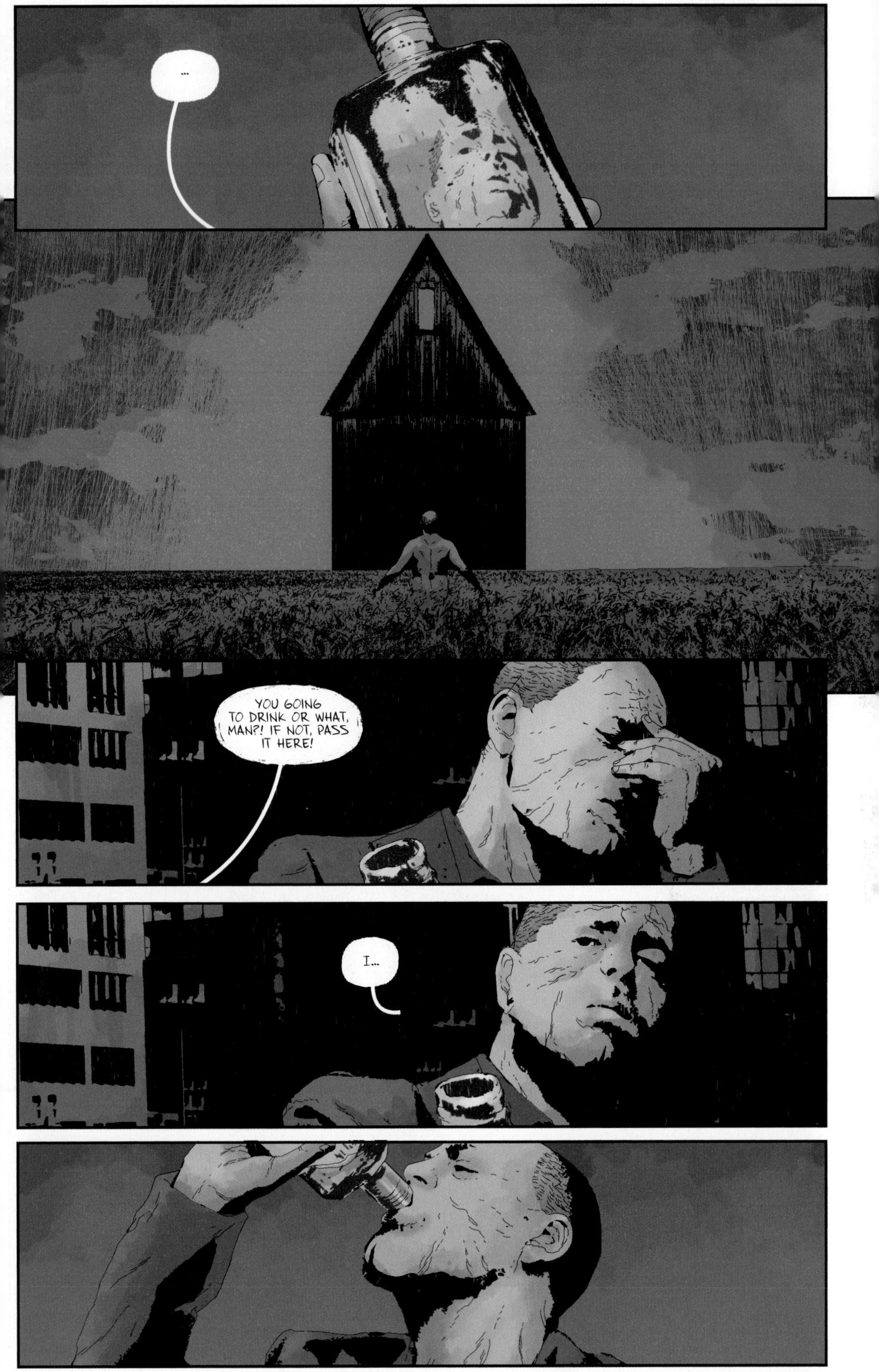
...
YOU GOING TO DRINK OR WHAT, MAN?! IF NOT, PASS IT HERE!
I...

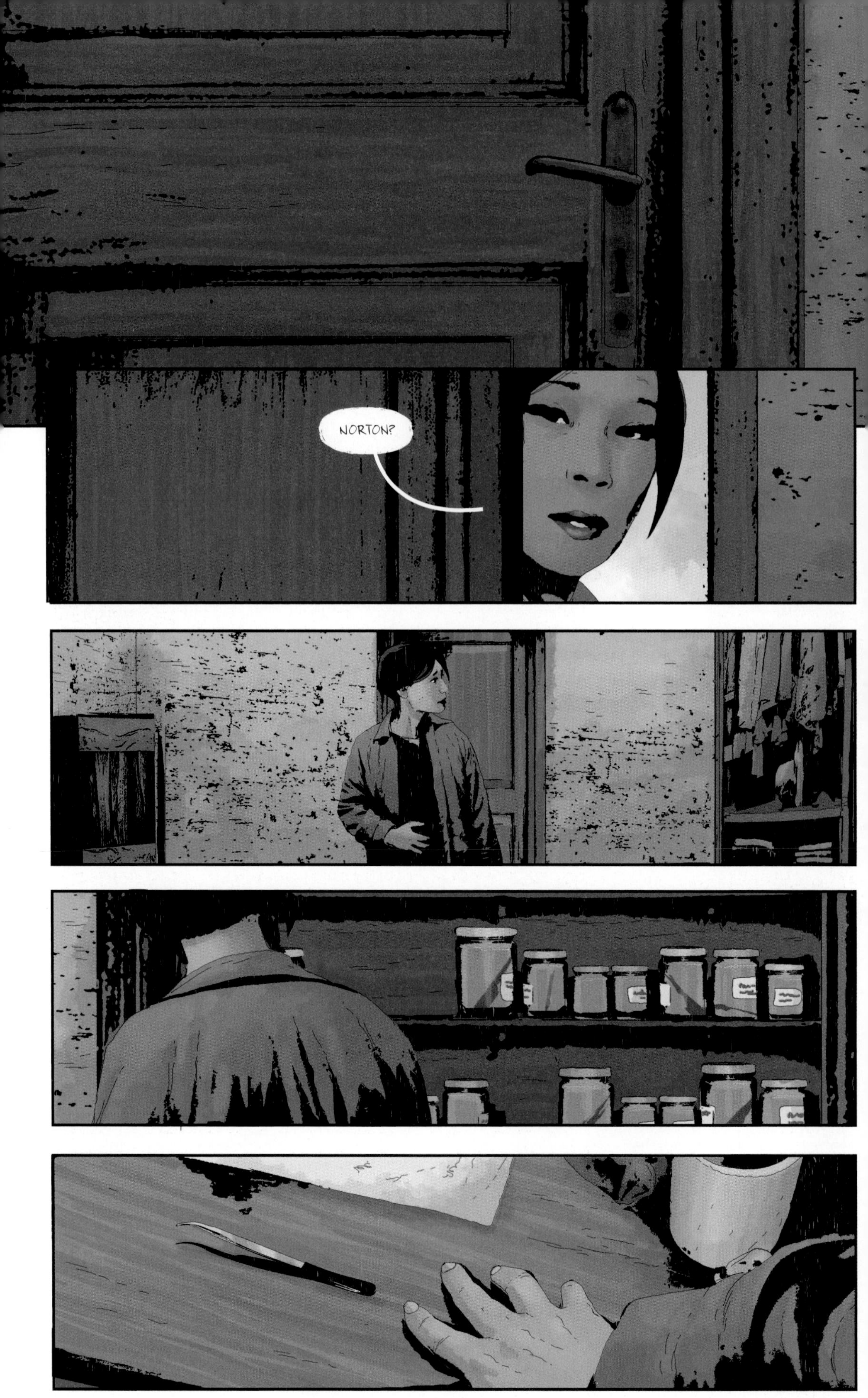
NORTON?

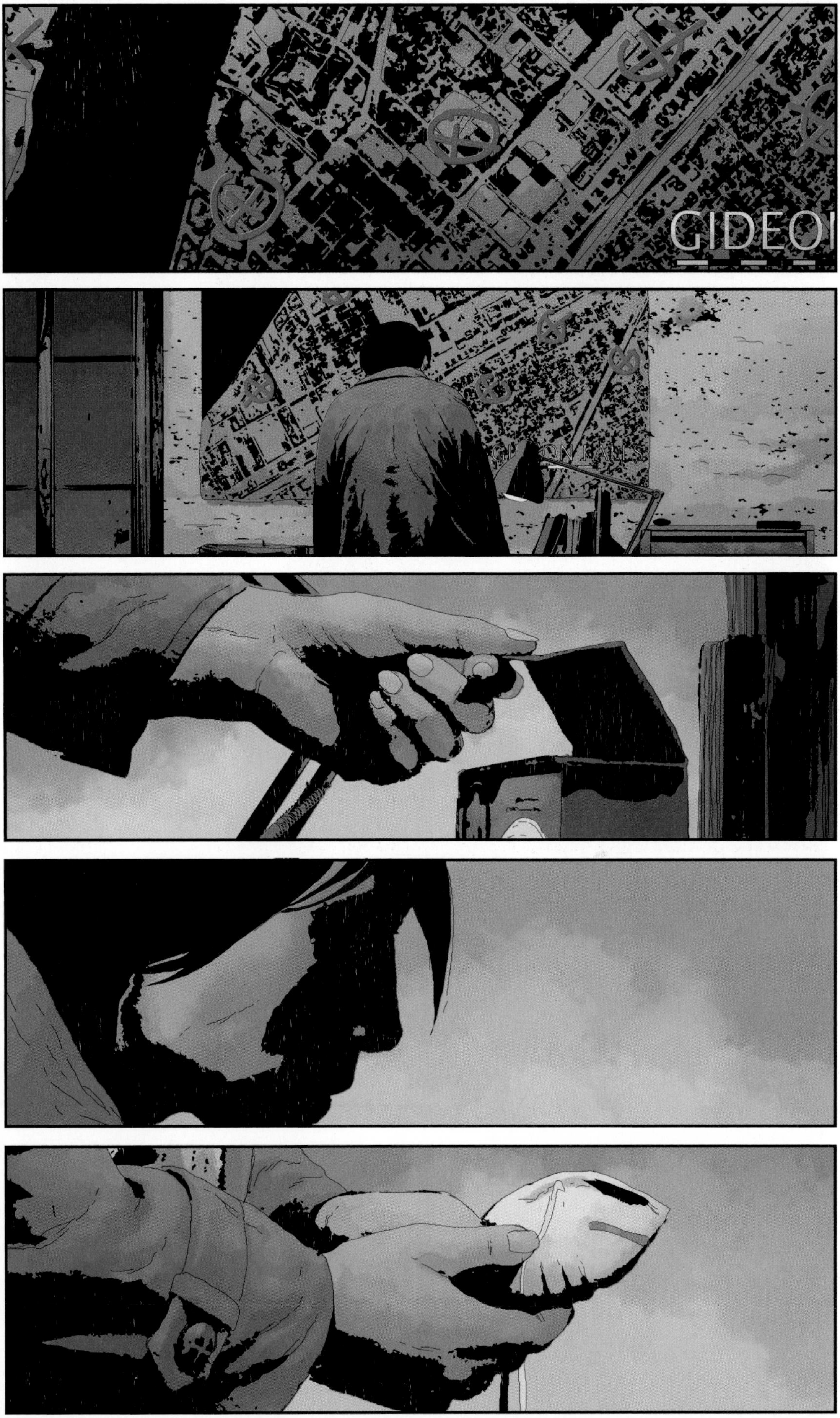
GIDEO

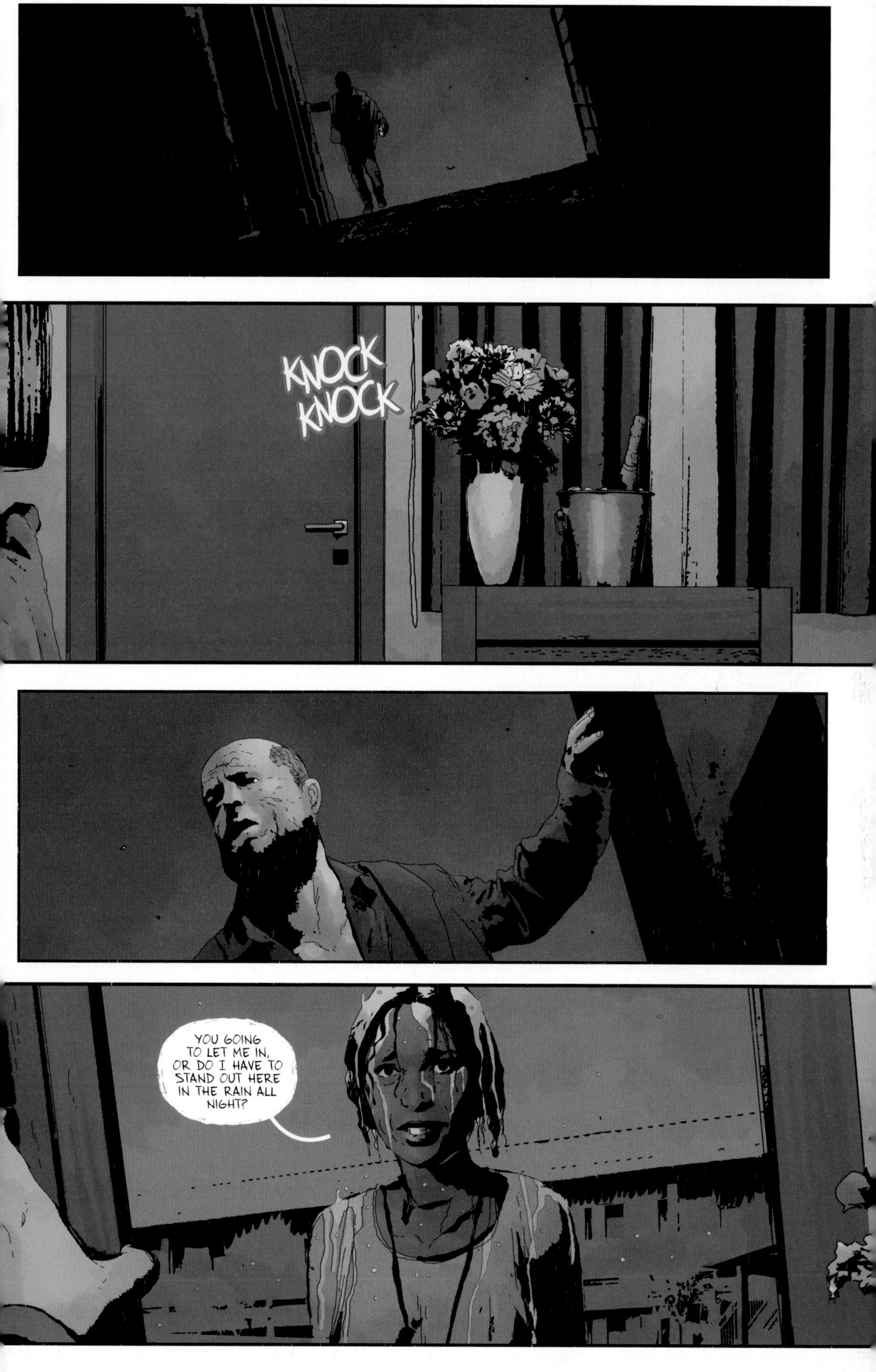
KNOCK KNOCK
YOU GOING TO LET ME IN, OR DO I HAVE TO STAND OUT HERE IN THE RAIN ALL NIGHT?

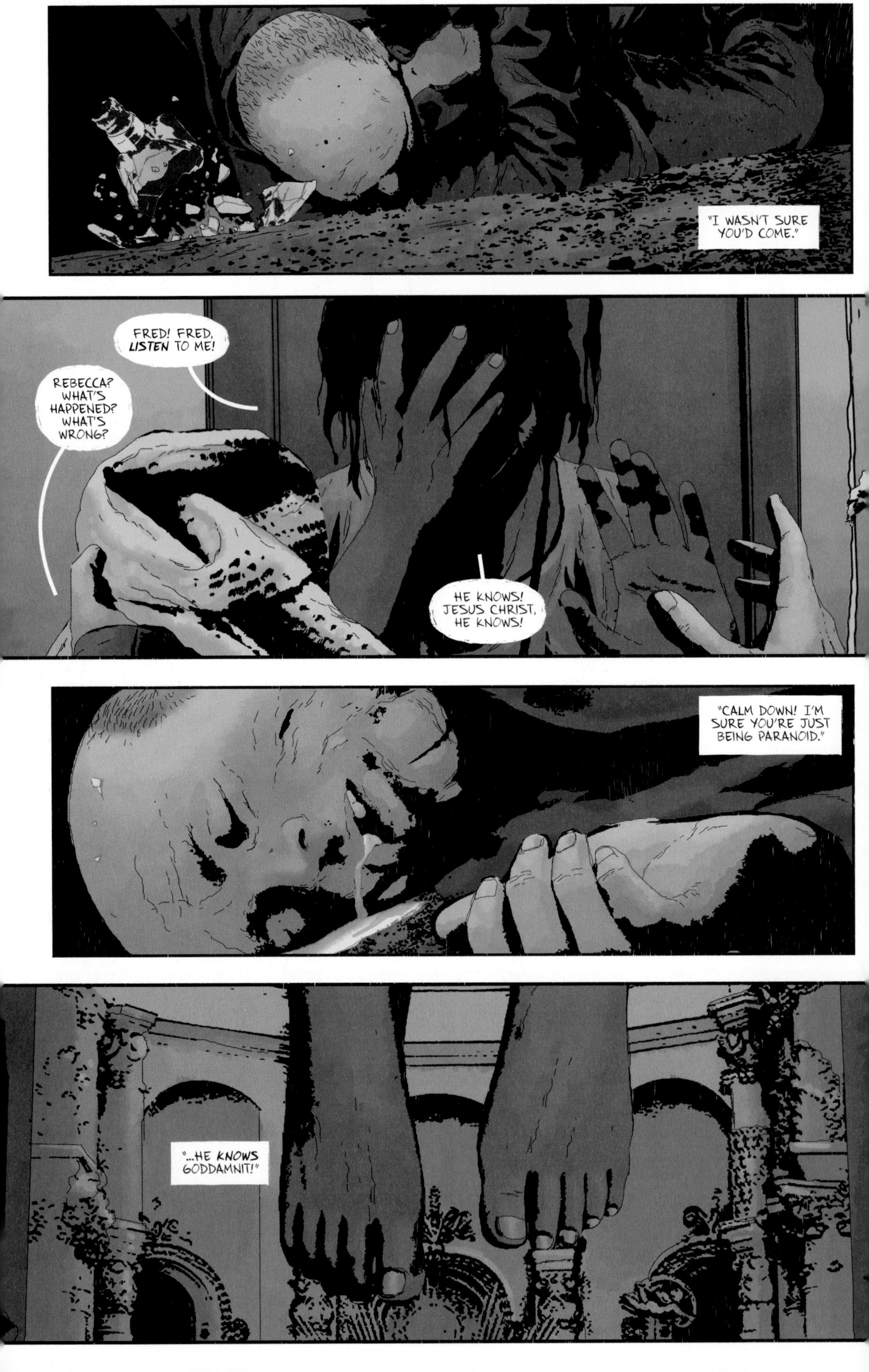
"I WASN'T SURE YOU'D COME."
FRED! FRED, LISTEN TO ME!
REBECCA? WHAT'S HAPPENED? WHAT'S WRONG?
HE KNOWS! JESUS CHRIST, HE KNOWS!
"CALM DOWN! I'M SURE YOU'RE JUST BEING PARANOID."
"...HE KNOWS GODDAMNIT!"

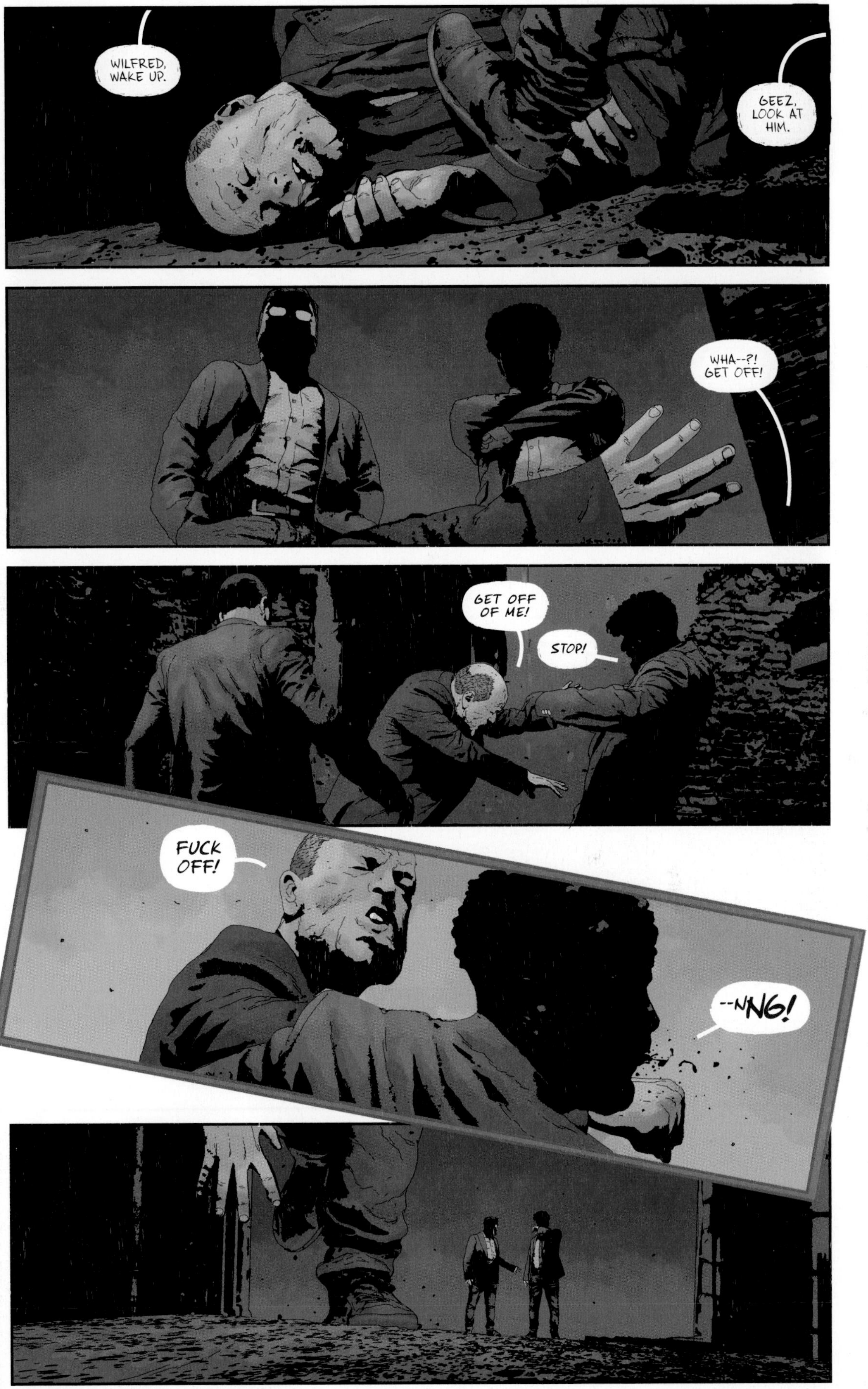
WILFRED, WAKE UP.
GEEZ, LOOK AT HIM.
WHA--?! GET OFF!
GET OFF OF ME!
STOP!
FUCK OFF!
--NNG!

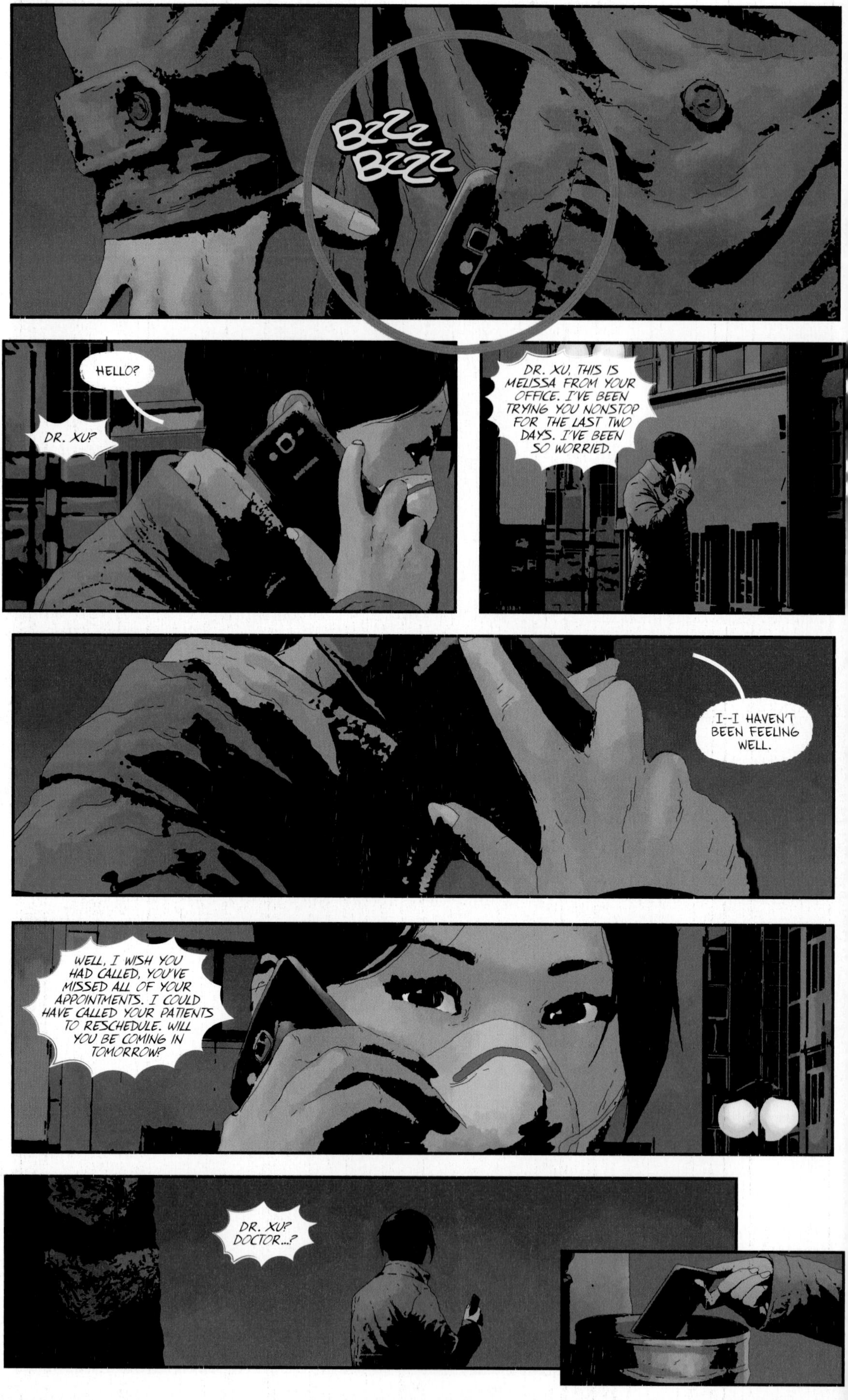
BZZZ BZZZ
HELLO?
DR. XU?
DR. XU, THIS IS MELISSA FROM YOUR OFFICE. I'VE BEEN TRYING YOU NONSTOP FOR THE LAST TWO DAYS. I'VE BEEN SO WORRIED.
I--I HAVEN'T BEEN FEELING WELL.
WELL, I WISH YOU HAD CALLED, YOU'VE MISSED ALL OF YOUR APPOINTMENTS. I COULD HAVE CALLED YOUR PATIENTS TO RESCHEDULE. WILL YOU BE COMING IN TOMORROW?
DR. XU? DOCTOR...?

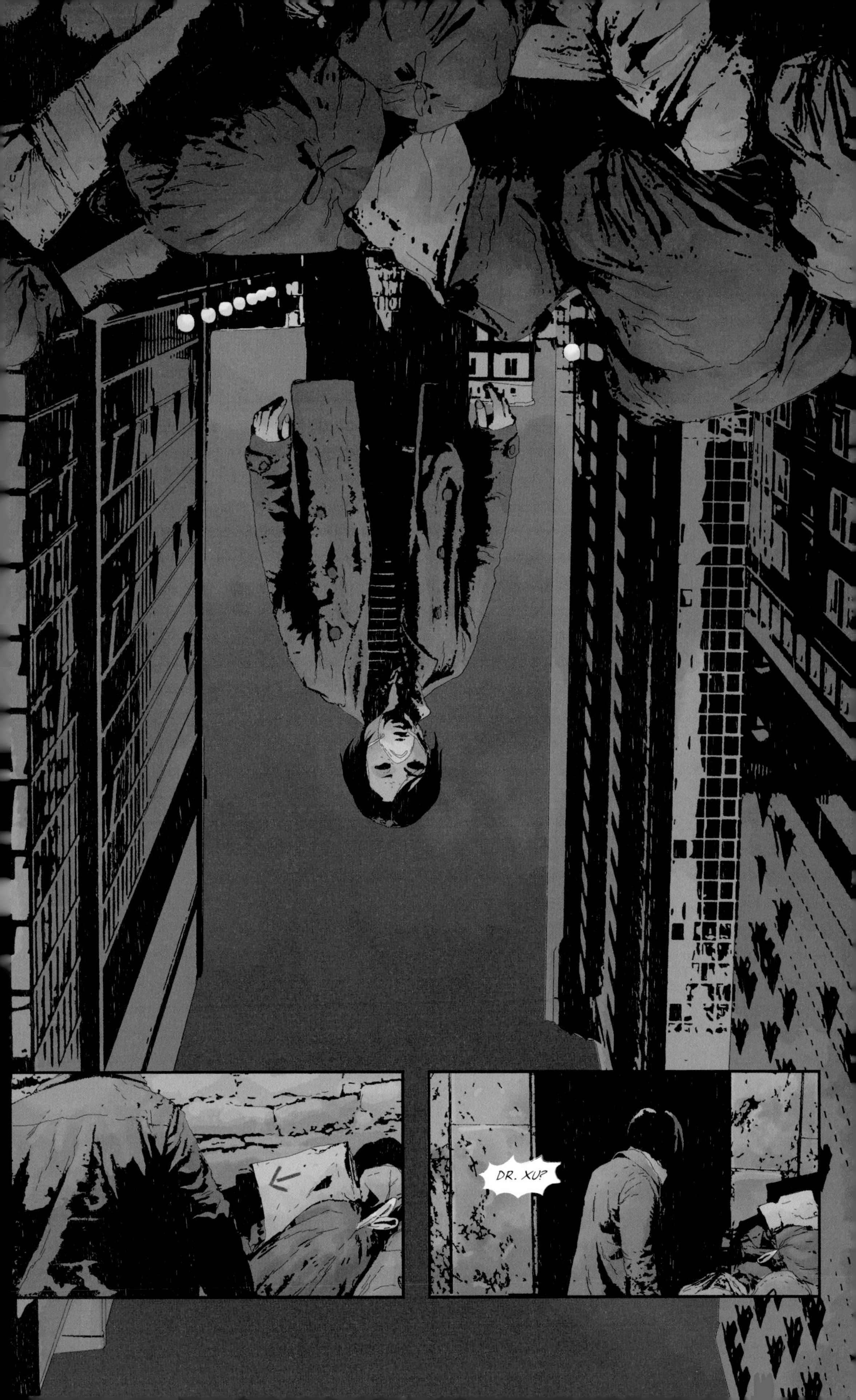
DR. XU?

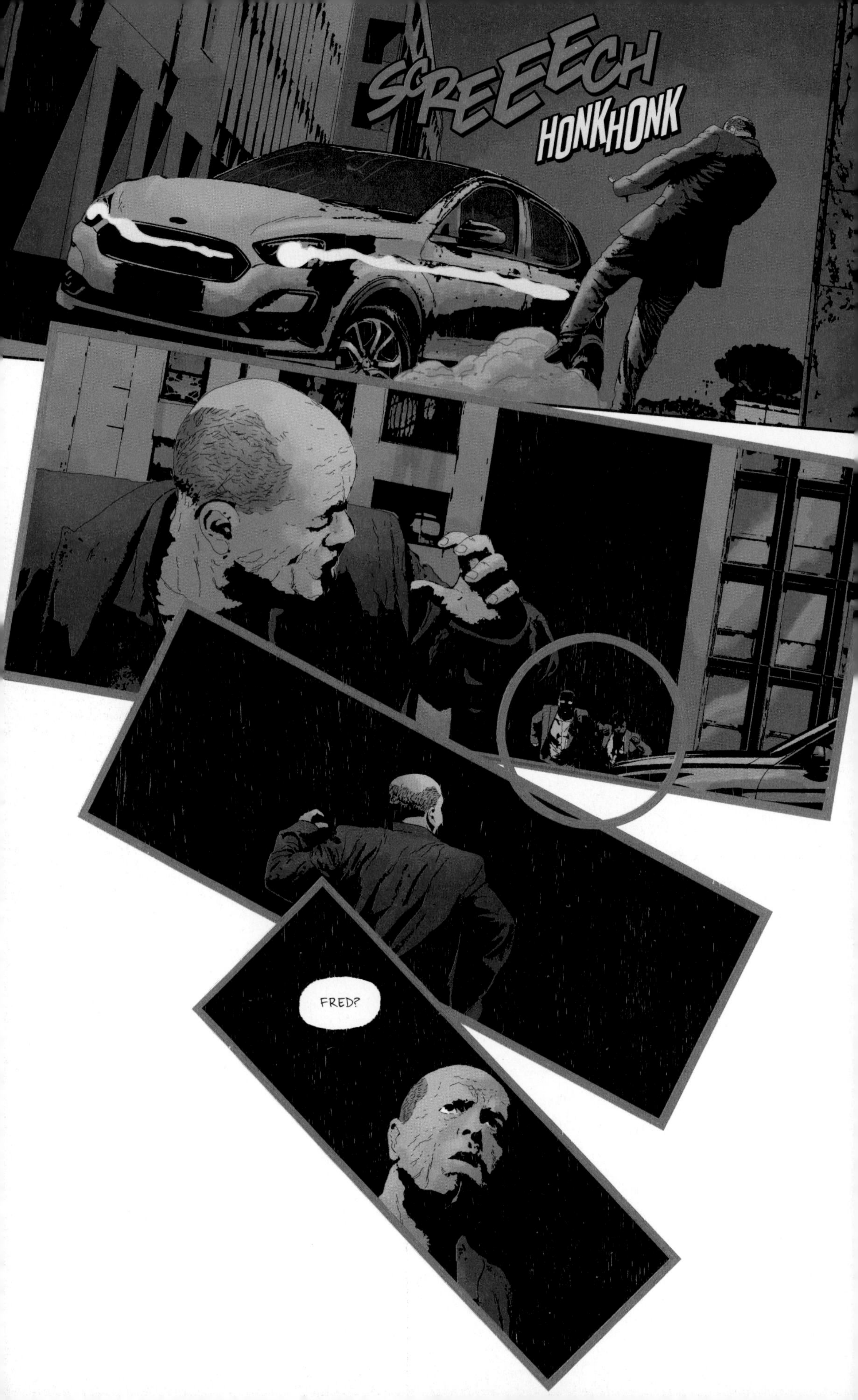
SCREEECH
HONKHONK
FRED?

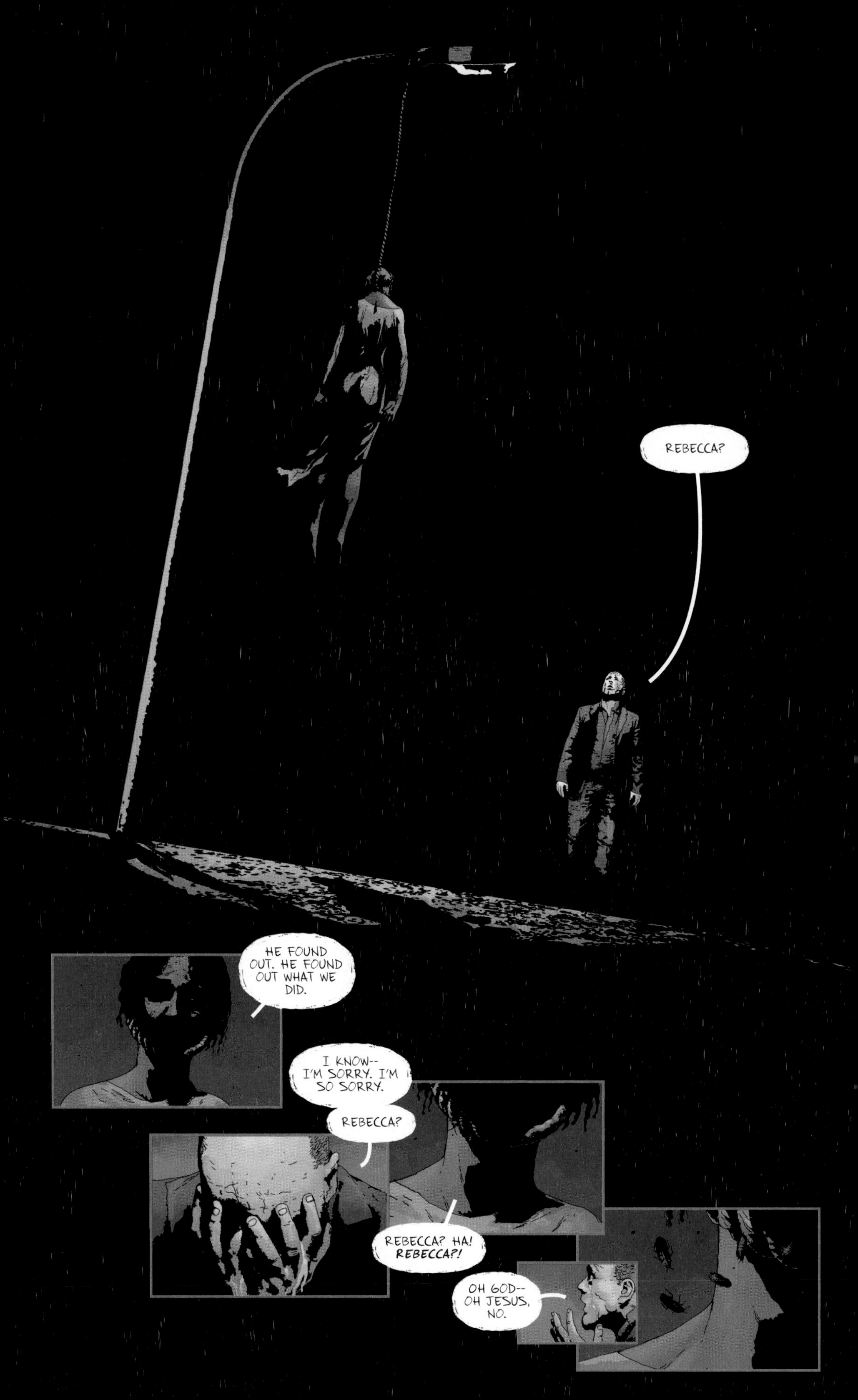
REBECCA?
HE FOUND OUT. HE FOUND OUT WHAT WE DID.
I KNOW-- I'M SORRY. I'M SO SORRY.
REBECCA?
REBECCA? HA! REBECCA?!
OH GOD-- OH JESUS, NO.

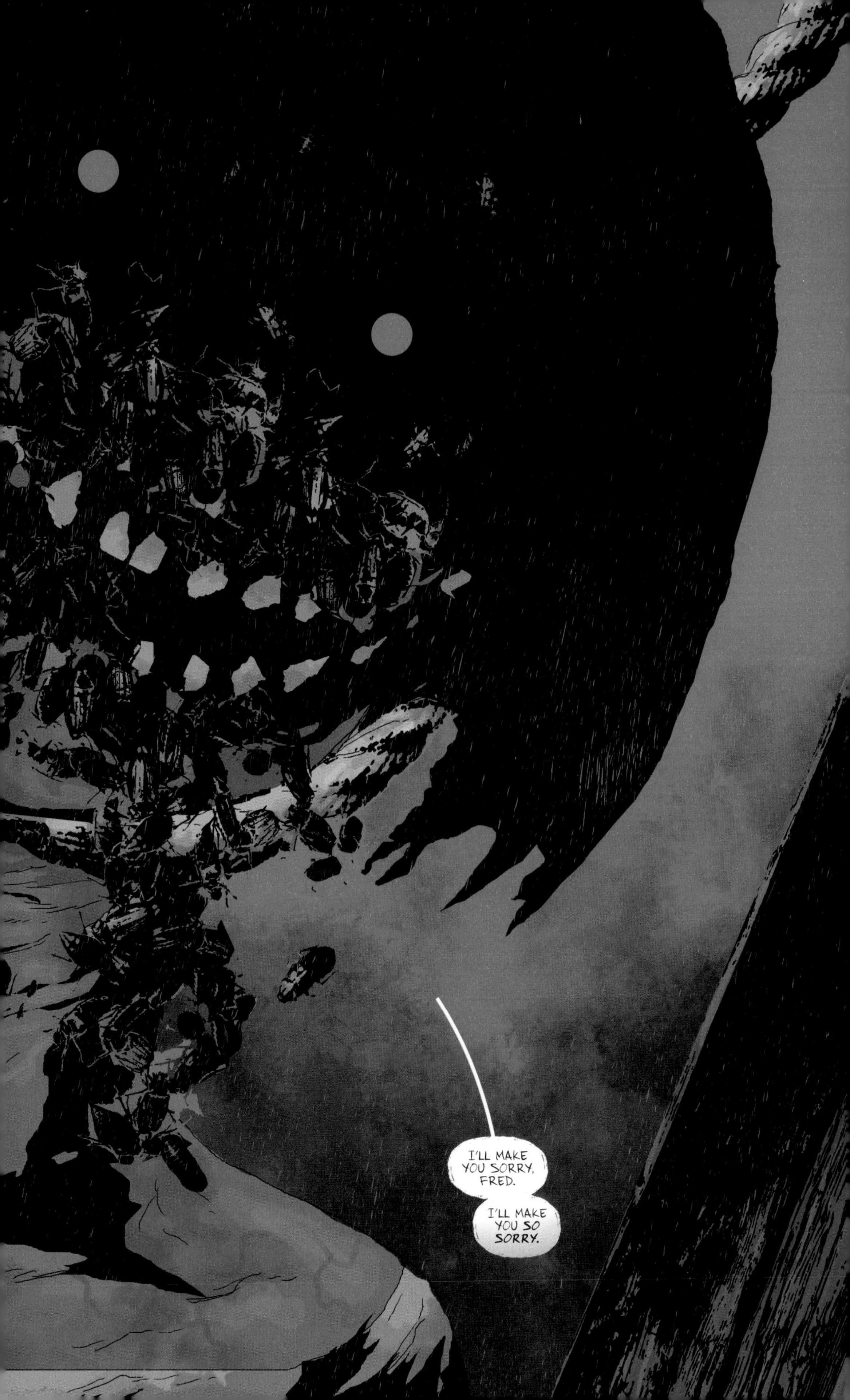
I'LL MAKE YOU SORRY, FRED.
I'LL MAKE YOU SO SORRY.

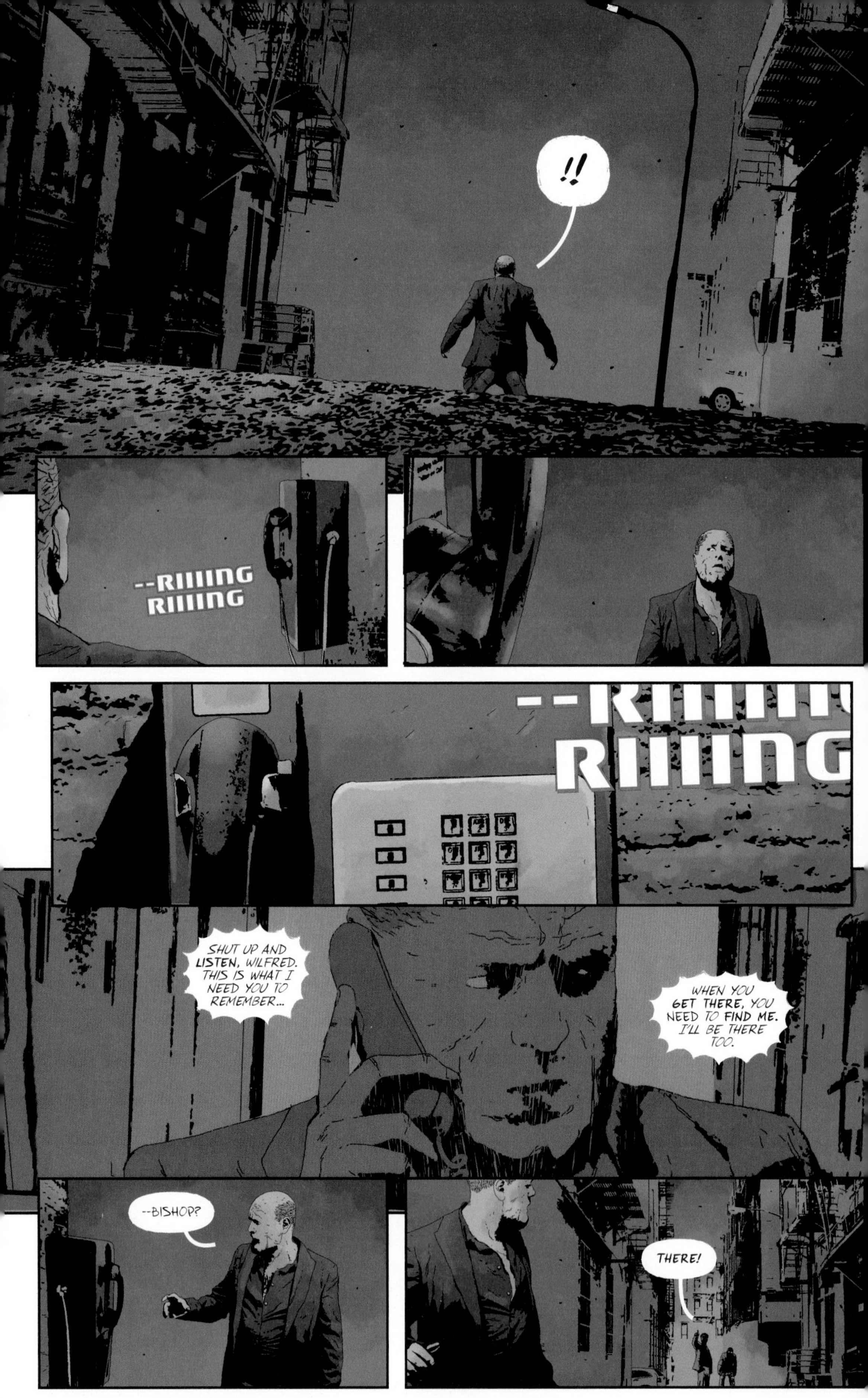
!!
--RIIIING
RIIIING
--RIIIIN
RIIIING
SHUT UP AND LISTEN, WILFRED. THIS IS WHAT I NEED YOU TO REMEMBER...
WHEN YOU GET THERE, YOU NEED TO FIND ME. I'LL BE THERE TOO.
--BISHOP?
THERE!

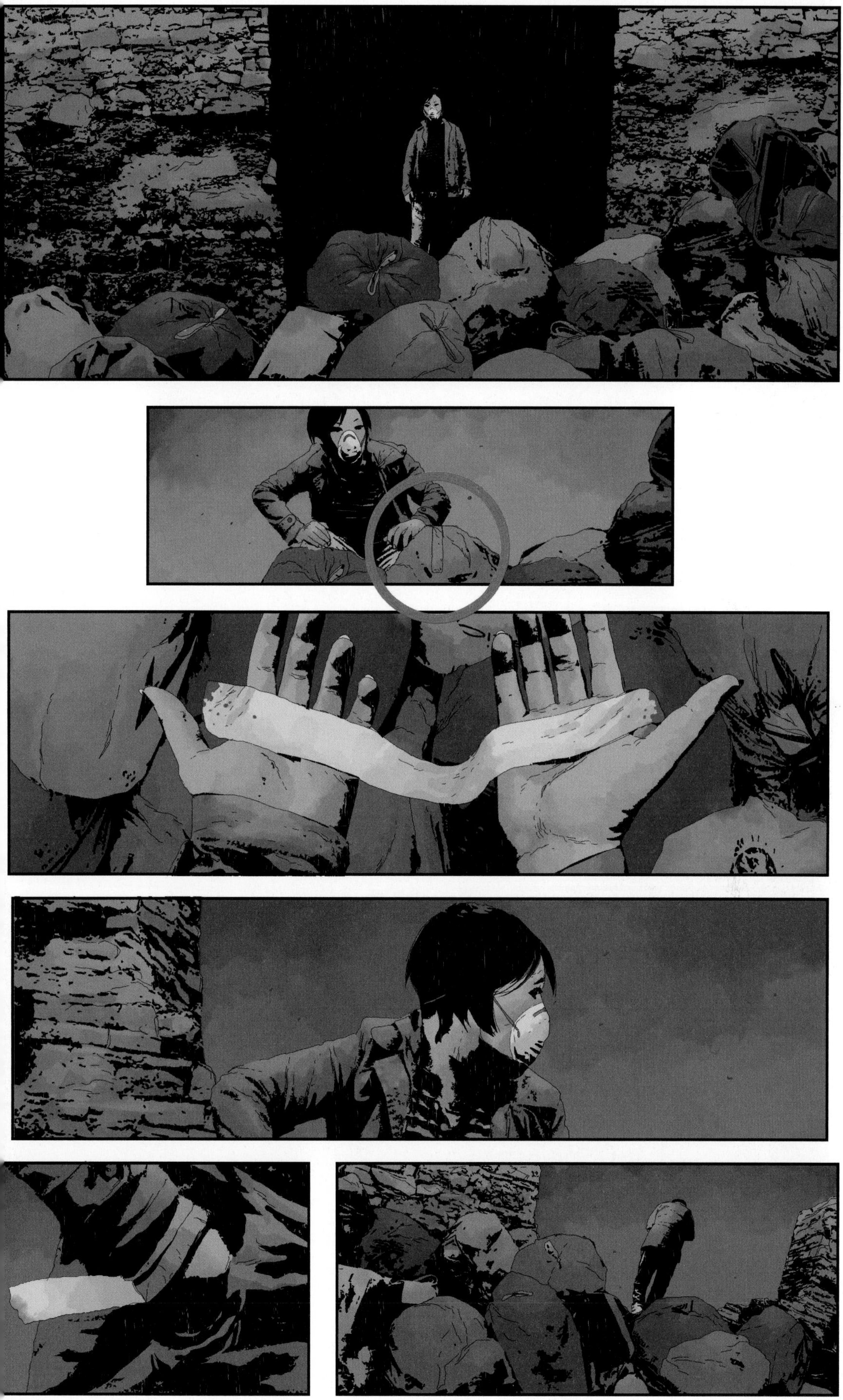

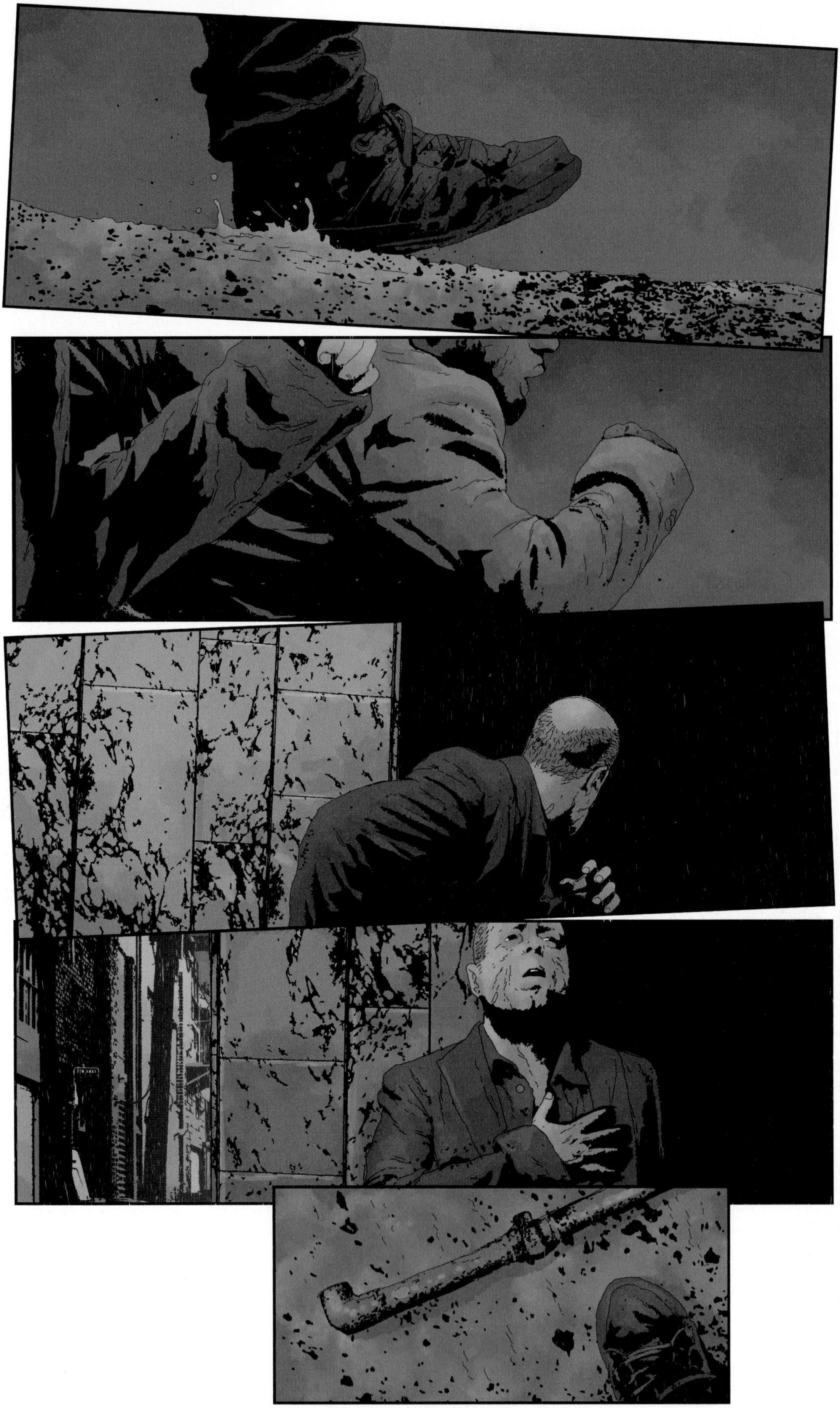

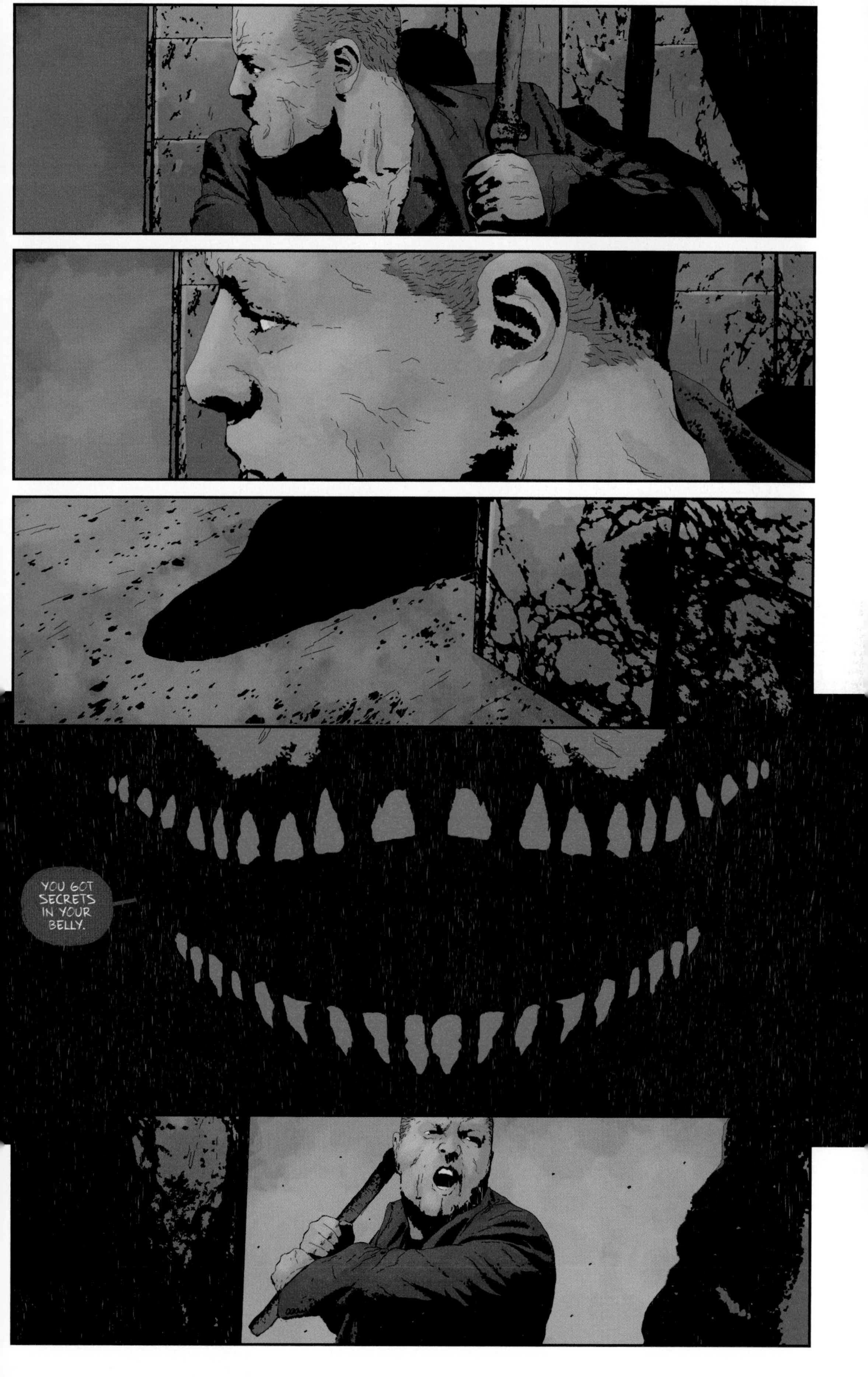
YOU GOT SECRETS IN YOUR BELLY.

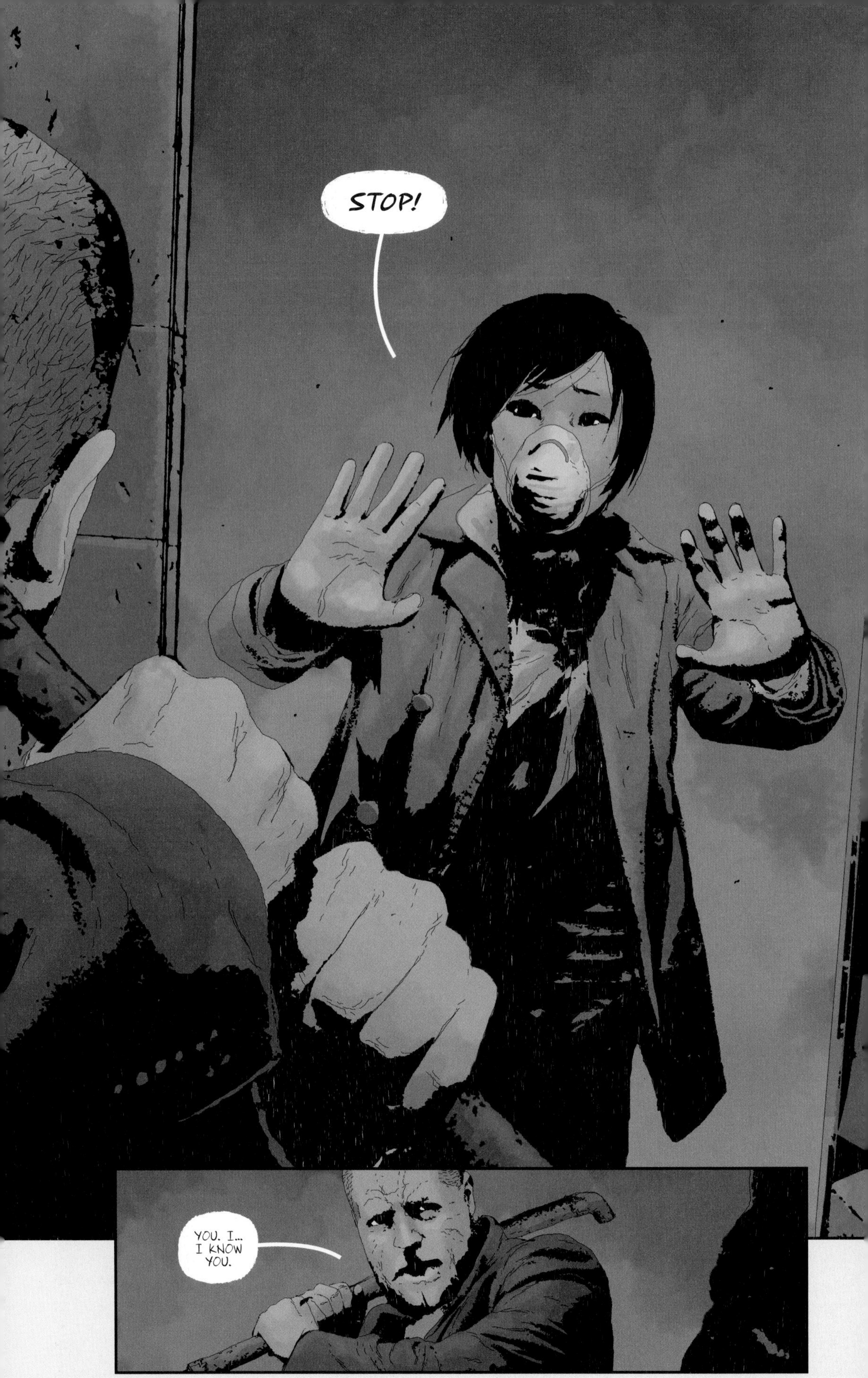
STOP!
YOU. I... I KNOW YOU.

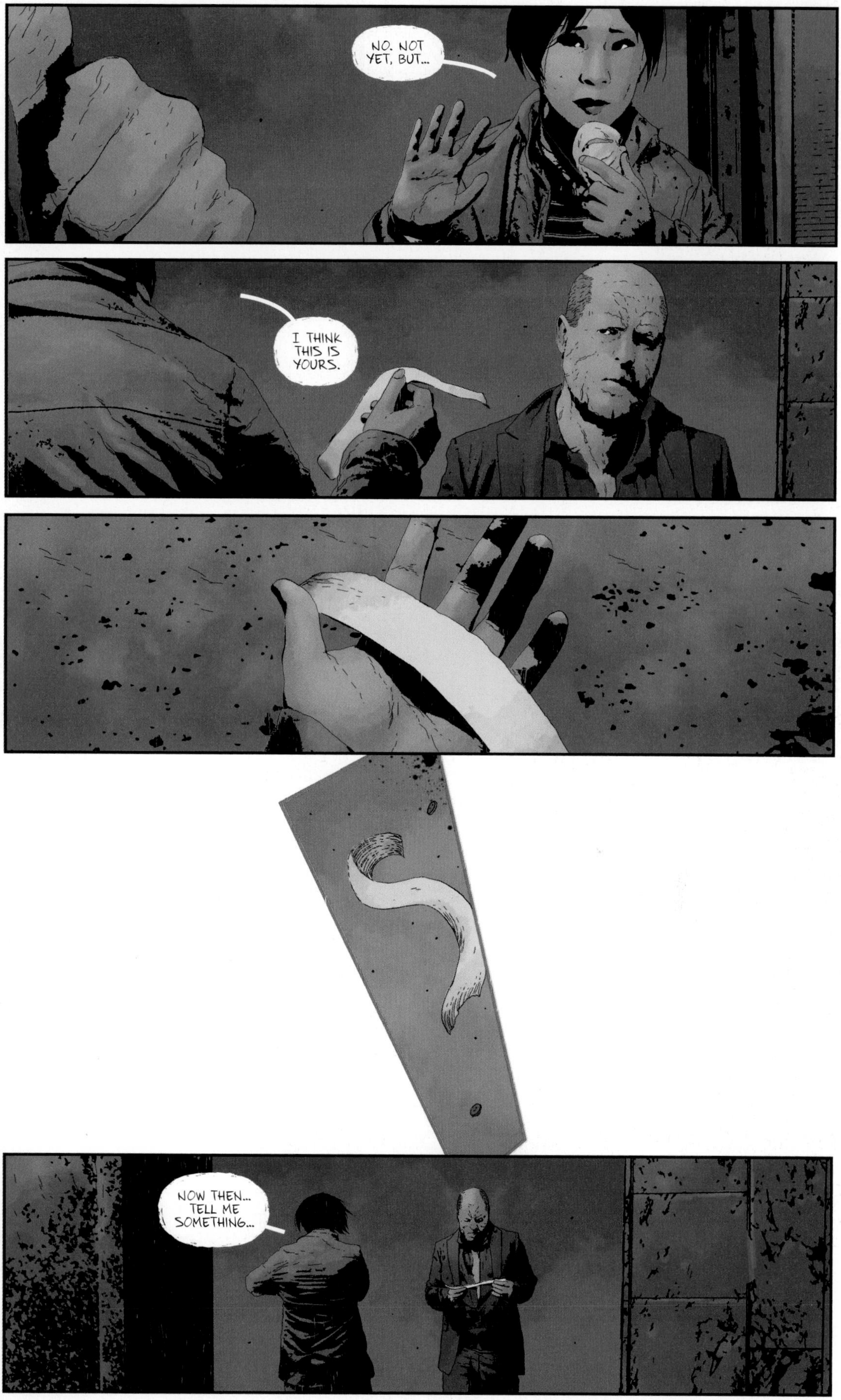
NO. NOT YET, BUT...
I THINK THIS IS YOURS.
NOW THEN... TELL ME SOMETHING...

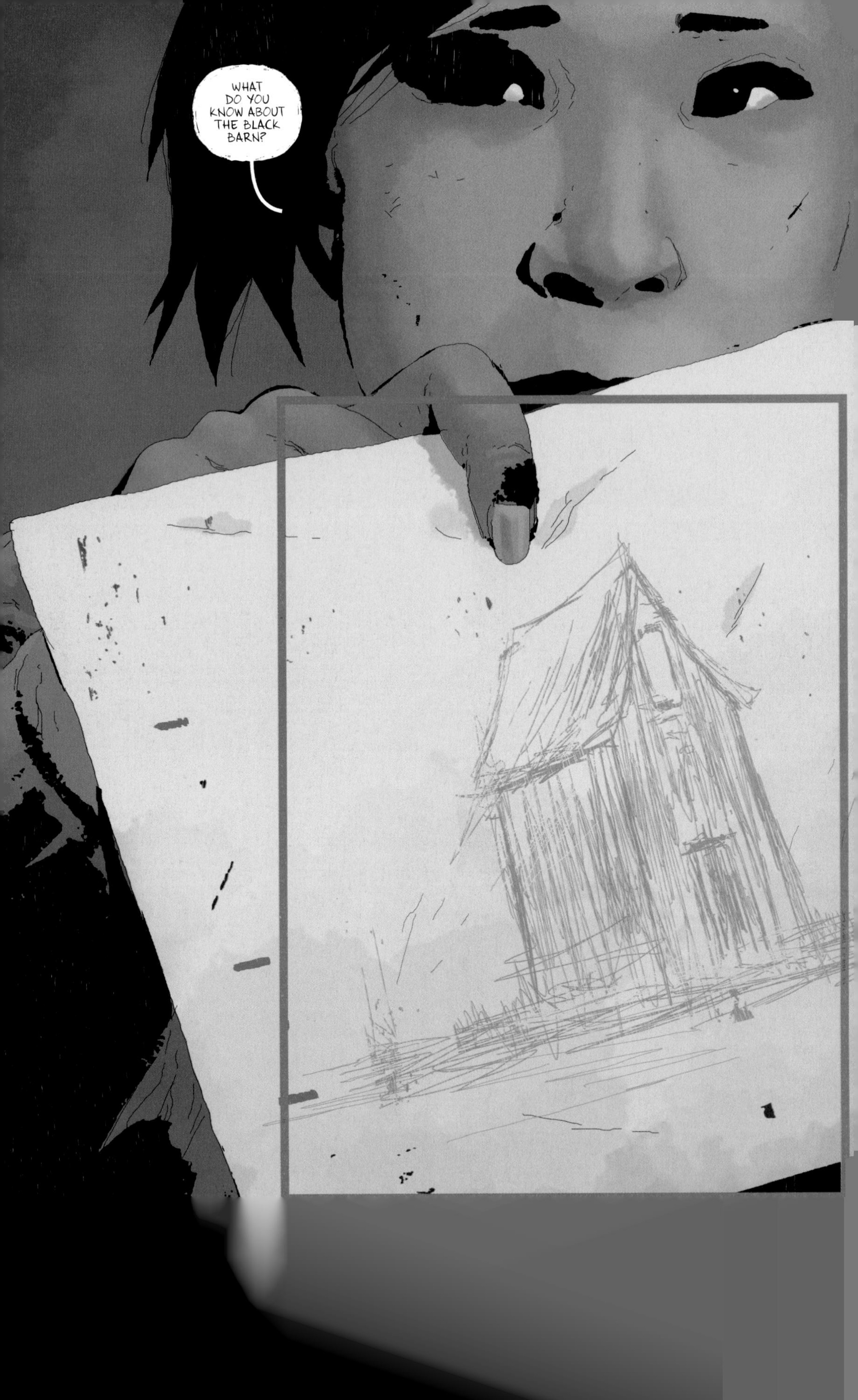
WHAT DO YOU KNOW ABOUT THE BLACK BARN?

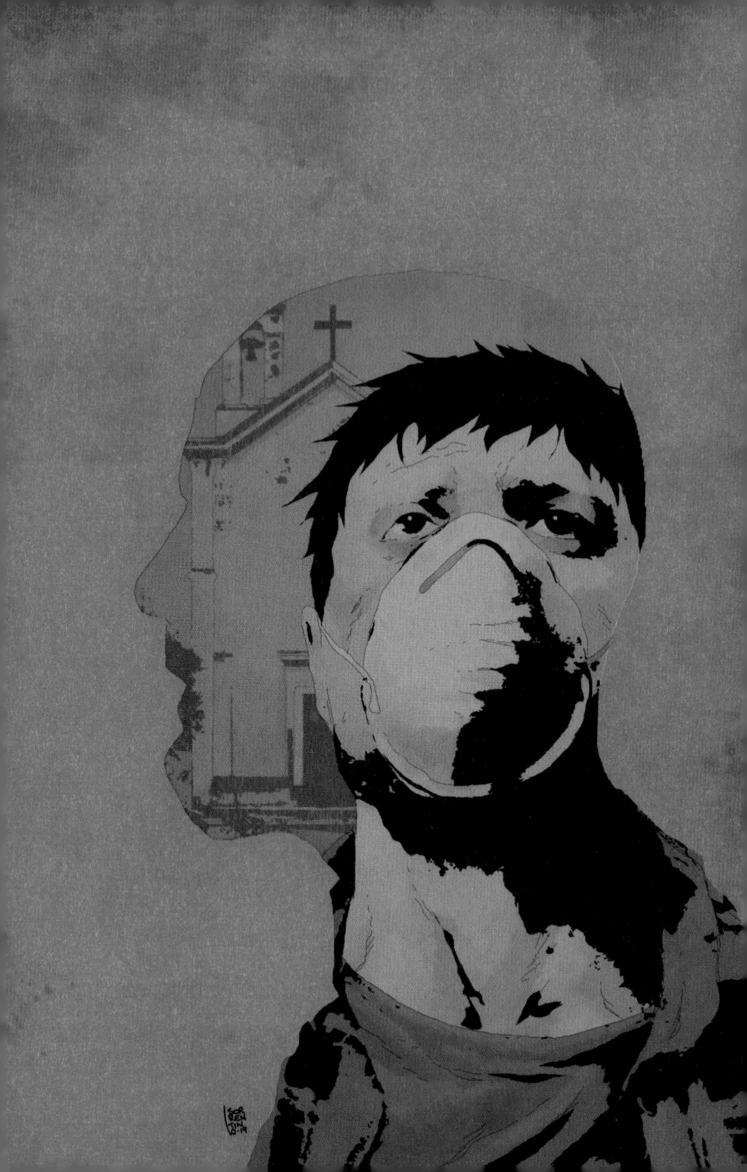

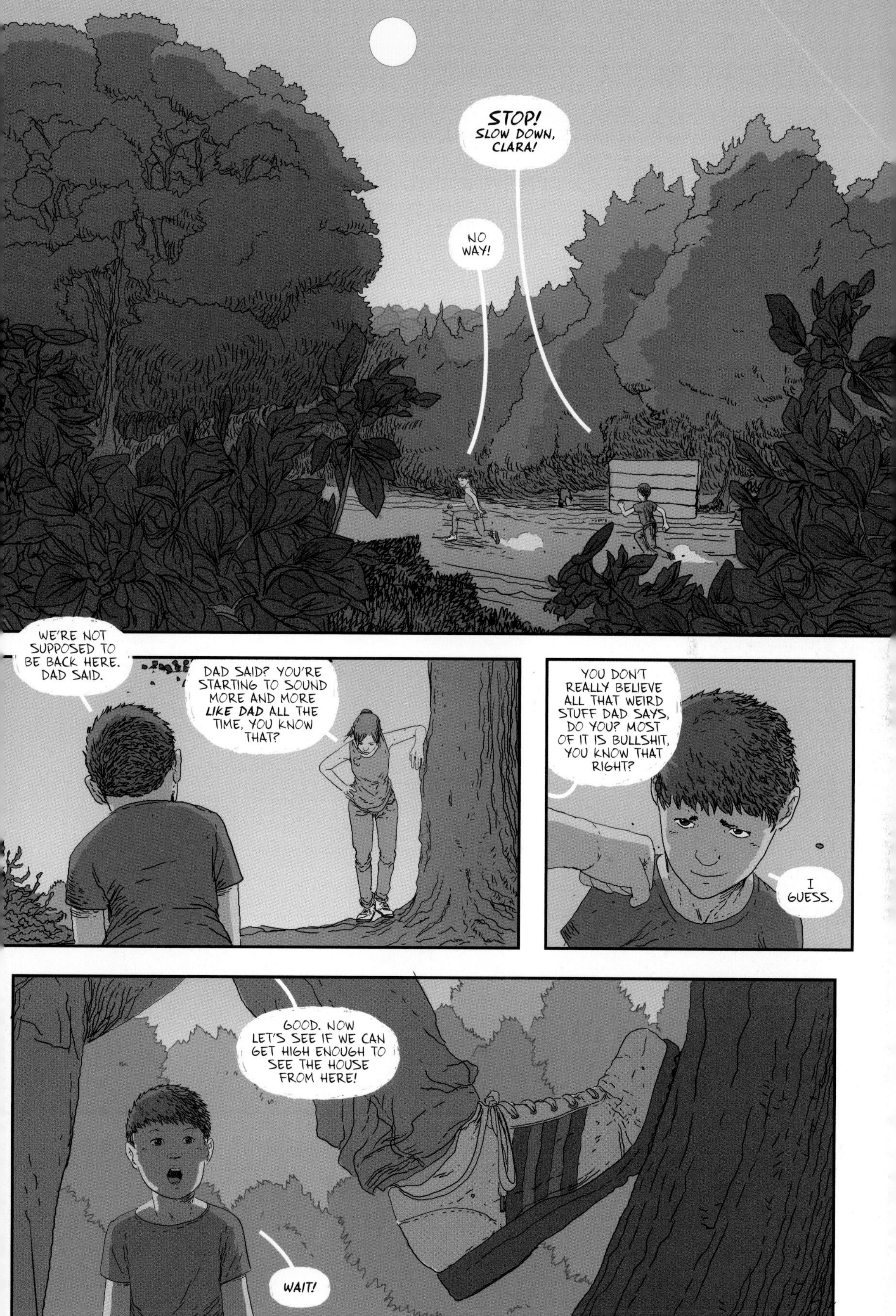
STOP! SLOW DOWN, CLARA!
NO WAY!
WE'RE NOT SUPPOSED TO BE BACK HERE. DAD SAID.
DAD SAID? YOU'RE STARTING TO SOUND MORE AND MORE LIKE DAD ALL THE TIME, YOU KNOW THAT?
YOU DON'T REALLY BELIEVE ALL THAT WEIRD STUFF DAD SAYS, DO YOU? MOST OF IT IS BULLSHIT, YOU KNOW THAT RIGHT?
I GUESS.
GOOD. NOW LET'S SEE IF WE CAN GET HIGH ENOUGH TO SEE THE HOUSE FROM HERE!
WAIT!

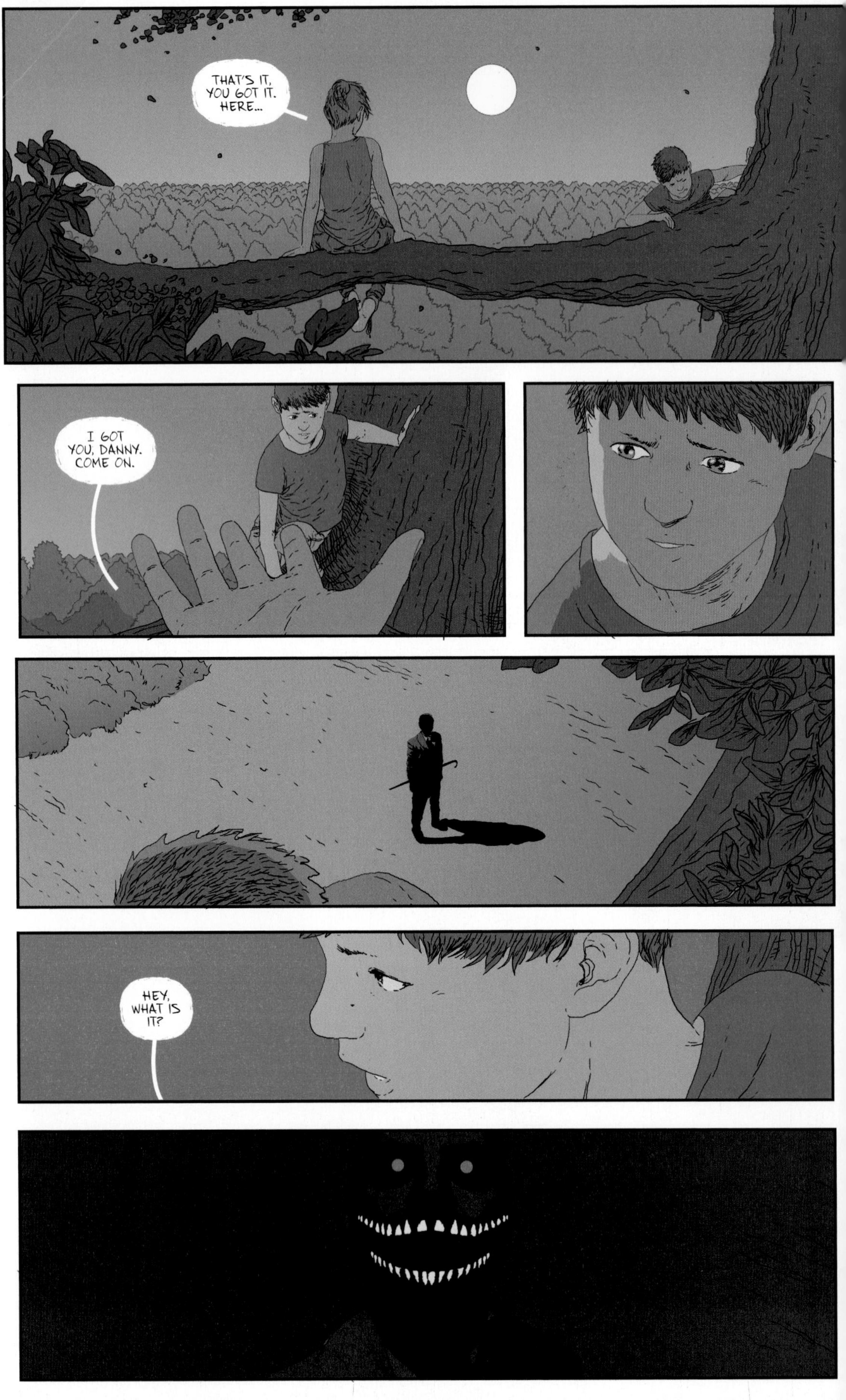
THAT'S IT, YOU GOT IT. HERE...
I GOT YOU, DANNY. COME ON.
HEY, WHAT IS IT?

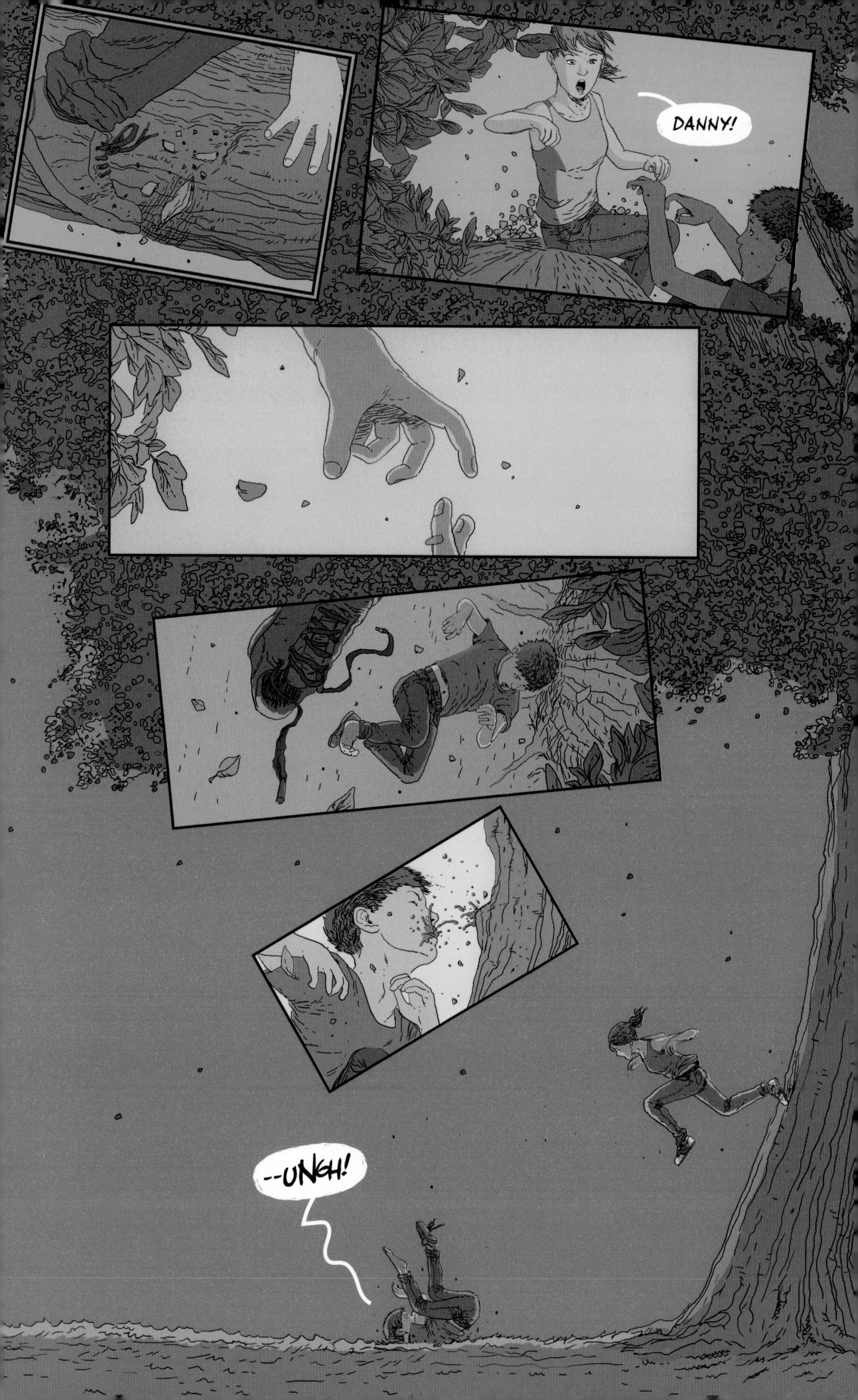
DANNY!
--UNGH!

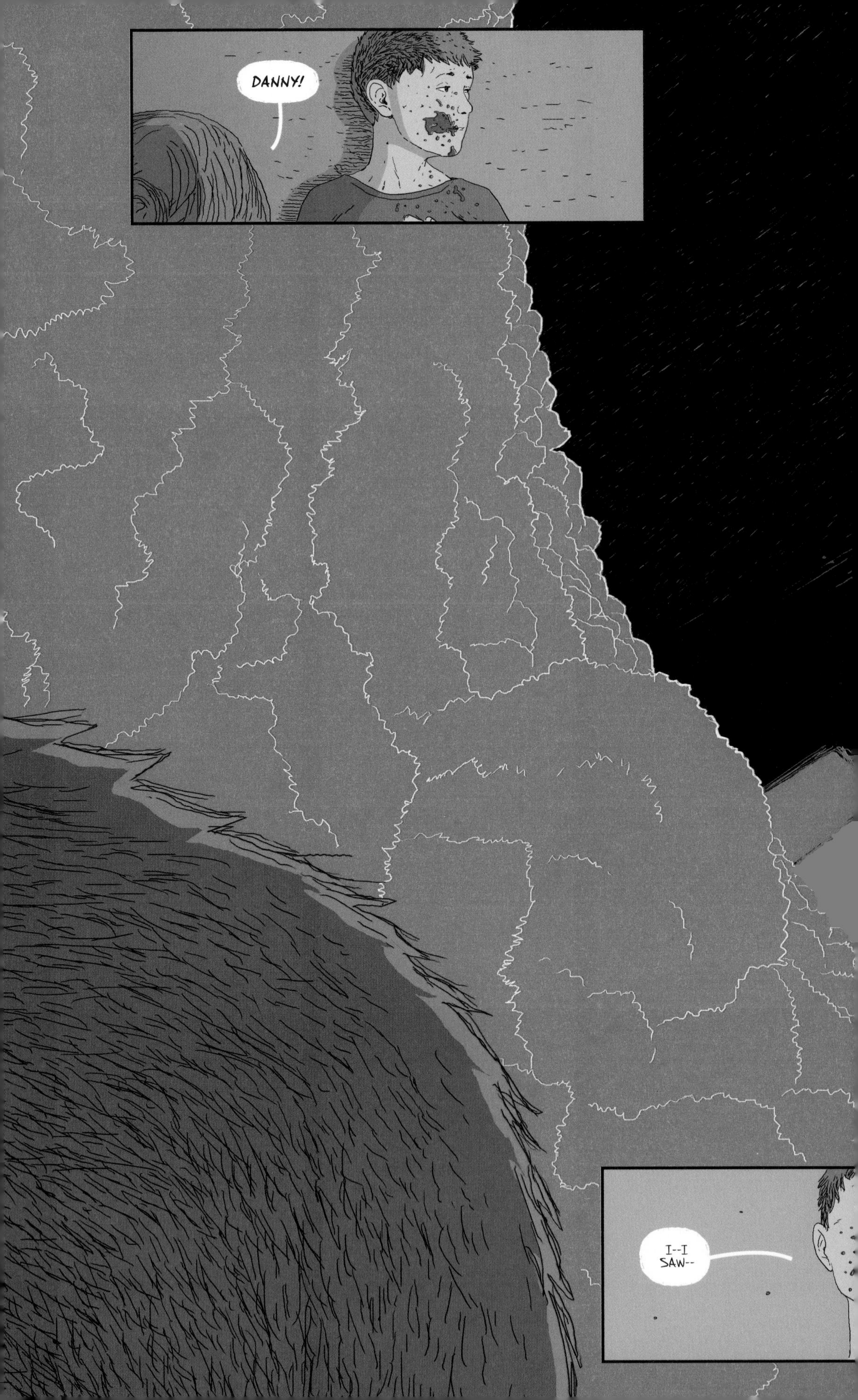
DANNY!
I--I SAW--

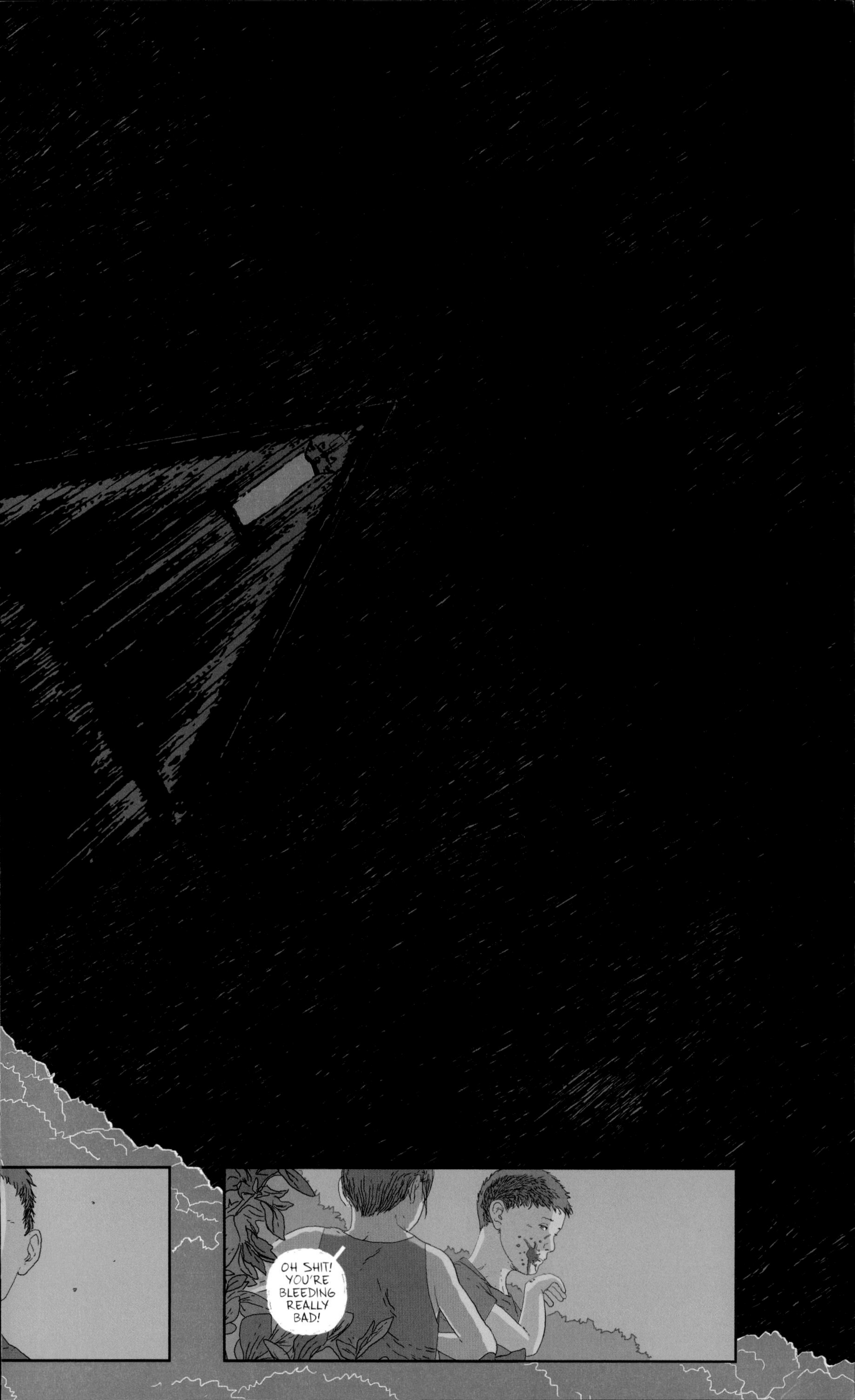
OH SHIT! YOU'RE BLEEDING REALLY BAD!

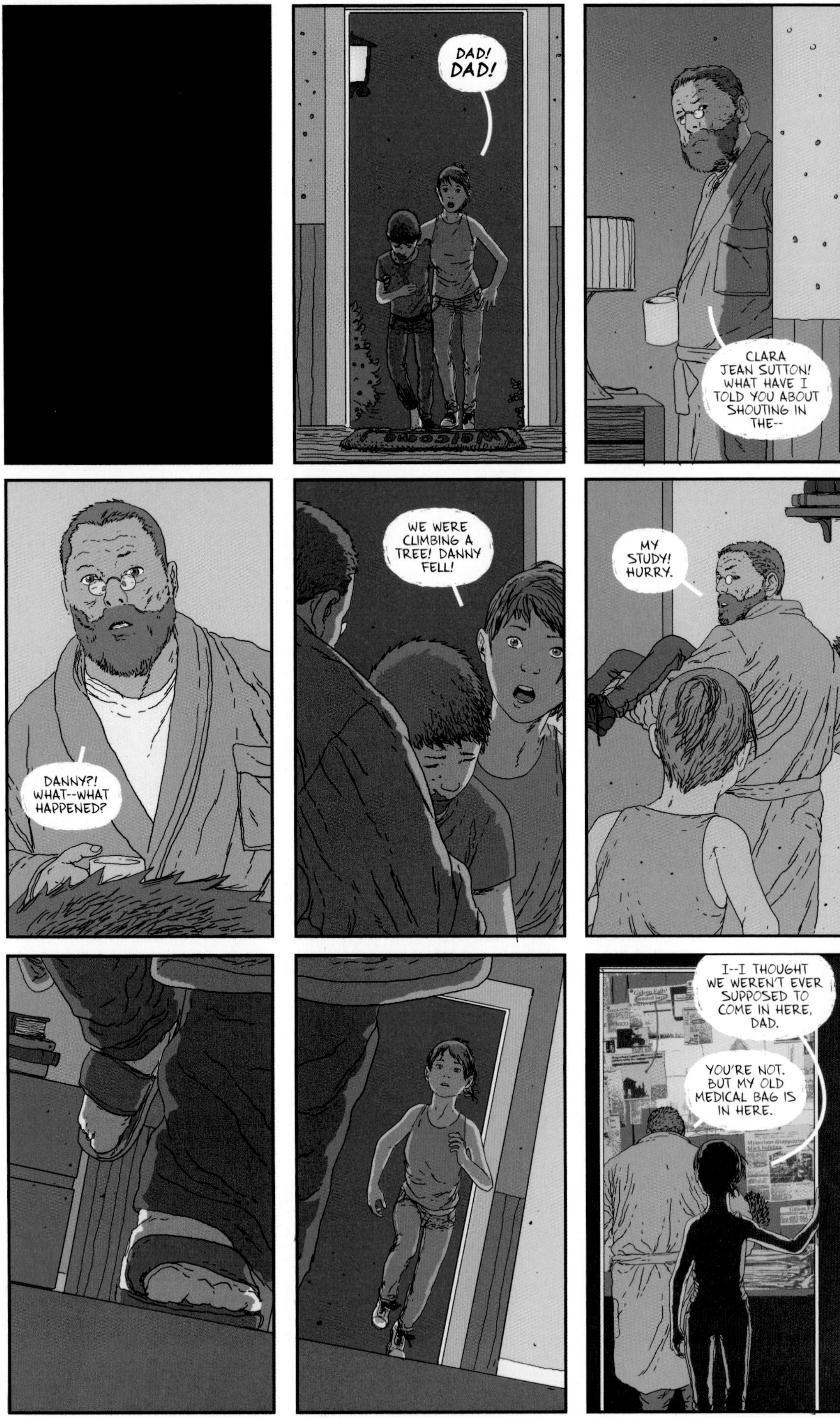
DAD! DAD!
CLARA JEAN SUTTON! WHAT HAVE I TOLD YOU ABOUT SHOUTING IN THE--
DANNY?! WHAT--WHAT HAPPENED?
WE WERE CLIMBING A TREE! DANNY FELL!
MY STUDY! HURRY.
I--I THOUGHT WE WEREN'T EVER SUPPOSED TO COME IN HERE, DAD.
YOU'RE NOT. BUT MY OLD MEDICAL BAG IS IN HERE.

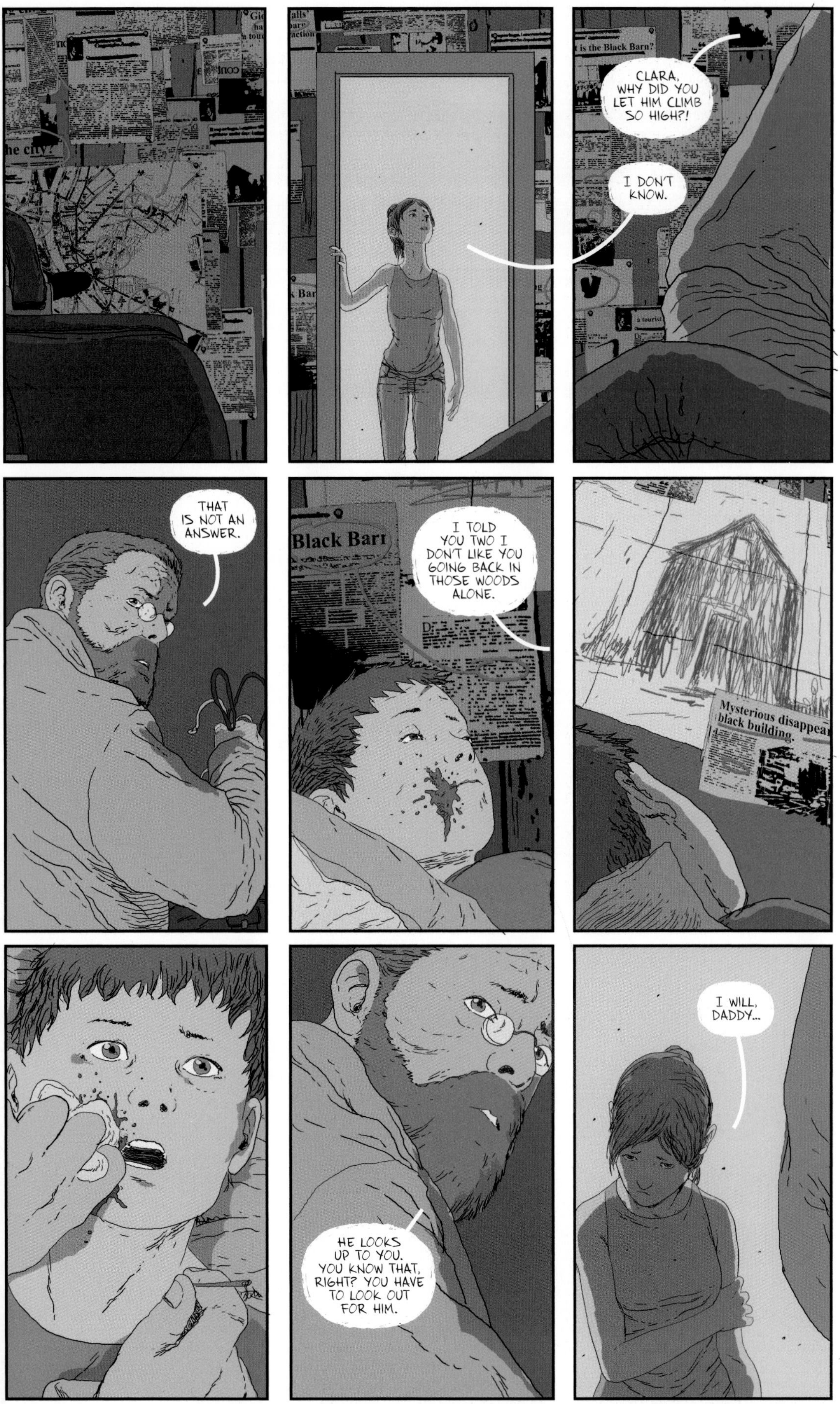
CLARA, WHY DID YOU LET HIM CLIMB SO HIGH?!
I DON'T KNOW.
THAT IS NOT AN ANSWER.
I TOLD YOU TWO I DON'T LIKE YOU GOING BACK IN THOSE WOODS ALONE.
Mysterious disappear black building.
HE LOOKS UP TO YOU. YOU KNOW THAT, RIGHT? YOU HAVE TO LOOK OUT FOR HIM.
I WILL, DADDY...

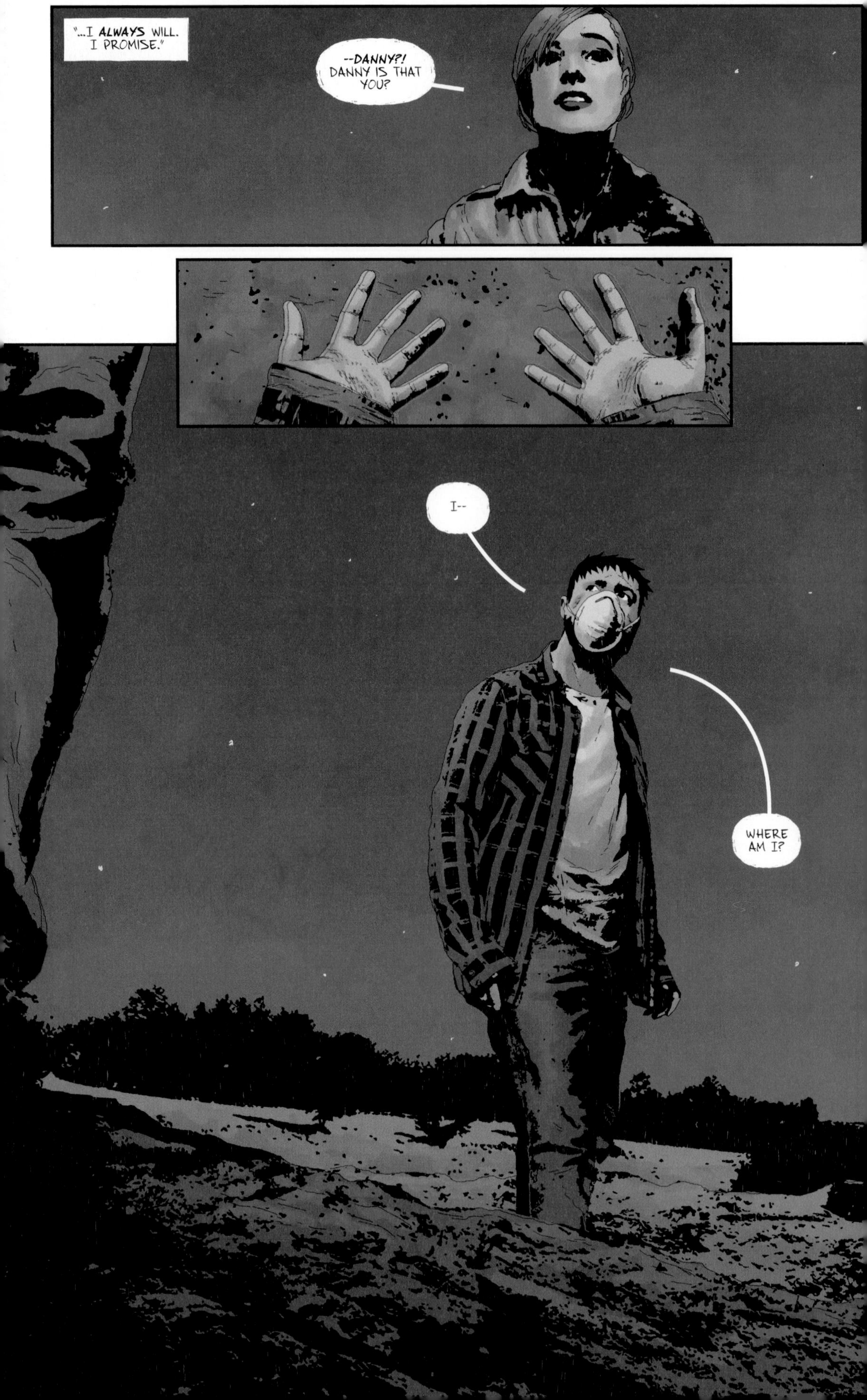
"...I ALWAYS WILL. I PROMISE."
--DANNY?! DANNY IS THAT YOU?
I--
WHERE AM I?

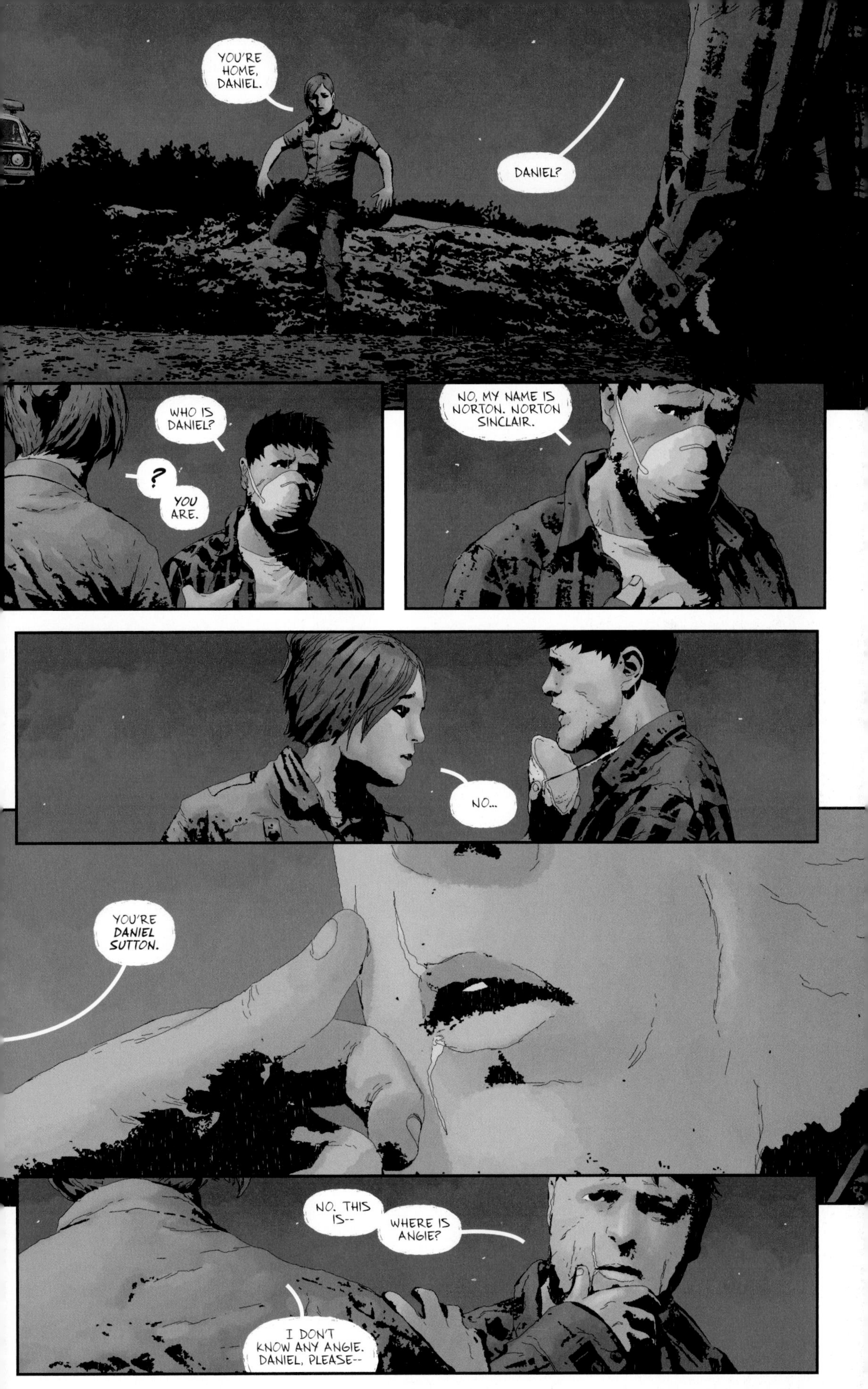
YOU'RE HOME, DANIEL.
DANIEL?
WHO IS DANIEL?
?
YOU ARE.
NO, MY NAME IS NORTON. NORTON SINCLAIR.
NO...
YOU'RE DANIEL SUTTON.
NO. THIS IS--
WHERE IS ANGIE?
I DON'T KNOW ANY ANGIE. DANIEL, PLEASE--

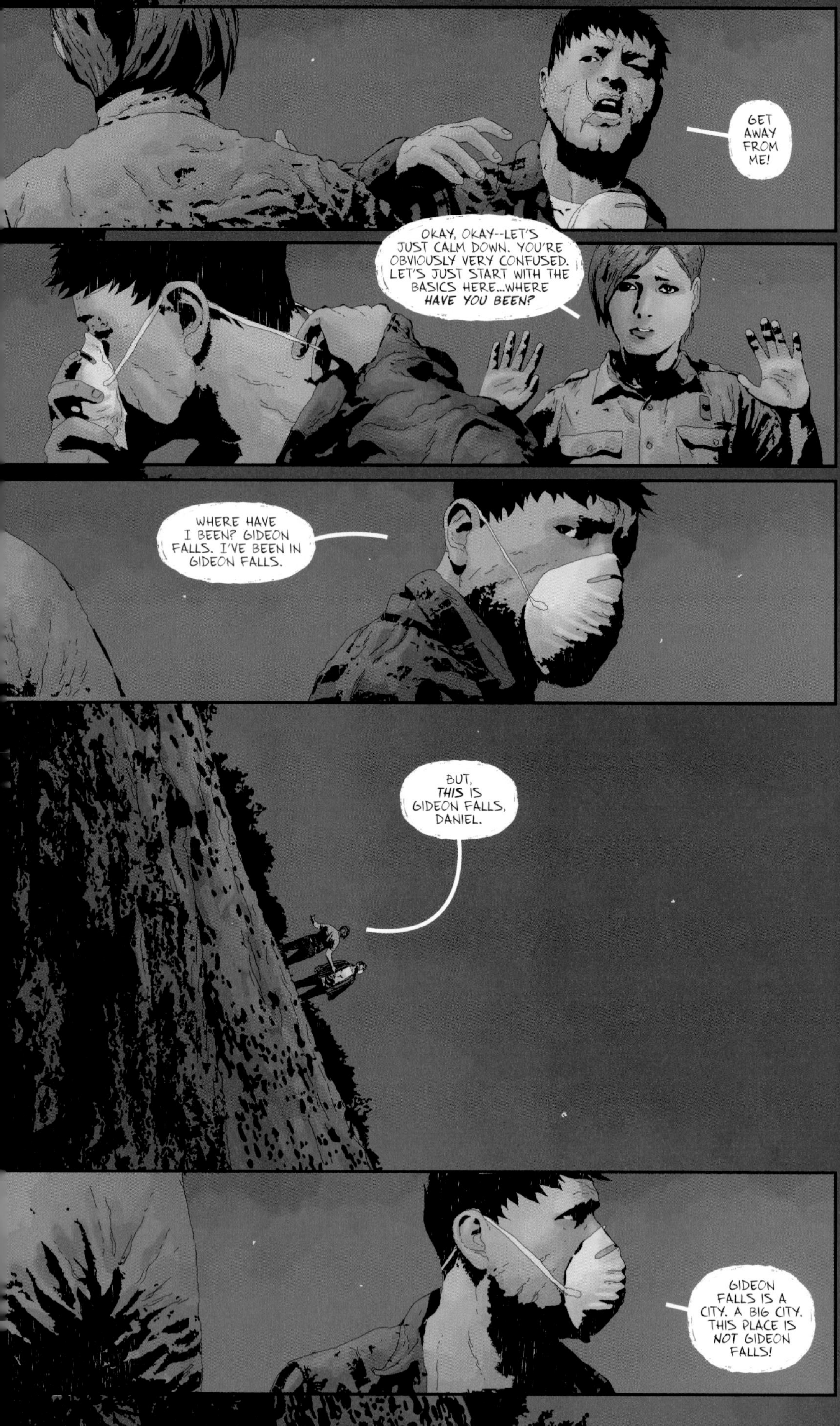
GET AWAY FROM ME!
OKAY, OKAY--LET'S JUST CALM DOWN. YOU'RE OBVIOUSLY VERY CONFUSED. LET'S JUST START WITH THE BASICS HERE...WHERE HAVE YOU BEEN?
WHERE HAVE I BEEN? GIDEON FALLS. I'VE BEEN IN GIDEON FALLS.
BUT, THIS IS GIDEON FALLS, DANIEL.
GIDEON FALLS IS A CITY. A BIG CITY. THIS PLACE IS NOT GIDEON FALLS!

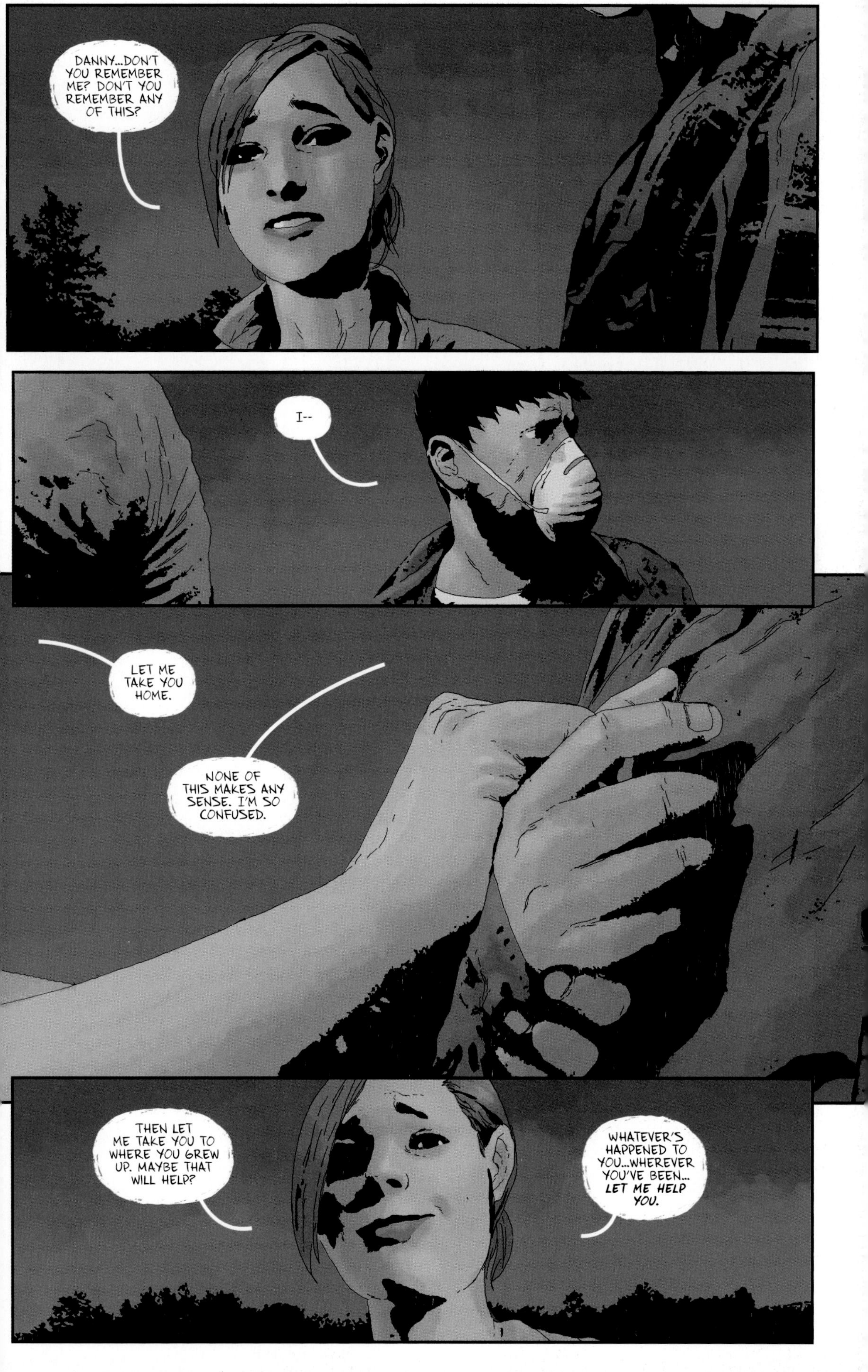
DANNY...DON'T YOU REMEMBER ME? DON'T YOU REMEMBER ANY OF THIS?
I--
LET ME TAKE YOU HOME.
NONE OF THIS MAKES ANY SENSE. I'M SO CONFUSED.
THEN LET ME TAKE YOU TO WHERE YOU GREW UP. MAYBE THAT WILL HELP?
WHATEVER'S HAPPENED TO YOU...WHEREVER YOU'VE BEEN... LET ME HELP YOU.

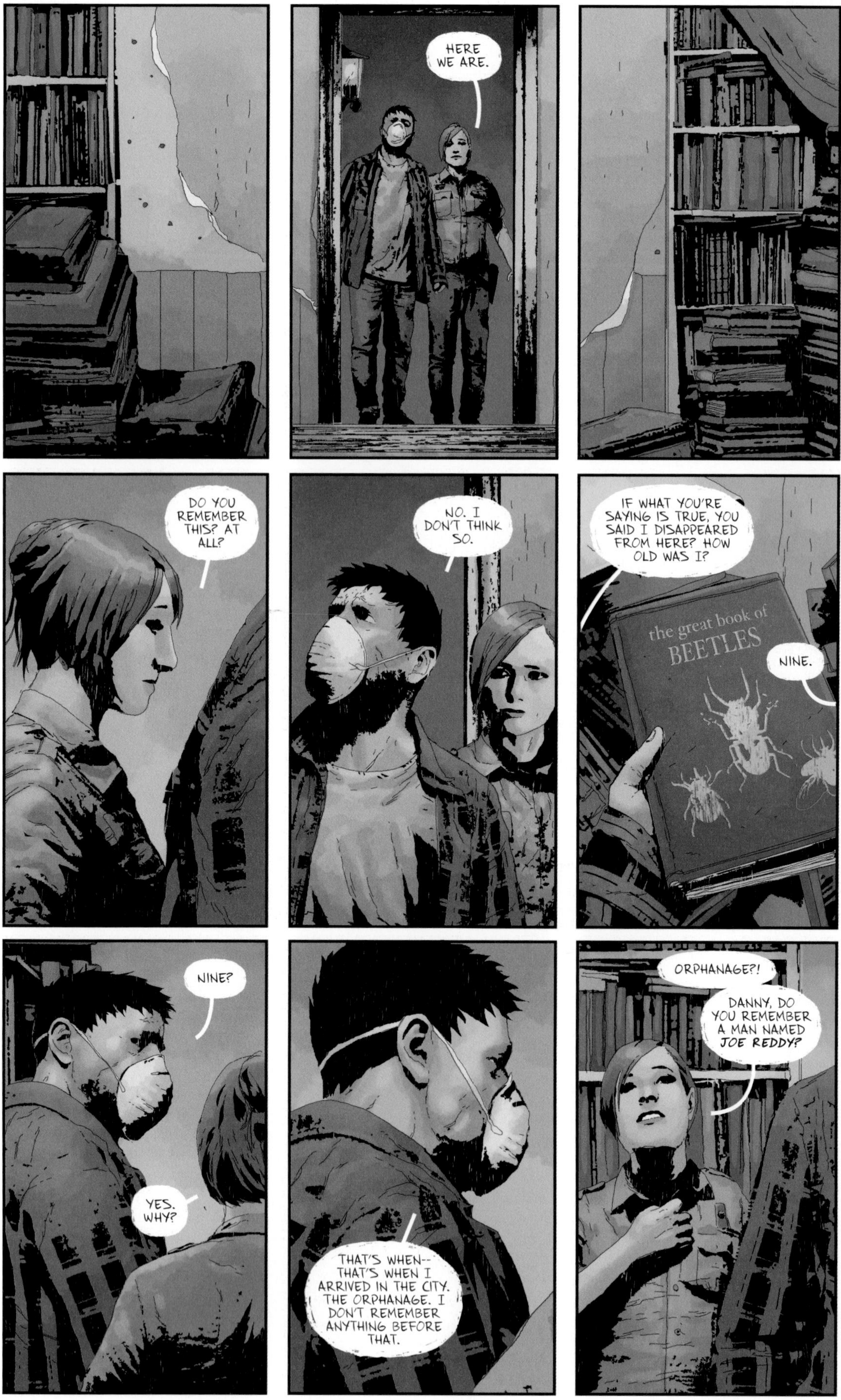
HERE WE ARE.
DO YOU REMEMBER THIS? AT ALL?
NO. I DON'T THINK SO.
IF WHAT YOU'RE SAYING IS TRUE, YOU SAID I DISAPPEARED FROM HERE? HOW OLD WAS I?
the great book of BEETLES
NINE.
NINE?
YES. WHY?
THAT'S WHEN-- THAT'S WHEN I ARRIVED IN THE CITY. THE ORPHANAGE. I DON'T REMEMBER ANYTHING BEFORE THAT.
ORPHANAGE?!
DANNY, DO YOU REMEMBER A MAN NAMED JOE REDDY?

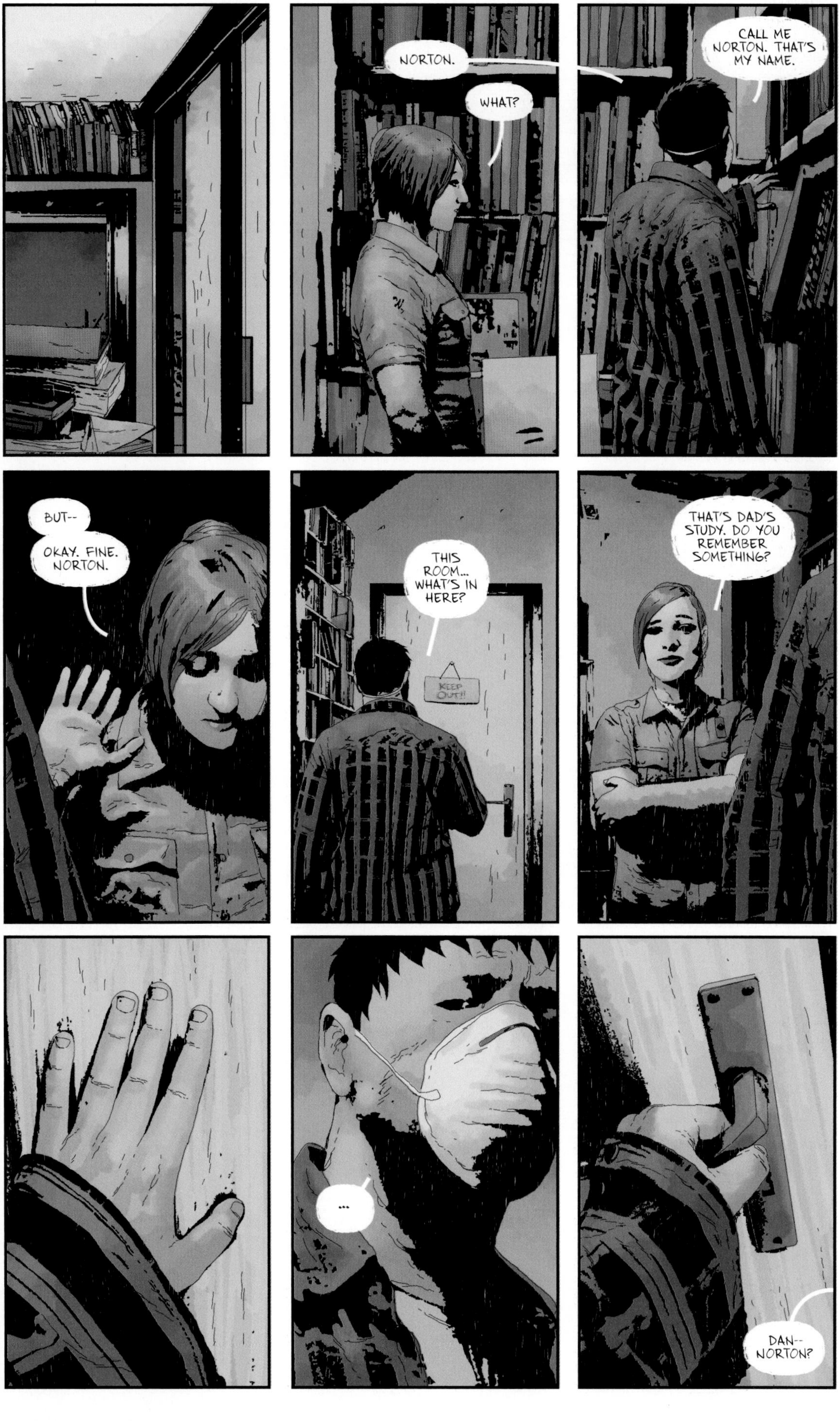
NORTON.
WHAT?
CALL ME NORTON. THAT'S MY NAME.
BUT--
OKAY. FINE. NORTON.
THIS ROOM... WHAT'S IN HERE?
KEEP OUT!!
THAT'S DAD'S STUDY. DO YOU REMEMBER SOMETHING?
...
DAN-- NORTON?

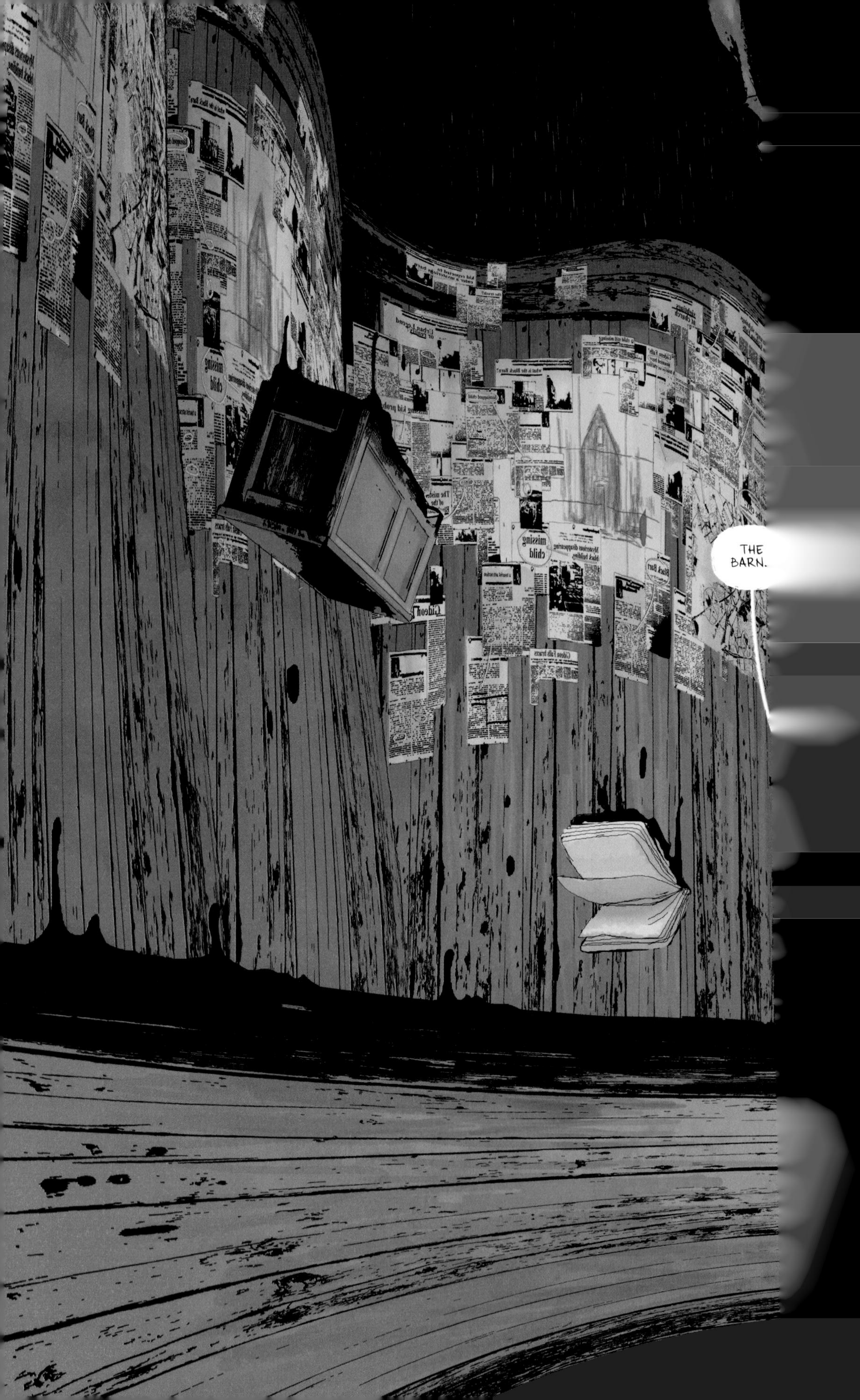
THE BARN.

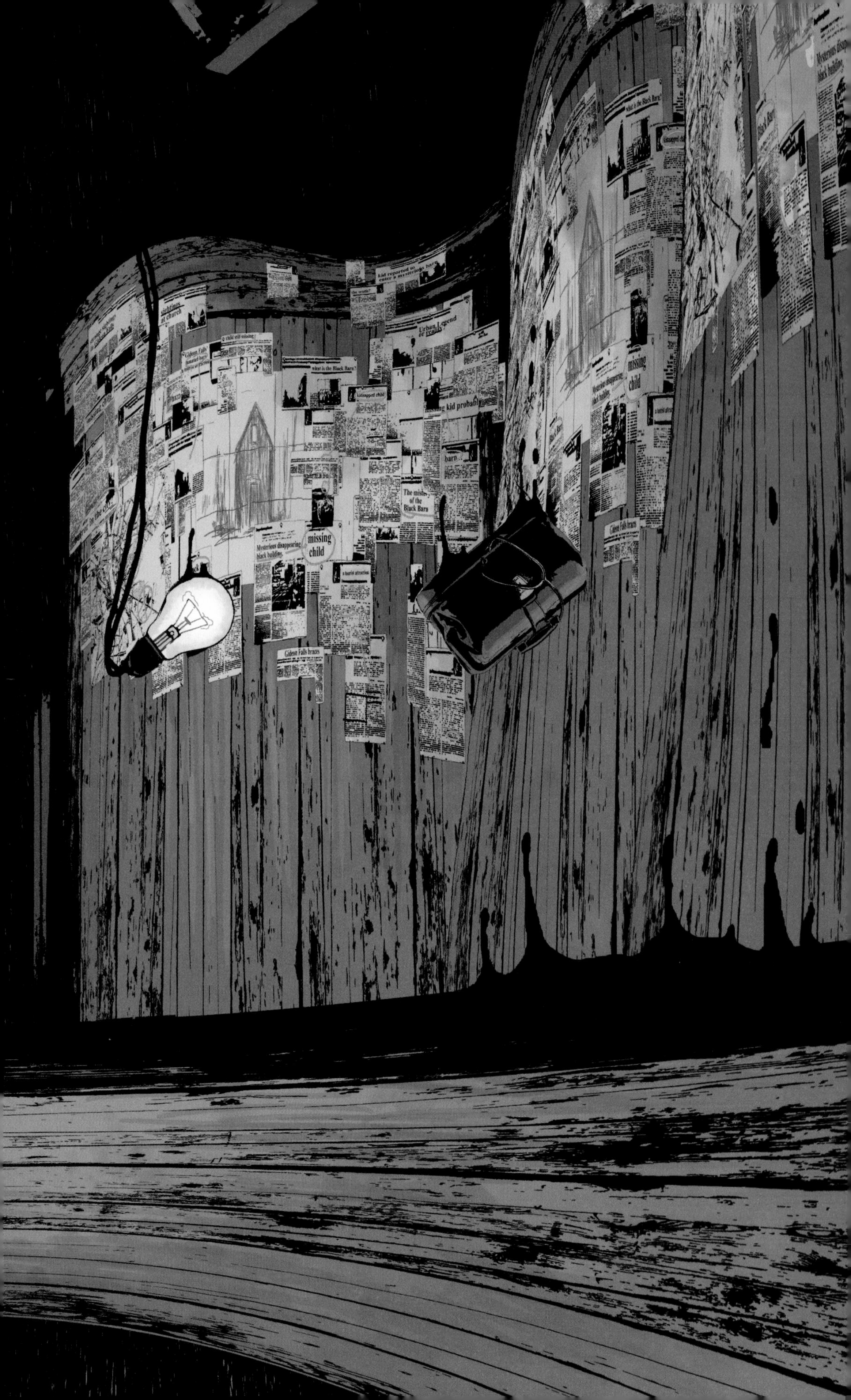
sightings at church
kid reported to enter a mysterious barn
child still missing
Urban Legend or reality?
what is the Black Barn?
kidnapped child
barn
The mistery of the Black Barn
Mysterious disappearing black building
missing child
a tourist attraction
Gideon Falls braces
what is the Black Barn?
missing child
Mysterious disappearing black building
Gideon Falls braces

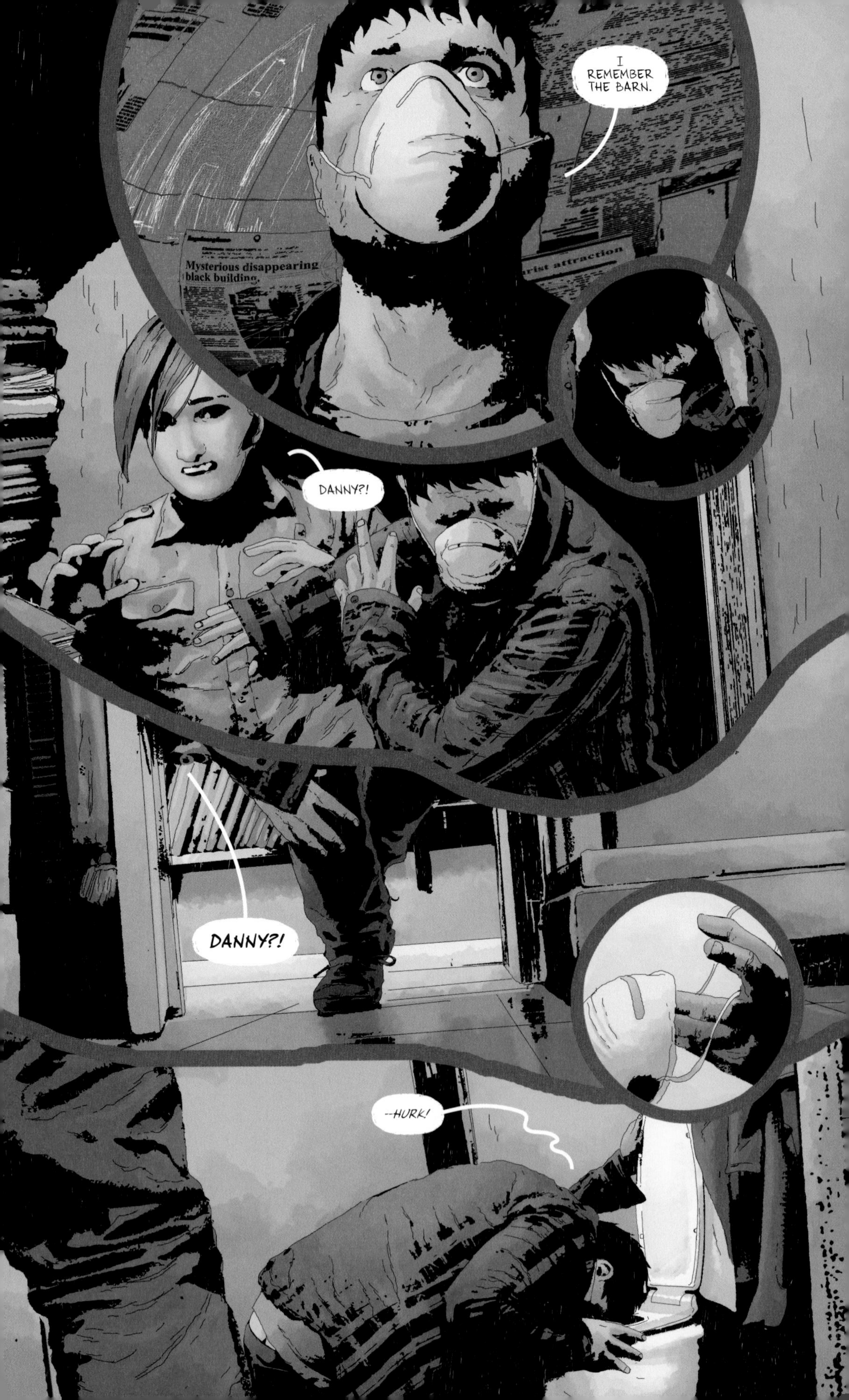

Mysterious disappearing black building.
I REMEMBER THE BARN.
DANNY?!
DANNY?!
--HURK!

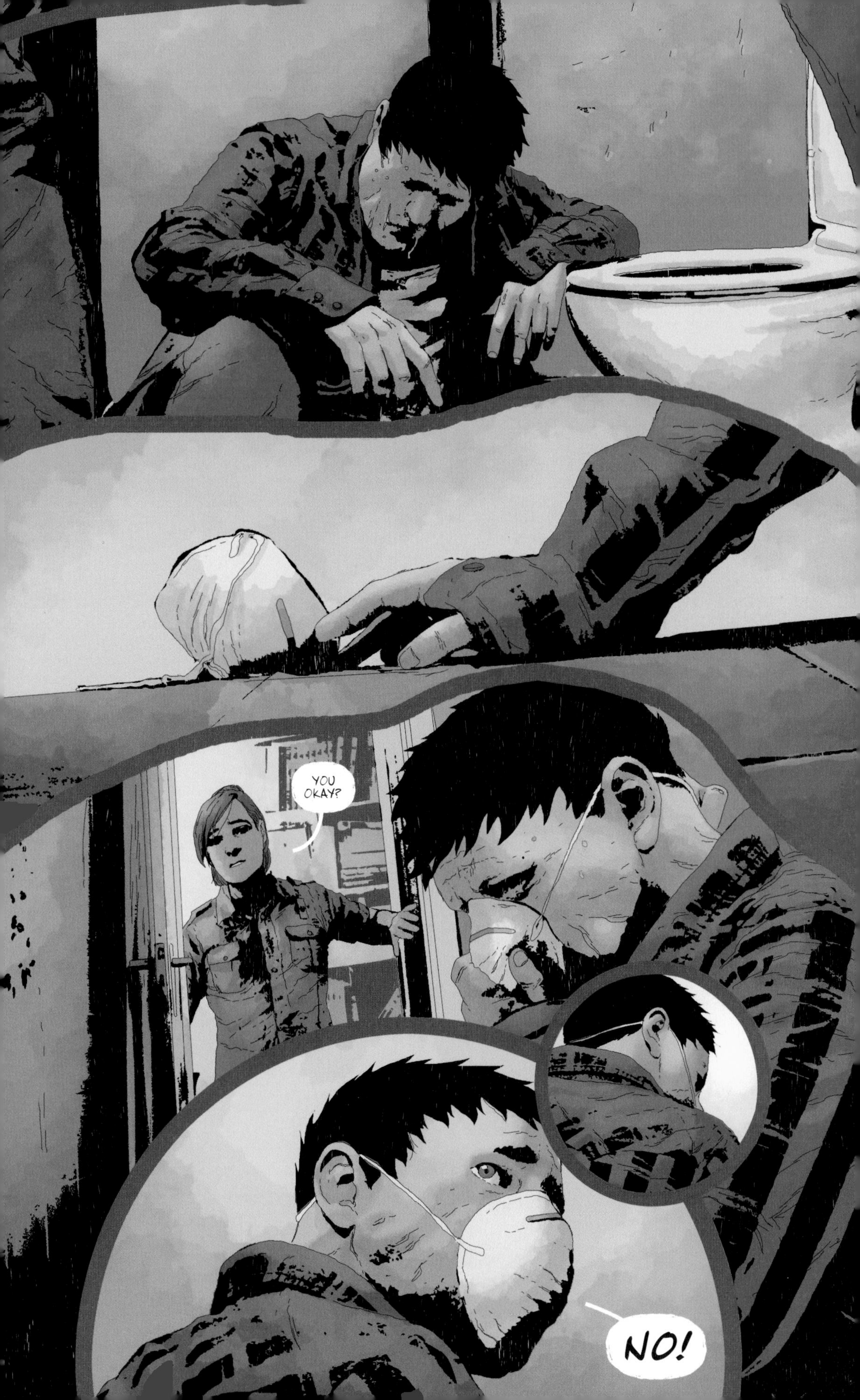
YOU OKAY?
NO!

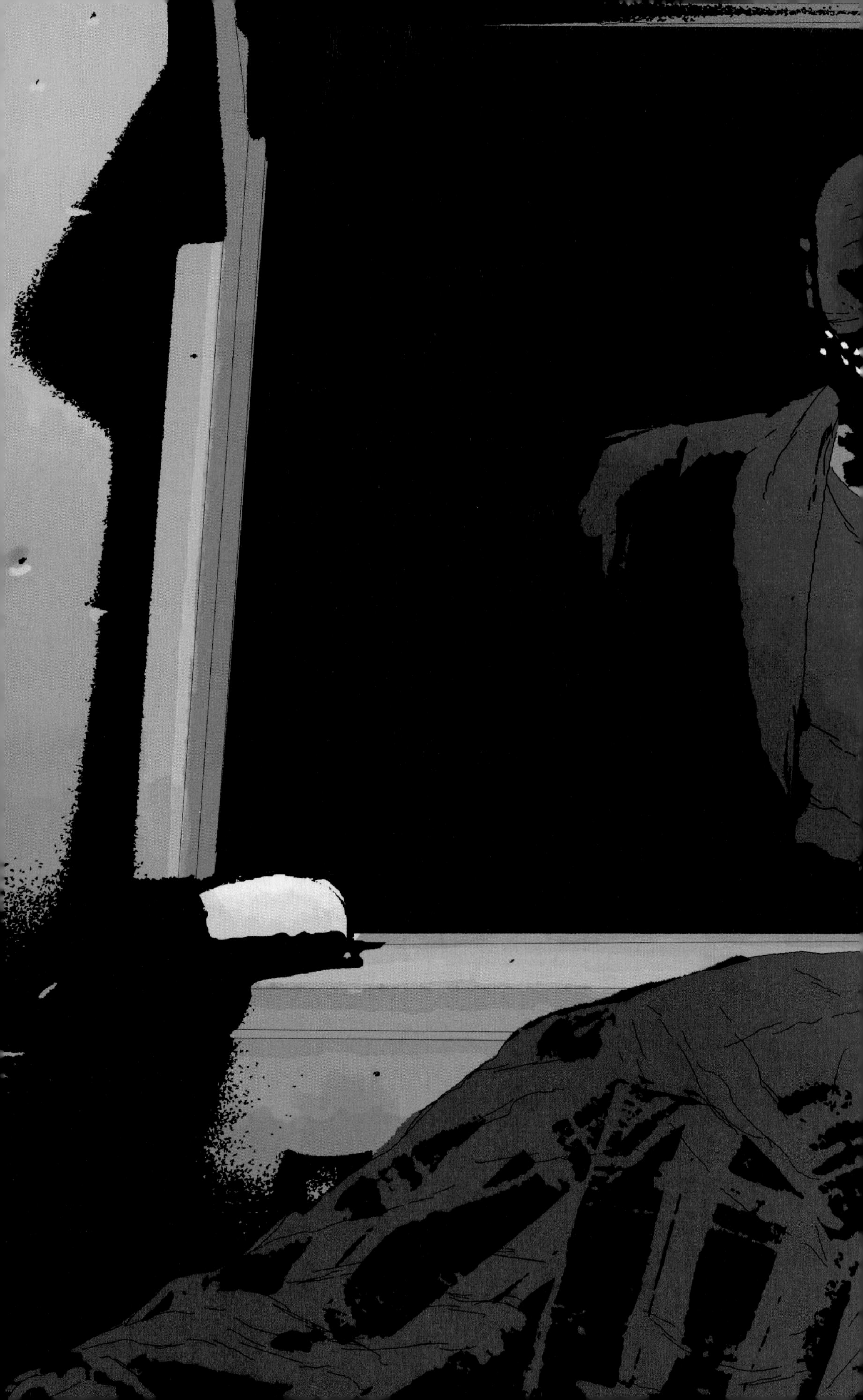

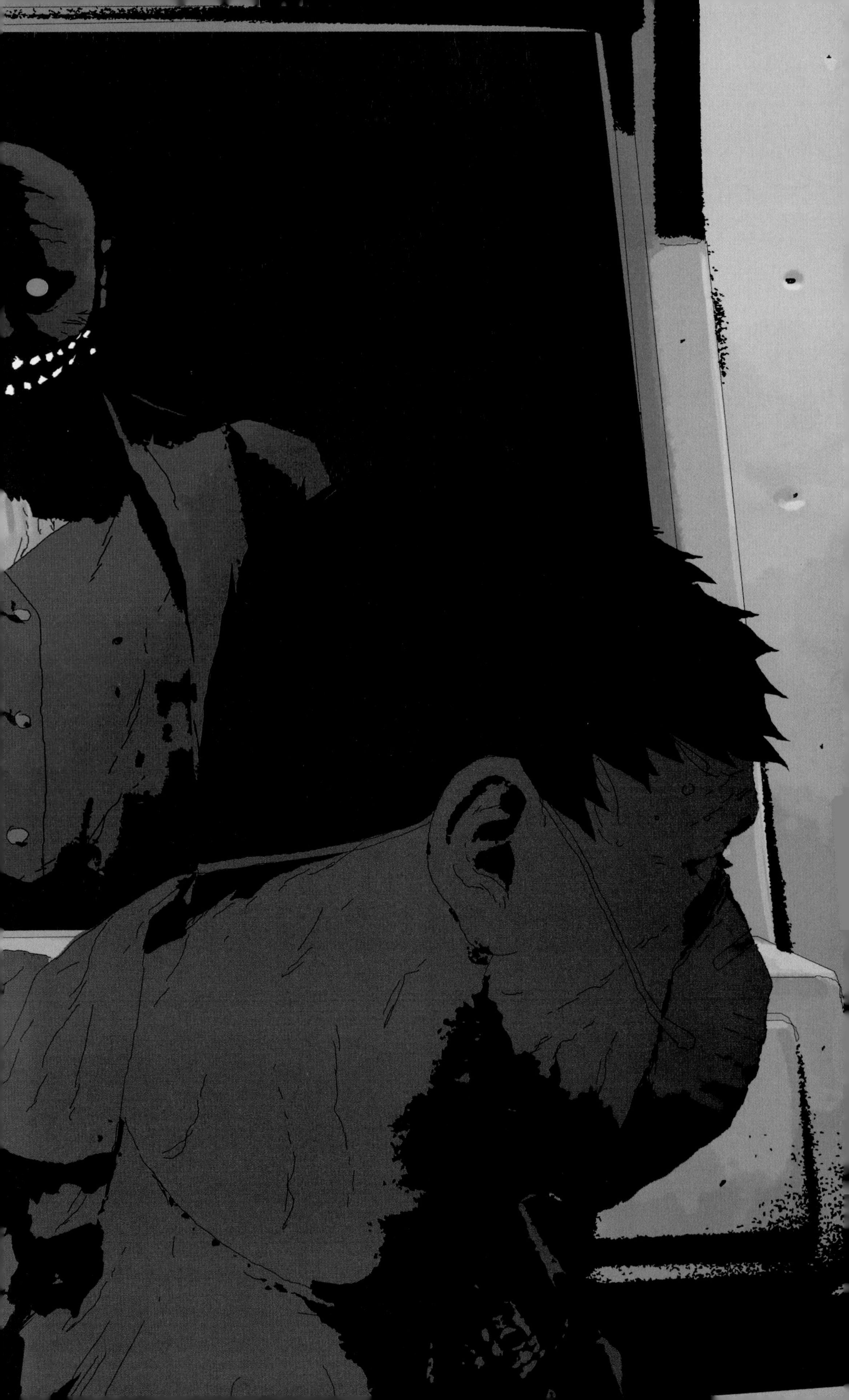

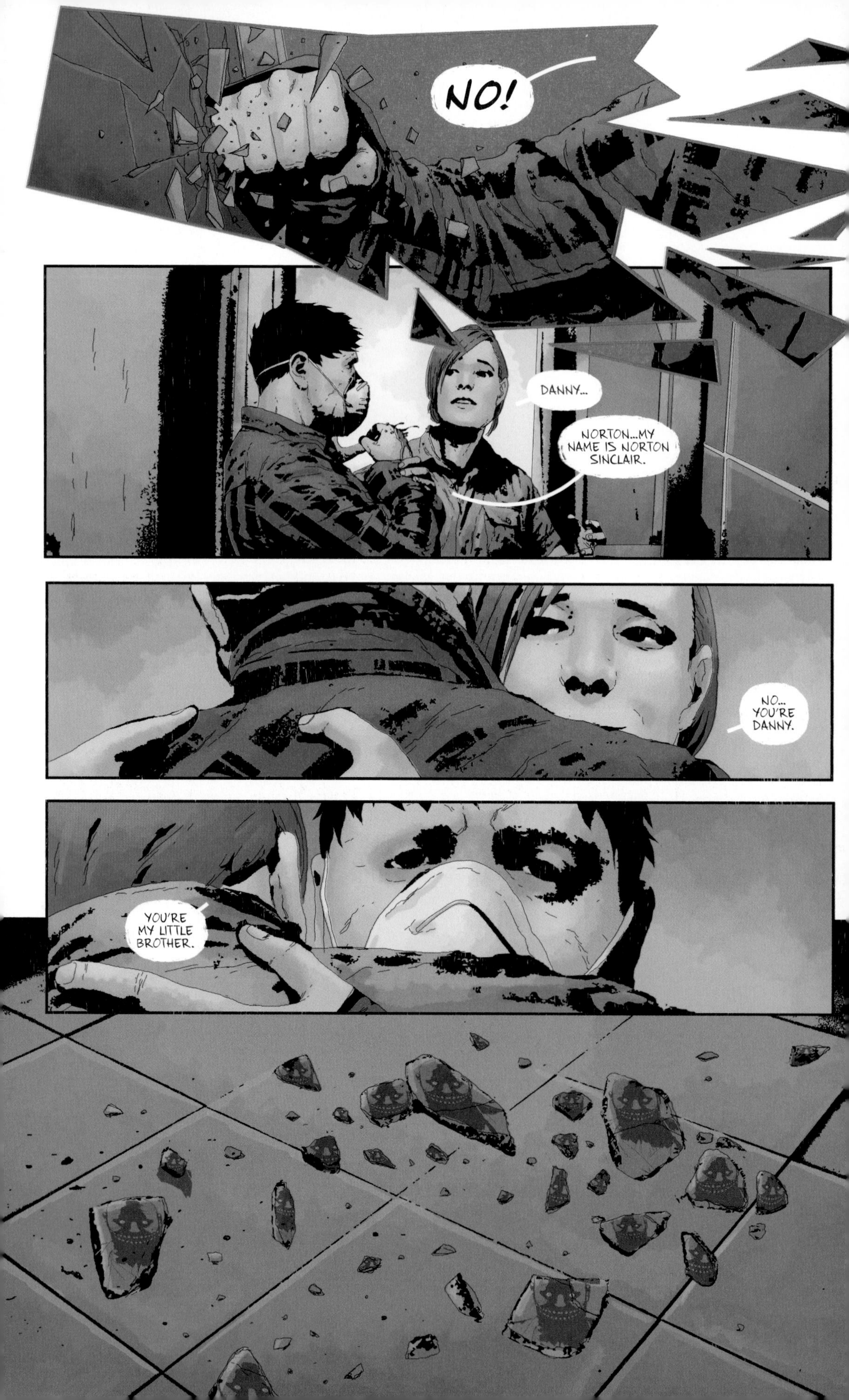
NO!
DANNY...
NORTON...MY NAME IS NORTON SINCLAIR.
NO... YOU'RE DANNY.
YOU'RE MY LITTLE BROTHER.

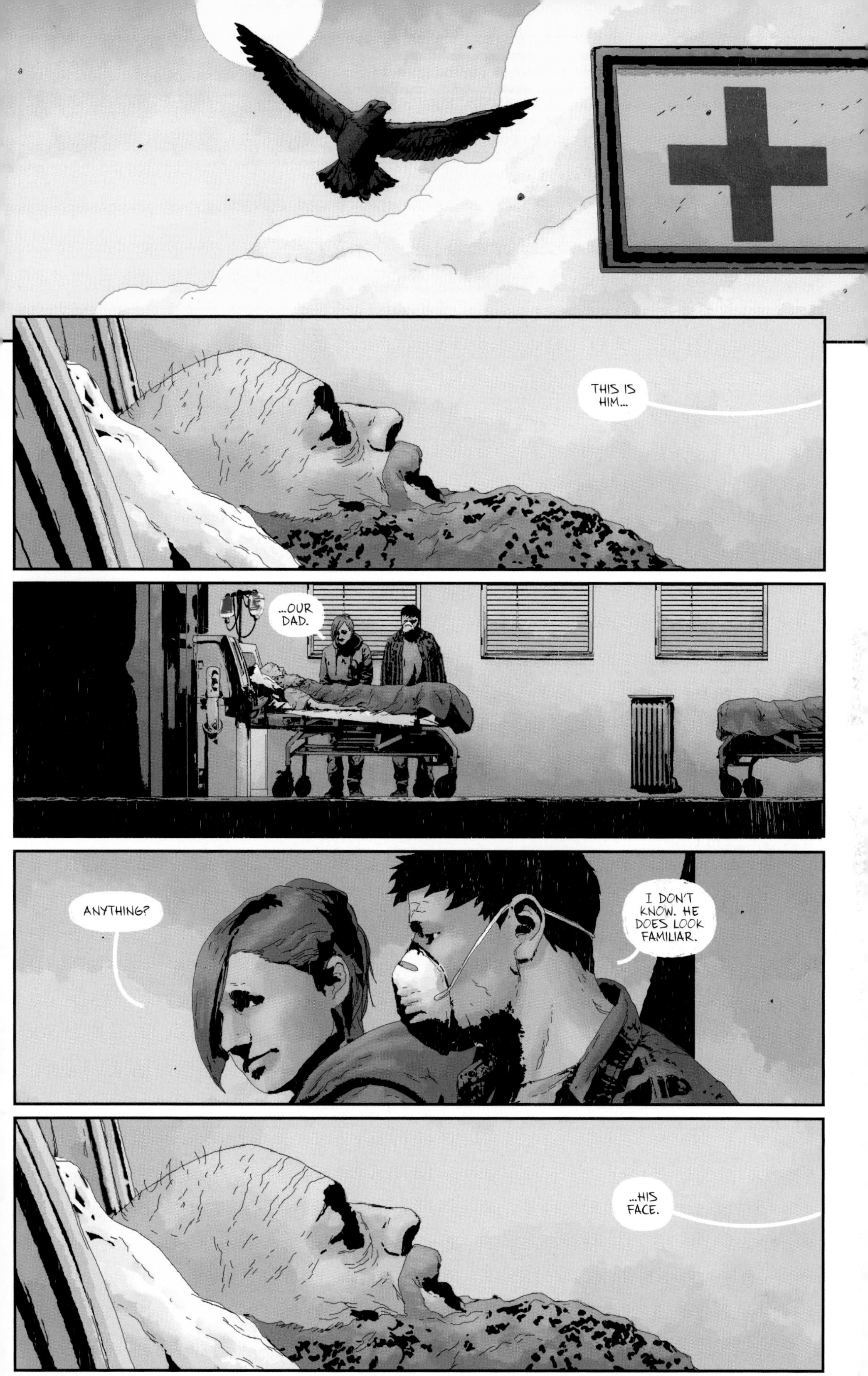
THIS IS HIM...
...OUR DAD.
ANYTHING?
I DON'T KNOW. HE DOES LOOK FAMILIAR.
...HIS FACE.

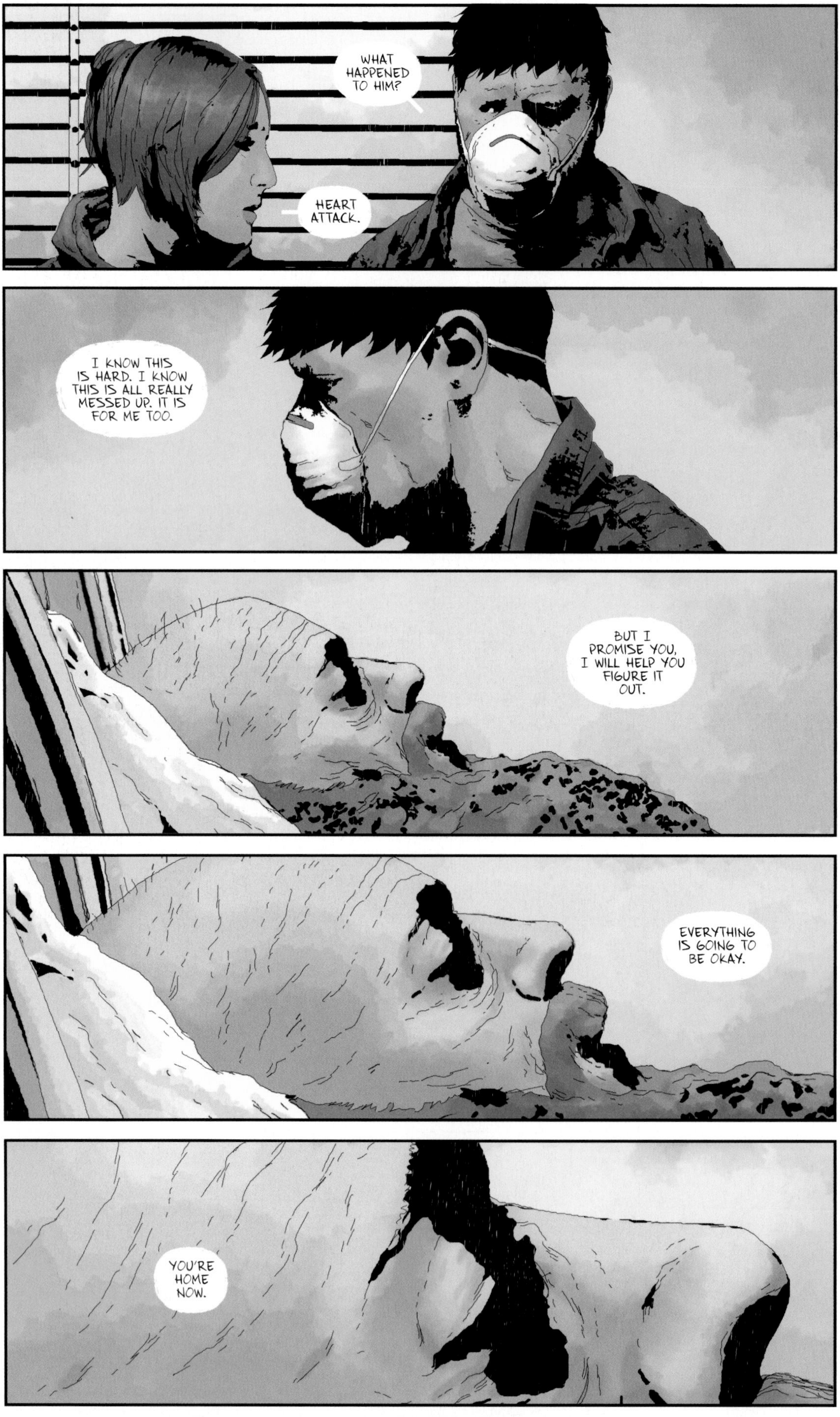
WHAT HAPPENED TO HIM?
HEART ATTACK.
I KNOW THIS IS HARD. I KNOW THIS IS ALL REALLY MESSED UP. IT IS FOR ME TOO.
BUT I PROMISE YOU, I WILL HELP YOU FIGURE IT OUT.
EVERYTHING IS GOING TO BE OKAY.
YOU'RE HOME NOW.

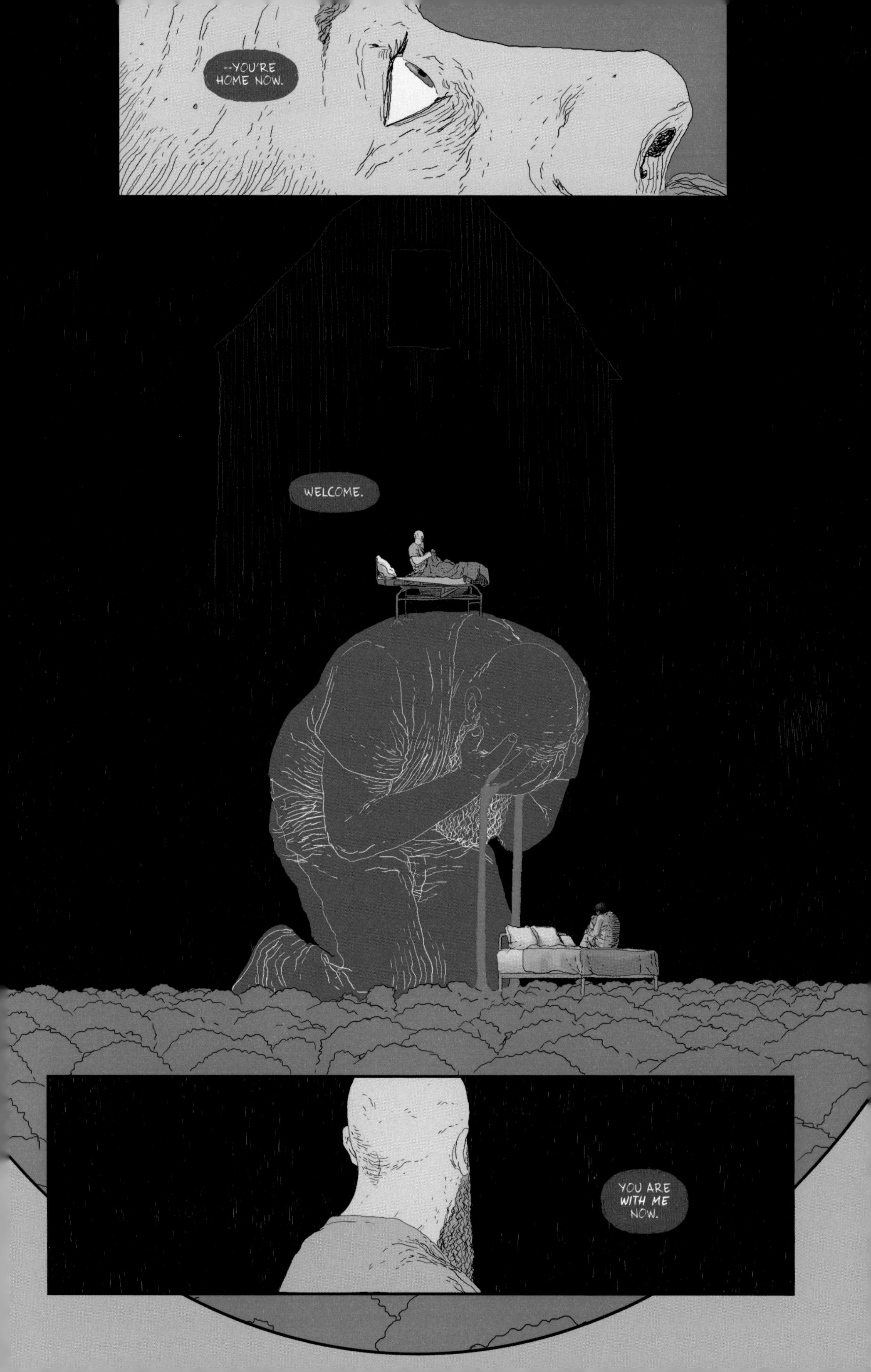
--YOU'RE HOME NOW.
WELCOME.
YOU ARE WITH ME NOW.

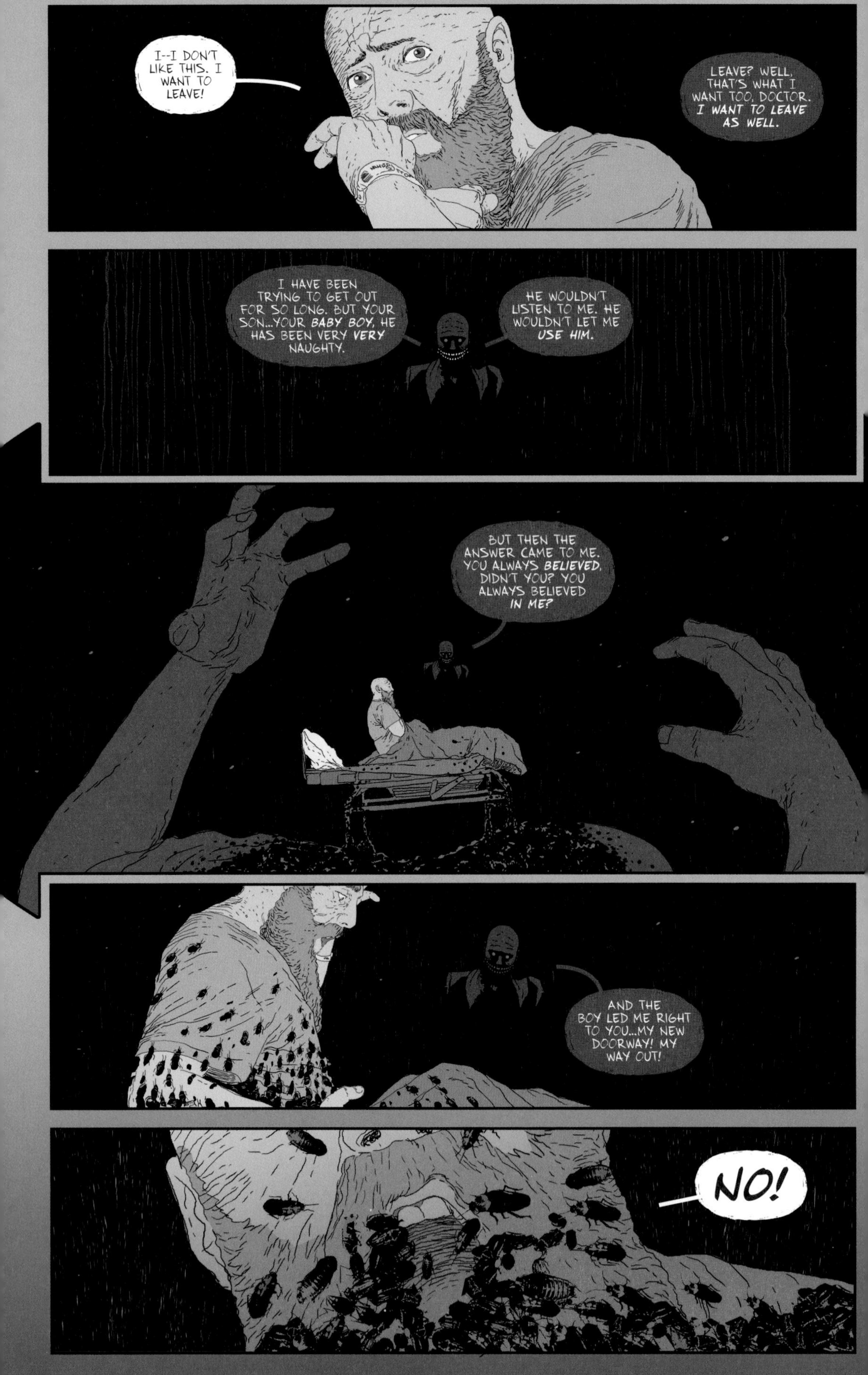
I--I DON'T LIKE THIS. I WANT TO LEAVE!
LEAVE? WELL, THAT'S WHAT I WANT TOO, DOCTOR. I WANT TO LEAVE AS WELL.
I HAVE BEEN TRYING TO GET OUT FOR SO LONG. BUT YOUR SON...YOUR BABY BOY, HE HAS BEEN VERY VERY NAUGHTY.
HE WOULDN'T LISTEN TO ME. HE WOULDN'T LET ME USE HIM.
BUT THEN THE ANSWER CAME TO ME. YOU ALWAYS BELIEVED, DIDN'T YOU? YOU ALWAYS BELIEVED IN ME?
AND THE BOY LED ME RIGHT TO YOU...MY NEW DOORWAY! MY WAY OUT!
NO!

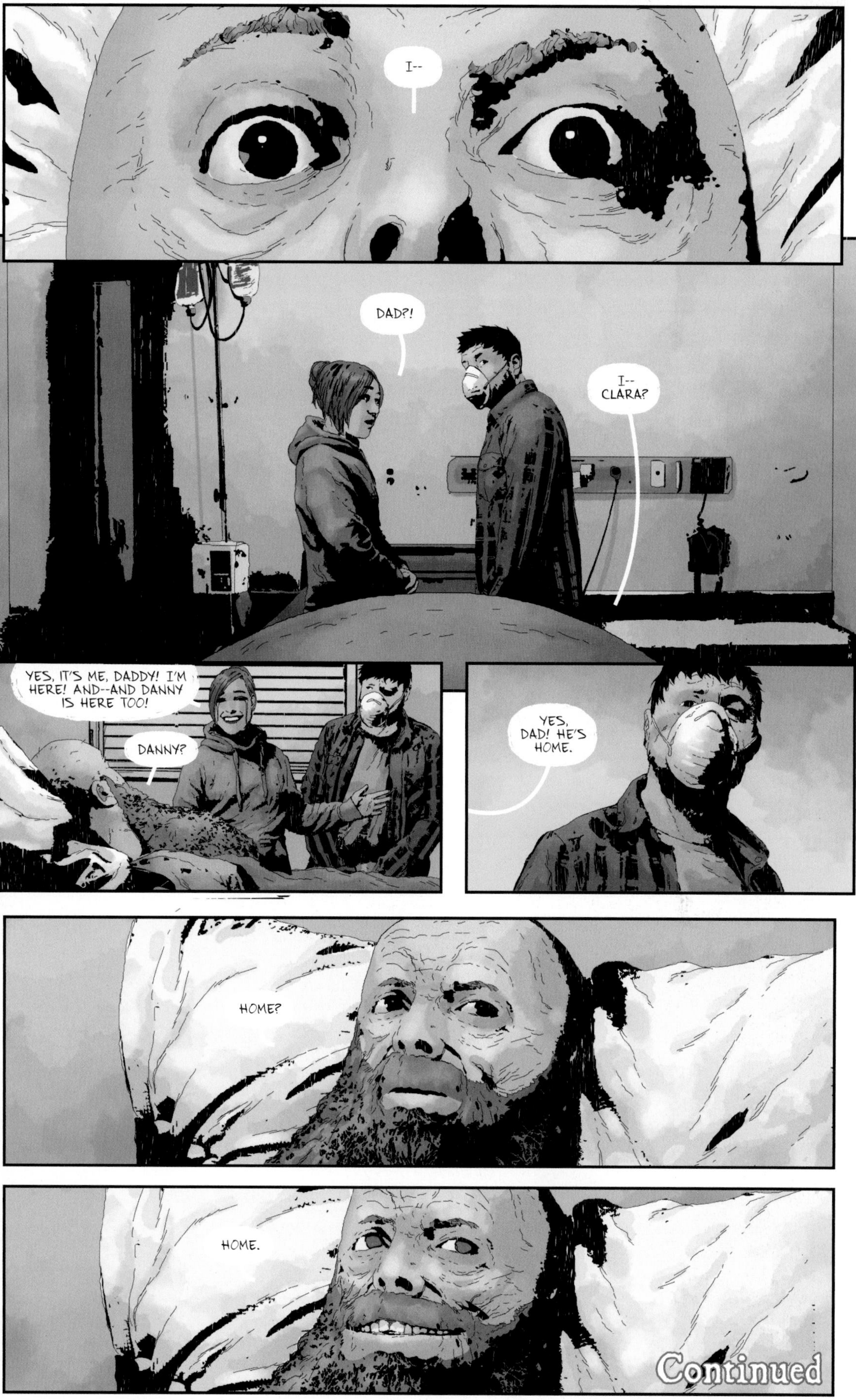
I--
DAD?!
I-- CLARA?
YES, IT'S ME, DADDY! I'M HERE! AND--AND DANNY IS HERE TOO!
DANNY?
YES, DAD! HE'S HOME.
HOME?
HOME.
Continued

COVER GALLERY

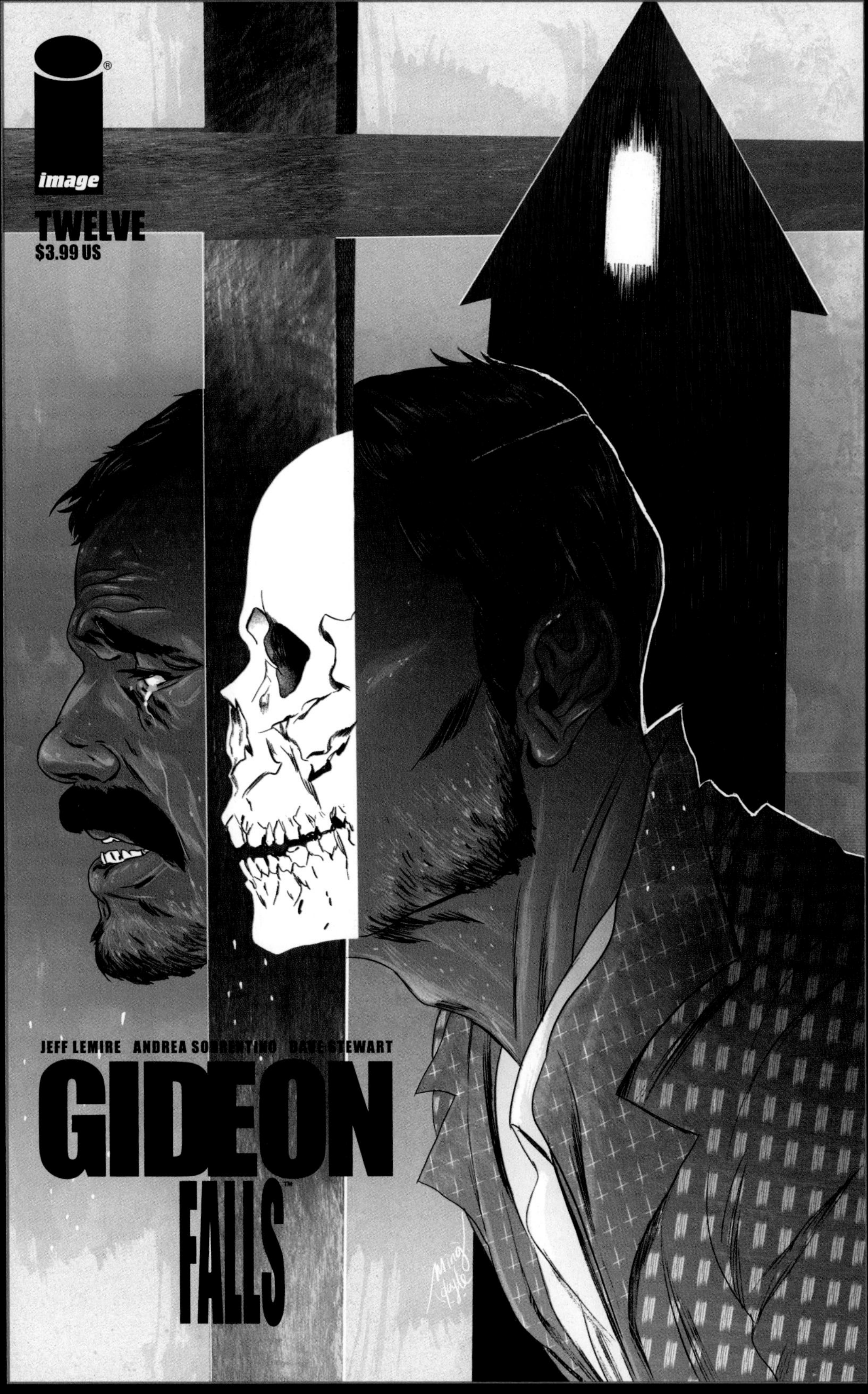
image
TWELVE
$3.99 US
JEFF LEMIRE ANDREA SORRENTINO DAVE STEWART
GIDEON FALLS™

#12B - MING DOYLE

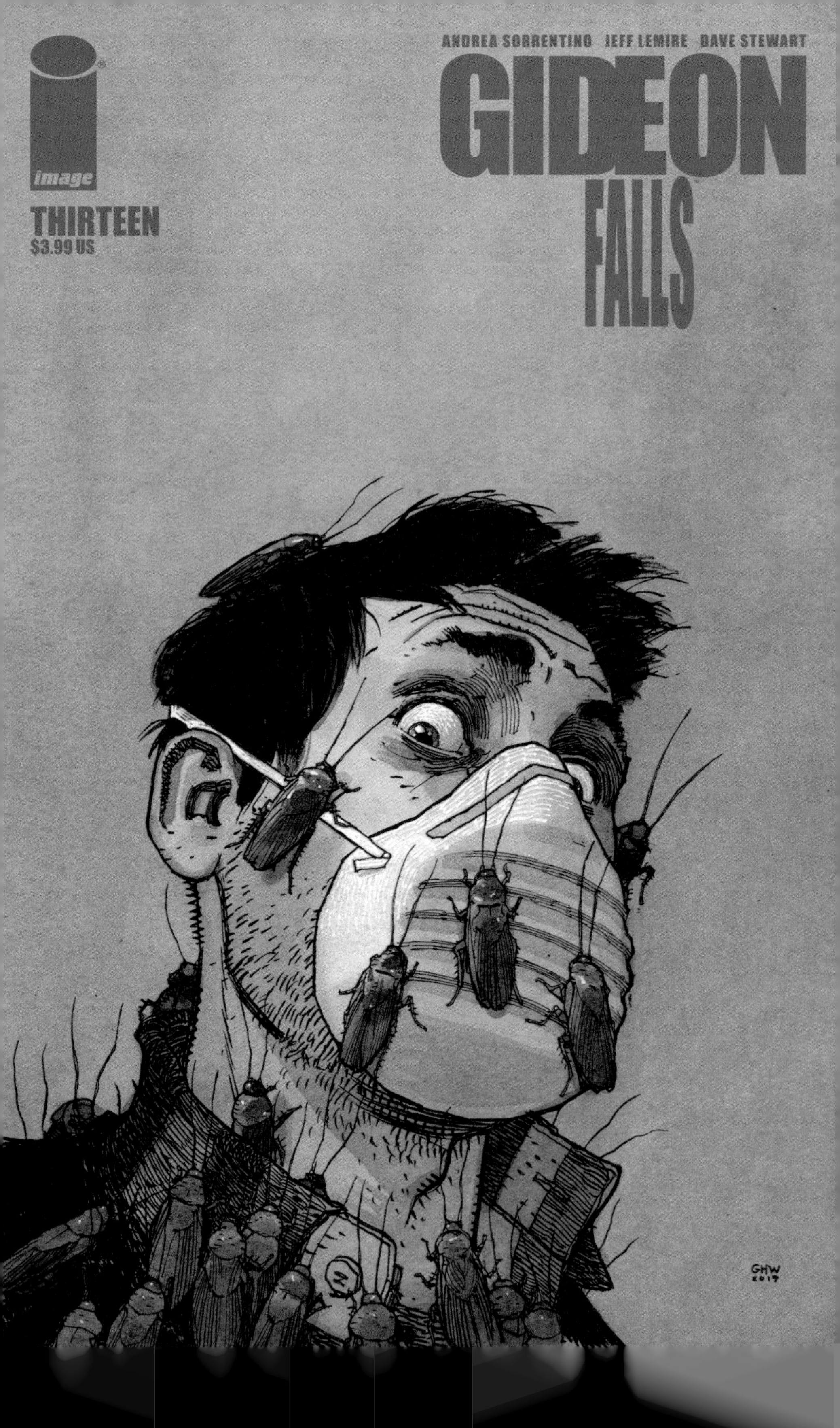
image
ANDREA SORRENTINO JEFF LEMIRE DAVE STEWART
GIDEON FALLS
THIRTEEN
$3.99 US
GHW
2017

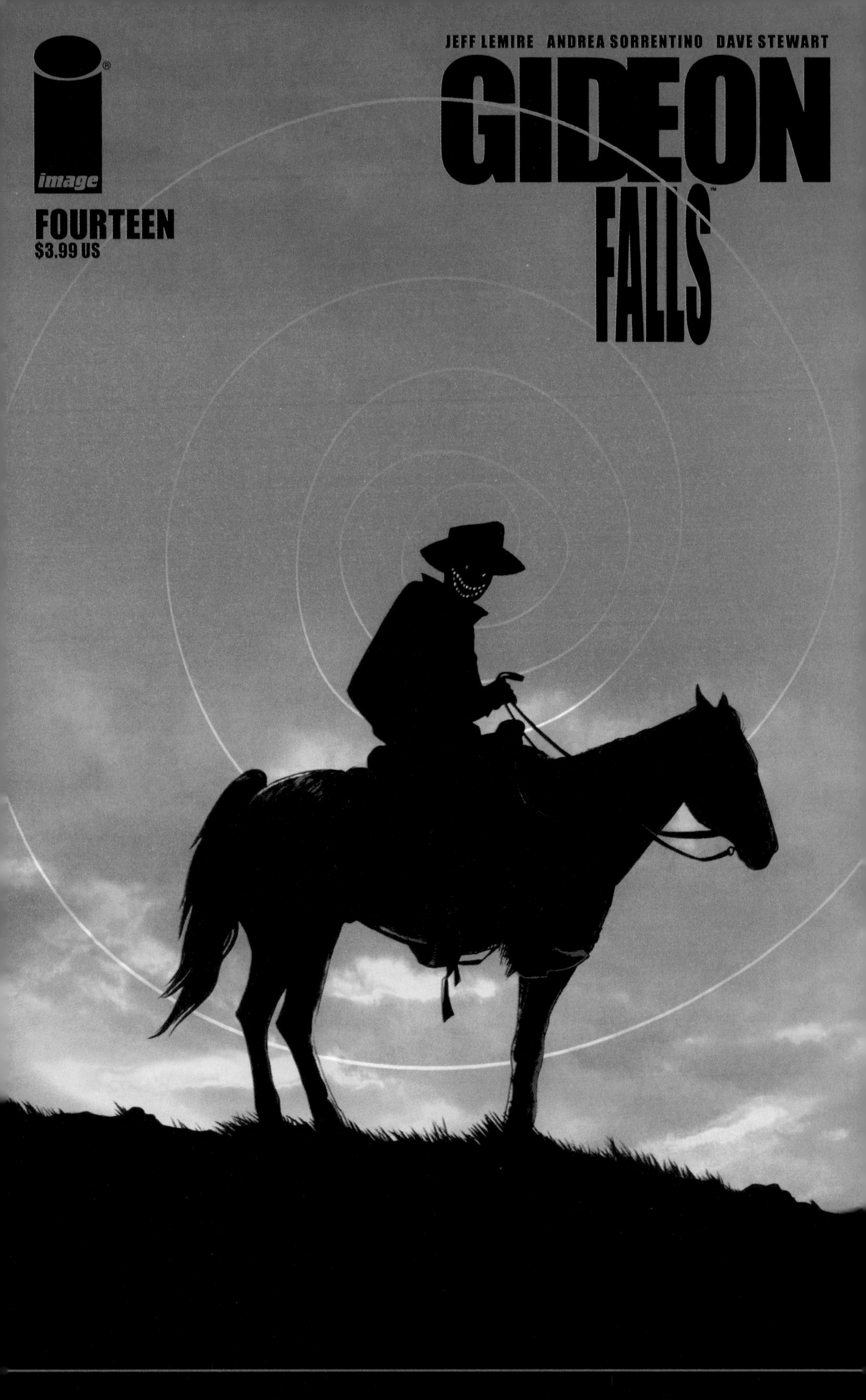

JEFF LEMIRE ANDREA SORRENTINO DAVE STEWART
GIDEON FALLS
image
FOURTEEN
$3.99 US

#14B - VERONICA FISH

ANDREA SORRENTINO   JEFF LEMIRE   DAVE STEWART

GIDEON
FALLS

FIFTEEN
$3.99 US

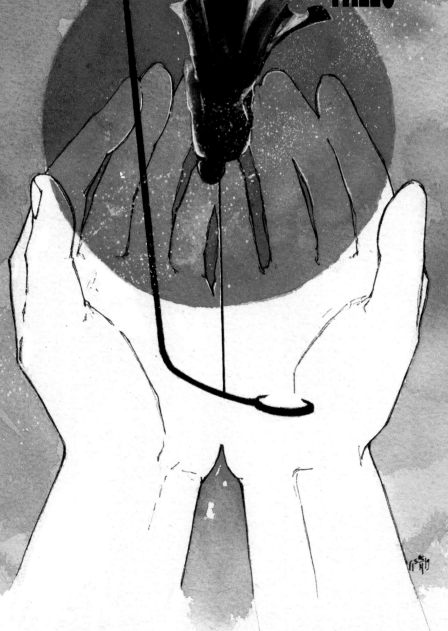

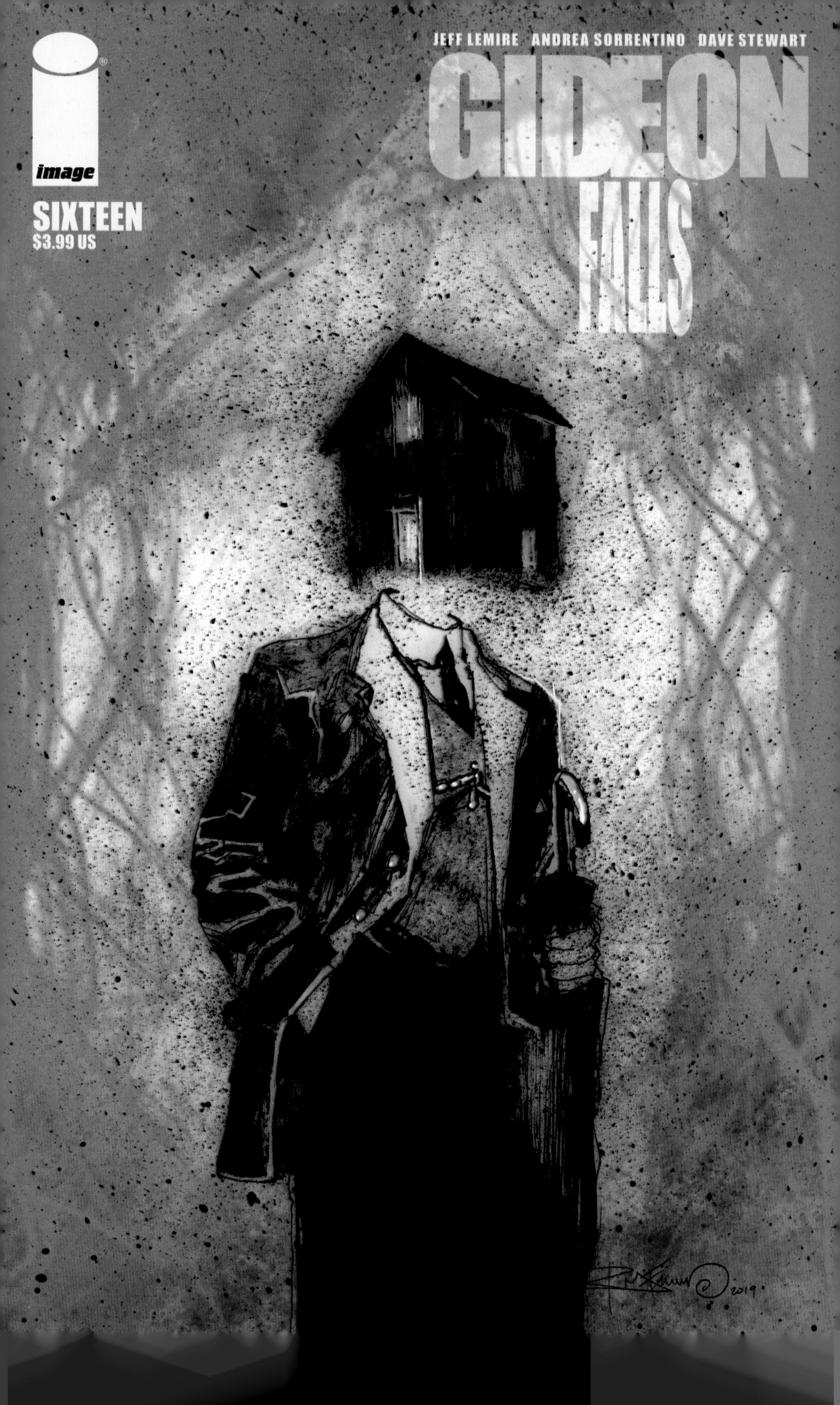
image
JEFF LEMIRE ANDREA SORRENTINO DAVE STEWART
GIDEON
FALLS
SIXTEEN
$3.99 US

GIDEON
FALLS